Dungeon World

Drifters

Book 2 in the System Apocalypse – Relentless
an Apocalyptic LitRPG series

By

Tao Wong & Craig Hamilton

License Notes

Dungeon World Drifters

Published by Starlit Publishing
PO Box 30035
High Park PO
Toronto, ON
M6P 3K0
Canada

www.starlitpublishing.com

Ebook ISBN: 9781778550614
Print ISBN: 9781778550621
Hardcover ISBN: 9781778550638

Books in the System Apocalypse Universe

System Apocalypse: Relentless

A Fist Full of Credits

Dungeon World Drifter

Apocalypse Grit

Main Storyline

(complete series with 12 books)

Life in the North

System Apocalypse: Australia

(3 books with more to come)

Town Under

Anthologies and Short stories

Comic Series

Contents

Prologue

"Welcome back to *Dungeon Rules: Royalty Edition!* I'm your host Amryl a Jorra."

The face of a lanky, pale-skinned Movana filled the viewscreen, the elf's magenta tapered pompadour bobbing as the announcer ran while holding the recording device that captured the broadcaster's image and voice.

"For those of you just joining us, we're on Earth now, in the mountain range the natives call the Colorado Rockies," Amryl explained to his unseen viewers. "It's been just over a local year since the Galactic Council inducted this planet into the System as its latest Dungeon World, and over ninety percent of the native sentient population has been wiped out in the last twelve months by System-spawned creatures."

The elf spun the recorder around to give viewers a quick glimpse of the surrounding snow-covered, jagged peaks. The Movana turned the focus of the device back onto himself, holding the recorder in the "selfie style" that had become popular since material from Earth's "Internet" hit the Galactic scene. Not that it was really new, but the influx of new cultures always brought up old trends.

"We're about to see some of those monsters in action!" Amryl exclaimed. "Today's challenge is for Prince Arturios Arfuriosa III, heir to the throne of Demarcia, to take down a dozen ferocious Frost Drakes."

A roar echoed from somewhere nearby, followed quickly by several more.

"Sounds like the action has already begun," said the elf. "Let's catch up and see it happen live!"

The view whirled as the Movana crested the mountain ridge to look down upon a scene of furious combat.

A pack of stocky, white-scaled quadrupeds with thick, spiked tails swarmed out of a wide-mouthed cavern, the lizards' blue-clawed limbs leaving deep tracks as they bounded through the snow drifts to assail a group of four armored adventurers.

The lead adventurer, a green-skinned humanoid clad in a lightweight, armored jumpsuit with a mountain camouflage pattern, opened up on the Frost Drakes with a snub-nosed energy carbine as the lizard-like creatures encircled the party. The drakes snapped at the adventurers with long, pointed maws filled with rows of sharp fangs. Crimson beams from the Hakarta's carbine stitched across the advancing monsters, leaving glowing orange traces gouged deeply into the creature's scales.

"There's Kargut Fura, the prince's Level 49 scout, kicking things off with his trusty auto-beamer," said Amryl, narrating the developing combat. "Most Wasteland Trackers tend to be the solitary types, but that Hakarta spends as much time carousing with the rest of the crew as he does using his Class Skills to track down the prince's next trophy."

Behind the gunner, a staff-wielding wolfman waved in a complicated gesture and a wall of flame sprouted up between the adventurers and the cave. A trio of drakes stood trapped between the party and the flames, while the rest of the monsters shied back from the fiery obstruction, their advance halted until the creatures pushed out around either side of the blaze.

"Good move there by Ruby Emede," Amryl continued. "A flame wall placed by a Level 47 Firewalker will give the team time to deal with the first few drakes without getting completely overwhelmed by the entire nest."

Next to the fire mage wolfman, a bark-skinned dryad, the party's third member, tossed a handful of spikes that stuck into the ground in a line that led up to one side of the flame wall. Translucent blue shields popped up from the spikes, closing off one side of the group in an overlapping protective barrier.

"There's Lilisae following up with more protective measures," Amryl commented. "Since no one has taken any hits yet, there's no one for the Prismatic Channeler to heal with her repertoire of Level 45 spells. Those portable shield generators will block off another avenue of attack from the drakes and limit the directions the team will need to defend."

One of the largest drakes bounded through the fiery wall with a roar, heedless of the scorching flames that charred the edges of the monster's scales, and pounced on the Hakarta gunner, driving the tusked adventurer to the ground before the orc could dodge the attack.

"That's not looking good for Kargut, but fortunately for him, Prince Arturios is already getting to work!"

The view zoomed in through the chaos to focus on the fourth, and final, member of the party, a humanoid in articulated power armor. The towering figure plowed through the massed creatures, knocking the large drake clear of the prone Hakarta and sending it flying back through the curtain of fire toward the mouth of the cave.

His silvery armor lacked a helmet, showing off the luxurious mane that fringed the prince's leonine head. Rounded ears with blond fur poked through the dark brown mane and matched the golden hue of the prince's protruding muzzle, lips drawn back in a furious snarl as the hulking lion man swung a massive greatsword through the melee.

The sword gleamed brightly in the sunlight, almost too bright to look upon. Over a handspan in width, the razor-sharp blade cleanly severed a drake's neck in a single sweep.

"The Judgment of the Dawn," Amryl breathed, eyes wide in reverence. "The prince's heirloom sword has a presence you can feel anytime it's drawn from the sheath."

Two more casual swings of the gigantic sword chopped the two other drakes into multiple pieces and gave the group breathing room to organize themselves to deal with the remaining monsters.

Kargut climbed back to his feet as several drakes charged around either side of the flame wall. The team ignored the ones that encountered the shield generators, monstrous claws skipping and sliding off the energy barriers without gaining purchase. Instead, the adventurers focused on the ones flowing around the other side of the flames.

Arturios stepped up beside the flaming barrier, his silver armor protecting him from the intensity of the heat, and stood with his greatsword at the ready. The first drake to round the wall of fire promptly met its end, cleaved in half. Lengthwise.

"Look at that power," Amryl cheered. "Also at Level 49, he's an unstoppable Battlefield Tyrant!"

The prince roared in triumph as the next monster leapt over the carcass of its clutchmate, only to be met with a hail of energy fire from Kargut's beam carbine. The beast recoiled and Arturios diced the creature into pieces before it recovered.

All of the drakes to circle around the flames died in similar fashion, stunned by the attacks of the prince's support crew and finished off by the devastating power of the relic weapon. The pile of carcasses was higher than the prince's waist by the time the flame wall spell dissipated.

"That is excellent teamwork," said Amryl, still looking down on the gulch below from the crest of the ridgeline. "Magical support and focused fire to bring down a superior number of monsters. Very coordinated. That just speaks to the experience this team has together. Well done."

Two more drakes waited beyond as the fire died down, and Arturios charged toward them. Only bare stone remained at the mouth of the cavern, with the snow melted away by the intense heat of the spell, and sparks flew from beneath the prince's armored greaves as he danced between the remaining monsters.

The creatures soon lay in multiple pieces, and Arturios roared once again, posing heroically in the mouth of the cave as his party cheered him on.

Amryl zoomed the view away from the leonine figure, bringing the whole party into the frame while still keeping it centered on the prince.

Then a shadow fell over the entire group, and Amryl glanced up.

"Oh, no."

The ground shook as an ivory-scaled dragon slammed into the snow, the massive creature nearly filling the depression beneath the ridgeline. One clawed limb crushed Kargut into a pulp with a sickening squelch, while another smashed two of the shield barriers with an audible pop.

The dragon's jaws snapped down over Arturios before the prince could do more than gape in horror. The dragon lifted its head, chewed twice, then spun around to face the pair of living adventurers before shaking its head from side to side as it swallowed.

The dragon opened its mouth and jutted its neck forward as it breathed toward the last two members of the group. An icy mist flowed out of the gaping maw and engulfed the terror-stricken adventurers, entombing them within solid blocks of ice moments after the breath flowed over them.

As the dragon jerked its head forward to unleash its breath, the prince's greatsword tumbled free of the dragon's maw. A severed arm still gripped the hilt as the weapon plunged down into a snowdrift.

Focused on the fallen sword, Amryl looked up to find the dragon's angry gaze fixed upon him.

The dragon pounced, and the announcer dropped the recorder as he attempted to flee.

It was far too late for that.

A moment after the recorder hit the ground, a brief scream cut off with an audible chomp and the crunches of grinding bone.

A rush of wind filled the air as the dragon took flight.

Only silence remained.

Left in the center of the recorder's view, the prince's greatsword stood almost upright. The hilt stuck up out of the snow with nearly a foot of the blade exposed, a hand still tightly clutching the hilt. The severed forearm steadily dripped blood from ragged flesh around the exposed, broken ends of the radius and ulna bones until the liquid froze.

Day passed, then night.

Sheets of ice built slowly over the sword and over the recorder, the view growing increasingly blurry as the layers accumulated, until only a white blur remained visible at the height of daylight.

Then the device's stored Mana ran out, and the transmission, finally, went dark.

Chapter 1

The setting sun dropped behind the mountain at my back, slightly easing the heat of summer as I slipped down the forested crest of the ridgeline. Though I remained far enough inside the tree line to remain shrouded from sight, I kept an eye on the lone figure patrolling the pedestrian bridge that spanned both lanes of I-68 through the man-made mountain pass below.

On the far side of the cement walkway lay the Sideling Hill Welcome Center, the scenic rest stop which currently housed a band of highwaymen who'd been blockading this route through the Appalachian Mountains of Maryland—and taking their toll in theft, rape, and murder on anyone seeking to travel through.

The bandits' iron grip on this pass ended tonight. They just didn't know it yet.

Shifting through the trees unnoticed was easy enough with the stealth training my employer had provided, and only the sound of my feet swishing through the grassy undergrowth marked my passage as I navigated farther down the slope. The heavily forested southern side of the cut above the parking lot for the eastbound side of the interstate covered my approach, though I cautiously slowed my descent each time the guard reached the far end of the bridge and walked back in my direction.

Nothing in the man's status gave me cause for alarm, since we'd already scouted the bandits' position. No significant threats were found, so my boss had agreed that we could dispatch the bandits and made the call to engage.

I reached the end of the walkway and ducked beneath it, listening carefully for footsteps until the guard turned to patrol back across the bridge once more. Leaning out from beneath the walkway, I scanned the back of the man with the large rifle as he ambled toward the visitor's center on the far side of the pass.

David Moore (Rifleman Level 44)

HP: 520/520

MP: 440/440

"Go."

The silent command from my employer over party chat propelled me into motion, the System communication unheard by anyone else in the vicinity. Her Diplomatic Contact Class Skill more closely resembled telepathy than talking out loud and transmitted far more securely than any radio transmission.

With one hand grabbing the top of the chain-link fence, I vaulted silently onto the walkway, landing lightly on the paved surface and summoning my knife into my hand as I accelerated into a sprint at the marksman's exposed back.

Along with providing a passive durability boost to my equipment, Quality Over Quantity—one of the tier-3 Class Skills I'd unlocked at Level 31—had finally granted me the opportunity to declare a personal weapon. Rather than opt for one of the plethora of pistols I tended to use, or something flashier like a sword, I'd selected a trusty combat knife. The straight-spined, seven-inch blade now filling my grip ended in a slight concave clip point with a sharpened swage. The matte finish on the blackened material completed the deadly appearance of the weapon and made it ideal for stealthy wet work.

And, most importantly, it would never run out of ammo.

A recall enchantment imbued into the soulbound weapon was a part of its very essence. It allowed me to summon the knife directly into my hand at any time, so now I truly never would go anywhere without a knife.

My high Agility boosted my stealth, and the rifleman never heard my approach as I sprang onto his back. The weight of my tackle carried the guard to the ground as I slashed my knife through his neck with Rend activated. The active Class Skill inflicted a bleeding effect on foes damaged by my weaponry and only exacerbated the fatal wound left by my blade.

The guard's loosely held rifle tumbled free as we crashed to the ground, and it clattered away until it slid to rest against the chain-link fence that enclosed either side of the pedestrian walkway.

Even with his windpipe and both arteries severed, neck cut back to the bone, the bandit guard still tried to push himself up.

Damned video-game bullshit.

My free hand grabbed a fistful of greasy hair and yanked back before I plunged the knife into his exposed throat once again. Hot blood splashed over my blade hand, slicking the grip of the weapon as the spreading crimson pool underneath us stood out sharply on the cement. I twisted the weapon as I pulled it free, then slashed it across the man's wrist, just below the cuff of his armored jumpsuit, as he continued to push himself up. The limb collapsed, and the man fell prone once again.

Though he continued struggling and kicking beneath me, the mortally wounded guard failed to gain purchase on the blood-slicked pavement, and his movements gradually slowed. Continuing to bleed out, the rifleman finally ceased moving all together.

I could have cast Cleanse, but instead I opted to conserve my Mana, wiping my blade and blood-slicked hand clean on the man's armor before I stood and chucked the body into Meat Locker, one of my extra-dimensional System storage spaces. This one was specific to, well, meat. My kills.

Then I continued across the bridge, scooping up the fallen rifle and storing it in my Inventory. I'd worry about the rest of the dead man's loot later.

Despite the lack of warnings over our party chat, I remained alert for any sign that my takedown of the patrolling guard had been noticed. When I reached the corner of the Welcome Center without incident, the tension in my shoulders eased a little.

The structure showed only a few System improvements, highlighting the bandit group's failure to take advantage of the location's Fort designation. Other than reinforced walls and a lone manually controlled turret, the structure retained most of its pre-System appearance.

In the tall windows of the building, I caught a brief glimpse of myself in the glass panes. A head of brown hair and a face bearded in perpetual stubble stared back at me from the window, which was covered on the inside by a "Discover Mountain Maryland" static decal. The tight-fitting dark gray armored jumpsuit with pistols holstered on each hip only emphasized my athletic frame.

I passed the windows and found the upper entrance to the building unlocked, only for a foul stench to assail my nose as I eased the door open. I had to regret the acuity of my Keen Senses as I slipped through the entrance into the upper level of the multi-story building. The coppery tang of blood mingled with the nauseating foulness of unwashed flesh and human excrement.

The stench of death, an old friend, lingered here.

I eased the door closed with nary a click before I stalked into the shadowy interior.

"David hasn't checked in for a bit." The throaty female voice came from around the corner ahead of me. "I'm going to go see what he's up to."

A gruff snort responded. "You're just going to jump his bones again."

"Tsk, tsk," replied the unseen woman. "Don't be jealous."

Another snort. "Hardly, I have plenty of play toys here."

The sharp smack of an impact on flesh echoed through the building, followed by a terror-filled whimper. The woman and the man chuckled darkly at the moan.

"Have fun," the woman said, and I sank back against the wall as footsteps approached the corner.

The woman rounded the corner with her head down. Short black hair hung down to cover the woman's face as she focused on tying the sleeves of her unfastened armored jumpsuit around her waist, leaving her only in a sports bra to cover her muscular torso and tan skin—likely in preparation for her intended tryst with the now deceased rifleman.

Elena Sanchez (Fighter Level 37)
HP: 640/640
MP: 210/210

My activation of Hinder affected the woman before she ever realized she was under attack. The Class Skill slowed my target's physical movements, giving me the advantage as I erupted out of the shadows with my knife slashing across her throat before she managed to look up at me.

One hand clutched her throat desperately as blood trickled between her grasping fingers, but the wound failed to be as devastating as it had been against the more fragile rifleman outside.

Despite the severity of her injury, the fighter displayed good instincts and swung at me with her free hand. Only the slowing effect applied by Hinder saved me from her attack as a spiked mace materialized in her grasp as I ducked beneath the strike.

While I dodged her blow, the woman tried to call an alarm over her shoulder, but she only managed to exhale a gurgling gasp.

Thrusting forward, I buried my knife in her stomach and dropped her health further before springing beyond the range of her sweeping mace. As she staggered and looked at me, I tossed the knife from my right hand to my left and watched the fighter's eyes track the blade through the air. While I caught the knife in a reverse grip, my right hand pulled the survival axe from the Mana-powered clamped sheath at the small of my back.

With a weapon in each hand, I launched myself back at the fighter. The woman parried desperately against my sudden offensive, but she only had a single weapon to my pair. Suffering from Hinder and accumulating wounds, she moved far too slowly.

Nicks and cuts slowly sprouted along her unprotected arms and torso, the blood dripping from the minor injuries to mingle on the floor with the fluids cascading from the still bleeding wounds in her neck and stomach.

I caught the haft of her mace under the hooked beard of my axehead and spun her off balance as I stabbed her in the torso once again. The metallic clang as our bound weapons tangled echoed through the building and finally alerted the brigand around the corner.

"Is that you, Elena?" the gruff voice called. "What's going on?"

The woman wrenched her weapon free and backed away from me as she slammed the mace loudly against the wall in an effort to warn her compatriot. Stone shattered beneath the blow and sent the scattered chips clattering across the room.

I had no desire to fight two-on-one, so I needed to end this. Fast.

I charged toward the fighter, who choked up her grip on the mace as she prepared to unleash a charged-up attack. The woman swung the weapon—which glowed brightly now—as I reached her, but her eyes went wide in confusion at the malicious glee in my expression. Before her attack landed, I dropped to my knees, sliding across the blood-slicked floor beneath the wild swing too quickly for the fighter to compensate for my movements.

My axe hacked into the back of her leg as I slid behind her. My momentum carried me past my target and wrenched the blade free as the woman collapsed. I continued along the floor and popped back to my feet, skidding to a halt as the woman hit the floor with only the barest strands of flesh and muscle holding her knee together.

Before I could finish the woman, footsteps pounded toward us from around the corner and I turned to face the incoming threat. Still hunched over while buttoning his trousers, the shirtless man towered over me by at least four inches.

What was it with half-naked bandits today?

Clyde MacAskill (Pugilist Level 38)
HP: 840/840
MP: 160/160

The gigantic man looked up from fastening his pants, glaring through a greasy mop of tangled red hair that hung down over his face. A scraggly beard of ginger curls cascaded down onto a chiseled torso of freckled, pasty white skin.

As he caught sight of the wounded fighter, the big man squared up into a boxing stance, fists held to his chin, and shuffled toward me. I feinted toward the boxer, and he responded with a lightning-fast jab as I pulled up short. Before the man's arm had pulled back into a defensive position, I activated Hinder on him and lunged forward in an attack of my own.

Despite the slowing effect of my Class Skill, the pugilist still managed to deflect my weapons. Something told me he had Resistances to physical hindering Skills. As it was, my blades caused little more than minor nicks to the outside of the man's arms as he batted the attacks away from his torso.

The fact that my blades failed to cut deeply into his forearms, and that he had consciously kept my attacks away from his torso, told me the pugilist had defensive abilities that reinforced his arms but hinted that his center might be more vulnerable.

A slight squelch from behind alerted me to a threat from the other fighter, and I jumped away from both enemies in time to avoid a sweeping strike from the woman's mace as she lunged on her good leg. My movement took me out of her range, and the fighter flopped onto the blood-covered floor as her attack failed to connect. The pugilist took advantage of the distraction and charged me, his fists flying at my head.

I shifted from side to side, bobbing and weaving to avoid the incoming strikes. Despite backpedaling constantly, I circled around the hall until I managed to put the pugilist between myself and the fighter. While the woman struggled to push herself upright with hands slipping on the bloody tiles, I focused on turning the fight against the boxer.

I couldn't wait too long, not with the System constantly healing her.

Suddenly, an energizing heat swept through me. Both of my opponents' movements faltered as a haunting chord resonated throughout the building. The chord held, reverberating in a steady tone before it combined with the next note, building one upon another until a melancholy tune filled the air.

You are affected by the Whispering Strings' Dirge of the Death Lotus.

I recognized the music and the status effect, bolstering my movements and attack damage while weakening those of my enemies.

Sounds of distant combat followed the notification, along with a whoosh of flame and clanging weapons, confirming that my employer had joined the fray against her own target.

Or targets.

I frowned. The sounds of fire and magic were expected from the sole Advanced Class mage we'd observed while scouting, but the clash of weaponry told me that my employer now fought more than one person. Which meant we had likely missed at least one of the brigands in our reconnaissance of the pass.

Though she hadn't asked for help over party chat, I needed to end my current fight.

"Playtime's over," I growled and sheathed my weapons.

The pugilist and the fighter exchanged a glance of confusion when I pointed an empty hand at each of them. Then the pair grew wide-eyed as a submachine gun appeared in each of my hands, summoned from my Inventory.

The Right Tool for the Job never failed to surprise, the Class Skill offering a separate equipment Storage that allowed me to instantly swap out weapons and gear for a minimal amount of Mana.

I squeezed the triggers while aiming a weapon at each of my foes, and gunfire thundered in the enclosed space of the hallway as a hail of bullets tore into my targets.

Before the System, firing an automatic weapon on full auto with one hand would have been a good way to waste ammunition, as the recoil would drift the barrel upward and off target within a few shots.

Now though, my physique and coordination were beyond superhuman. My increased Strength attribute easily permitted me to control the firearms, despite the bucking recoil. Advanced Agility and Perception attributes combined to allow me to fire the weapons independently with each hand, while keeping them centered on my separate opponents.

The System-adapted short-barreled MP5Ks had a cyclic rate of fire of 900 rounds per minute, and I emptied the 30-round magazines in just over two seconds. Dismissing the depleted weapons back to my Inventory, I took in the damage to my targets.

The fighter slumped to the floor and lay unmoving, her chest and neck a ruined, gory mess.

The pugilist remained on his feet, proving that I was not the only beneficiary of the System's improvements. All those superhuman bonuses were also given to others, leveling the playing field.

A little.

Blood sprayed from the man's mouth with every gasping breath, matting his beard before flowing down to join the blood streaming from his perforated torso. He staggered toward me a single step, then toppled forward onto his face before he lay still. A growing puddle of blood seeped across the floor around the body, and no sign of further movement occurred.

A quick check of my notifications confirmed that I had gained experience for each of the kills, and I left the bodies as I moved toward the sound of ongoing combat farther in the building.

I'd finished one fight, but the battle over the bandit stronghold was far from over.

Chapter 2

Around the corner, a haunting vista greeted me.

Battered and bloody figures lay chained to the wall, and the stench of human filth grew to a nearly unbearable level. Most likely the survivors of the missing travelers, though several of the prisoners lay entirely unmoving. Only the suspension of their restraints kept them upright.

At least one of the still bodies looked as if their skin had been flayed completely, and from the amount of blood around that particular corpse, the torture had occurred while the victim still lived.

The System had brought with it a host of horrors, only adding to the tortures mankind could inflict upon each other. I could only imagine the Class Skills used to bring pain and suffering to the dead and injured cowering here against the wall.

I rushed past as the more alert prisoners either moaned in fear or begged for help, but I had no time for them now—my employer needed my aid.

At the end of the hall, a balcony overlooked the floor of the lower level, and I peeked over the railing at the fighting below. In the center of the open space, just inside the main entrance, a pair of shadowy figures were locked in a close-range melee. A cloud of darkness surrounded both figures and flowed out in waves that swirled around the room below. The liquid gloom obstructed my view and made it impossible to identify either of the combatants.

While I could tag them with my Greater Observation ability, I realized that even if I knew which of the combatants was my boss, the two were so close to each other that any attack on one would be likely to hit the other.

Which was probably why the third figure below stalked angrily around the room with magical fire held in each fist, chanting as he waited for the opportunity to unleash a gout of flame on my employer if she failed to keep her quarry close enough. Heat rippled around the mage, likely indicating some kind of magical shielding defended him.

John Keith (Flamecaster Level 4)

HP: 470/590

MP: 980/1120

The mage's depleted health indicated that my employer must have gotten in a good hit before the missing stealth bandit had made their unaccounted-for presence felt. Still, the Flamecaster was a problem I could deal with now, and the chanting meant that the Advanced Class mage was using more complex spells, not just Class Skills, to bolster his attacks.

Unnoticed by the combatants, I ducked out of sight below the railing and pulled my largest weapon out of my Inventory. The Banshee II Hybrid Gauss Rifle was a unique weapon that utilized Mana like a beam weapon but used that energy to propel physical projectiles to hypersonic velocities.

Like any projectile weapon, the hybrid rifle could boost its damage further depending on the quality of the round fired and the shell's payload. The most cost-effective option remained solid state projectiles, but there were numerous options for the discerning connoisseur. The selection ranged from armor piercing and explosive, up to poison-gas-filled rounds or shells that unleashed raw elemental magic.

For this situation, I slotted a magazine of anti-magic rounds into the rifle's magazine well. Specifically designed to disrupt spellcasting and penetrate magical shielding, the rounds should be perfect for dealing with the mage.

Locked and loaded, I popped up from my crouch and swung the weapon in line with the Flamecaster before squeezing the trigger. The weapon whined as energy built, the sound piercing through the haunting melody that filled the building. The Flamecaster glanced to either side, looking for the source, but it only took a second for charge to accumulate, and in that brief period, the mage never thought to look up.

The rifle kicked back into my shoulder as it discharged, a brilliant beam of coruscating energy streaking down to drive the weapon's projectile into the chest of my target. The Flamecaster's heat shield rippled away from the point of impact as the round punched through the defensive barrier, and the mage staggered backward from the force of the attack.

Keeping the rifle centered on the caster's torso as the man stumbled off balance, I pulled the trigger again. Light flashed through the building as the second shot punched completely through the mage's stomach. The man hunched over with one flaming hand clutching the wound, screaming as he staunched the gaping injury with the cauterizing heat of his ability. The flow of blood pouring out over his hand slowed as he burnt the blood vessels shut.

The afterimage of the rays from my shots still hung in the air, like the retinal imprint left behind by a bolt of lightning. They highlighted my position on the balcony to the mage, who finally recovered enough to turn his head up toward me.

The man snarled with surprise at the sight of me preparing to fire at him yet again. With one hand still covering the wound from my previous shot, the mage thrust his other flame-wreathed hand up at me. An arc of fire reached toward me, rushing through the air like water shot from a high-pressure hose.

I shuffled sideways along the railing just ahead of the cascade of flames that pursued me, but I ran ahead of it, leaning out over the ledge and aiming at the caster once again. Firing on the run before the System had required a high degree of practiced training rarely seen outside of highly skilled military units. Even then, most movements were repeatedly drilled into soldiers who performed at the highest levels of their physical capability. Entering close quarters battle, those operators relied on muscle memory and instinct to identify threats and take down targets.

On the first day of the System Apocalypse, the human average would have been around 10 for most physical attributes: Strength, Constitution, and Agility. A Special Forces soldier or an Olympic-level athlete might have scored as high as 14 in those categories. By the time I reached Level 15 less than two weeks after that, and fully unlocked my Class Skills, my lowest physical attribute was a 31 in Strength and my Agility was double that.

Fast forward another year to now, and my attributes have continued to grow. In short, the old rules no longer applied. Even if the scale of growth wasn't a straight line but more a logarithmic curve, the gains were astounding.

I vaulted over the burning railing, fired at the mage in mid-air, and landed on my feet a story below without breaking stride before firing again.

The Flamecaster's face gaped in surprise and pain as he flailed backward after taking two more rounds to the chest in short succession. His arm still pointed up at the balcony where I had been only moments before, though the stream of magical fire died out as his concentration faltered. The man looked down at his hand and shook it as a questioning look crossed his face. The anti-magic rounds were finally taking effect.

The poison-like substance carried by the projectiles disrupted the Mana within their target, briefly disabling their regeneration and interrupting the ability to actively cast spells if the poison's concentration grew high enough.

The sounds of blades whistling through the air and flesh impacting on armor echoed from the shrouded area between us. I ignored the shadowy melee that still dominated the center of the room, and I circled the floor before launching myself toward the caster.

It took only four loping strides to reach him, and I had dismissed the hybrid rifle back to my Inventory after the first of those steps. My melee weapons were drawn back out by the third, and I stabbed out with the flat of my knife blade held horizontally in front of me as I took the final step.

The blade slipped between the Flamecaster's ribs, and the man gasped before gritting his teeth against the pain. He lifted his hand against my chest and tried to push me away, beginning his chant once again. Flames ignited in his palm and searing heat singed my skin, even through the armor of my jumpsuit. The scents of burning metal and flesh filled my nose as blazing pain spread across my torso.

I ripped the knife from the man's chest, twisting the blade so that its edges scraped across his ribs on the way out, and used the momentum of the caster's push against me to spin myself around. Pivoting on one foot, the head of my axe swung around on the backswing and chopped into the side of the man's neck as I finished my revolution.

The blow hacked through the Flamecaster's throat and severed his spine. The head flopped backward, the last few strands of connecting flesh tearing free as gravity pulled it down and the decapitated body collapsed to the floor.

With the Flamecaster's death, I could focus on the last combatants.

Turning back to the writhing mass of shadow at the center of the room, I concentrated on the fighters within. Greater Observation, another of my Class Skills, allowed me to obtain information on targets if I focused enough attention on them. Pulling the information directly from the System, it was a forced approach that could alert a potential foe of my scrutiny.

With both figures already locked in combat, I no longer needed to worry about alerting a target, and I hit the shadowy mass with the full force of my ability. Though the pair remained shrouded from sight, Greater Observation reached into the murk and detailed the figures within. I sensed their Status, which exposed why the shadows hindered neither combatant.

Countess Dayena Baluisa, Sultana of the Whispering Strings, Mistress of Shadows (Agent Provocateur Level 37)

HP: ???/???

MP: ???/???

Sarah Farnsworth (Shadow Flayer Level 8)

HP: 433/880

MP: 630/960

I'd expected the first figure's Status, but the second came as a surprise.

Another Advanced Class, this one higher leveled than the Flamecaster we'd identified as the initial threat but nowhere near the Level of my employer. Not that Levels were the only thing that came into play when it came to combat—after all, a pure Combat Class would be able to beat a pure crafter even if the crafter was significantly over-Leveled.

I couldn't see either woman through the massed shadows, but Class Skills didn't always need a visual if you could locate the target. The System allowed me to lock on abilities within the sphere of my observation, doing all the heavy lifting.

Since I could assist the Countess, an activation of Hinder on the now-identified bandit grabbed hold of the human woman, and the tempo of the fight shifted dramatically as she slowed.

A moment later, a human figure flew out of the gloom at the center of the room and streaked through the air before bouncing off the wall. A long-bladed dagger with a jagged edge tumbled free on her impact with the wall and clattered to the floor, the woman dropping to her knees beside it.

Covered in scrapes and shallow cuts, none of which looked critical, the petite brunette looked more like a flayee than a Flayer. Several of the wounds over her scalp had shaved away parts of the woman's pixie cut and left her hair a matted mess as blood trickled down her neck from the nicks around her head. Reddened from exertion and fury as she picked up her fallen weapon, the pale-skinned woman stared toward the center of the room with an ugly expression on her face.

The shadows enshrouding the center of the room faded into nothingness, revealing the lithe figure of my employer, who stood poised on one leg. Dayena slowly, deliberately lowered her upraised leg back to the floor, her serene expression in stark opposition to both her opponent and the forceful violence of her kick.

Clad in a matte black armored jumpsuit that clung to her supple form, the dark elf's amethyst eyes watched the Flayer recover the dropped dagger. Her lips were pulled back in a smirk, revealing brilliant white teeth that shone from her onyx skin. Pointed ears peeked out through the platinum hair that framed her shapely face, but the silvery strands transitioned to intertwining weaves of cerulean and crimson as her twin braids descended past her shoulders.

The Truinnar noble flourished her weapons in a display of arrogance designed to enrage her adversary, the pair of silvery swords the length of my forearms flashing through a languid kata.

Her graceful movements before she settled into a ready stance reminded me of our first encounter. Back then, I'd thought that Dayena was just another bard busking for Credits, an athletic elf dancing across the tiny stage of a Gimsar dive bar hidden away in the small town in western Pennsylvania where I'd paused during a quest to deal with a serial killer.

In actuality, the dark elf was something far more than a simple troubadour. Chameleon, spy, or assassin—a Countess with a ceremonial title who complemented her graceful deadliness with ridiculously stacked Charisma. I'd learned far too late that she bent people to her will as easily as she breathed.

I'd discovered that fact when I'd become the object of her interest following our chance meeting in that dingy bar.

After I'd dealt with the serial killer problem, the town's Galactic owner had objected to my methods, and the ensuing argument almost led to my summary execution by the Baron's guards. While I'd debated whether to take down the arrogant alien before his bodyguards could take me out, the Countess showed up and halted the impending violence. Mesmerizing everyone into inaction with her appearance, the Countess informed the town owner that I worked for her—while offering me a System contract which would make her bluff a statement of truth.

Not particularly keen on dying, I'd accepted the employment contract.

Without reading the terms.

Now I watched the Countess catch her breath during the lull in the combat, though the dark elf's face showed none of the frustration or anger evidenced by her human foe. While the Countess also bore a handful of minor injuries, the dark elf looked more than comfortable continuing the battle without my assistance.

The Flayer glanced at where I stood over the body of the fallen Flamecaster, and a hint of panic reached her widening eyes. A twisted smirk crossed my face as I folded my arms across my chest, content to keep watch for any other foes we'd missed while the Countess finished her fight. I enjoyed the reversal of fortune, though it paled compared to the tortures the bandit had inflicted upon her victims on the floor above.

The Countess tossed one of her short swords into the air, focusing all attention upon her. The Truinnar coolly raised the now free hand to beckon her opponent to return to the fight. The taunting motion completed, Dayena opened her palm as the hilt of the airborne blade dropped back into it.

The casual showmanship and nonchalance enraged the Flayer beyond reason. An unhinged, warbling scream echoed through the hall as the crazed woman charged back at the Countess.

Even if we were fourteen months after the System's integration, most people had been civilians beforehand. Fighting, controlling your emotions and reactions during a fight, none of that came naturally.

Didn't hurt that the Countess was turning the full brunt of her massive Charisma pool on the Flayer for the taunt either.

The dark elf stepped forward to meet her enemy, and blades flashed as the two joined together in a deadly dance. The slightly longer short swords gave the Countess the edge in reach over the Flayer's knives, but both sets of weapons were designed for close-in fighters. Metal clanged as the women parried and scraped their blades against each other.

No longer concerned with being roasted by the now-deceased Flamecaster, the Countess devoted her full attention to the fight. Each movement was a study in perfection and control, every fluid motion only shifting the Countess the minimal amount required to deflect the wild strikes of the enraged flayer.

A chill ran down my spine as I realized the Countess was toying with her opponent. The difference in Levels, training, and practical experience meant that the Flayer had no chance now that the combat was one-on-one.

A flash of blades passed between the combatants, and the Flayer sank to her knees, disemboweled and gurgling from a slashed throat. The Countess stepped around behind the woman, ending her suffering by scissoring her paired short swords through the back of the woman's neck and severing her spine.

The body slumped to the floor, and silence filled the room as the haunting melody which had filled the building finally ceased.

Thankfully. As great as the effects were, classical music had never been my thing.

Chapter 3

"Nice of you to finally show up."

The Countess spoke without looking in my direction, cleaning her weapons with a cast of the Cleanse spell before returning the blades to the sheaths belted at either side of her narrow waist. "Are there any survivors?"

"Upstairs," I replied, ignoring her initial comment. "They'll need cut free before we try to move them to town. They're in bad shape from an item or a Skill."

The elf nodded and gestured to a shadow that hovered just inside the main entrance to the building, a pocket of gloom which I hadn't even noticed until now.

Hovering in the air at shoulder height, the umbra faded to reveal a stringed instrument, not unlike a violin. Constructed from some kind of blackened metal, the sinuously curved body of the apparatus tapered into a longer neck which bore a half dozen strings and ran the length of the instrument.

A bow of ivory bone strung with strands of blue-tinged black hair fluttered just above the instrument's strings, as if an unseen musician were ready to play at a moment's notice.

Tier I Luitsalin (The Whispering Strings)

Base Damage: N/A

Durability: 6000/6000

Special Abilities: Umbral Shroud (Level 40), Etheric Performance (Level 37), Dirge of the Death Lotus (Level 34)

The Whispering Strings, an heirloom relic instrument, passed down through Dayena's family for at least two generations before her. Mastery over the soulbound Luitsalin bestowed on the Countess a title, boosting her already significant abilities in conflict, both in more physical combat and the social skirmishes of Truinnar politics.

Most of the time, the instrument resisted my use of Greater Observation, so the abilities listed in its status were only the ones I personally witnessed in use. Beyond that, the instrument tended to slip from awareness unless I focused on it intentionally or came under its effects when it boosted our party. The relic's full capabilities remained a jealously guarded secret, and I didn't blame the Countess for keeping them under wraps.

Wars had been fought over weapons of similar power, near sentient items with the ability to Level independently of their user.

The relic floated through the air and drifted down, locking itself into place on a harness clamp behind the Countess's left shoulder. While the Luitsalin could play itself, the semi-sentient instrument generally tended to disguise that fact.

Dayena watched me eye her prized relic with an amused air, a smirk just barely evident in the upraised corner of her lips before she leaned over to loot the body at her feet. Her motion prompted me to action, and I began my own looting with the corpse of the Flamecaster.

The dead man gave up a fair number of Credits, and I lamented that only Credits could be looted from Inventory, with all other items lost to the ether and the System. A few bits of jewelry that seemed to carry minor enchantments, so I helped myself to them.

Ring of Fire Magic +1

Effect: Increases the damage of fire-based spells and Skills by the owner by 10%.

Necklace of Adurkarthan

Effect: Boosts armor penetration strength of fire magic by 20%.

No wonder the flames had burned right through my armor.

I chucked both items into my Inventory. While I owned a fire spell purchased from the Shop, it was more to ensure I carried a full spread of elemental damage so that I had options if I encountered a creature with resistances to my usual methods of dealing out destruction.

Generally, that meant shooting, stabbing, or hacking things to bits.

I stood from stripping the corpse, and a chill ran down my spine. Goosebumps formed on my arms, and the hair on the back of my neck stood up.

Distant attention focused upon me, sizing me up and assessing me as if weighing my worth. Looking around, I saw nothing—but then, I never did.

The feeling almost always swept over me after I'd been involved in a violent confrontation. The mysterious watcher, or watchers, didn't seem to care whether I fought humans, Galactics, or monsters. That I emerged from those conflicts victorious seemed the only concern.

Dayena saw my glance around the room. "Your watchers again?"

I nodded in confirmation at the elf's raised eyebrow. As my employer, she'd long since known the truth of my hidden Class. However, even our combined Shop research failed to reveal the source of my unknown observers. The absolutely astronomical cost in Credits for the answer to that particular question remained out of reach even for an individual with the resources of the Countess.

While that answer eluded us, we successfully managed to obtain a small bit of information on my unique Advanced Class at a lofty, but still affordable, price.

The Class originated from the Fey homeworld, the planetary kingdom of Perisreien, which was well known for the limited export of high-quality magically infused steel. Beyond that strictly governed trade, little actual knowledge of the restricted solar system seemed available. Beyond the fact that any outsider setting foot upon the planet acquired an automatic death sentence.

I could only hope to find more information before reaching Level 50 and progressing up to the next Class tier.

For now, I ignored the fading sensation of being observed. Dayena handed over the useful items she'd stripped from her vanquished foe before I dragged both of the bandit corpses into my Meat Locker storage space. Once we were finished, I planned to either dump them out of sight in the wilderness on the way back to town or sell them off at the Shop if I didn't find better monster carcasses on the trip.

Morbid, but even after a year as part of the System, researchers across the Galaxy still paid top Credits for fresh human cadavers.

Either way, no sense in letting the survivors see the bodies of their tormentors on their way out of their former prison.

By the time I stored the corpses, the Countess had headed to the prisoners upstairs and started removing the manacles chaining them to the wall.

With the imminent threat of combat eliminated, I now took the time to look over the survivors. Four women and two men still breathed, while two other unidentifiable figures also hung limply from the chains. One of the two dead was the flayed prisoner I had noticed before but the other appeared to have been beaten into a literal pulp. Still shackled to the wall, neither were remotely recognizable in their current shape.

A sharp click indicated Dayena's success with the first set of manacles and the woman they'd held slumped to the ground, curling up into herself defensively with a moan.

Dayena glanced at me, and I jerked my head to the next of the prisoners before kneeling next to the woman on the ground. While I left the Countess to deal with the lockpicking, I cast Improved Minor Healing on the first of the freed hostages.

Charlotte Miller (Scout Level 28)

HP: 28/280

MP: 30/300

The injured woman recoiled from my touch with a panicked shriek, which she quickly stifled as if afraid of my reaction to the sound. All this, despite the fact that my spell instantly more than doubled her low health. She pulled herself back against the wall and stared at me wide-eyed, wrapping her arms around her knees as she drew them up to her chest.

"Easy, Charlotte," I said. "You're safe now. We're here to help."

Charlotte's shoulders heaved as shuddered breaths came rapidly, almost panting despite my attempt to calm her panic.

My appearance as a heavily armed male figure was likely the trigger for her alarm. It would likely have been better to have the Countess attempting to comfort the woman, but I lacked the finesse to break the prisoners free from their shackles as quickly as the dark elf.

A quick glance at the manacles hanging above the quivering woman in front of me showed that my priorities were correct when I examined them with Greater Observation.

Consuming Manacles of Enslavement

Effect: While wearing these shackles, Mana and health are limited to 10% of their maximum values and all regeneration is disabled. No Class Skill or spell may be activated while worn. Drained regeneration from the wearer feeds back into the shackles to reinforce their durability. Consuming Manacles of Enslavement will not activate their special effects against targets of the Advanced Class tier or higher.

That effect meant that removing the shackles had to be our priority. Once freed, the former prisoners could start regenerating health and Mana naturally on their own. My Minor Healing spell would do the trick, but it had a sixty-second cooldown between uses.

The combination of the drain and disabling effects were likely why the prisoners failed to escape, despite their own System-granted abilities.

"Easy," I repeated myself, dragging the word out. "I'm going to put my hand on your arm, so I can cast another healing spell on you, okay? I'm not going to hurt you."

The woman watched, wide-eyed, as I gently reached forward and set my hand on top of her arm that remained wrapped around her knees. I kept my hand still once it touched the bare skin of her arm and triggered a second healing spell, Minor Renew, even as the woman shook beneath my touch.

Another click from the next prisoner over indicated that the Countess had freed the next of the prisoners, so I needed to move on.

I patted the woman's arm. "I'm going to move on to help the others, Charlotte. I'm not going far."

The woman still trembled as I removed my hand and slid over to the next prisoner, a young man who's tattered shirt showed the slashes cut through both fabric and flesh over his torso. The wounds had been allowed to heal and then sliced open once again.

James Jackson (Porter Level 24)

HP: 36/360

MP: 18/180

James clutched tenderly at his wrists where the skin remained chafed and raw underneath where the manacles had rubbed. There were scabs on his reddened flesh that looked painful, and his eyes stared sightlessly straight ahead.

"James, we're going to get you out of here," I said.

The young man blinked at my words but otherwise failed to respond. I cautiously placed my hand on one of his outstretched legs and cast both of my minor heals, one after the other. His health ticked upwards with the spells but nothing else seemed to change.

"You're free now, James. Are you still with us here, buddy?"

Another slow blink of unseeing eyes followed my question but still no response. I sighed, knowing that even with the System's miraculous healing, the traumatized victims here would need lengthy therapy to deal with the torture they'd endured. I patted the young man on his leg before moving on to the next of the wounded prisoners.

The remaining four were freed and healed in short order, though each exhibited signs of their ordeal that ranged between the panicked hysteria and the unresponsive catatonia of the first pair.

Darkness fell over the pass by the time I finished burying the dead prisoners and dumped the bandit corpses for nature to take its course. Those who used their power to abuse others received no dignity from me in their deaths.

The Countess got the survivors outside the visitor's center by the time I returned. Since only the Countess and I had working bikes, we couldn't carry all the survivors even if we doubled up. That lack of transportation meant our trip out of the mountains to the nearest town would be on foot.

Our slow-moving group left the visitor's center behind and headed downhill to the east, out of the cut. Leaving behind corpses and bad memories. If there was ever a case for the non-existence of ghosts and haunts, the entire damn planet these days would be a good one.

Nightmares, human and alien made, everywhere.

Chapter 4

"If you are still reading what I think you are, you will not find what you seek."

Before my deployment to Afghanistan, I'd gone with my best friend from high school to an underground jazz club. How Roger had managed to get an in there, I'd never found out. It was the kind of back-alley place with an unmarked door that only let you in if they knew you or, in my case, if someone vouched for you.

I didn't remember much from that night after the whiskey started flowing, but one thing stuck with me. The crowded stage at the far back of the dark room had somehow squeezed a double bassist and a saxophonist in between a drummer and a full-sized piano, though the musicians faded into the background as soon as the spotlight came on and highlighted the vocalist with a thigh-high slit in her blood-red dress.

Her voice filled the room with an intoxicating, velvety warmth that dripped sex and sensuality. I couldn't recall a single lyric, but I remembered the intensity of the moments when her eyes met mine during her performances throughout the night.

The sultry smokiness of the voice calling over my shoulder reminded me of that speakeasy singer. Her words sent a tingle down my spine before I reminded myself it was just the dark elf's damn Charisma at work.

"Again." Her single word chimed with unrestrained mirth.

With a sigh, I closed the System window, dismissing the blue box of text that detailed the terms of the contract between myself and my employer. I looked back at the Truinnar noble, who hurried to catch up to me in the dark as I led the way toward the nearest town. My focus on the now-dismissed document and deterring attacks from the local monster populations had led me to ranging farther ahead of the survivors than I'd intended.

Efficient Trail, a tier three passive Class Skill enhancing my movements, meant that I crossed rugged terrain more swiftly than most others. Since I usually only had the Countess around, her high Agility allowed her to keep up if she worked at it, but the line of recovered humans behind her looked a bit more strung-out than I felt comfortable with.

I hoped at higher Levels, the Class Skill would apply movement bonuses to my party, but that would likely take more points than I wanted to spend with the number of passive Skills already eating into my Mana regeneration.

The dark elf met my gaze, and I rolled my eyes at her confident expression.

Truth be told, I didn't mind working for the Triunnar noble. She wanted to Level up as much as I did, and she rarely acted like the spoiled heiress she pretended to be in more airified company. Instead, she eagerly listened to me when it mattered, and we'd earned a number of Levels working together.

Something of my thoughts must have shown on my face, because Dayena winked at me before turning back to the curving exit ramp that left the highway just in front of us.

The highways of the former United States had fared poorly over the last year, with the complete lack of maintenance leaving crater-sized potholes and cracks just from the changes of the seasons. Fallen trees, washed out bridges, and monster damage only added to the obstacles encountered on the roadways.

After nearly five miles over the broken asphalt of I-68 and a half dozen furious monster assaults from out of the night, we had finally brought our group of rescuees within sight of the walls of the Village of Hancock, Maryland. The town's main gate sat about a quarter mile south of the interstate interchange with US Route 522.

The silvery barriers stood just over two stories high and glinted in the nighttime darkness from the floodlights spaced at regular intervals along the upper rim. Outside the perimeter, all vegetation had been stripped back nearly one hundred yards to provide a clear field of fire, though the actual defenses were sparsely distributed automated turrets that barely covered the entirety of the open area.

The defenses, which ran in an oblong arc from one end of town to the other along the northern side of the Potomac River, were courtesy of the town's latest Galactic owner. Ostensibly independent, the alien was another Triunnar like the Countess and claimed to "administer the Village on the benevolent behalf" of the Dragon's Teeth Guild—since Guilds were not permitted to own settlements.

While the administrator was certainly not a Dragon's Teeth Guild member, there were clearly some strings attached between the Guild and their puppet bureaucrat. So far, the Guild seemed content to set up the town as a midpoint port on a canal operation based on the restoration of the old Chesapeake and Ohio Canal. All in an effort to establish a major east-west transportation route from the east coast to the burgeoning starport outside of Pittsburgh, Pennsylvania.

Though they had made good time for the first part of the trip, moving easily with their physical wounds healed, the former prisoners showed more signs of enthusiasm and liveliness as they crossed the final stretch into town than they had displayed since their rescue. It made sense, the walls a tangible sign of safety and protection that the survivors had been without for so long.

The gates slid open silently before I reached them, and I stepped to the side, waving the rest of the group through. Just inside the light pouring from the newly formed opening, a boar-headed alien guard grunted an unintelligible greeting as Charlotte entered. On a chain around the guard's neck hung a fang no larger than my index finger, proclaiming the alien's affiliation with the Dragon's Teeth Guild.

Scrofalori Gunner (Level 36)
HP: 420/420
MP: 220/220

Without being obvious about it, I kept an eye on the gunner while everyone passed through the gate, though the stocky, furred alien allowed them to pass without any sign of concern. That air of indifference fell away when the hirsute alien's black eyes caught sight of the Countess bringing up the rear of the party. The Scrofalori blinked, and its head slowly rotated to follow the dark elf as she stepped past me without seeming to notice the scrutiny. The dark elf had a habit of drawing attention with her high Charisma.

With the Countess entering the town, that left only me outside the gate, so I stepped in after the others, still leery of the alien guard.

My eyes flicked to the pair of notifications that appeared as I set foot inside the walls, but I left them unacknowledged and waited until I heard the gate snap shut, leaving the guard well behind. The first notification was one I had received before, and I dismissed it as soon as I saw nothing within the text had changed from my initial visit.

You Have Entered a Safe Zone (The Village of Hancock)

Mana flows in this area are stabilized. No monster spawning will happen.

This Safe Space includes:

Village of Hancock City Center

The Shop

FastCharge Mana Replenishment Vehicle Station

The second notification was the successful completion of the Quest that had led the Countess and me up to the mountain pass in search of the bandits.

Quest Completed: Clear the Pass

Bandits have blockaded the Sideling Hill Road Cut along Interstate 68, cutting off the flow of pedestrians and goods through the Appalachian Mountains. The inhabitants of Hancock, Maryland, have put up this Quest to reward the removal of the problem.

Rewards: 5,000 Credits; 5,000XP

Optional Objective Completed. Bonus Rewards: 500 Credits per Each Survivor (3,000 Credits Received); 250XP per Survivor (1,500XP Received)

While neither the Credits nor experience rewarded were significant, every little bit helped, and the experience gained from the deaths of the higher-Leveled crooks made the trip worthwhile.

The Quest completion triggered a new update to my status, one I was more than happy to see.

Level Up!

You have reached Level 38 as a Relentless Huntsman. Stat Points automatically distributed. You have 2 Free Attributes and 8 Class Skill Points to distribute.

"Finally," I muttered as I closed the update without taking the time to assign either set of points.

While I planned to spend the Free Attributes during my next downtime, I'd been hoarding the Skill points for when I hit Level 46 and unlocked the fourth tier of my Class Skills. Having several available points to dump into those new abilities would be a huge boost.

I'd already been reserving several points for my third tier of Class Skills when my employment with the Countess began, and I quickly learned that one of the advantages of working for a Triunnar noble meant access to her deep pockets. Her payments for my services were significant enough for me to purchase Class Skill points from the Shop and largely offset any actual resentment I might hold for the way she'd snared me into her service with a Contract.

At my murmured exclamation, the Countess turned back to face me, and it only took me a couple strides to reach her. The dark elf matched my pace when I caught up.

"Congratulations," the Countess said.

I nodded. "Thanks. It's taking longer, the higher I Level."

"That is why so few reach Master Class," the Countess explained. "Or beyond. The higher you strive, the more dangerous it becomes to continue pressing onward."

"I don't plan to stop," I said.

"No, I imagine not." She grinned. Despite the brilliance of her white teeth shining from the onyx skin of her face, it was a dark smile that beamed at me, and her eyes glinted with a dangerous fire. "I have plans of my own."

"I'm aware," I said. "It seems I'm stuck with you for a while."

"Ah, yes," the Countess said. "Your perpetual search for loopholes in our Contract. I assure you, there are none."

I sighed. The elf still read me like a book, despite the Levels I had gained since our first meeting.

Looking for a change of subject, I gestured at the building ahead of us. Though the broken sign standing at the edge of the road proclaimed the building across the parking lot to be a Save-a-Lot, the honest-to-goodness castle which stood in its place was only one of the many manifestations of the changes the System had wrought upon the world. Smoothly carved marble blocks stacked in offset rows three stories high made up the fortress that housed the Village's City Center and the local access point for the System Shop.

"Shop?"

"Yes," she replied, smirking even while she allowed me to change the topic. "I have a few upgrades I want to look into."

An ecstatic cry from ahead of us pulled my attention from the Countess and back to the survivors who had continued down the street. A handful of people gathered along the street to meet the former prisoners, with more rushing out to join the small throng from farther within the town. The majority were half-dressed or in night clothes of one sort, evidence of the late hour and the haste with which they'd assembled.

The townsfolk who had contributed to the Quest must have been notified of its completion and rushed to greet their returned friends and loved ones. Charlotte had already been engulfed in the arms of her family. James and the rest were all quickly smothered in hugs and tears of joy.

I glanced at the Countess and jerked my head toward the Shop. At her nod, the pair of us slipped away from the excitement and managed to enter the building unnoticed.

The entryway into the City Center building resembled an airlock more than the medieval exterior the structure presented, but the automated security system allowed Dayena and me to pass through without issue. Past the screening, the passage opened into a larger, dimly lit room that took up most of the first floor. Several desks used by the town's administrators sat empty at this late hour, but a glowing crystal off to the side of the area indicated the Shop's access point.

After I placed my hand on the crystal, I blinked at the sudden shift from the gloomy room to a brightly lit hall as I found myself transported to my personal Shop. A long hall, reminiscent of a museum, brimmed with cases that displayed all manner of weapons, armor, and equipment.

"Adventurer Mason!" the cheerful voice boomed out to greet me. "Welcome back!"

"Shopkeeper Ryk." I nodded in greeting to the quadrupedal Bariadur, the centaur-like alien with the body of a ram, humanoid torso, and curled horns. The corner of my mouth twitched upward in a wry smirk. "You just saw me less than a day ago."

"One never knows what may happen on a Dungeon World," Ryk replied. "Survival is far from guaranteed."

I shrugged to acknowledge the ram-like alien's point. He wasn't wrong, but I'd never been one to dwell on my mortality. Sure, life tended to be pretty risky these days, but in my opinion, the advantages provided by the System's superhuman abilities more than offset the danger.

Or maybe I was just an adrenaline junkie now.

Either way, I couldn't change the world, only do my best to meet the threats and continue to survive.

I waved toward the shopkeeper, sending him an update to my munitions inventory. Ryk's eyes went unfocused for a moment as he processed the data, then he nodded as he focused back on me.

"Before I forget," Ryk said, "I have a message for you."

"A message?" While there were Class Skills that allowed one to communicate across vast distances, Shops were often used as intermediaries or post offices.

The communication appeared in a window before me, and I read it quickly. Apparently, some former allies had a job offer for me, though it would mean heading back toward the Pittsburgh area. I had avoided the city in an effort to let the heat die down after my actions had led to a conflict between two Galactic factions. Actions to which those factions remained ignorant.

Ryk noted that I had finished reading the message and brought my attention back to the present. "Pretty light on your hunting this time?"

"Don't worry. I've still got some goodies for you."

It didn't take long to unload my Inventory of the bandits' equipment and the loot from the monsters slain along our round trip through the mountains, receiving a tidy sum of Credits in exchange. If I restrained myself, I might come out ahead on this Shop trip. A rare occurrence indeed. Normally, I spent almost everything I got in upgrades to my gear, the occasional spell to bolster my limited casting abilities, or the rare new Class Skill.

"Anything else for you today?" Ryk asked.

"No," I replied. "I just need a moment to spend some attribute points, and I'll be on my way."

The shopkeeper nodded and moved off to give me some space, puttering around the display cases farther down the lengthy hall. Far enough away to provide the illusion of privacy, but still close enough to respond.

I brought up my Status screen and gave my attributes a quick look, wincing as I saw my Credit balance. I wouldn't be buying any more Class Skill points for a while.

As far as my attributes went, my Agility and Constitution far outpaced all of my other attributes, with Agility standing out as the higher of the two values.

Back when I gained my Advanced Class, my Class Skills had been locked, due to my overall attributes lacking the minimum prerequisites for the Class. The attributes would always be missing since I'd skipped over the Base Class tier completely when I'd selected Relentless Huntsman instead of a more common Basic Class like Soldier or Marine.

In turn, I'd gained almost triple the attribute points per Level when compared to the more standard Classes and a lower XP cost per Level. The cost being the inability to access my Skills until I raised my attributes to the minimum required, along with never having a Basic Class and its variety of Skills.

I still didn't regret the choice, though I had far more points in Agility than I really needed these days. It would have been nice for my attributes to be a little more evenly distributed. But the speed it gave me let me stand in the face of focused melee classes that I really shouldn't have been brawling with otherwise.

I'd been trying to break my bad habit of mixing things up at close range and stick to my pistols, but I'd spent nearly ten months stretching every

Credit to the max and conserving ammo before getting on the Countess's payroll. Her funds provided high quality ammunition for my projectile weapons, which let me spend a bit more profligately.

Those considerations pretty much decided where I needed to put my latest points. While Luck held the distinction of being my lowest attribute overall, almost no one added points to that characteristic. I still dropped a couple points into Luck every ten Levels, just on the principle that I had survived when so many others had not.

For now, I added the first of my available points to my lowest practical attribute, Willpower. Then I put the second point into Perception, the attribute besides Agility most critical for my particular brand of marksmanship.

I finalized the selections, only to have another blue box pop up asking if I wanted to use my unspent Class Skill points. The window showed the full tree of my available abilities, highlighting the tempting options of places I could spend the points.

The tree showed the three branches "Utility," "Pursuit," and "Combat."

From Utility, I'd already unlocked Meat Locker, Right Tool for the Job, and Quality Over Quantity. Pursuit held Keen Senses, Greater Observation, and Efficient Trail. Finally, my Combat options were Hinder, Rend, and Expose.

Between the main branches were a few other Skills. On the Hunt, Implacable Endurance, and Resilient Nature rounded out the last places I could spend my points now.

At the top of each tree were the final choices, which I couldn't select now. More Where That Came From, Apprehend, and Kill Shot remained grayed out and unavailable.

At Level 46, those tier four options would become accessible, and seeing them waiting only strengthened my decision to hoard my accumulating points.

I closed the popup and took another look over my updated Status.

Status Screen			
Name:	Hal Mason*	Class:	Hunter*
Race:	Human (Male)	Level:	38
Titles			
Galactic Iron Bounty Hunter, Sharp Eyed* (*Title hidden)			
Health:	1200	Stamina:	1200
Mana:	870		
Status			
Normal*			
Attributes			
Strength	68	Agility	131
Constitution	120	Perception	82
Intelligence	87	Willpower	62

Charisma	86	Luck	22
Class Skills			
Efficient Trail	1	Expose	1
Greater Observation	2	Hinder	2
Implacable Endurance	1	Keen Senses	1
Meat Locker	3	On the Hunt	3
Quality Over Quantity	1	Rend	1
Resilient Nature	2	Right Tool for the Job	2
Non-Class Skills			
Blood Scent	1		
Perks			
Gut Instinct			

Combat Spells
Earth Spike (II), Firespray (II), Frostbolt (VI), Frostnova (IV), Greater Healing (I), Greater Regeneration (I), Lesser Disguise (V), Minor Healing (IV), Minor Renew (II)

The asterisks that dotted my Status sheet caused a smirk to briefly tug my normally stern expression into one of amusement. Those marks denoted information "adjusted" using On the Hunt, the Class Skill that allowed me to manipulate the information displayed to others by the System and even hide the alterations from all but the most focused high-ranked analysis Skills.

I closed the window and wiped the mirth from my face before I looked around for Ryk. The shopkeeper rubbed a cloth across a display case farther down the hall, wiping imagined smudges from the already spotless surface.

"Heading out, Ryk," I said with a wave. "Take care of yourself."

"You as well, Adventurer Mason." Ryk paused his cleaning and faced me before bowing his human-like torso. "You take care as well."

The museum-like hall of the Shop faded from around me, and I found myself back in the dim administrative town center. There was no sign of the Countess, so I walked over to the exit from the building.

If she took as long shopping as she usually did, I might have time to find my way to the bottom of a whisky glass or two.

Chapter 5

The outer airlock doors slid open with a faint squeak, and I paused with one foot outside the building, seeing a half-dozen figures in an arc surrounding the entrance. Moonlight highlighted the two silver-haired Truinnar in the center of the group, one male and one female, who were involved in a serious conversation.

The first Truinnar wore modern gear, a high-tech suit of plate power armor painted in mottled shades of gray and black which covered him from neck to toe. The suit's helmet sat in the crook of one arm and the dark elf's other hand gripped the haft of a two-handed mace, the spiked head of which sat on the ground by his feet.

The dark elven woman wore a blood-red bodysuit beneath a shimmering black corset that highlighted her slender waist and emphasized her hourglass figure. Turned half toward her male partner, the side profile she presented to me showed off her well-formed backside. A closer look at the corset revealed that the glinting came from light reflecting off the fine scales that covered the entire garment. I blinked as I realized the attire wasn't just decorative. It was armor. A dragon-scale corset.

The two dark elves glanced at me when the doors opened, my arrival interrupting their conversation. They looked me over, the male dismissing me almost instantly and returning to lecturing the female, but her gaze seemed to linger, her purple eyes sparkling as she sized me up. The male snapped his fingers in front of the woman, sneering as she turned her attention back to him.

"You can stare at humans you find pretty later," he scoffed. "We have a mission to complete."

The female dark elf bristled at her partner's belittling words, and I realized that the male had spoken in Truinnar, not English. Neither of them realized I'd understood them—courtesy of a purchased language pack from the Shop—but his words, combined with his abrupt dismissal of my appearance, let me know I wasn't their quarry.

Split with a pair on either side of the two dark elves, a quartet of human mercenaries waited with bored and tired expressions. They'd focused on me initially but dismissed me as a threat after my arrival was ignored by the pair of Truinnar.

The three men and a woman were all armed but looked as though they'd just rolled out of bed, since none of the four wore combat armor. Two carried rifles pointed at the ground, but neither shooter held their hands in position on the pistol grips of their weapons, so they weren't in any position to fire right away. The third man carried a heater shield with a sword belted in a scabbard at his waist, while the lone woman leaned on her staff and yawned.

None of the humans wore the dragon tooth pendant of the local Guild, nor did they display a Truinnar House standard. Like the rose-and-fanged-skull emblem on the shoulder of the dark elf male's powered armor. That lack of insignia meant the mercs were local hires, likely contracted on the cheap.

Which meant there would be no consequences if the Countess or I eliminated them.

At least, not from the Truinnar.

Certain municipal authorities tended to get pissy when you killed people in their towns, as I'd found in the past.

That little instant analysis of the situation and potential ramifications meant that all my studies were paying off. Learning the politics of the System and the major players on Earth after beginning my employment with the Countess had been annoying but strategically useful.

The mercenaries all had Levels in the upper 40s, but it was the pair of Truinnar that held my attention as I scanned their statuses.

Creynora Baluisa (Heart Guard Level 46)
HP: 860/860
MP: 940/940

Rhegnah Baluisa, Fist of Judgment, Deputy Adjudicator (Dominator Level 34)
HP: 1980/1980
MP: 2190/2190

With those last names, there could be no mistake. They could only be here for my employer.

Worse, the massive Health and Mana values on the male Truinnar meant he had to be an Advanced Class, with his level nearly equal to the Countess's. And I had no way to warn the Countess about the danger, since party chat didn't work unless the group happened to be together inside the same instance of the Shop.

No evidence of my thoughts crossed my face as I stepped outside and turned to my left, the door sliding closed behind me as I walked alongside the building. I continued beyond the group's loose perimeter before stopping to lean casually against the corner of the building, my arms folded across my chest while I took in the conspicuously empty area. Both the streets and the parking-lot-turned-courtyard in front of the castle-like admin building had cleared of the townsfolk celebrating the return of their loved ones, leaving the space abandoned but for the Truinnar and mercs.

I couldn't even hear the footsteps of the usual guild guards on the ramparts two stories over my head, though the floodlights from the structure's walls illuminated the lot.

It took several minutes before any of them noticed I hadn't wandered off and stood in a position to flank them, which didn't speak well of their situational awareness. Then again, my Skills tended to make me rather inconspicuous unless someone actively paid attention to my presence.

"This doesn't concern you." The nearest rifleman, standing on the group's flank, had finally turned to me.

The man growled menacingly when my only response was to regard him with a raised eyebrow. He didn't say anything further, and I took my time responding.

"Looks like you're about to put on a show."

"Keep. Moving."

I caught the faint sound of the admin building's inner doors sliding open just behind the merc's growled command.

"You've got a family welcoming committee waiting for you out here," I thought over party chat. *"Two relatives and four human mercenaries."*

The Countess barely hesitated in her reply. *"Understood."*

A moment later, the sound of the administrative building doors opening pulled the attention of the man questioning me toward the Countess as she stepped out of the building. My employer wielded an icy glare at the two Truinnar facing her, her hands resting only inches from the hilts of her blades, thumbs looped through her belt.

She ignored the presence of the mercenaries as they readied for the impending confrontation, shifting from foot to foot and clutching their weapons nervously.

I nearly sneered in disgust. They weren't professionals. They were pretenders playing at soldier, thinking that System abilities substituted for training and discipline. Beyond their woeful preparedness, the most critical thing for the mercs though was that they'd completely forgotten my presence at the Countess's appearance.

Tension built as the weight of silence grew. No one wanted to be the first to speak.

Finally, the male Truinnar swung his mace up onto his shoulder with one hand and stepped forward, the weight of his power armor crunching the broken asphalt of the former parking lot with each stride. He stopped a handful of paces from the Countess and looked down at my employer with hate-filled eyes. Despite the Countess standing above my own 6' 2", the power armor added almost eight inches to the Royal Adjudicator.

"Cousin." His haughty tone dripped with disdain as the armored elf barely acknowledged my employer and blinked, hesitating, as his eyes traced over her lithe figure. "You've certainly grown."

Higher pitched than I'd expected, the lusty hunger in the adjudicator's voice felt more than slightly creepy. I had to acknowledge that the Truinnar appeared rather handsome, despite the severe expression on his angular face. I wondered if Truinnar always placed their Free Attribute points into Charisma when they Leveled, though I appreciated the attractive appearance of the curvier Truinnar woman far more.

"Cousin Rhegnah," the Countess replied with barely a nod, her facial expression completely blank, before bowing her head toward the other elf with slightly more respect. "Cousin Creynora."

The dark elf in the sanguine bodysuit acknowledged the greeting wordlessly with a nod of her own before a lull descended over the area once again.

"It's time to end this wayward journey of yours and return home," Rhegnah said. "His Grace grows tired of the delay in your marriage, and his patience with our family grows thin."

The Countess sneered as the adjudicator spoke. "I will not be auctioned off as a broodmare just to satisfy the lusts of some ancient noble."

"It is your duty to meet your family's obligations," Rhegnah shot back.

"Duty?" The Countess spat angrily to her side, the spittle splashing onto the asphalt. "I am no pawn. Nor am I a child, and I refuse to be treated like one."

"I see there is no reasoning with you." Rhegnah sighed. "I look forward to seeing you being taught your place."

The adjudicator lifted his arm, waving at the Countess in a clear signal to the surrounding mercenaries.

"Take the mercs," the Countess commanded over party chat as the mercenaries closed in around her.

Thunder and flame blossomed into the back of the nearest rifleman's head as my paired projectile pistols were drawn from their holsters and fired in a quarter of a second. I continued the barrage as I pushed off from the wall and lunged forward to close the space between myself and my target.

The roar of my unexpected attacks surprised the group surrounding the Countess, and all of the hostile combatants turned toward the sudden threat. That instinctive reaction gave the Countess the opening she needed to close the distance to the Deputy Adjudicator and kick the helmet from the crook of her cousin's arm. The helmet bounced away across the parking lot as the Countess kept her momentum, running up the chest of the adjudicator's power armor and kicking him squarely in his vulnerable face. The armored elf lurched backward under the force of the impact.

My sustained fusillade reduced the head of my target to a gory stump. As I reached the already collapsing corpse, return fire blazed toward me from the merc on the far side of the encirclement. Ignoring the energy beam that sizzled past me, I crouched in the shelter of the first crumpling human as I centered myself on my next target. Then I sprang forward with my weapons blazing.

This time, my rounds failed to catch the target unawares, and a translucent blue barrier popped into place around the staff-carrying mage. The magical defenses deflected my rounds, but I continued firing as I ran to close the space between us, circling to place the mage bubble between myself and the man with the beam rifle.

Meanwhile, the second dark elf had engaged with the Countess, the two Truinnar women fighting in circles while the adjudicator swung his mace at my employer with heavy sweeps that she managed to dodge. Though she remained hard-pressed by her two foes, I had no aid to give the Countess as the sword-and-board merc charged me around the mage's shield.

I ducked under a slash of the warrior's sword and kept up my fire on the mage. The magical shield sparked as it deflected each shot. Despite my predicament, I grinned at the panic on the woman's face as each round pushed deeper into the shield, circular ripples washing outward from the impacts as Expose ramped up.

The Class Skill applied increasing damage bonuses to attacks against personal defenses, like the shield around the mage, and my fire soon tore through the faltering barrier. It gave way with a sudden pop before fading out of existence completely.

Before I could capitalize on the now-defenseless mage, a lunging stab from the warrior forced me to leap away. The warrior followed up the stab with a slash on the backswing. Even though the mage remained the greater overall threat, the immediate danger from the warrior forced me to deal with the sword-wielding mercenary first.

I stepped sideways as the man stabbed at me again. This time I let the blade glance off my armored ribs and continue through between my arm and torso. Before the warrior could recover, I clamped my elbow down on his extended arm and dropped my pistol to firmly hold the warrior in place.

Shock filled the man's eyes as I pulled him toward me and twisted as I fell backward, my Advanced Class Strength at least equal to the warrior's in this moment of surprise. I drew my knees up to my chest as the two of us fell backward, planting my feet on the man's chest as my back hit the ground. Releasing my grip on his arm as I kicked off explosively, the warrior catapulted over my head and into the air. The airborne man let out a startled scream as his body collided with the unshielded mage, the pair collapsing to the ground in a tangle of limbs.

A crimson energy beam seared across my chest as I rolled to my feet, the last rifleman finally landing a shot now that I lacked the shelter of the mage's shield. The heat from the laser weapon left a steaming scorch mark on the surface of my armored suit but only shaved away a sliver of my overall health.

More beams flashed toward me, but my charge toward the pair on the ground threw off the attacks. I fired the last couple rounds from my remaining pistol into the prone mercenaries as they struggled to untangle themselves. The pistol slide locked open with the magazine depleted, and I dismissed the weapon back into my Inventory, replacing it in an instant with a fully loaded, identical weapon.

I shifted my fire to the rifleman as I ran past the struggling mercenaries on the ground and summoned a plasma grenade into my other hand. A flick of a finger armed the grenade, and I tossed it over my shoulder with my next step. Two strides later, I heard a *thunk* as the metallic casing of the grenade bounced off one of the warrior's skulls behind me.

A brilliant flash pierced the darkness from behind me with a roar, illuminating the area with a blinding azure radiance and forcing the man firing at me with the beam rifle to squint against the glare. He jerked a finger on the trigger of the rifle, squeezing the weapon tightly as I bore down upon him. The rifle glowed as it overcharged with the activation of some ability before a storm of fire erupted from the weapon.

Lances of energy showered over me in a crimson cascade, though as many beams glanced off or missed as actually landed. My health trickled lower with every one of the blistering bolts that struck, but I steadily returned fire without flinching. A beam seared completely through my cheek and continued on to savage my right ear.

I pushed through the pain and sent six shots in less than half as many seconds into a tight grouping on the man's chest, which staggered the rifleman and interrupted the deluge of laser fire. Before the man could recover, I batted aside his rifle with my free hand. He squealed in pain as my pistol jammed into his eye, the hot barrel sizzling flesh and bringing with it a whiff of cooking flesh.

Then I made his day worse. I pulled the trigger.

The man dropped the beam rifle and flailed at me in a vain attempt to push me away, but I pushed forward against the rain of blows and continued to fire my weapon into his skull. Eye splattered, bullets went in, even as the System Constitution and resistances fought against basic physics.

Three shots later, the man collapsed limply, and I dismissed the gore-coated weapon back to my Inventory. A quick glance at my notifications confirmed the experience gained from the downed mercenaries, which remained the fastest way to confirm an opponent was no longer a threat.

Turning to where the Countess fought her opponents, I took in the conflict between the trio of combatants.

From the ragged state of her armored jumpsuit and the blood that trickled from the wounds beneath the tatters, it became apparent that Dayena fared more poorly now than she had in her last two-on-one fight. Her eyes darted between her opponents as she continually turned, parrying and dodging as they attempted to circle her.

The Heart Guard's face remained blank as she harassed the Countess with a gold-hilted saber that stabbed and slashed the weapon's sharpened tip through any gaps in my employer's defenses. She employed an attack style that featured quick footwork that matched the blinding speed of her thrusts and feints. An unused pistol rested in a holster on the duelist's hip, and part of me wondered why the Truinnar hadn't employed the weapon to overwhelm the Countess completely.

Maybe Creynora was more sympathetic to Dayena's situation than she let on.

In contrast to the cool expression on the first dark elf adversary, the Deputy Adjudicator bared his gritted teeth in a frustrated snarl as he continued to swing his mace in heavy blows that would crush the Countess should any connect. He moved quickly, but my employer remained a hair beyond his reach for almost every attack.

Still, penned in between the sweeping strikes of the spiked mace and the lightning attacks of the saber, the Countess failed to avoid every attack, and damage from the glancing blows had been accumulating while I had dealt with the mercenaries.

Time for me to even the odds.

A moment later, the comfortable weight of my upgraded hybrid rifle settled into my hands. I slammed a magazine of black-tipped rounds into the weapon before snuggling the stock tightly into my shoulder as I sighted in on my target. Rhegnah's bulky power armor filled my sights, the slow-moving Truinnar the ideal mark for my weapon.

The rifle whined as I squeezed the trigger, but only the Heart Guard cocked an ear in my direction. The Deputy Adjudicator remained lost to his rage, but the saber-wielding Truinnar's momentary distraction allowed the Countess to finally land a blow.

My employer leapt over a wild swing of Rhegnah's mace and twisted in the air to thrust, slicing into the shoulder of her corset-wearing cousin. Before the Countess landed back on the ground, my rifle kicked into my shoulder and discharged a coruscating bolt of light that slammed a hyper-accelerated projectile into the Deputy Adjudicator's shoulder.

The outer jacket of the projectile shattered on impact with the armored surface, but the hardened inner core of the round continued on, boring deep into the joint. Small cracks formed in jagged lines that radiated out from a central crater.

The attack halted Rhegnah's reckless assault, the dark elf looking around for the source of the attack. As the Truinnar's eyes settled onto me, an angry scowl crossed his face, and I fired again.

The elf rocked back on his heels as larger cracks spiderwebbed out from the impact site along the armor's shoulder, thanks to the damage boost from Expose. A large chunk of the power armor gave way, and a piece fell free of the armor frame, bouncing off an armored knee as Rhegnah stepped in my direction. The dark elf visibly reined himself in and looked at where the Countess and Heart Guard continued their duel.

"Deal with the human, sister," Rhegnah commanded, apparently unwilling to leave dealing with the Countess to another.

Creynora leapt backward, out of range of Dayena's short swords, and looked at the Deputy Adjudicator dubiously.

"I can handle our wayward cousin," the male dark elf growled at Creynora's expression.

The Countess watched the exchange, her expression of concern quickly replaced with one of her perpetual smirks. While the elves bickered, I took the opportunity to fire at Rhegnah again.

The Deputy Adjudicator saw my attack coming and reacted in time to shift just enough that the round didn't hit the exposed section where the plate had fallen away from the suit. Instead, the armor penetration round hit the suit's armored pauldron. The shoulder plate fractured, slivers of shrapnel blasting out from the impact and shredding the side of Rhegnah's face.

Blood trickled from the marred skin of the dark elf's cheek, and fury clouded his face once again. With a wordless scream, Rhegnah flung himself recklessly at Dayena. The Countess danced away from the series of strikes, though the attacks came at an even faster rate than before.

Creynora shook her head disgustedly at her compatriot's adjudicator's loss of control but pivoted toward me as I shifted my aim to her. With a flick of her wrist almost too fast to follow, the saber's tip swept up into the coruscating beam extending from my rifle. My eyes narrowed as my shot went wide, deflected by a parrying Skill.

Damn cheating System that disregarded real world physics whenever it wanted.

I backed away, firing again. This time, the dark elf's Skill failed to fully deflect the shot and my round scraped across her already wounded arm. The elven woman winced, but she still launched herself at me with the tip of her sword pointed at my chest. Her speed increased as she closed the distance, her outline blurring as a charge ability activated.

I freed one hand from my rifle to cast Frostbolt at the rushing Truinnar. My improved version of the spell summoned a jagged shard of ice the length of my forearm to stab the dark elf in her stomach. The spell's impact and slowing effect stalled the dark elven woman with the tip of her saber only a handspan from my chest.

Jerking to the side, I twisted as the tip of her weapon tore through my jumpsuit, tracing a line of stinging fire along its path before continuing across my chest.

I dismissed my rifle, the bulky weapon too unwieldy to maneuver against an agile opponent in close quarters, and retreated in an attempt to open up the range between us. The speed with which she pursued prevented me from gaining any distance, and her constant rapid swings with the saber's curved blade scored a number of cuts across my forearms and torso within seconds.

Creynora's graceful movements as she thrust and cut at me with the saber reminded me of the fighting style used by the Countess. Though the weapons differed, the stance and footwork highlighted Creynora's tutelage under the same weapon masters as my employer.

With crystal clarity, I realized the difference between most of the previous foes we had encountered and what we now faced. While still only an unusual Basic Class, Creynora rated as a serious threat due to the combination of that Class rarity, highly enchanted equipment, and a lifetime's worth of quality training.

My health dipped with each harassing attack, her blistering speed barely dampened by the slowing effect of my Frostbolt. Reluctant to reveal any of my Class Skills this soon, I resorted to another holdout option.

A quickly chanted spell left my lips, and an icy wind surrounded me with a cold so severe that traces of frost formed on the edges of my armor.

The temperature dropped precipitously for a moment before blasting outward in all directions. The Frostnova spell left a frozen white layer in a perfect circle on the ground around me.

With both feet frozen to the ground, Creynora teetered precariously as she recovered her balance. Almost immediately, her strength began to stress the ice. I took the opportunity to rearm myself while moving farther beyond the reach of her blade.

"Your brother is kind of a self-centered asshole." I spun, my words thrown over my shoulder in a distraction as I used my body to shield my first summoned object as it dropped to the ground at my feet.

I continued to step away as I retrieved two more projectile pistols from my inventory and turned the rest of the way around to fire them at the frozen Truinnar with every step.

"Mayhaps," Creynora replied, glancing at the corpses of the mercenaries while working to free herself from the freezing spell. "You appear not so different though."

I shrugged, continuing my attacks. "I'm not trying to drag someone off to an arranged marriage."

Creynora flinched, but it still took her less than three seconds to free her feet from the rime-covered ground. She started toward me, drawing her pistol to return fire. The energy beams from her shots seared into my chest, and I grunted with each burn.

Creynora rushed at me, focused entirely on her pistol shots and getting back into melee range. I almost grinned but managed to keep my face blank. Both of the Truinnar seemed to go for the straightforward approach, and I'd counted on that behavior.

An explosion erupted under the dark elf's feet, flinging her airborne as the mine I'd placed detonated.

The predictable trajectory of the Truinnar's arc through the air left her an easy target, and I emptied both pistols into her before she slammed into the ground.

Despite the damage from the explosion, pistol fire, and heavy landing, the dark elf remained alive with a sliver of health remaining. I approached the fallen elf warily, reloading my weapons with spare magazines from my Inventory. Creynora groaned, wheezing for the air knocked from her lungs by her fall. I extended my arm, pointing my pistol at the Truinnar's head.

"Wait!"

I froze with the tension on the trigger, poised at the firing point by the sudden cry over party chat. I kept the weapon aimed at the dark elf before me and glanced at the Countess to find her standing on the fallen Deputy Adjudicator's power armor. I tilted my head to the side in a wordless question.

"She is family," the Countess explained. *"I am in enough conflict with my house for rebelling against the will of my father. Slaying a blood relative would only lead to further hardening of their desires to hunt me down."* She paused, intensely staring at me across the parking lot. *"I am not yet prepared to take that step."*

I nodded and eased my finger off the trigger. I slid my pistol into its holster and reached down to pry the weapons from the wounded Truinnar's hands. I stored the saber and pistol in my Inventory before I patted her down, adding several small trinkets and a fancy dagger to my loot in the process.

The dark elf groaned as I left her lying on the ground and walked back to where the Countess waited by her fallen opponent. The Deputy Adjudicator seemed to be out cold, blood trickling down his face from a crooked and broken nose. I looted the Truinnar's mace then looked at the damaged power armor, still worn by the unconscious dark elf.

The Countess saw my appraisal and rolled her eyes as she waved dismissively. By now, the Truinnar noble had accepted my habit of looting anything not nailed down for a few extra Credits, but she remained unconvinced of that trait's usefulness.

"You want them disgraced, don't you?" I asked.

The Countess considered my question for a moment before her eyes lit up, and she abruptly stalked over to where her other cousin lay.

I pried the unconscious Rhegnah out of his armor, only stopping to deliver a single blow to render him senseless again after a moan and several twitches revealed signs of wakefulness. Once I'd finished removing his armor, I stuffed every bit of it into my Inventory. Then I stood and glanced over to find the Countess stripping the blood red jumpsuit from her cousin. She had already slipped on the dragon scale corset, clearly intending to use that piece of armor personally, though she had yet to tighten the fastenings over her own armored bodysuit.

Dayena looked up and found me watching, then motioned for me to do the same to Rhegnah. I sighed and removed the elf's thin, skin-tight jumpsuit, the only thing he'd worn beneath the power armor.

Once we'd completely stripped the pair, a wicked grin appeared on Dayena's face. I raised a questioning eyebrow as two pairs of familiar manacles appeared in the dark elf's hands.

"Those only work on Base Classes," I reminded the Countess.

"I have a Skill for that." Dayena tossed me one set of the cuffs and nodded toward Creynora. "Get her."

Kneeling beside the naked elven woman, I rolled the unconscious Truinnar onto her stomach before binding her wrists behind her back. Then I stood with a sigh. As much as I admired the view, I required my partners conscious and consenting for that kind of play.

I stepped back as Dayena tossed a small device between the two restrained Truinnar and, a moment later, the dome of a red emergency shield covered the pair.

"No sense in leaving them defenseless for some idiot to kill before they wake up," the Countess said as she looked around. "No one showed up to investigate the commotion."

I scooped up the few worthwhile pieces of gear carried by the dead mercenaries.

"No," I said, recalling the way the gate guard had watched the Countess on our way into town. It hadn't been because of her Charisma, but because she wasn't the first Truinnar to come into town this evening. "I'm guessing the guild was warned to stay away from this little confrontation."

The Countess nodded. "That sounds like the way Rhegnah operates."

"We should probably make ourselves scarce," I said.

"Where shall we go?" The Countess looked at me with a hint of worry.

I recalled the message I'd received in the Shop and glanced at the empty area around us. I saw no one, but we were still in potentially hostile territory.

"*Not here,*" I thought over party chat, unwilling to voice my plans aloud. "*I have something in mind.*"

Chapter 6

"You will not believe who I learned is on Earth."

Despite the rushing wind flowing past as we cruised westbound on the ruined highway, I easily heard the Countess over our telepathic chat as she finally broke the silence between us. We'd broken out our bikes after fleeing the Hancock city limits and were now making good time through the bright moonlight of the warm, summer night.

My Outrider retained the chassis I'd purchased on the second day of the apocalypse, though I'd upgraded the majority of the bike's parts at the behest of my employer. One enhancement enabled "hover mode" for the vehicle, the anti-gravity drives floating the bike half a yard over the ground. The upgrade allowed us to easily weave through the abandoned vehicles and overgrown wrecks that littered the highway, paying no mind to the numerous cracks and potholes of the former US highway system.

The Countess continued on excitedly, without waiting for my response. *"Lord Graxan Roxley, Corinthian of the Second Order and acclaimed Dancing Master of the 196th Ball!"*

The calm, collected facade my employer normally projected dissolved with her exuberance. With the similarities in our actual age and the mature front she normally displayed, that the Countess was considered little more than a teenager by the standards of the long-lived Truinnar regularly slipped my mind. At least until she fangirled out over one of her celebrities or high society gossip gleaned in her latest Shop visit. I'd learned that the dark elf's culture held their gladiatorial dancers in very high esteem, so it was best to humor her when this happened.

"Was he the winner who got the dagger or the one who got the sword?"

"The soulbound sword, Purity," the Countess replied. *"The dagger was the prize for the previous Ball."*

"Ah, right." At least I'd remembered the weapons. Those were interesting. It was taking me far longer to firmly grasp the nuances of the intricate relationships between the various Truinnar Houses and their positions at court. *"So, this Lord Roxley is on Earth now?"*

"He purchased a Village called Whitehorse in the far northwest of this continent and took possession just after the System initialization," she answered. *"The gossips are all ablaze because he shifted his allegiance from the Duke of Ravius to Duchess Kangana, while somehow extracting all of his people from his barony and moving them safely to his new holdings here on Earth."*

"Sounds like quite the coup for Duchess Kangana."

"Yes, not only has the Duchess gained territory here on Earth, but her rival Duke has lost both resources and status for his failure to meet the obligations in support of his vassal."

The Truinnar noble courts adhered to a labyrinthine political system. While cunning often outmatched raw strength and subtle maneuvering garnered more respect than the overt use of force, at the end of the day, it only mattered who climbed upward through the ranks and who had fallen.

"Do these developments affect us at all?" I asked.

The Countess was quiet for a moment. *"No, not in the near term, at least. The areas under Truinnar control are still widely separated and there are no signs of cohesion between the forces on the planet, though that may change as those territories expand and alliances develop in the future."*

"Are there any places we need to avoid in particular, especially now that your family has representatives on Earth?"

"That little brawl of ours earlier will have repercussions." The Countess bit her lip and glanced at me nervously. *"My family will be aware of your presence now and the threat you represent. They will likely target you in some manner in order to apply pressure to me."*

I nodded somberly. I had expected as much. That was why I'd held back the use of any Class Skills during my duel with the saber-wielding Triunnar.

"I think we need to stay on the move and avoid Truinnar strongholds if possible," I said. *"While we were in the Shop earlier, I received a message about a job that might fit both of those requirements."*

I raised one hand from the handlebars of my bike and flicked a System window toward the Countess, sharing with her the message I'd received.

Hal, the Shop says you're still alive and gaining Levels. There's an opportunity here with an allied Clan and your very particular set of skills would prove useful, if you're looking for work. You know where to find me if you're interested.
-B.

The Countess remained quiet for several minutes after she finished with the note, and the text faded as I let the blue window dissipate while she considered the contents of the message.

"This 'B' seems to have been checking up on you. Do you trust them?"

I pulled a flask from my Inventory and took a sip. The fiery liquid no longer burned my throat as it had the first time. It hadn't turned my whiskers pink either, so I felt content with the tradeoff. I chuckled at the thought. *"Yes, you could say that."*

"Then it would seem to be a timely opportunity."

"It only buys us a little time," I said. *"The next confrontation will be worse."*

"Yes." Sadness tinged her solitary reply.

"I noticed you didn't use the Strings."

"*Only my immediate family knows that I possess the relic,*" she said. "*My parents must not have informed my cousins, otherwise they surely would have first demanded that it be returned.*"

"*We still have an edge then,*" I mused, though how long that advantage lasted would be entirely dependent on the forces brought after us.

For several minutes, Dayena remained silent. "*I wanted to ask you something. I noticed that while you have no issues helping civilians and non-combat Classed individuals, you also have no issues with eliminating members of your own species otherwise.*"

"*There a question there?*"

"*Why?*"

I glanced over at the Countess. "*Why don't I have a problem killing humans?*" At her nod, I paused to collect my thoughts. "*Back when I served in my nation's military, there was this saying. There were a couple variations, but it was something like, 'People sleep soundly in their beds at night for rough men stand ready to do violence on their behalf.' I guess I'm one of those rough men.*"

"*That does not bother you?*"

I sighed. "*Once someone takes that step of threatening those who just want to live peaceably, they've placed themselves beyond the bounds of society. At that point, I have no issue removing the problem they've become.*"

Dayena scowled. "*That is a naive point of view under the System. Society is defined by the strong, and only those in power get to make the rules. If your peaceable people want to live for themselves, then they need to be able to defend that way of life.*"

I shrugged. "*I get that. I still feel the need to try when I can. Maybe it's not the most logically consistent worldview, but bullets and Credits have gotten me this far.*"

Dayena shook her head but seemed content to let the conversation lapse while I continuously checked for nearby threats on my minimap as we cruised along the ruined highway. Faded gray dots appeared from time to time, almost always cowering in place or scampering farther away when the lower leveled creatures sensed our presence.

For the next hour, we pushed on through the night. Without traffic and with our upgraded bikes' ability to float over most obstructions, we made far better time than we would have traveling the same route before the System.

The relaxing portion of the ride ended abruptly when we found both lanes of the interstate bridge collapsed over Cheat Lake, just east of Morgantown, West Virginia. The roadway slumped down into the debris-filled water less than a hundred feet out, and I slowed to a halt before I reached the shoreline.

"Our vehicles can handle the water," the Countess said, slowing to a stop beside me.

I shook my head. "It's not the water that concerns me. It's what's under the surface."

She glanced at me then took another look at the spot where the asphalt disappeared under ripples reflecting the moonlight. "I sense nothing."

"Look at the road and the barriers along the side," I said. "Gouges in the cement where something has crawled up out of the water and craters left by weapons fire or explosions."

The Countess blinked, clearly seeing the evidence I described. "The road is so clear, like nothing ever happened here."

"Yeah," I said. "That's what worries me the most. Whatever is here, it's smart enough to clean up after itself in preparation for the next ambush."

I looked about and spotted another bridge several hundred yards to the south. Though the other bridge was smaller and even closer to the water's surface, it stretched the full way across the lake. I pointed out the alternate route to the Countess and we swung our bikes around, back tracking until we managed to find our way off the highway and over to the other bridge.

I kept a part of my focus on my minimap, searching for threatening red dots as we cruised out on the second bridge. No threats appeared, but I couldn't shake the sense of unease.

Halfway across the span, the waters on either side frothed in sudden violence. Several large crustacean-like creatures vaulted out of the shallows and onto the roadway, their crab claws furrowing deeply into the sides of the bridge.

Hunched over, with a segmented carapace that reminded me of a lobster, the nine-foot-tall crustaceans were at least twice that in length and had four segmented legs in addition to their forward pincher arms. Dozens of purple tentacles writhed around the creatures' maws, the rubbery feelers dripping a greenish substance that matched the ugly, puke-colored shades of their shells. The liquid smoked where it splashed on the ground, likely an acidic substance best avoided.

The first monster's tentacles rubbed over each other, creating a rasping sound as the ridges vibrated, and the following monsters responded to the stridulation.

I swept Greater Observation over the nearest of the four monsters as I pushed off from my bike, storing the vehicle in my Inventory and skating nearly a dozen feet across the surface of the road in my armored boots before my momentum died.

Mature Chuul (Level 67)
HP: 1820/1820

A gesture flung a Frostbolt shard at the closest monster. I opened up with a beam pistol summoned from my Inventory before the spell landed, bathing the monster with a barrage of crimson energy beams as I backed away. The attacks lanced into the fleshy tentacles around the monster's mouth, severing several and making the beast flinch before it could close the distance between us.

Strands of music whispered in the night, the Countess and her Legacy instrument joining the fray as my employer sent a flurry of energy beams to impact another monster. The damn nest of monsters now blockaded the road and our way forward.

We retreated as the monsters pursued, though they seemed content to herd us along at a deliberate pace. Imagine my lack of surprise when another trio of red dots appeared behind us on my minimap, the new arrivals breaking from stealth as they hauled themselves from the water and cut us off from the shore.

I reversed course, charging the original ambushers and switching out my pistol for the higher damage firepower of the hybrid rifle. My first shot with the weapon's standard ammunition struck my original target in the face, staggering the chuul and dropping its health further down to half.

Next, I activated Hinder on my target. Ducking beneath an instinctive swipe from a clawed pincer, I ran up one of the monster's segmented legs and pushed off the middle joint to leap on top of the chuul. Despite the water-slicked nature of the smooth carapace, I found no issues keeping my footing steady as the monster lurched in an attempt to shake me off. I grinned at the monster beneath my feet, though it couldn't see my look of triumph as I fired the hybrid rifle straight down into the top of the monster's head. Efficient Trail treated large enough monsters as "terrain features," and the Class Skill enabled me to perform such ridiculous feats.

The carapace shattered, a circular hole appearing where the round punched through. The chuul slumped to the ground with its brain pithed by the shot. I calmly stepped from the fallen monster and swung my rifle toward the next creature.

Claws from the second and third chuul snapped at me, and I hurried to apply Hinder to both monsters as I proceeded to dodge, duck, dip, dive, and dodge away from their onslaught. I barely managed to intersperse shots from my rifle once the fourth of the monsters joined the fray, though the creatures failed to coordinate their attacks and often got in each other's way.

My unwieldy rifle complicated my movements, but I felt the penetrating power against the monsters' thick shells outweighed the need to switch out to my more agile pistols.

The sheer number of flailing claws meant that some attacks got through my hasty defense, leaving me battered and cut. I retained control of my weapon and avoided being grabbed by the pinchers though. I reapplied Hinder as the duration faded and finally built up enough damage to drop a second monster.

Still, my health was at nearly half between the spraying acid and slashing claws. I focused on taking the third out of the fight as quickly as possible.

Combat rang out in a deadly medley from behind me as the Countess battled her own trio of chuul, blades singing as they deflected off of and sliced into monster carapaces. The tempo blended with the somber melody from the Whispering Strings, and from the nearly full green bar of health in the party status at the corner of my vision, I knew the Countess was handling her end of the fight without trouble.

More red dots populated my minimap as I sensed additional monsters streaming in our direction from the collapsed bridge to the north. A quick glance showed visible wake lines churning the lake as the additional monsters swam toward us, just beneath the surface of the water. One wave outclassed the others by a significant margin, both wider and pushing displaced water even higher. I had a pretty good idea what that meant, especially with the cunning shown by setting up this alternate ambush on a lesser used route.

"Alpha inbound," I sent over party chat, my voice calm despite the sudden surge of adrenaline that coursed through my veins.

"Almost done here," Dayena replied. *"Are you finished yet?"*

I stomped on the only remaining claw of the last chuul, pinning it to the ground before firing point blank into the side of the monster's face. Ichor splattered the roadway as the round penetrated through both sides of the creature's head.

Only the eerie melody from the relic instrument remained as the echo from my shot faded, and I knew the Countess readied her own preparations for the more serious fight to come.

We could have run at this point, but I didn't bother to even give voice to that thought as I chugged a health potion. We both knew running wouldn't get us anywhere in the long run. Only by throwing ourselves into danger and facing more lethal enemies would we grow stronger. This kind of fight was exactly the reason we braved the wildlands between the holdouts of civilization on the Dungeon World that Earth had become.

But that didn't mean we weren't prepared for those fights. Knowing that the Alpha would prove more resilient than the monsters we'd faced so far, I swapped out the hybrid rifle's nearly depleted magazine of standard ammunition for a cartridge of armor piercing rounds.

With the incoming waves about twenty yards out, a nasty thought crossed my mind, and I summoned a grenade from my inventory. I tossed the orb just to the side of the Alpha's wake, and it splashed directly in front of a smaller ripple.

A geyser erupted a moment later as the explosive detonated, sending a column of water and steam into the air. I grinned evilly, knowing that even with the System messing with physics, underwater blasts transmitted the explosion's forces further than the same detonation would have through air. I threw another grenade to the Alpha's other side before alternating tosses of more explosives until the monster almost reached the bridge.

The improvised depth charges forced the smaller creatures away from the leading monster, which gave us some space to work with.

I moved to my left, farther across the bridge, as the Alpha's wave arrowed straight for me, likely identifying me as the source of the explosions. The Countess headed in the opposite direction, trading out her short swords for a beam pistol as she littered the roadway with scattered mines.

The surface of the lake lifted in a massive wave as the Alpha catapulted itself onto the bridge. Glowing yellow eyes shone through the curtains of water that cascaded from its curved back. The creature was triple the size of the first chuul, and the monster's back half still stretched back into the lake as it lunged forward.

Chuul Alpha (Level 71 - Boss)
HP: 5520/5740

I activated Hinder as the monster broke the water's surface, then I cast Frostbolt, noting that the handful of grenades hadn't done much more than piss off the monster. Giant pinchers extended toward me, attempting to snatch me, and I realized that unlike the smaller monsters, the Alpha had an additional pair of crab claw arms.

Despite the combined slowing effects of my Class Skill and ice spell, the edge of one claw raked across my side before I dashed out of range. Pain flared through me as the blow ripped through my armor, tearing away a chunk of flesh and scraping along my ribs. The blow spun me around, blood spraying from my side, and I tumbled from the force. I rolled along the road to put more distance between myself and the monster hauling itself farther out of the lake.

As I did so, I caught a whiff of the asphalt and water, nose wrinkling at the slight bitter-lemony scent in the sky. Not fishy, but a little off and wrong, like a bad combination of car air fresheners and body odor.

Beyond the massive monster, the Countess fired her beam pistol into the creature's back. Though the rays of energy carved small furrows into the armored shell, the attacks failed to do much damage before several smaller chuul swarmed out of the water. Forced to deal with the nearest threats, the dark elf shifted her attacks to her immediate pursuers. I knew she'd deal with them quickly enough. I just had to stay alive until she finished.

I popped back to my feet, fingers tightening against cracked and rough concrete as I levered myself up. I fired at the Alpha, aiming for the joint where the nearest arm attached to the giant crustacean's body. The curved carapace that protected the articulation point crumpled slightly from the impact of the round and faint cracks appeared in the shell, so I fired at the same spot once again.

This time my attack broke the carapace, and the arm drooped limply. The claw at the end of the arm was left to drag along the road, nearly tripping the Alpha as it shuffled along the bridge after me.

Several normal chuul attempted to clamber out of the lake and onto the bridge, but the Alpha battered them aside in its single-minded pursuit, crushing the legs of one creature and knocking a pair of the others back into the water completely.

Slowed slightly by knocking into the other monsters, and with the Alpha's damaged arm hindering its speed, I finally increased my separation from the giant crustacean. Outside the immediate danger from its waving claws, I kept up a steady rhythm of fire from my hybrid rifle and ignored the pain coming from my wounded side.

I took a moment to layer healing spells on myself between each shot, letting my health climb upward as I backed away from the monster. My barrage slowly chipped away at the massive creature's health as I continued to focus my shots on any location not covered by a solid carapace plate. The monster shifted and swayed in an attempt to throw off my targeting, but even my few missed attacks left damage all around the beast's eyes, mouth, joints between segmented limbs, and I even drove occasional shots between the ridges protecting the junction of the creature's head and thorax.

The damage built on the monster, and the Alpha's blind rage ebbed as it realized how much I'd hurt it. The glow in its eyes faded as the Alpha's intellect reasserted itself, along with the realization that it couldn't catch up to me with all of its numerous injuries.

The creature paused and threw up its head. A rumbling vibration filled the air, the pulsing noise a disconcerting cross somewhere between the screech of nails on a chalkboard and the intimidating roar of a jungle tiger. I felt the sound pass through me, resonating in my chest. My muscles seized as the effect warred with my resistances.

The Alpha clearly intended to freeze me in place with the force of the ability, my movements slowing as the monster's wail grew louder and gained in pitch. The sonic damage popped my eardrums, deafening me and threatening to scramble my brain. I felt warm liquid leak from my ears as they bled.

I hardened my will and forced my muscles to move. I wouldn't die here. Not when I'd already survived the advent of the System taking hold on Earth and the apocalypse which followed.

A notification appeared as I shook off the effect before it could slow me, though for a moment, the vision of a serpentine shape floating through a rippling blue portal above a city skyline etched itself into my mind's eye.

Fear Effect Resisted

The text's display banished the thoughts of my past and I focused on the present—a moment too late.

The Alpha's good claw pinched closed on my left bicep as I jerked backward. White-hot pain burned through my arm as the pincer snapped shut, scissoring through my arm and severing it completely.

My Status helpfully notified me of the Bleed applied when I lost the arm.

No shit.

I pushed through the pain and focused on retaining hold of my rifle. Holding the weapon awkwardly in one hand, I rushed toward the damaged arm of the Chuul Alpha. Another application of Hinder on the crustacean slowed the monster's reactions further, and I vaulted onto the limply hanging claw that dragged on the ground in front of the creature, a stream of blood pouring out along my path.

I ran up the monster's arm with far less ease than I had mounted the smaller crustacean earlier, my only hand clutching my rifle as I mounted the monster's shoulder. The Alpha's mouth tentacles slapped against the carapace at my heels, failing to trip me as I climbed the hunched shell behind its head. I paused out of their reach and grinned as I steadied myself.

Then I braced my feet in a wide-legged stance and fired my rifle one-handed, straight down into the protected back of the chuul's thorax. Over and over, the hybrid weapon's coils glowed with the energy I poured through the barrel.

My precision attacks on the same spot on the exoskeletal armor triggered the secondary effect of Expose as it finally punched through the thick carapace. The damage bonus of Expose against the armor reset, then began climbing once again as each round delved farther into the monster's core, orange ichor splashing out to coat my armored boots in the viscous liquid.

The Alpha bucked and heaved, growing ever more frantic as my attacks penetrated. I just barely managed to stay mounted on the writhing creature. If I hadn't damaged so many of the monster's limbs before I'd started this stunt, it may have been able to throw me off.

Then the monster turned sideways, and I felt the Alpha gather itself to spring back into the lake. If it managed that, then the other chuul could simply climb from the water right onto the Alpha's back and swarm me.

I ceased firing with my hybrid rifle and pulled a plasma grenade from my Inventory. I thumbed the activator and dunked it into the jagged hole in the carapace. I dropped a second live grenade after the first before I ran down the monster's spine.

Feeling me leave its back, the Alpha paused long enough for me to slide off the splayed lobster tail and roll back to my feet on the bridge.

Before it could pursue me once again, the plasma grenades detonated inside the Alpha. The force of the paired explosions flung me forward, peppering my back with shards of carapace and coating me in another layer of ichor. I bounced off the cement bridge rail, and the force of the collision twisted the rifle from my hand. Tumbling across the bridge, I rolled shakily to my feet and looked around.

The Alpha lay stretched across the bridge, obviously dead now, with a hollow gouged out of its middle large enough for a pickup to drive through. A couple of the normal chuul climbed back to their feet, but most of the monsters lay in discernable chunks strewn along the roadway, diced to pieces by the Countess and her blades.

The dark elf stood completely unaffected by the blast, with a foot on the head of a fallen chuul and prying one of her swords free from the monster's skull.

I debated looking for my rifle amongst the corpses and debris but opted to summon my trusty knife instead, quickly dispatching the final pair of disoriented chuul before the monsters fully recovered from the disorienting effects of the plasma grenade's detonation.

With the last of the monsters slain, I cast Cleanse on myself to remove the coating of gore that drenched me, then I treated my wounds with another round of healing spells. The spells did nothing for my missing arm beyond staunching the blood flow, but the pain from my side receded as the flesh mended itself.

Losing a limb always sucked. Normally it required most people to visit the Shop to purchase a means of healing or a replacement. Instead, increasing my Resilient Nature Class Skill allowed limbs to regenerate, in addition to boosting my overall regeneration. My arm would regrow over the next few hours, making the loss more of an inconvenience now that I'd survived the immediate threat of complete dismemberment.

Now that I'd dealt with my health, I searched through the carcasses scattered on the bridge for my lost rifle. I looted the chuul corpses as I went along, though it took a little longer than usual. I didn't bother storing any of the dead creatures in my Meat Locker storage. I had other plans for that free space.

Eventually, I located the rifle lodged partially under a fallen chuul and coated with orange muck from the Alpha's innards. I kicked the carcass clear of my weapon and picked it up with two fingers.

Ichor ran down the length of the weapon and dripped from the end of the barrel.

Gross.

Another casting of Cleanse removed the disgusting slime, then I awkwardly knelt with the rifle across my knee to perform a one-handed swap of the nearly empty magazine with a full one before returning the weapon to my Inventory. As had become habit after most combats, I performed a quick tally of munitions used and noted which items would need restocked on my next visit to a Shop.

By the time I'd finished my post battle cleanup, the Countess had completed her tasks and joined me beside the massive body of the dead Alpha.

"An armorsmith would pay dearly for that Alpha carapace," she said, glancing at me. She tactfully didn't mention the missing arm.

"It just needs harvesting," I replied.

Dayena blinked innocently. "Do you need a hand?"

"Right." There was the sarcasm.

I sighed and drew my knife, stepping up into the gaping hole in the giant monster's thorax to begin the gory task.

The glamorous life of a Relentless Huntsman right here.

Chapter 7

Vibrations from a deep roar filled the air, filling my chest with the thrum of reverberation like standing too close to the amps at a heavy rock concert. I looked up to find the source—a rectangular spacecraft the size of a skyscraper turned sideways that slowly floated downward in the sky overhead. The craft drifted until it reached the ground, settling into a berth between two other vessels just as large.

The starport sprawled out before us, massively expanded to meet the growing demand for interstellar transport since my last visit. Little of the old airport now remained. Along with the renovations, all signs of the abandoned and crashed terrestrial aircraft that once littered the area had disappeared.

The expanded airside terminal stretched from its original location all the way to the base of the traffic tower and merged with the control tower's attached administration building before continuing farther east. The tower, still topped by a massive quad-barreled turret, rose above the starport, but those were the only two original structures that remained. Other turrets, smaller than the gigantic Icarus suborbital cannon atop the control tower, lined the terminal roof at regular intervals.

Configurable berths for smaller starships took up most of the areas around the original terminal, while the new construction east of the tower supported the more massive interstellar freighters like the one which had just landed.

The Countess and I cruised forward with a moderate amount of vehicle traffic along an access road curving around the starport. A notification appeared as we passed between a pair of defense towers topped by beam turrets, highlighting the increase in the defensive perimeter since my last visit.

You Have Entered a Safe Zone (Pittsburgh Sprocketsworth Starport)

Mana flows in this area are stabilized. No monster spawning will happen.

This Safe Space includes:

Air and Space Traffic Control Tower

Passenger and Freight Terminals

Sprocketsworth Clan Headquarters

The Shop

Raw Material Processing Facility

More...

I dismissed the update as we followed signs directing us toward the "Raw Material Processing Facility." We weren't the only ones looking to unload our loot, as we found ourselves in a slow-moving line between a pickup and a flatbed truck. Heaps of monster carcasses were piled high in the beds of both vehicles, and foul fluids dripped from the tailgate of the pickup from the dead beasts inside.

The ripe smell of rotting meat intensified as the line of vehicles crawled forward and split into multiple lanes that led into an open-sided warehouse. A large conveyor belt ran through the middle of the warehouse with bridges crossing over it for each lane. A vehicle would pull partially up onto the bridge for their lane, and once parked, an antigrav platform moved into place next to it. Workers in full body hazmat suits swarmed the truck beds and shifted the dead monsters onto the platforms. Once fully loaded, the platforms were maneuvered over to the conveyor and tipped high enough that the carcasses slid onto the moving belt.

One lane toward the end of where the conveyor disappeared into the next warehouse sat empty with the sign above it reading "High Tier Monsters Only." A bored-looking gnoll wearing a neon hardhat and vest over an armored undersuit stood blocking the lane, likely to ensure only those with valuable loot used the reserved zone.

I swung my bike out of the general line and coasted over to halt in front of the humanoid hyena, who sniffed and glared suspiciously at me.

Gnagh Bonespear (Enforcer Level 39)
HP: 690/690
MP: 380/380

"Does an Alpha carcass count as 'High Tier'?" I asked.

Gnagh snorted and pressed a clawed finger down on a communication device attached to a belt at the gnoll's waist. "Boss come, she tell."

A door slammed, audible even over the machinery of the conveyor system and the bustle of the unloading vehicles. A gnome stormed out from an office next to where the conveyor hauled the monsters at the end of the open warehouse.

Emilyana Grindsaw (Supervisor Level 4)
HP: 890/890
MP: 1040/1040

Despite her rise to an Advanced Class, I recognized the Pharyleri stomping up to the gnoll as she jabbed a pointed finger at the brute. Interruptions to her work still clearly annoyed the green-haired gnomish woman, and despite towering over her, the gnoll looked at the Pharyleri meekly.

"Oi, thickskull!" Emilyana exclaimed. "What is it this time?"

The gnoll hurriedly gestured toward me, anxiously deflecting the attention of his boss. "Says has Alpha carcass."

"Hmmph." After skewering the gnoll with a lengthy skeptical look, Emilyana turned toward me. A moment later, her stern expression vanished into one of surprise, and she blinked. She gave the dark elf behind me a slightly confused glance before returning her focus to me. "Hal?"

"In the flesh," I replied. "Congrats on moving up to management from monster harvesting."

"Thanks. I certainly don't miss it, but I wasn't expecting to see you when bonehead here called me out," she said with a jerk of her head toward the gnoll beside her. Her initial cheerful demeanor quickly shifted back to business. "You've actually got Alpha bits though?"

I waved my regrown arm. "A Boss in the low 70s."

Emilyana whistled, clearly impressed. "We're seeing more Boss parts, but they're still not common. We'll pay a premium for them. The Clan Artisans will greatly advance their skills working with high quality materials."

She gestured for us to follow before leading the way to the reserved lane. I dismissed my bike to my Inventory, but Dayena chose to coast forward on hers, easily keeping up with the short-legged Pharyleri.

We reached the intake area where a sole platform floated at knee height next to our lane. The metallic sheet turned up at the edges with a slight lip, resembling a giant serving tray. I glanced at the plate then looked at Emilyana.

"You're going to need a few more of these," I said, waving at the floating rectangle.

The gnome raised an eyebrow to give me a skeptical look before summoning several platforms from other lanes with a gesture. While the plates floated toward me, I retrieved parts of the Alpha from my Inventory and stacked the bits onto the platform.

Massive organs, eyes large enough to fill my open palm, nerve tissues, and slabs of crustacean meat—all still dripping ichor and other fluids—quickly filled the first platform, and I tapped my foot with exaggerated impatience as I waited for the other trays to assemble beside the loaded platform. More meat and fibrous tendons loaded the second platform heavily enough that it sagged noticeably lower than the other floating trays. We required two more full trays and part of a fifth for the carapace pieces by the time both the Countess and I finished unloading our Inventory.

Despite my desire for Credits, I held onto several stacks of the carapace plates in the hopes that I could get a customized set of armor crafted out of them. It would certainly cost me, but the future confrontations with Dayena's family loomed, requiring better gear and Skills than those I currently possessed.

Emilyana shook her head when we finished depositing the bulk of the Alpha's loot, then she pulled a scanning device from her belt. She ran the scanner over the assembled monster parts and sighed before forking over a sizable sum of Credits. I split the bounty with the Countess, once again lounging on her bike while she waited for me to finish the transaction.

"I've got regular monster carcasses too," I said as Emilyana returned the scanner to her belt.

The diminutive gnome glared at me impatiently and pulled the device back out. The full platforms slid away, gliding out over the conveyor and moving along with it instead of dumping their valuable loads to be diluted with the lower value monster parts that filled the belt. Several more empty platforms floated over to me, and I emptied the remaining chuul carcasses out of my Inventory in exchange for a significantly smaller sum of Credits.

"Now are you done?

I grinned at Emilyana. "Yes, thank you."

"Good," she said. "The boss will want to see you."

I nodded. "That's our next stop, assuming his office is still in the same place."

"It is," Emilyana confirmed. "Follow the building to your right until you reach the small vessel terminal, then signs will give you directions to administration. Now get out of here. Some of us have work to do."

I bid the surly gnome farewell with a wave, but she was already stomping back to her office.

"It has been some time since I was so thoroughly ignored," Dayena commented, dismissing her summoned vehicle and falling in alongside me as we headed toward the main terminal.

"I think you'll find the Pharyleri an enterprising and resilient bunch, especially for a clan of Artisans," I said. "For just over a year, they've maintained a hold on this area, building this place into one of the largest transportation and trade hubs on the continent."

My nose twitched from the scents of death emanating from the next building we walked alongside, but I'd smelled the like, if not worse, far too often to really be affected. From the shouts and the whining of saws, the structure housed the workers and equipment processing of all the monster parts dropped off by Adventurers like us.

"It is impressive," Dayena replied.

An open section of tarmac separated the resource processing buildings from the walls of the terminal proper, and we crossed the open space quickly, dodging through the zooming starport transport vehicles hauling linked carriages full of goods between the various starport structures. Only slightly larger than pre-System baggage tractors, the haulers with their train of dollies stretching out behind bore an uncanny resemblance to the old airport vehicles and almost gave a sense of normalcy to the scene.

A solid stone wall protected the small craft end of the terminal and kept us from directly accessing the area. The seamless nature of the construction indicated that Skills and Mana had played a significant part in the defensive barrier's creation. A dozen yards from the wall itself, bright yellow hazard stripes marked the tarmac. Accompanying signage warned individuals that the area signified a defensive zone covered by turrets that would open fire upon trespassers.

Staying clear of the danger zone, we circled the wall until we located an entrance. A Pharyleri supervising a pair of Gimsar mercenaries attended the gate. The heavily armed and short, bearded mercenary guards nodded in greeting, scanning us thoroughly as we entered the terminal.

I didn't recognize the supervising gnome sitting in the open cockpit of an armored mecha, but the Pharyleri gave me a double-take after reading the Status above my head. The gnome's expression vanished almost as soon as it appeared, but he gave me a subtle nod before pointedly looking away with an air of boredom. Since the gnome's armor stood behind the mercenaries, neither of the guards noticed his actions as they waved us through the security checkpoint.

Once we were inside the terminal, a throng of beings moved in either direction through the long concourse that still bore some of the paint and signage from the structure's prior life as the Pittsburgh International Airport. The individual gates once used by planes now led to small craft berths, with each vessel's berth separated by a wall of the same stone construction that encircled the entirety of the terminal.

None of the gates were manned by local flight attendants or starport personnel. Instead, from the diversity of the aliens at each station, it seemed as though each craft was responsible for securing their own berth.

Across the terminal from each other, two heavily armed groups faced off as they guarded their individual gates.

On one side, a squad of green-skinned Hakarta in matching beige-and-brown tiger-striped armor mean-mugged any creature passing too close to their gate. Their angry expressions encouraged passersby to give them extra space.

Directly across the terminal from the armored orcs, another set of aliens secured the entrance to their starship's berth far more casually but with no less intimidation. Just as tall and broad as the Hakarta—which said something considering the orcs had a good eight inches in height and probably a hundred pounds on me—the towering humanoids with catlike features more resembled lions than the everyday housecat. Full manes fringed the heads of the male leonids, with most of the dark golden hair braided with beads and metallic decorations.

One Hakarta—what I assumed was an officer from the more ornamental version of the combat uniform worn by the others—prowled through the orc formation. I recognized a surprise inspection when I saw one.

The leader of the lion-like aliens stood with arms folded and an expression of amusement while watching the Hakarta squad leader across the way, and I delicately swept Greater Observation across the pair in a subtle attempt to get a feel for their strength.

Hakarta Lieutenant (Cyber-Phalanx Level 35)
HP: 4960/4960

Demarcian Knight-Commander (Ebon Breaker Level 39)
HP: 5240/5240

I pulled my attention away from the pair as soon as their information appeared in my vision. They were so far out of my league that they could swat me like a gnat. I really didn't want to draw their ire, though with the traffic flowing through the terminal, it looked as though neither had noticed my inspection.

I slipped into the crowd and began down the terminal toward the administration facilities. The Countess followed and kept pace, just behind my shoulder and off to one side. I glanced back at her, and she nodded, indicating that I take the lead for now.

We reached the passage that led to the admin wing and split off from the flow of traffic. I noted several recesses in the walls and ceiling that likely hid deployable turrets or other defenses. The short hall ended in sealed blast doors that slid open at our approach.

The opening only allowed us to enter one at a time, and when I passed between the doors, I found myself in an armored antechamber. Even more of the defensive weapons mounts greeted me, less subtly disguised than the ones in the hall. At least the turrets remained ensconced behind their armored plating.

Once the Countess had followed me into the room, the doors closed. Only once they'd closed completely did the matching security gateway ahead of us slide open to reveal a pair of armored suits standing in the doorway.

A gnome-sized canopy took up most of the mecha's torso, and the arms carried a variety of weapons systems. Clearly upgraded from what I remembered, the suits were similar to the systems worn by the Pharyleri when we'd cleared the airport over a year ago.

The pair of suits stepped apart and gestured us forward, indicating that we should proceed ahead of them down the hall and farther into the administration wing. I stepped between them and swept my observation over the suits, finding them shielded from my analysis. All that was revealed was the armor rating and weapons of the mecha instead of details of the pilots inside.

The mecha clomped along the wide hallway behind us without a word as I led the way, following the signs through several intersections toward the clan offices. The halls were mostly empty, but Pharyleri clustered in out-of-the-way side passages and peeked out of half-closed office doors as we passed. I caught my name mentioned in between snatches of conversation in the Pharyleri's native tongue, a language that I regretted not picking up in the Shop.

I sighed mentally. There would always be something else I needed to purchase if I wanted to keep growing stronger. A better weapon, additional knowledge, another Skill. Stagnation equaled death in the System, especially on a relatively lawless Dungeon World like Earth, where the powerful did as they pleased.

The health totals alone on the Hakarta Lieutenant we'd passed earlier illustrated how long the road ahead of me still lay, and I couldn't imagine how much stronger someone in the higher ranks, like a Major or even a General, might be than that lowly Lieutenant.

The mecha guided us up a flight of stairs and down a long hallway on the second story. We passed a lounge with a reception desk and were directed toward a pair of fancy double doors that opened into a well-furnished office.

"Adventurer Mason!" The aged voice carried excitement like the bubbling of a brook through the ancient stone of a glacier-carved gorge. The speaker, a gray-haired gnome, stood as I entered the room and hobbled out from a large hand-carved wooden desk while leaning on a cane for support.

Clan Leader Borgym Sprocketsworth, Pharyleri Clan Elder, Prime Administrator, (Chief Executive Level 41)

HP: 5670/5670

MP: 7880/7880

"Clan Leader." I greeted the old Pharyleri formally since I didn't recognize the other gnome present, who remained seated in one of a trio of chairs before the desk. The comfortable chairs were upholstered in a rich, chocolate-colored leather fastened with golden rivets.

She sat quietly, observing Borgym's greetings without her expression giving anything away.

Borgym snorted dismissively as he shook my hand. "Hal, I know it's been a while, but there's no need to be formal after everything you've done on our behalf. I'm just glad to see you got my message."

The clan leader made a gesture to the armored suits, and they quietly closed the office doors, leaving the Countess and I alone with the two older gnomes.

"I'm afraid I do have to be a little formal for at least the introductions," I replied. "Clan Leader Borgym Sprocketsworth, Pharyleri Clan Elder and Prime Administrator, meet my current employer, Countess Dayena Balusia, Sultana of the Whispering Strings and Mistress of Shadows."

"Countess, it is a pleasure to meet you despite your unfortunate situation." Borgym bowed to the dark elf in a formal greeting, but his tone more than implied he understood all about the strained relationship between the young dark elf and her family.

"Thank you, Clan Leader," Dayena said, returning the bow. "My circumstances certainly are complicated, but Hal has provided excellent services as my advisor on this Dungeon World."

The gray-haired gnome glanced at me. "Hal, you should know that playing bodyguard to renegade Truinnar royalty is a dangerous game." His look turned into a stern glare. "But it's not the first time you've played out of your league, hmm."

I twitched my shoulders in a slight shrug. The old gnome had a point, but I wasn't about to get into the reasons I'd stayed clear of Pittsburgh for the last year, not when the clan leader already seemed to have a pretty good idea. I also didn't know the still-seated gnome or how secure the room might be, though it made sense for the clan leader's office to hold strong wards against scrying and other high-tier anti-spying defenses.

Borgym picked up on my hesitancy and sighed, beckoning for us to take the other seats in front of his desk to move the discussion along. While we seated ourselves in the extravagant leather chairs that automatically conformed into a position of maximum comfort as we sank into them, the clan leader circled around to the back of the desk and sat in his own chair, which had lowered to allow the tiny humanoid to climb into it easily. Once Borgym took his seat, the chair raised back up so that he was clearly visible on the other side of the broad desk.

"You've got great timing, Hal." Borgym gestured to the seated gnome. "This is Clan Leader Nesdyna Pistongrinder."

"Greetings, Adventurers," Nesdyna said. The female gnome nodded respectfully to Dayena and me before continuing. "Thank you for responding to Borgym's missive."

Broad streaks of bright neon green highlights ran through her hair, which was as gray as Borgym's, pulled back into a pair of braided buns.

Clan Leader Nesdyna Pistongrinder, Pharyleri Clan Elder (Logistics Coordinator Level 31)
HP: 4780/4780
MP: 5260/5260

Dayena nodded and settled back in her chair. From the elf's relaxed posture, it seemed she expected me to take the lead in the conversation on her behalf.

"Greetings, Clan Leader Pistongrinder," I said. "Borgym's message mentioned an opportunity for work, but we would like to know the details before agreeing to anything. While I am contracted to the Countess, neither of us are opposed to joint employment if the work will give us the chance to earn both Credits and experience."

Nesdyna looked at Borgym when I finished speaking. "Perhaps it would be best if you filled them in on the background to set the stage for everything going on."

Borgym steepled his fingers together in front of him on his desk. "You understand that the largest exports of a Dungeon World, beyond the experience and Levels gained from slaying monsters, are the components harvested from those monsters, as well as the raw materials gathered in areas of high Mana density, like dungeons. The problems then lay in moving these goods from the Dungeon World out into the galaxy at large.

"While the Shop provides teleportation services, those services are cost-prohibitive when looking at large scale mass transport of raw materials. It's generally only utilized on an individual basis, with fees as a portion of the cost of the goods sold."

Borgym paused as Dayena and I nodded our understanding of the gnome's explanation of Dungeon World Economics 101.

Nesdyna picked up the dialogue. "The starport serves well enough as a collection point for the local area, but the challenge in bulk transport is getting sufficient quantities of goods here to be shipped off world. Enough groups have arrived on Earth now that the System initialization is complete that goods are being stockpiled across the planet. However, there are still a limited number of ways of transporting the materials into the wider Galactic economy.

"The Pistongrinder Clan is looking to bridge that gap by establishing a rail network using the starport as a hub. We will be building from the skeleton of the former continental railway system in order to move goods and personnel."

"You want to use trains?" I raised an eyebrow as I looked at Borgym.

The Pharyleri answered my question with one of his own. "You've seen how we've expanded the footprint of the air defenses?"

"Yes," I replied, thinking about the towers we'd passed on our way into the starport. "High elevation with good sightlines."

"Exactly," Borgym said. "They're more for air defense against the increasing populations of higher Leveled airborne monsters. Just last week, we had a pack of griffins harassing our orbital traffic, though we managed to deal with them. Fortunately, we haven't had anything really nasty set up nearby, like the Ice Dragon up in the Yukon or the Frost Dragon in the Colorado Rockies."

"Anything that powerful means the area around it is pretty much a no-fly zone for hundreds of miles," Nesdyna said. "You might get a freighter in and out once if you've got a pilot with the right Skills, but regular air traffic is just a good way for lots of people to die."

"Got it," I said. "Air transit is out, so you've got to move goods on the ground. What about roads?"

"Roads? On a Dungeon World?" Borgym snorted. "Your asphalt highways will break down faster and faster without the territory they're in being purchased and regularly maintained. Only within Safe Zones where the System provides the upkeep will they remain passable, and that isn't feasible outside of high population areas."

"What makes railways more stable than roads?" I asked. "You're still crossing large stretches of unclaimed territory, just like with highways."

Green-streaked hair bobbed as Nesdyna nodded excitedly. "That's a good point, but we've developed specially designed rails to project a sliver of Mana stabilization around the tracks in order to preserve the system once it's in place. After that, regular use will keep them clear. The work will be upgrading the existing tracks from your old routes, but we have a locomotive with a system specially designed to do the rail conversion."

"That sounds like a lengthy project," I said. "My history is a little rusty, but I seem to recall the construction of the American Transcontinental Railroad taking years."

"Ah, yes," Borgym said, sharing a pointed glance with Nesdyna. "We researched that bit of your world's past when preparing for this project. It's a miracle that the railroad was ever completed with all the fiscal mismanagement, corruption, and fraud that occurred. Not to mention the mind-boggling treatment of your fellow humans."

With a fair idea of where this discussion seemed headed, I raised a skeptical eyebrow. "Galactic society doesn't seem overly concerned with indenture, serfdom, and outright slavery, despite what platitudes might be voiced about groups like the Krym'parke."

"That's hardly the same as oppressing groups of your own species based on such minor differences as the melanin content of their epidermis!"

"Perhaps," I said, remaining calm despite Borgym's outburst. "I find it hard to believe that Earth is the only place in all of the galaxy where prejudices exist. I bet in the System, there are those judged for the planet they were born upon or even their Class or Skill allocations."

Borgym and Nesdyna looked away from me at my last point and even Dayena seemed abashed. Something I said must have struck a nerve with the Pharyleri's own past, while I knew that Dayena's advancement to Agent Provocateur had been one of the initial points of conflict with her family.

"I'm only responsible for my own actions, as are you, and not the entire sum of our species' history." I shrugged. "To bring us back on track, I'm guessing that you want combat support for this railway conversion."

"Yes," Borgym said. "As you may have noticed on your way through the starport, the majority of our combat forces are mercenary in nature, like when we employed you in the past."

When I nodded, Nesdyna continued. "The Pistongrinder Clan is similarly focused on Artisan pursuits, so we've hired several combat Classed individuals to provide additional security for the expedition, and we're looking for a trusted individual to lead the team."

"And I'm the trusted individual in question."

"Borgym speaks quite highly of your performance during the clearing and initial construction of the starport," Nesdyna said. "That you took grievous wounds but still pushed through your injuries. All to complete the Quest you'd accepted on behalf of those you were assisting."

"Others sacrificed far more," I replied, looking pointedly at Borgym.

Nesdyna shook her head. "Those actions are only expected from clan members on behalf of the greater good. You had no obligation of blood or duty beyond that of coin and Quest."

Truth be told, I had been out for both Credits and experience at the time. While growing stronger remained my primary motivation even now, the Pharyleri were the first Galactic group I'd met that hadn't immediately oppressed the surviving human population—like later alien groups I had encountered. Sure, the gnomes might be in the starport business for a profit, but there was no denying they were providing useful services.

"On the subject of coin and Quest then," I said, "what are you offering in exchange for my leadership of your combat team?"

"It's just going to be the external security team," Nesdyna replied. "We have a small team of Pharyleri who will remain onboard the train at all times. We're looking for your team of Adventurers to keep monsters as far away from the tracks as possible while staying in range."

I nodded in understanding. "Let's talk details."

Borgym waved a hand over his desk, and a holographic map sprang up to float above the surface. The outline of the continental United States hovered for a moment before the focus of the display narrowed in on a green line that twisted and curved across the Midwest from Pennsylvania to Colorado.

I stood and leaned over the desk as I looked over the display. "This is the route?"

Small sections of yellow and red in varying lengths broke up the solid line of green running across the continent.

"We paid a considerable sum of Credits for a track survey from the Shop," Nesdyna explained. "Yellow indicates a blockage of the tracks that will need to be cleared. The red shows damage that requires repair."

I looked up from the map at the elderly logistician. "How are those problems being addressed?"

"A track-mounted repair drone will run ahead of the train to address small issues like broken tracks and welds. Larger problems will require the train to stop so that crew's mechanics and laborers can fix the track or clear the obstructions."

I exchanged a glance with Dayena. "Anytime those crew members are off the train outside of a Safe Zone, they'll need protection, or they'll be monster chow."

Nesdyna sighed. "Yes. Your team will be primarily responsible for clearing incoming monsters drawn by the rail conversion system while the train is moving, then additional combat pay to clear danger zones and guard the work crew during all of these repair stops."

Dayena leaned forward in her chair at the mention of pay, and I let her take over the negotiations at her signal of interest. Her high Charisma and social Skills ensured that she would get a better rate for us than anything I would be able to obtain.

I returned to my seat and turned to Borgym, pulling the elder into a side conversation as the Countess put her talents to work. "The starport is far larger than I remembered."

The old gnome smiled. "Yes, we've established trade agreements between several local and Galactic groups for exclusive access to goods and landing rights. That allowed us to expand the initial transit hub and build out berths for bulk freighters. We still get a decent amount of unaligned traffic, Adventurers looking to venture out in search of Dungeons, or various military groups sending forces for training experience."

I completely tuned out the discussion between Dayena and the Pistongrinder elder as I caught up with Borgym. My talk with the old gnome continued until a prompt appeared to inform me of the Quest being offered, halting our side conversation.

Quest Received - The Pistongrinder Express I

Provide combat support against monsters and other hostile forces as you escort the crew of the Pistongrinder Express locomotive to its destination in Denver, Colorado. Completion of this Quest grants acceptance of a subsequent Quest with additional rewards granted for a successful return journey with a loaded train of goods.

Reward: Variable depending on the condition of the locomotive and surviving crew.

I glanced at Dayena to confirm that the terms matched the results of her negotiations before accepting the Quest. Nesdyna smiled warmly as the notification disappeared.

Borgym rubbed his hands together excitedly before jumping down from his chair. "Who's ready to see the train?"

Chapter 8

The wide doors hissed, air escaping due to the pressure differential, one significant enough to be audible even over the squeal of metal on metal. The massive doors ground slowly open to reveal the structure's interior, bringing with it a real sight.

I whistled appreciatively as doors came to a halt. "That's a train all right."

A female gnome, her bobbed hair the same shade of bright green as the streaks in Nesdyna's braids, stepped out from the train house to greet us and drew my attention. The younger gnome, clad in beige coveralls over an olive-green tunic, glared at me critically for a moment before giving Dayena a similar examination. I returned the inspection, confirming my suspicions of the new Pharyleri's family resemblance.

Ismyna Pistongrinder (Stalwart Operator Level 29)
HP: 960/960
MP: 1370/1370

"A train is the entire series of connected units," Ismyna explained, tension filling her words. "This is an engine. Locomotive works too."

I raised an eyebrow and glanced at Borgym, who shrugged at me.

"Impressive engine then," I said, hoping the praise might smooth over whatever had offended the operator.

"Hmmph." Ismyna turned away from our group after blowing off my compliment and giving Nesdyna a half-hearted wave.

Ismyna's expression softened as she looked over the locomotive for a moment, then she marched back toward the now open structure that housed the engine, the gravel surrounding the tracks crunching beneath her combat boots. Despite the tone of the young gnome's initial greeting and whatever about my presence that upset her, the young gnome's pride in the gleaming locomotive remained evident.

A second gnome stood near the engine and scowled at me as Ismyna stomped toward him. The middle-aged gnome wore an armored jumpsuit similar to mine, though it was the same olive color as Ismyna's shirt, with a pistol holstered on one hip and a baton of some kind on the other. The black material of the armor appeared brand new, with that fresh-from-the-Shop feel of equipment yet to see use. He lacked the bright neon hair sported by most of the Pharyleri. Instead, his slicked back hair was a midnight blue so dark that it glistened nearly black from the overhead lighting shining out of the enginehouse. The gnome also sported a ridiculously drooping mustache that curved down past his jawline on either side of his pointed chin.

With the intensity of the stare the gnome held fixed on me, I knew that he was analyzing my status and I blatantly returned the inspection.

Dicenyk Crushcrank (Security Troubleshooter Level 19)

HP: 980/980

MP: 840/840

As Ismyna stepped into the enginehouse, she looped her arm through Dicenyk's and tugged on the Security Troubleshooter. The sour-looking gnome shot a final dirty look my way before going with her.

"Well, I've got a starport to run," said Borgym. "I'll leave you in Nesdyna's capable hands." The old clan leader shook my hand. "Good seeing you again, Hal."

He said farewell to Dayena and hustled off the way we had come from, heading back to his offices.

"Anything you want to tell me, Clan Leader?" I asked the lone Pharyleri who remained with the Countess and me.

Nesdyna sighed. "My daughter and her paramour believe your assistance is unnecessary."

"How so?"

"The durability of the Pistongrinder Express is considerable." She gestured to the locomotive.

Only the front profile of the engine lay visible from where it rested, ensconced within the structure the size of a barn. The locomotive nearly filled the gaping doorway of the enginehouse, standing nearly the height of a two-story building and half that in width.

Ballast ground beneath our feet as we followed Ismyna toward the structure, though the irregularly shaped rocks soon gave way to the paved surface of the building's interior when we passed through the doorway.

Curved bars of shining coppery metal formed a cowcatcher that nearly scraped the tracks beneath the giant locomotive and stretched around the full width of the vehicle to either side, where they seamlessly joined with armored plates of the same material. Currently powered off, headlights sat on either side of the engine, above and just forward of where the cowcatcher merged with the thicker side armor. Another curved plate sat behind the cowcatcher and ran upward in an armored ridge that protected the vehicle's centerline, an airhorn affixed to the crest at the top of the engine.

Though trains hadn't needed cowcatchers in years before the System's arrival, I supposed the danger of roaming monsters crossing the tracks warranted the precaution.

Beneath the protection of the bulky plates hid the barely visible surface of the engine itself, which glistened with a sleek bronze-like material, significantly darker than the brighter armor overtop. Wires, gauges, and gears covered the undercarriage of the engine, like some kind of steampunk amalgamation beyond my comprehension.

Hopefully, the crew on this trip thought to bring along someone capable of fixing the locomotive when it inevitably broke down or got smashed by some rampaging monster. This was Earth. Rampaging monsters were sort of our thing now.

I stepped up to the front of the locomotive and rapped my knuckles against the armor. A flare of light appeared under my fist as it made contact and rippled out from the center of the sharp impact. My touch revealed the reactive magic embedded within the armor itself. I peered closer and probed at the armor with all of my senses, engaging Greater Observation and digging through the coppery metal until I found the source.

Enchantments.

Serious runework so deeply integrated that nothing stood out as visible from the surface.

I stepped back and walked around the side of the engine, the change in perspective revealing the wheel assemblies that traversed the tracks beneath the behemoth.

One of the triple-axle trucks sat forward, just behind the cowcatcher, while the second set of axles rested beneath the narrow window slits of the operator cab located at the rear end of the locomotive. Both wheel assemblies were nearly hidden by the glimmering armor plates that protected the side of the engine, but they appeared similar in form to the wheel assemblies from diesel-electric engines used by railroads before the System's arrival, though the vehicle here stretched out slightly longer than those pre-System locomotives.

Dayena, walking ahead, continued around the locomotive in Ismyna's wake.

"It seems formidable," I said. "But armor isn't impenetrable. You need to deal with the threat before it shatters completely."

Nesdyna nodded. "You're entirely correct, Adventurer Mason."

"Call me Hal, please."

"Very well, Hal," Nesdyna said. "There are some weapon stations on the engine, but it's primarily designed to take a beating and keep the train moving."

"Speaking of moving, how does the propulsion system work?" I asked. I didn't need to be an expert but knowing how the engine operated would help me defend it from attack.

Nesdyna pointed at a large cylinder that rose from the engine, halfway down the locomotive's length. My first thought was that it looked like a smokestack from an old steam engine, but the numerous forward-facing vents made that unlikely. "Mana collection sieve. With Earth now fully integrated into the System, Mana density will continue to increase. That means that collecting Mana as a power source is more practical here than almost anywhere else outside the Forbidden Zone. When charging the Mana batteries is unnecessary, the collector can be lowered to achieve higher speeds."

I nodded in understanding when the older gnome glanced at me, and she pointed lower, at a section of the engine hidden behind the copper-colored armor plates, and then farther down at the wheel assemblies. "Mana batteries store any excess energy until it's needed, while the rest is supplied directly to the traction motors on the wheel assemblies. Mana also powers the blower units that cool the motors and prevent them from overheating during use."

My brow furrowed. "Is the power system hardened against null grenades or Mana draining Skills?"

Nesdyna peered at me. "You're not just thinking about defending against monster spawns, are you?"

I shook my head, thinking back to the bandits holding the pass over in Maryland. "Sooner or later, someone will try to take it from you, and you'll need to fight to protect what's yours."

"You have a very cynical view of the world."

I turned away from my examination of the locomotive and looked at the diminutive older gnome. "A year ago, the people on this planet only worried about paying their bills and the concerns of everyday life. Now most of those people are dead, and the rest of us are just trying to survive another day." I gestured toward the Countess as she climbed up the back ladder of the locomotive. "From what I've learned of Galactic politics, our perspective isn't really all that unique."

Nesdyna sighed. "You asked about the effects of Mana draining attacks?" At my nod, she continued. "The resistances that are integral to the engine provide some defense, but high-tier Skills often bypass them to some degree. We've installed redundant systems in as many places as possible to combat that."

"Good. I'd like to get a full walkthrough of the engine to familiarize myself with the systems and any failure points." I held up my hands to forestall Nesdyna before she could protest. "I need to be as familiar with the vehicle as any attackers who get their hands on the schematics. If there are any weak points in the design, I need to know."

"You'll have full access," she said. "What else do you need?"

"What about the crew and their Skills?"

"While the primary crew does have some hybrid Classes with Skills that can be used offensively, their traits are focused on securing the infrastructure and transport directly rather than eliminating external threats."

"Primary crew?" I asked.

"My daughter has a hand-picked team of the Clan's best for this first run," Nesdyna replied. "We've also hired another pair of Adventurers as security contractors to assist you in combating monsters."

I raised an eyebrow. "When do I get to meet the crew and the contractors?"

"Most of the crew is off until the morning of departure, but the two contractors will report in here at the enginehouse at dawn tomorrow."

Staring over the locomotive, I nodded absently. "I'd best get started with some hands-on familiarization now then."

Though I didn't voice them, I also held concerns over the pair of mercenaries for hire. Would they be reliable? Could I trust them at my back?

A plan formed for a way to answer the first question. The second would remain unanswered until I got to know them.

After walking to the back of the locomotive, I climbed the ladder set into the rear corner of the engine. A narrow platform of grated metal ran around the exterior of the operator cabin and an open hatch led the way inside.

I ducked through the opening and found myself in a compartment filled with control screens, buttons, and display screens. A holographic display projecting over the walls of the cabin presented an impressive three-hundred-sixty-degree view around the engine in perfect detail that almost made it seem as if there were no walls in the compartment.

Leaning over Ismyna's shoulder for a better look at the controls as the green-haired gnome explained various systems, Dayena glanced at me as I entered but returned her attention to the engineer. Nesdyna climbed into the cab after I moved aside to make room, but the small space felt crowded with the four of us inside.

The rest of the day was spent learning the fundamentals of the various sensor readouts and understanding what those readings meant, along with the basics of the controls for the locomotive. It never hurt to be prepared, though I never expected to be driving the engine.

Once I felt comfortable with the controls and the cabin displays, I followed along as Ismyna performed an inspection of the entire engine, inside and out, from the plow-like cowcatcher nose to the coupler at the tail. At one point, she demonstrated how a ruptured Mana battery could be ejected in an emergency, reminding me of those old TV shows where a starship would jettison the warp core.

I even crawled beneath the locomotive to familiarize myself with the undercarriage. I knew well the kind of System technology that could hide a device used for tracking an enemy, but at least now I would have some chance to notice anything out of place in the future.

When I finally clambered out from beneath the engine, Ismyna stood alone alongside the engine, waiting for me. I stood before stretching, reveling in being out from the cramped confines of the narrow service pit between the tracks where the locomotive rested. The tight maintenance area had been designed for the much smaller Pharyleri and fitting down there hadn't exactly been a comfortable experience.

At least it had been sparklingly clean.

"You really are taking this seriously," Ismyna said when I lowered my outstretched arms.

Looking at the gnome, I raised an eyebrow. "Why wouldn't I?"

"None of this means anything to you," Ismyna said, gesturing to the engine. "The effort and hopes and dreams that went into building this to make a future for my clan. It's just a job and some Credits to you."

"When I say I'll do something, I do it at my best. I keep my word." I grinned and raised one shoulder in a half-hearted shrug. "I do like Credits though."

Ismyna snorted and headed toward the tall doorway where the Countess chatted amiably with Nesdyna beside the opening that displayed the darkened sky outside the enginehouse. I followed the gnome, and the conversation at the doorway dropped off as we approached them. The sky beyond the doors showed no sign of daylight, the sun having set some time ago.

"What is your timeline?" I asked when I reached the group at the doorway.

"Departure the day after tomorrow," Ismyna replied.

I frowned. "That doesn't leave me with much time to shake down the Adventurers you've hired into a cohesive party."

Nesdyna shrugged. "We need to get the project started. It's going to take weeks to reach the projected endpoint of our initial line. You'll have time to work out any issues with your team on the way."

"First few days could be rough, but we'll do our best to figure something out."

We left the enginehouse, finding that Nesdyna had arranged lodging for Dayena and me in the quarters for transient spacers that adjoined the starport. We parted ways for the night shortly afterward, only stopping long enough to grab a bite from a food vendor in the terminal itself before we reached the hotel and crashed for the night.

Tomorrow was going to be fun, what with meeting my technical subordinates.

Chapter 9

An odd pair waited outside the enginehouse to greet us when we returned in the morning.

The first stood only a little higher than my waist with shoulders half again as broad as mine. The pale-skinned dwarf had tied his black hair back in a ponytail, with a greasy beard of the same color covering most of the dwarf's chest and falling nearly to his waist. A faded brown jumpsuit covered the Gimsar, but he carried no weapons that I could see.

The dwarf leaned against a quadrupedal robot that looked like a large dog, complete with sharpened blades that gave the appearance of clawed paws and a protruding snout filled with jagged triangular teeth. The antenna sticking up from the back of the dog's head suggested that the dwarf used some sort of remote control to direct the robot. A pair of drones hovered behind the Gimsar, each with a central weapon system suspended between dual rotor cylinders.

A wrist-mounted computer took up the dwarf's left forearm, and a metallic band circled his head. Several small antennas stuck up from the band, which connected to a tiny translucent red square that the dwarf flipped up from covering his eye as we approached.

Nargen Cragbreaker (Drone Animator Level 40)

HP: 480/480

MP: 820/820

Just as wide as the Gimsar, the second figure towered above the dwarf, easily standing nine feet tall. A single horn stretched out from the right side of the humanoid's bull-like head before curving to point forward, but only a broken stump of ivory remained on the opposite side. Mismatched plates of various shades armored the massive humanoid, and the riot of colors only highlighted the golden tan of the minotaur's hide, visible where his head stuck up from a raised gorget.

Though the incongruous panels of the armor spoke to a frugality that bordered on excess, there seemed to be nothing wrong with the Yerrick's weapon of choice. The minotaur leaned on the haft of a weapon that actually stood taller than the creature himself. A sharpened spear point topped the weapon shaft, glinting in the morning light, above a curving axeblade that matched the Class of the weapon's wielder.

Kurak Thunderfury (Halberdier Level 41)

HP: 920/920

MP: 410/410

The notable fact about the Yerrick was that their world had been one of the first Dungeon Worlds. With their population decimated by the System's arrival, much like humanity during our own System initiation, and their world fallen to chaos, the Yerrick spread far across the galaxy. With no homeworld to call their own, the Yerrick clung fiercely to their identities as members of their clans and always put the needs of their tribe above their own.

The Pharyleri were footing the bill for these Adventurers, and I'd taken the job, so I'd just have to get over my reservations and work with what I had for now.

"Adventurer Cragbreaker and Adventurer Thunderfury." I greeted the pair as the Countess and I approached within speaking distance.

The two non-humans had watched our arrival and gave us each a shallow nod.

"Adventurer Mason," Kurak rumbled, his voice reverberating with a gravelly bass. "Countess Baluisa."

"Morning," muttered Nargen. The Gimsar's gaze fixed on the space above my head, scanning my status with his targeting headset, and a scowl crossed the dwarf's face as he folded his arms across his broad chest. "You're to be our team leader?" The incredulous tone highlighted the Gimsar's thready voice, contrasting sharply against his stern appearance as the dwarf stood fuming.

"Yes," I replied as I fixed Nargen with an icy glare. Best to shut down this attitude now before it grew to something that caused problems down the line.

The dwarf scoffed, failing to take the hint. "Psh, what's a human hunter know about the wilds of a Dungeon World?"

I waved dismissively. "Oh, I don't know, I've only been living in them for just over a year."

Nargen harrumphed and rolled his eyes. "A year, he says."

Stepping in front of the Gimsar, I leaned down and stuck my face right in front of his. "And just how many years did it take you to earn your forty Levels?"

The calmly asked question surprised Nargen, given my confrontational posture, and the dwarf blinked as he considered my query. I stood up straight with my hands on my hips, allowing the Gimsar time to consider his next words carefully.

My apparent Basic Class level nearly equaled his own, and I'd accomplished my thirty-eight Levels in only a year. I wasn't the highest Leveled human on Earth, but Levels by themselves weren't everything, and I certainly was no slouch either.

"Bah, fine." Nargen spat the words disgustedly. "You're in charge. What's your plan?"

"Well, first we'll need to figure out how to work together as a team," I replied. I nodded to Dayena, who extended party invitations to Nargen and Kurak. Both appeared in my party status menu a moment after they accepted. I grinned. "We're going to run a Dungeon."

***

Less than an hour's drive later, we pulled into the main parking area at McConnells Mill State Park. Only a few abandoned pre-System vehicles sat scattered across the lot as the Countess and I parked our bikes. Kurak pulled in behind us, driving a four-wheeled ATV that seemed decidedly undersized for his large frame. Nargen brought up the rear, riding on his robodog drone.

Before the apocalypse, the park around the historic gristmill had been a popular outdoor recreation spot for people who enjoyed hiking, kayaking, and fishing. Now with the System stabilized, the Mana density in this section of the Slippery Rock Gorge to the south and west of the mill had increased and converted the ravine into a permanent Dungeon.

Dismounting my bike, I double-checked my loadout, having swapped out the projectile pistols for beam weaponry in the holsters at my hips. No point in burning through Credits by expending ammunition when I more wanted to get a feel for our new party members than I needed to do damage myself, at least if things went well. Just in case though, I had added a second pair of beam pistols in a shoulder rig, with the energy weapons hanging holstered under each armpit.

"What's the plan?" Kurak asked, carefully extracting himself from the tiny frame of his vehicle.

I waited until Nargen and Dayena were also listening, then I pointed toward the edge of the parking lot. "The trail down the hill leads to the historic location that marks the entrance for the Dungeon. It's a gauntlet-type Dungeon with constant encounters along a scenic trail that loops down one side of the gorge and back up the other."

"You've run this Dungeon before," Kurak said.

I nodded. "I was part of the group that earned the first clear bonus."

That first clear had been too late to save the residents of nearby Portersville from the monster wave that spawned from the overflowing Dungeon after its initial formation. The tide of creatures had swept over the town in a stampede that reduced the few buildings that remained after the apocalypse into rubble and ground the inhabitants into paste. Once the danger of the overflowing Dungeon was identified, a Quest issued by the Truinnar noble who'd purchased nearby Zelienople had mobilized enough Adventurers and human survivors to deal with the problem. Several groups coordinated to punch through the tide of monsters, and my team, led by a trio of Yerrick Adventurers, reached the Dungeon first.

While selfish interests in protecting his own holdings had motivated Lord Daxily to issue the Quest, he had likely saved a number of lives in the process. Still, I wouldn't mind punching out the smug dark elf for other reasons if I ever ran into him again, though that likelihood remained slim since the Countess and I had been politely barred from town after my last visit.

"What should we expect inside?" Nargen's question pulled me from my reflection of the past.

"Mostly mutated animals of Earth origin," I replied. "We'll want to stop when we find the roaming Boss and swap out to gear you don't mind pitching out."

The three non-humans all looked at me quizzically. Adventurers rarely discarded anything that might still be useful or worth Credits.

"The Boss is a giant skunk," I explained.

Three uncomprehending stares looked at me, and I sighed.

"It's a beast with a corrosive spray that smells beyond foul, so keep an eye out for a black furred animal with white down on its back and tail."

"My equipment will be fine," Dayena scoffed. "Superior quality materials and manufacture will supersede anything a Dungeon below Level 100 can throw at it."

I shrugged and headed for the trailhead that led over the hillside and down toward the mill below. "Don't say I didn't warn you."

Usually the Truinnar noble took my advice at face value, but every once in a while, the dark elf felt the need to show off her superiority. Typically, I let her find out for herself that she could still be wrong.

The trio followed me after a moment, and I led them down the switchback trail until we reached the bottom. Along the bank of Slippery Rock Creek stood the restored gristmill and the red covered bridge which spanned the white-water-filled ravine.

I walked down the slight incline from the side of the mill toward the bridge and stopped at the covered information board beside a tiny parking area, only large enough for maybe four cars. The board displayed the map of the park and a chalkboard marked with bright neon letters reading "Check-In Here."

Frowning, I noticed that the check-in date for the last group on the board was over two weeks prior, and the line lacked a check-out time.

"Problem?" Kurak rumbled over my shoulder.

"The last group to attempt the Dungeon never checked out," I replied, scanning the previous entries on the board. "Maybe they forgot to check out, but it looks like they were regulars, and nobody has cleared it since."

"You still want to go in?" Nargen's voice cracked in fear.

Instead of replying, I grabbed the piece of chalk that dangled from the board on a bit of string and scrawled my name, along with the date and time. I'd fought this Dungeon back from an overflow once before. I'd do it again before I let another wave of death sweep another town of survivors off the face of the Earth.

Pivoting on one foot, I marched toward the shimmering field to the left of the covered bridge, my boots clomping over the asphalt drive. The light denoted the entrance to the Dungeon, along the southern bank of the wide creek. At the portal's threshold, I paused.

"Are you coming?" I asked without looking back.

The nervous shuffling of feet was the only response to my question, and I turned around to face the others, resting my hands on my hips.

The Countess stood only a pace behind me, her footsteps so quiet that only her presence in the party system and our experiences together informed me of her position while I'd faced away from her.

Kurak looked as though he'd only taken a couple steps toward the Dungeon entrance after I'd walked away from the sign. The minotaur looked back and forth between Nargen and me, confusion and reluctance written plainly on his bovine face.

The Gimsar stood with his arms folded, back beside the chalkboard, his usual scowl firmly in place as he shook his head. "No, no, no." Nargen finally snapped out under the weight of my stare. "A Dungeon overflow is a one-way trip. We go in there, we ain't coming back out."

I snorted. "You haven't been here long, have you?"

"What?" Nargen blinked at the non sequitur.

"You're on a Dungeon World with more than ninety percent of the native population wiped out. An overflowing Dungeon is just another Tuesday."

"It's not Tuesday though," Kurak offered hesitantly.

I sighed, looking at the minotaur. Sometimes Galactics cheaped out on their translation packs, and it became painfully obvious when a colloquialism showed up in conversation. "It's an expression to indicate an everyday occurrence."

My attention returned to Nargen as Kurak mulled over my words. "I picked this Dungeon because it fit our Levels, though if I'd known it was close to overflowing, then I'd have chosen it anyways. Get over your fears and get used to seeing places like this, since there are far worse locations already overrun across the continent and the world. Or you can head back to town with your Contract cancelled to look for employment elsewhere." I shrugged. "It's your call."

Then I turned away from the reluctant Adventurers and drew the pair of energy pistols from the holsters on my hips before stepping through the Dungeon entrance. The condensed Mana of the barrier holding the Dungeon in check washed over my exposed face like passing through a curtain of water. When I entered, the piercing cries of mutated animals echoing in a shrieking cacophony hit me with almost physical force.

A blurred brownish-orange shape already flying toward me exploded in a burst of overheated gore as the energy beam from one of my pistols lanced through the airborne creature. A tide of similarly colored squirrels, overgrown to the size of small dogs and with six legs instead of the usual four, poured out from the undergrowth and rushed toward me.

Dozens, if not hundreds, covered the trail and still more came, squealing maniacally from mouths full of aberrantly pointed teeth.

Squirrexail (Level 48)
HP: 220/220

A quick sweep of Greater Observation revealed that the squirrel creatures lacked much in the way of health or durability but made up for that shortcoming with an overabundance of numbers.

Normally at the start of a Dungeon, Adventurers got a bit of room to sort themselves out and get into formation. On the brink of an overflow, no such safe space existed. The monsters swarmed me in the wake of the first mutated animal now blasted into atoms by my pistol.

Jamming one pistol back into its holster, I stepped forward to clear the entrance space for whoever came through next and opened fire with my remaining weapon. With my free hand, I summoned a plasma grenade and chucked it into the midst of the swarm as the first wave pounced.

Summoning my knife, I slashed the seven-inch blade deeply into the bodies of the beasts. Blood and entrails sprayed out of the wounded and dying animals as they fell, and I continued forward as the grenade detonated. The edges of the blast swept over me, a wave of fire and pain that savaged the monstrous swarm far more than it did me. I lunged into the center of the space created by the explosion.

My pistol picked off tumbling creatures, and my knife cut through any that recovered enough to fling themselves at me once again.

I didn't catch them all. The monsters gnawing and biting at my ankles were held off by the armor. For the moment. I could sense my armor's durability dropping.

Then the swarm gathered itself, and the rabid animals launched themselves at me from every direction. Clawing and biting, the squirrels latched onto me and refused to be dislodged as I stomped and spun to throw off my attackers.

No matter how many I cut and shot, another took its place until the angry beasts hung from almost every portion of my armored jumpsuit. Though they hadn't managed to get through, my hands were full keeping the creatures away from my face.

"Are you planning to leave any for the rest of us?" Dayena called from behind me as the beams from her pistol joined my assault on the swarm. "Or are you just making yourself a fur coat?"

"I didn't have the chance to ask if they'd mind waiting to start the party," I replied, still hacking and shooting at the swarm.

Heavy footsteps thundered up from behind, and a flash of steel passed in front of my face as a precision slice of Kurak's halberd cut away the squirrels that clung to my torso.

I winced as one nasty little bugger clambered up my back and bit the back of my neck. My shoulders hunched involuntarily, and I cursed as I dropped my knife before yanking the squirrel free, tearing loose a chunk of flesh in the process. I flung the creature against one of the many rocks that lined the trail, splattering the beast with a satisfying *thunk*.

Then I turned my attention to clearing the rest of the swarm, despite the trickle of blood that ran down the back of my neck.

Bodies littered the trail as Kurak's halberd cleared swaths of the creatures. A sudden line of small explosions rippled through the swarm, gouts of flame and the scent of charring animal flesh filling the air as squirrels flew with every detonation. A glance revealed the source of the explosions as another barrage of miniature missiles launched into the swarm from one of Nargen's flying drones. The reluctant Gimsar stood alongside Dayena, firing a beam rifle after finally joining us, though the dwarf's expression remained twisted in a scowl so deep that his eyebrows nearly touched.

A moment later, Nargen's robodog plunged into the fray alongside Kurak and snapped the squirrels in half with each chomp of its artificial jaws.

Dayena saw my glance and grinned in amusement at the situation, though part of her amusement originated at finding me clad in a living fur coat. It was humorous in hindsight, and I couldn't help but smirk before I returned to the morbid business of monster clearing.

The fight didn't last much longer, even as the lone beam pistol I used completely depleted its charges as the last of the abnormally large rodents lay twitching in pieces.

"Loot fast," I commanded, already stooping amongst the carcasses. "We need to keep moving forward or the Dungeon will push the next waves even faster."

Kurak joined me in crawling along the gore-coated trail as we touched each dead squirrel to loot bits of fur, bones, and other animal parts.

Nargen spoke up from behind. "We could just leave?"

Clearly, the Gimsar still didn't care to be in the nearly overflowing dungeon.

I stood from looting and frowned at the Gimsar. "You want to let the Dungeon overflow? Maybe wipe out another town or village?"

"It's fine, Nargen." The minotaur attempted to wipe some of the blood covering his gauntlets onto the plant leaves that lined the trail. "If we want to keep our Contract with the gnomes, we need to prove we can get the job done."

"I've seen the results of an overflowing Dungeon. A full run that slays the Boss stems the tide from continuing to push monsters outside, then one or two more clears after that usually gets things back to normal." Having said my piece, I left Kurak to convince his companion and returned to sorting through the dead monsters, copying the Yerrick's hand-cleaning method once I'd finished looting the last of the monster corpses near me.

Looking back toward the Dungeon entrance, Dayena approached me while Nargen appeared to be loading additional missiles into the launchers on his drone. Nodding in approval, I swapped out the spent beam pistol for another fully charged one from my Inventory.

Once the dwarf and his trio of drones caught up to where Kurak and I waited with the Countess, I looked solemnly at our group. "Conserve your ammo and Mana whenever possible. This is going to be a long slog, and we're just getting started."

Kurak and Nargen exchanged a nervous glance, while Dayena just gave me a look that my words were something obvious.

I scouted ahead along the creekside trail, the burbling water a deceptively relaxing backdrop to the dangers that lurked in the rocks and trees. It didn't take long until I found the next group of creatures, then I fell back to engage the beasts with my team's support.

Another group of mutated squirrels attacked us next, their slightly higher Levels putting up more of a fight than the first swarm our party had dispatched.

Then alongside a stretch of trail where a placid section of the brook ran, a flock of mutated turkeys ambushed us from the woods. Their flapping wings and overly large bodies jumped on us, pinning our group against the water's edge.

Nargen's drones drifted over the water, providing fire support from a range that the gliding turkeys couldn't reach. At least until a giant trout leaped out of the water and tried to swallow one of the drones like a bug. The drone moved upward at the last moment, narrowly escaping being swallowed whole by the massive fish.

After that incident, the drones stuck closer to the group and remained hovering above their Gimsar controller. Fortunately, once we'd cleared that stretch, the trail curved away from the water's edge. I briefly considered dynamite fishing but chose to conserve ammunition.

Maybe on the way back. Mutated trout made for good eating.

After nearly thirty more minutes of constant combat along the four hundred paved yards of the trail, our group reached the wooden bridge beyond which the trail narrowed and grew rockier.

Deep scratches marred Kurak's armor, and our jumpsuits sported numerous rents and slashes. The burbling rivulets of water falling over the rocky terrain above the bridge provided a scenic backdrop as we recovered from our latest encounter.

Then we returned to the fray.

Chapter 10

Sticking with the theme of native wildlife mutated in size and deadliness, the native Pennsylvania creatures continued to rush us from all sides as we delved onward.

Giant chipmunks, winged raccoons, snapping turtles with spiked shells, and shadowy mink whose fangs dripped with poison that sizzled when it splashed on the ground, all assaulted us unceasingly and in groups numbering in the dozens.

The monsters battered us repeatedly, and our gear looked more and more ragged. After a chipmunk with incisors the size of my thumb gnawed through one of my pistols, I stuck the sparking mass into my Inventory. Chips and rolls marred the once-sharp edge of Kurak's halberd from repeated impacts on the impossibly hard shells of the snappers.

One of the raccoons had dived into a front leg of Nargen's prized robodog and twisted it so badly that the leg now pointed almost straight backward as the drone hobbled along on its three good limbs. Swaths of Dayena's blistered skin glistened as it slowly healed after the corrosive spittle from an ambushing mink ate through her armor and into the flesh beneath.

Despite the peril, somewhere amidst the constant tides of death that threatened to sweep us away, our group found a rhythm that carried us through surging monsters.

Kurak's armored bulk served as the bulwark upon which the waves broke, the Halbardier's namesake weapon hacking through the ranks of teeming creatures and leaving behind only mangled bits. Nargen's flying drones hovered over him, their firepower directed into the thickest bits of the swarms while the limping robodog guarded its master's back.

By unspoken agreement, Dayena and I held our abilities in reserve, instead supporting the party with our weapons only. Precision beam fire from our pistols riddled the oncoming monsters until they reached Kurak, at which point we switched to melee weapons and waded into the fray on either side of the massive minotaur.

Though Kurak and Nargen were allies due to their contract with the gnomes, their ultimate loyalties remained unknown. Until things with Dayena's family settled down, the less anyone saw of our Class Skills, and the longer we kept our full potential hidden, the better our chances stood in the long run. While information could always be purchased from the Shop, it would be better to let them see the expected and save the surprises where we could.

Nearly three hours passed before we finished the eastern half of the loop, and Kurak's armored hooves clomped down the wooden framed stairs that descended to Eckert Bridge from an elevated section of the trail.

"Hold up," I called to the minotaur, trying to keep my voice from carrying too far.

Kurak snorted and paused on the last stair, pulling himself out of his mindless plodding forward and looking around for the source of the caution in my tone.

"It's been too quiet," I said when I reached the halted warrior.

Kurak shifted uncomfortably, the wood creaking beneath his movements. "Yes, we should have encountered another wave several minutes ago."

"Wait here." I squeezed around Kurak and hunched over as I crept the dozen feet that separated the stairs from the opening in the guardrail that led to the poorly maintained access road.

I crouched at the gap and listened, my enhanced senses straining for anything out of the ordinary. Wind rustled through the leaves overhead, the trees swaying with the breeze. The creek's rushing water flowed and burbled over rocks as the brook passed beneath the bridge that led to the north bank. Then I heard scratching and the churning of earth as something pawed at the ground, and a faint acrid stench burned the insides of my nostrils.

I slowly eased forward, leaning out to look to my right. Across the bridge, a mass of black fur, easily the size of a pre-System grizzly bear, waggled a bushy black tail that stuck straight up into the air. A white streak of fur ran down the center of the giant skunk's back as it dug into the far side of the ravine, dirt flying up behind the monster as it tore into the ground.

With the monster clearly distracted, I focused on it with Greater Observation.

Giant Skunk (Boss Level 67)
HP: 4890/4890

I frowned at the analysis and the lack of mutations visible from where I stood. Every other monster we'd encountered in this dungeon sported multiple unique mutations, and the boss only looked larger than I remembered from the previous clear. I continued to watch the beast and noticed that the air seemed to ripple around it, like waves of heat over asphalt in the summer sun.

Or fumes from the opening of a gas can.

A moment later, the beast's claws latched onto something, and it wiggled backward out of the hole dug into the hillside. An oversized groundhog impaled on the skunk's elongated claws squealed as the larger creature dragged it from the burrow. The skunk's muzzle snapped down on the unfortunate rodent, silencing the bleating groundhog.

I crept back from the trailhead as the boss devoured its prey. Maybe the aggression wasn't really even an additional mutation, since normally skunks were scavengers that ate insects and smaller game like moles, snakes, or frogs. The groundhog was just larger than its usual pre-System prey.

Keeping my voice low but above a whisper, I informed the group of my observations.

"I assume you have a plan?" Dayena asked.

"Tank and spank," I replied, pointing first at Kurak then gesturing to the rest of our group. "The tricky bit is that the Boss looks bigger than normal. Also, the air around the monster still looks like it has the corrosive aura. So, change out your gear into things you can afford to lose."

The minotaur nodded and took a moment to swap out a few pieces of gear, though he kept on his heavy plate armor. Then he clomped past me down the last of the stairs to the trailhead. We followed, spreading out behind Kurak to clear our firing lanes as he jogged across the bridge. The pounding of the Yerrick's greaves over the cement drew the attention of the skunk, and it turned toward Kurak with its bushy tail raised as he sped into a sprint.

Less than a half dozen paces from the Boss, Kurak reached the edge of the corrosive aura that surrounded the monster, and the minotaur visibly flinched as the fumes swept over him. The tank's confident rush devolved into an uneven stagger as he coughed. The skunk, obviously anticipating that, prepared to lunge at the distracted minotaur.

Crimson rays streaked past Kurak and swept across the Boss's snarling face, narrowly missing one eye as I opened fire with both beam pistols. The beast flinched, providing a moment that allowed Kurak the opportunity to adjust to the pain of the corrosive aura. The minotaur recovered enough to swing his halberd toward the skunk's fang-filled maw. The glinting weapon narrowly missed the Boss as it jerked away before snapping forward in an attack of its own.

Kurak spun away from the closing jaws in a surprising display of agility, narrowly escaping the sharp teeth that clacked together beside him. Pivoting on the blade of his halberd, Kurak kicked the side of the monster's head. Though the minotaur put the full force of his body behind the attack, the blow barely nudged the creature's head, and Kurak stumbled back a pace as he regained his footing.

Beam fire stitched across the beast from the combined attacks of the rest of the party. The energy attacks singed the skunk's fur, charring patches in the white streak that ran along its upper flanks. Despite the flurry of shots, none of the attacks burned through the fluffy pelt.

Our attacks drew the beast's attention, and it spun around with its tail pointed straight up. I dove for the side of the bridge and vaulted onto the guardrail to launch myself, but I was too slow.

The spray from the skunk's backside washed along the length of the bridge and splashed into my side as I pushed off the railing. The liquid sizzled and popped over the surface of my jumpsuit and ignited a burning sensation that seared the exposed skin of my face and hands.

The pain was a minor annoyance in comparison to the smell. Tears formed at the fumes, blinding me as I squeezed my eyelids shut. Off balance, I fell from the bridge. The noxious, acrid stench of the spray seared my nostrils, and I coughed—just in time to smack into the creek in a painful belly flop.

The creekwater filled my mouth and nose, soothing the pain of the skunk's attack enough that I managed to override my instinctive attempt to breathe in more liquid. I dismissed the weapons I'd somehow held on to back into my Inventory.

With my hands now empty, I kept my mouth shut against my heaving chest that burned with the water it wanted to expel and kicked for the surface. My feet pushed off the creek bed rocks, and my head broke free of the water's surface a moment later. Damn thing was only about six inches deeper than I was tall.

I coughed, spurting up the water I'd swallowed, while I bobbed and bounced toward the far shore. Audible over my splashing were the sounds of coughing and hacking mingled with the noise of combat. The fumes from the skunk spray lingered at the water's surface and burned the back of my throat slightly with every breath, but it remained far from the full force of the initial toxic blast.

Scrambling from the water, I clambered on all fours up the bank and onto the old Hells Hollow trail that ran along the far side of the creek. Though no one had hiked the path since the Apocalypse, it remained cut into the side of the hill, and I used the worn trail to quickly return to the fight.

The path led up beside where I'd first seen the giant skunk tunneling into the hillside, which meant I found myself behind the Boss as it had rushed past Kurak and onto the bridge after the rest of my team.

The skunk stood with its forelimbs atop Nargen's robodog in the center of the span, metal shrieking as the beast clawed and tore at the sparking mess of wire and metal with a single-minded fury. The rest of the team appeared to be taking advantage of the drone's sacrifice, retreating out of range of the skunk's aura.

The scattered pieces of the drone seemed to melt under the destructive influence of the skunk's aura. Like an ice cube on a hot plate, shredded chunks of armor that lay scattered across the bridge's cement surface turned to liquid then evaporated.

Tears streamed down Nargen's face as he reluctantly backed away from the Boss. From the Gimsar's stricken expression, the demise of his prized drone seemed as likely a source of the dwarf's weeping as the tear-inducing fumes. Despite mourning his drone, Nargen continued to fire his beam rifle.

A barrage of energy rays from Dayena and Nargen's hovering drones also poured into the Boss, and the stench of burning flesh joined the skunk's acrid odor in a truly nauseating combination. At least the energy attacks seemed to pierce through the protection of the monster's fur once they'd burned enough of it away.

The surface metals of the floating drones appeared warped from the caustic effects of the skunk's attack. I wondered how they still managed to fly with rotors contorted unevenly by the damaging ability.

The corrosion had also done a number on the jumpsuits worn by Nargen and Dayena. Little more than tattered rags remained of the purely fabric sections of their armor, while their armor's plates sagged and warped like the drones floating above them.

At the rear of the monster, Kurak's complete suit of plate armor drooped similarly under the corrosive aura, though it appeared mostly intact despite having been in closer proximity to the source of the acerbic damage. However, in contrast to the rest of the team on the monster's front, Kurak struggled to damage the monster's backside. The minotaur tank swung heavy two-handed blows into the rear, but the stiff fur resisted his assault.

Physical attacks might be successful once through the fur, but Kurak couldn't strip that outer layer of defenses.

"Fall back, Kurak," I commanded the Yerrick over our party chat.

Kurak jumped away from the monster instantly. I holstered one pistol long enough to summon a plasma grenade into my palm and chucked the small sphere into the now open area. The grenade sank into the coarse fur of the giant skunk's side and detonated in a burst of rippling plasma that swept over the monster's flank. The skunk screeched in agony as its fur burned away, exposing the flesh beneath. Flesh that bubbled and burned in the wake of the plasma's intense heat.

The monster spun around to face the source of its new torment, and I lit it up with a flurry of fire from my beam pistol. Doing so, I knew that my attacks would fully earn the beast's ire. The Boss hissed angrily as my energy fire lanced into its face before it charged with eyes blazing in fury.

Kurak circled the twisting Boss and laid into the newly exposed flank with his blade. I had no time to appreciate the rest of my party's attacks as I sprinted to the hillside. I launched myself up the steep bank and grabbed a nearby sapling, using the small tree to fling myself horizontally as the Boss crashed into the spot I'd just vacated.

The monster pursued, snapping at my heels as I stumbled along the hillside in a zigzag route that twisted back on itself multiple times. Trunks shattered and fell, sending out splintering sprays that lanced through my armor. The beast bowled through the green woods as if the trees were no obstacle at all.

Time and time again, I barely evaded snapping teeth and swiping claws, and I knew that without the movement bonuses provided by Efficient Terrain, I would have been monster chow a dozen times over.

Finally, the explosive sounds of skunk deforestation stopped behind me, though the whine of a few more energy beams echoed for good measure. I slowed, glancing back to ensure the monster truly lay finished. Then I skidded to a halt along the torn hillside as the skunk wheezed out one last breath and slumped limply.

Notifications flashed in the corner of my vision, but I ignored the prompts for now. There would be time enough to read through the updates once we'd fully completed the Dungeon and made it back outside.

Though the corrosive aura faded quickly with the death of the Boss, the acrid stench still lingered. I retraced my steps to the fallen monster and looted the creature before activating Meat Locker to dump the carcass into my extra dimensional storage. With the body no longer present, the stench dissipated on the gentle breeze that wafted through the ravine.

I crouched on the hillside, resting my back against one of the few remaining trees. Though I'd survived by pushing my speed to its limits, my prodigious stamina pool had dropped to dangerously low levels. At times like this, I felt supremely jealous of Classes who got teleport abilities.

Dayena approached while I pondered yet again why I hadn't bought a teleport Skill from the Shop instead of boosting my other Class Skills. The dark elf seated herself beside me after brushing the ground, as though it would clean the earth. "That was not pleasant."

I shrugged. "I warned you."

She pulled spare gear from her Inventory then paused to glare at me. "Wait, why is your gear fine?"

A flick of my fingers waved a Status screen into being and toggled the window into visibility before pushing it over in front of her.

Quality Over Quantity (Level 1)

Equipped gear is resistant to environmental and passive aura effects. Only direct damage to worn items will cause durability loss so long as it remains equipped and may have durability loss repaired directly by the user actively channeling Mana into the item. The user may also designate a soulbound Personal Weapon. Personal Weapons cause an additional 5% damage. Mana regeneration reduced by 5 Mana per minute permanently.

Dayena snorted in disgust when she finished reading the text and stood, retreating around behind the tree at my back to replace her tattered jumpsuit.

"Don't worry, I won't peek," I called over my shoulder. "There's nothing you haven't shown off before."

A bare leg flashed around the tree in a kick that would have snapped into my shoulder but smacked into the trunk instead. I had already started down the hill, smirking as I ignored the Truinnar curses that echoed from behind the tree.

Kurak waited at the bottom of the hill by the end of the bridge, replacing individual armor plates that were too damaged, while Nargen knelt in the center of the bridge beside the few bits of wreckage that remained of his robodog. The Gimsar seemed to move on autopilot, mechanically scooping into his Inventory the scattered gears, wires, and armor plates that had survived the skunk's pummeling. Piece after piece disappeared until the cement lay empty, and the dwarf squatted alone on the bridge, staring at the ground.

I walked across the bridge toward him, and the dwarf didn't even look up when I stopped several paces away.

"Once we've finished the Dungeon, we'll see if the Pharyleri artificers can help put your drone back together." I extended a hand to the Gimsar.

Nargen sighed and looked up, staring blankly at my hand for several seconds before allowing me to help pull him to his feet.

"Okay, thanks." Nargen's tone remained listless, completely void of his earlier displays of fear and anger. The loss of his primary drone had really upset the dwarf.

I clapped my free hand on his shoulder. "The hard part is over. We just have to fight through the return trail on this side of the creek, and the Dungeon will be cleared."

"Good," rumbled Kurak from over my shoulder. "I'm ready to be done with this place."

"Then let's get going," I said.

The return path along the western bank of the creek traveled upstream, and the terrain varied a bit more than the first half of the looping trail to include several sections of rock stairs which provided verticality both ascending and descending. More mutated monsters rushed us at regular intervals, though for the most part, the creatures were ones we'd already dealt with on our way through the park.

The only new mutation was a group of oversized toads with poisonous pustules that burst when an opponent drew near. We found that out the hard way when the creature's lengthy tongues flicked out to grab us and dragged Dayena into range of the toxic bursts.

The noxious attacks from the toads failed to faze anyone after our exposure to the much more virulent ability of the Boss. In contrast, the toads' ability felt more of an annoyance than a threat as we slaughtered our way through the muddy stretch of the trail where the toads resided.

At last, we reached the end of the trail and passed through the one-way portal that led onto the park access road, across which we'd first entered the Dungeon.

Our tired party clomped across the bridge, the wooden planks trembling beneath the heavy footsteps of Kurak's armored form. The rest of the group headed past the historic gristmill and onto the trail that led up the hill to the parking area.

But I paused at the covered information kiosk and signed out on the chalkboard, indicating that our group had completed the Dungeon's entire loop. For a moment, I contemplated the unfinished line before my entry. Then the chalk squealed as I drew a line through the names above mine, highlighting the loss of a party for any groups that would follow. Hopefully, they would take the Dungeon more seriously if they knew another party had met their ends within.

I lowered the chalk to hang at the end of the length of string, twisting and tapping against the board as I released it. Then I headed up the parking lot trail, leaving McConnells Mill behind.

With Nargen's robot mount destroyed in the Dungeon, the Gimsar rode behind me on my bike for the drive back to the starport. There was plenty of room for the dwarf who sat reversed and looking back down the road behind us. Since the hover system wasn't rated for the added weight of a second passenger, my bike remained in ground mode for the return journey

On one of the few stretches of relatively undamaged roadway, I took the opportunity to address my pending notifications. Beyond all the experience updates for the numerous monsters slain on our run through the Dungeon, two updates stood out.

Congratulations! McConnells Mill Dungeon Cleared!
+10,000 XP

Overflow Clear Bonus
For clearing the McConnells Mill Dungeon while in an overflow state due to unmitigated Mana buildup, you have been awarded an additional +2,000 XP and +1,000 Credits.

The first came as no surprise after the flood of monsters that had attacked as soon as I entered the Dungeon. The lump of experience for both the clear and the bonus gave me a nice jump toward my next Level, but I still needed more to rank up.

Title Gained!

For the repeated actions of battling your way into and through overflowing dungeons on a Dungeon World, you have been awarded the title "Dungeon World Delver" to acknowledge your survival. All damage dealt to monsters +5% and all damage received from monsters -5% when within a dungeon or on a Dungeon World.

The second notification was unexpected. As soon as I finished reading it, I brought up my Status screen and used On the Hunt to toggle the title into invisibility. The less information readily available to Dayena's family, the longer they would continue to underestimate us both.

Or so I hoped.

Other than a couple of spells and swapping weapons, I'd kept my use of abilities minimal during the first confrontation with her cousins. The fact that I'd been there at all had been a surprise during that fight, so that advantage was now gone. With any luck, they would think I was a simple Hunter and not look deeper.

But counting solely on that subterfuge to hold seemed unwise with the stakes of our lives on the line. I dismissed my Status screen and notification windows as I continued down the old interstate with the rest of my party, letting my mind churn over potentialities and ways to further surprise our foes in the future.

I chuckled as my thoughts reminded me of a saying from my old platoon's gunnery sergeant. Prior proper preparation prevented piss poor performance, indeed.

Chapter 11

The sun had set by the time we made it back to the starport, and I handed off Nargen to a team of Pharyleri crafters who promised to set Nargen up with a workshop where the dwarf could repair his drones. Then I spent more time finding repair kits and replenishing supplies with Kurak and Dayena for the mission ahead of us. Finally, I emptied my Inventory of monster parts and carcasses at the starport's slaughtering yard.

As I left the harvesting area's stench behind, a pair of familiar gnomes blocked my path.

"You think you know someone." The first gnome scowled, addressing his words to the gnome beside him. "You fight monsters together, you lose a friend alongside them, you get absolutely stinking drunk together. And then what happens?"

"Oh, I know the answer to this question," the second gnome replied. "That someone you thought you knew disappears for over a year after setting half of downtown Pittsburgh on fire. Then when he does show back up, all he does is run off to a Dungeon with a couple of Adventurers he just met instead of checking in on old friends."

I stopped, facing the two Pharyleri, and folded my arms across my chest. "You know, you two really should stick to your day jobs. You make terrible comedians."

Ipbar broke first, snickering.

Alryn kept his scowl and shook his head. "Let's go get a drink."

Alryn and Ipbar really hadn't changed much in the year since we'd cleared the starport together. Alryn remained quiet as Ipbar took the lead, showing us back to the same bar where we'd celebrated a wake in the aftermath of the Pharyleri taking possession of the starport. We found the watering hole surprisingly crowded with Galactics, a significant change in scenery from my last visit where I was the lone human in sight and the only other patrons were gnomes.

Once we snagged a table, Ipbar ordered some kind of dark-colored, high-proof alcoholic drink to no one's surprise. It smelled like spiced rum to me.

When I took a moment perusing the unfamiliar drink menu, Alryn insisted that I try an Apocalypse Ale. The label on the bottle of amber-colored lager described the brew as originating from a surviving Canadian brewery in the Yukon territory and highlighted using locally sourced materials found entirely on Earth. Their ad campaign and distribution seemed to be effective, since a glance around the bar showed several aliens drinking from identical bottles.

Notes of toffee and a hint of chocolate filled my first sip of the ale, the rich flavor masking the strong alcohol content and making for easy drinking. Though I normally considered myself a whiskey guy, I could see myself finding a taste for the beer. If it threw a few Credits to fellow human survivors, all the better.

"So, what have you been up to lately, Hal?" Ipbar asked after a sip from a black cocktail that fizzed inside a rocks glass.

"Wandering around, completing quests, killing monsters, clearing dungeons." I shrugged and took another drink. "Playing the part of the wandering Adventurer."

Alryn snorted. "He's up almost forty Levels in just over a year and acts like that's nothing."

I sipped my drink and frowned. "Most humans are at least above thirty by now, and I've seen some who have made the jump to an Advanced Class after hitting Level fifty."

138

Ipbar nodded. "You're right, but we've seen you fight. I think we all know by now that you're not really a Hunter."

The two gnomes stared at me intently, and I raised an eyebrow. "I'd really prefer you keep that bit of speculation to yourselves."

"Told you," Ipbar said, looking at Alryn and holding out an open palm.

The dour gnome sighed and placed something in the outstretched hand, which disappeared into Ipbar's Inventory before I got a good look. Clearly they'd bet something of value on my Class.

Rather than dwell on their speculations about my Class, I opted to move the conversation along. "What do you both have going on these days?"

Alryn jerked a thumb in Ipbar's direction. "This joker is the head of starport security now, if you can believe that."

"Oh, that sounds important," I said. "Did all the monster slaying back when we cleared the starport convince you to give up your Artisan ways?"

The gnome rolled his eyes. "It's more exciting than all the logistics I used to do, though I still oversee all the acquisitions for the security force."

I chuckled. "I guess I know who to talk to about spare gear now."

Ipbar glared at me in mock anger as Alryn laughed with me.

The conversation devolved into far less serious topics as the drinks flowed, and I ended up leaving the bar with a slight stumble just before dawn. Improved Constitution and fairly high resistances meant that I'd processed the majority of the alcohol in my system by the time I reached my quarters for a bit of rest. Those same attributes meant that a little sleep would suffice to get me through another day.

Two hours of sleep and a hot shower later, I felt only a little bleary as I wandered through the starport toward the Clan Pistongrinder enginehouse. On the way, I detoured long enough to find the starport's Shop.

Ryk quickly took care of my Dungeon loot, and the shopkeeper's eyes glinted as the Credits poured into my account from the transaction. I knew from his expression that the wily shopkeeper had something in mind to reduce that balance in favor of his own.

Before Ryk could act on his scheme, I extracted the gear I'd looted from Dayena's cousin from my Inventory and displayed it.

The gleam faded from Ryk's eyes as he looked over the power armor and the massive maul. One eyebrow shot upward as he caught sight of the skull-and-rose emblem on the armor's pauldron. "Making friends, I see."

"More teaching a lesson, I hope."

"You play a dangerous game." Ryk shook his head and waved, a considerable sum of Credits appearing before me as a trade offering that I quickly accepted.

Noticing the glint returning to the shopkeeper's expression as my Credit balance increased again, I fixed the shopkeeper with a firm stare. "So, what fancy bits of gear are you going to parade in front of me now?"

Ryk blinked innocently, but a moment later, the shopkeeper waved theatrically as a pair of boxes with a matte metallic sheen appeared on the counter beneath his gesturing hands. Despite the plain exterior of the cases, their quality remained evident.

"Since you've been such a high value patron of this establishment, I've managed to obtain these as something of an upgrade to your current arsenal." With a flourish, Ryk raised the lids on the twin cases, revealing two beautiful pistols.

The right-hand case contained a hand cannon with a matte black body and barrel, so dark that the weapon seemed to absorb the light around it. Gilded brass detailing along the barrel shone brightly against the darkness, turning the menacing weapon into a work of art. Carved from a wood that looked like black walnut, the curved grip of the pistol called out to me, and I wanted nothing more than to fit the weapon into my hand.

My hand drifted toward the weapon almost involuntarily, and I ignored the smirk that plastered Ryk's face as he observed my response. Instead, I swept Greater Observation over the weapon to learn more about it.

Last Word (Tier I Projectile Pistol)

Customized by Master Armscrafter Malphyr, the enchantments engraved into the body of this hand cannon are guaranteed to deliver the final statement in any firefight with increased armor penetration added to any ammunition fired through this weapon.

Base Damage: N/A (Dependent Upon Ammunition)

Ammo Capacity: 12/12 (Standard cylinder-style magazine)

Effect: +15% Armor Penetration

Despite the allure of the first weapon, the pistol in the second case was no less of a masterpiece. Parts of the pistol shared the same murky matte finish of the first weapon, but it contrasted those black surfaces with a ridge of white along the top of the barrel and a pair of diagonal white slashes halfway down the weapon's length. The grip of the pistol matched the shape of the first hand cannon's, though it was a black polymer instead of wood.

Ace (Tier I Projectile Pistol)

The twin enchantments worked into the frame of this hand cannon by Maestro Gunsmith Syx Cayde provide a minor enhancement to the wielder's reload speed and additional shield penetration to any ammunition fired through this weapon.

Base Damage: N/A (Dependent Upon Ammunition)

Ammo Capacity: 12/12 (Standard cylinder-style magazine)

Effect: +12% Energy Shield Penetration, +10% Reload Speed

Ryk was speaking, detailing the function of the unique pistols, but I barely paid any attention as I drank in the appearance of the weapons. "Both hand cannons are semi-automatic but utilize a unique reloading system that allows the wielder to swap out the cylindrical magazine set in the middle of the weapon frame, similar in some ways to the function of the firearms you called revolvers here on Earth."

"They're beautiful," I whispered in awe. I wanted them. I needed them.

Then I saw the price tags affixed to the weapons, and my eyes grew wide. I could buy almost a half dozen Class Skill points for the cost of purchasing these two pistols.

I glared at Ryk, but the shopkeeper beamed at me. I knew that he knew I'd want these weapons as soon as I saw them.

I sighed and forked over the Credits for the pistols, then paid out additional for two scores of extra magazine cylinders so that I could load them and keep them prepared in my Inventory.

The two master crafted weapons also went into my Inventory for the time being. I wanted time to practice using and reloading the weapons before I worked them into my regular combat rotation. My usual tactic of swapping out the entirety of a depleted weapon with a fully loaded replacement wouldn't work with these unique pistols.

Ryk slid a harness across the counter toward me. "I think you'll appreciate this accessory to complement your new firearms."

From the positioning of the holsters within the straps, I recognized the piece of equipment. "A shoulder holster?"

"Ah, but this is far more than a simple shoulder holster," the shopkeeper said as he held up the harness against his own torso with one hand. With his opposite hand, Ryk pressed the dangling strap that would attach the shoulder harness to a belt at the wearer's waist.

A shimmering blue field of energy swept up along the strap and out along Ryk's arm as the shopkeeper extended his limb until the faintly glowing energy formed a triangle between the dangling strap, Ryk's palm, and his armpit. I looked at the field for a moment, trying to puzzle out the device's purpose. It couldn't be a shield since it didn't actually cover any vulnerable spots, unless the user was trying to make themselves wider to shield someone behind them.

A lightbulb went off. Wider. Increased surface area.

"It's an energy wingsuit," I said.

Ryk grinned proudly and held out the harness. "Correct!"

Elysian Drop Harness Mk. IV (Modified)

This shoulder rig began life as a standard grav-chute issued to a member of the Elysian Home Guard. The air-mobile troopers of the Guard are known for lightning-fast deployments and guerilla attacks behind enemy lines. This particular harness was customized by a Guard trooper to carry twin pistols into battle and was promptly disposed of as surplus after the non-regulation modifications were discovered by a superior officer.

I sighed and sent over the additional Credits, then stored the new shoulder rig in my Inventory.

Ryk smiled at me contentedly. "Just let me know if you change your mind and decide to spend more of those Credits I just gave you."

"I'm pretty sure I've already spent them and then some, thank you." I sighed. "But I might be out of touch for a bit, so give me double my standard ammunition loadout and four of my usual light armor jumpsuits in dark gray."

The shopkeeper's smile grew even wider.

I equipped the harness while Ryk put together the new requisitions. The rig looped over my shoulders and crossed in the middle of my back, with the weapons holsters hanging under my armpits on either side, then a strap dropped down to connect to my belt. Once the lower strap fastened to my belt, the whole ensemble seemed locked securely in place, fitting snugly over my jumpsuit.

Though I had initially planned on waiting until I'd practiced the reloads with my new projectile pistols, I slipped the new weapons into the holsters at my waist. Weapons were meant to be used and they did me no good waiting in my Inventory. A pair of beam pistols went into the holsters underneath my arms on either side of my torso.

By the time I finished adjusting the harness, Ryk had returned with my requested supplies. I exchanged a fraction of the dwindling Credits left in my account with him, all while ignoring the shopkeeper's knowing smirk.

The Shop proprietor was far too effective at separating me from my funds.

Chapter 12

It took little time to make my way from the Shop in the starport concourse over to the enginehouse, where I found the area roiling with activity.

The locomotive sat outside the structure, several new additions stretching out behind the engine. I looked over the additions as I approached. The entire assembly gleamed far too brightly for the slight hangover throbbing behind my eyes, the early morning sunlight reflecting off the armor panels and mechanical components.

I'd have to watch that Apocalypse Ale in the future.

Directly behind the locomotive sat a half dozen train cars, all protected with the same bronze alloy armor. Segmented panels in several places along the lead carriage indicated sections that could be opened outward, though the operation of those doors would require further investigation. Other than those seams in the armoring, there were only a couple narrow windows along the length of the car.

The bodies of the second and third cars resembled more traditional train passenger cars, with an upper and a lower level. A row of narrow windows ran down the length of the two boxy cars on both levels, lending weight to my speculation about their likely purpose as passenger carriers.

Large windows made up the walls for most of the fourth carriage and, from the tables within, it appeared to be a dining car with a scenic window view of the countryside.

The fifth car also shared the large viewing windows, though the inside looked more like a lounge with comfortably padded seating running the length of the interior.

The final carriage was a heavily armored boxcar.

Kurak stood stoically on a platform at the rear of that final boxcar, leaning on his halberd and barely fitting within the platform. The entire thing was enclosed by multiple chains strung between posts which served as a guardrail.

Gnomes swarmed the length of the train, calling to each other as they completed their tasks in preparation for the upcoming journey, but the noise failed to mask the quiet footsteps approaching me from behind.

"And where did you get off to last night?" Dayena said.

I yawned. "Catching up with old friends."

"You have friends?" Dayena blinked in affected surprise.

"Har har," I replied. "What did you do after I wandered off?"

"Busked for extra Credits at a few of the friendlier starport bars."

"Putting those Courtesan Class Skills to work, I see."

"My Basic Class was Midnight Courtier," Dayena said, gritting her teeth and smacking my shoulder hard enough to bruise. "Not. Courtesan."

"There's a difference?" I grinned, and the Truinnar noble glared at me then back at the train.

"I happen to enjoy performing," Dayena said quietly, letting her affronted expression fade. "The music I play reminds me of happier times."

I didn't know what to say, so I remained silent. I wasn't artistically or musically inclined in the slightest. I respected people with the talent for creation, but I wasn't one of them. My talent lay in the other direction.

"You're very good," I said after the silence dragged out.

Dayena glanced at me sharply, gauging whether my words were sarcasm as she searched my expression, then looked away before speaking. "Thank you."

I looked at the noblewoman, examining the shapely profile of her face as she watched the Pharyleri and their preparations about the train. Despite her desperate efforts to grow more powerful, the Truinnar culture of intrigue and betrayal, and her affected air of worldly experience, something about the elf still seemed innocent.

Though our age in years may be similar, the Countess remained little more than a teenager by the standards of Truinnar culture. In accepting her contract several months ago, I'd committed to guide and protect her. Despite her being my boss, I needed to remember sometimes that she was barely out of adolescence, though from her elder cousin's attitude at our first meeting, that cusp of adulthood might be subject to some interpretation.

"I like the new weapons. They suit you."

Before I could respond to Dayena's comment, Nesdyna hurried over. The clan leader seemed harried by the number of preparations going on as she joined us to watch the busy gnomes at work.

Nesdyna pointed at the passenger car in the center of the train. "Final preparations are nearly completed. The rest of your party are already settled on the train."

I turned to the older gnome. "Speaking of the train, I wasn't expecting so many passenger accommodations."

"Areas for the support staff and the technicians, along with supplies in case more extensive repairs to the engine are required."

I narrowed my gaze. "It would have been nice to familiarize myself with the new additions."

Nesdyna waved away my concern. "You're not responsible for the condition of the remaining carriages, only the locomotive and whatever crew you are able to protect. The clan security team will provide defenses for the additional cars."

"This is starting to feel pretty rushed."

She shrugged. "It is necessary. A project like this cannot be done by only a few Adventurers without support. You'll need crafters and support personnel to work through any problems we haven't foreseen. And there will always be problems with any endeavor of this magnitude."

I shared a glance with Dayena, then nodded to the gnomish elder. "We'll do our best. See you when we get back."

Dayena also bid Nesdyna a terse farewell and followed me to the train, where I walked alongside the carriages. Other than the doors set into the middle of the lower level on each car, there were no obvious access points to climb up between the cars of the train. Even the couplings were protected by an articulated covering that extended from the bottom of the cars on either side and provided an additional defensive measure against any external forces attempting to separate the train's cars.

With our attributes, it would be easy enough to jump onto the roofs of the carriages. That prospect for any boarders would be far more challenging if the train were in motion, but not an impossibility. That was exactly why active defenders were needed.

"Adventurers Mason and Baluisa, right this way!"

The cheery voice chirped from a gnome who stood by the open center door on the lower level of the forward passenger car. He was clad in an olive-green three-piece suit consisting of trousers, vest, and jacket, all with bronze buttons that matched the armored plates of the train's exterior. A matching metallic chain ran from one of the waistcoat's front buttons and disappeared into a side pocket. The gnome's bright orange hair contrasted sharply where it stuck out from beneath the uniform's matching brimmed cap.

Wrefen Fixwhistle (Conductor Level 30)
HP: 360/360
MP: 520/520

The gnome waved for Dayena and me to precede him into the car.

"It's such a pleasure to meet you both. I'm Conductor Wrefen Fixwhistle and I'll be seeing to any needs you might have as passengers. Yes, Adventurer Mason, I know you are in charge of our security contingent, but my hospitality staff will treat you like passengers. Especially on our outbound journey, since the experience provides a training opportunity to my new team members before we take on paying passengers for the return leg."

"Thank you, Conductor," I said, finally interjecting as the gnome took a breath. "If you'll show us our cabins, I'd like to head up to the engine before we depart."

Something in my words seemed to shake Wrefen from his prepared remarks, and the gnome shifted his attention to the Countess before looking back at me.

"Oh, uh, I'm sorry," Wrefen stammered. "I'm afraid there may have been some confusion about the nature of your relationship, and we have you both slated to share a cabin."

I chuckled, looking back in time to catch Dayena's uncomfortable expression before the dark elf resumed her stoic facade. I turned back to the flustered gnome. "There is nothing romantic about the nature of our partnership. Does the cabin have separate bunks?"

"Oh, yes, of course!" Wrefen seemed happy to meet that condition, at least. "Please head inside the car and turn right. You'll take the stairs to the upper level and head to the front of the car. You'll be in Compartment Number 2, and your other party members will be next door to you in Compartment Number 3."

The gnome guided us to the upper level and along the corridor that ran along the outer wall on one side of the carriage toward the front of the train. Windows were evenly spaced along the passage, opposite the doors that led into the individual passenger cabins utilized by the train's crew. Door after door filled that side of the corridor with very little space on either side of the sliding hatches.

My former military experience prepared me for cramped quarters, but I was concerned by the lack of apparent space. On a lengthy journey, which this cross-country trek promised to be, personal space would quickly become a morale issue with the crew if not properly addressed.

Then I paused, considering if that was an issue at all. For me perhaps, but I was talking about aliens. Perhaps the Pharyleri wanted, or needed, close quarters. It wasn't as though I had spent enough time with them to really know.

When we reached the door with a bronze plate that labeled the cabin as #2, the door slid open to reveal a surprising amount of space and allayed my fears. The doorway led into a narrow passage of the same width between a pair of bunk style beds, each raised above a space split between a storage compartment and a desk. A comfortable office chair was pushed under the desk. The two sides were configured opposite, such that the desk beneath the right-hand bunk was directly across from the closed storage bays under the left bunk. If both office chairs were in use, the occupants would be sitting beside each other but facing their own desk.

A small mirror sat beneath the windows on the back wall, above a tiny sink.

It was an efficient use of the space, and I noticed that somehow the interior of the compartment managed to be wider than the exterior dimensions indicated.

Wrefen clearly saw me looking at the sides of the compartment door and comparing the location of interior walls against the start of the next cabin. "Don't try to figure out the use of dimensional space. The cabins were built by Artisans using spatial Class Skills to maximize the interior square footage before being assembled into the overall carriage construction."

"Got it." I nodded in understanding. Though the System had raised my Intelligence from the eating-crayons stage of human development, I felt no desire to dabble in dimensional physics and the quantum interactions between overlapping physical spaces. "Where's the head?"

"The what?" Wrefen looked confused. Apparently the System's translation packages didn't account for military jargon.

"The bathroom."

The gnome pointed back toward the rear of the train. "The second and third doors from the end are the bathrooms. The last compartment is the shower."

I gave our sleeping compartment a long look through the open door. I had a feeling I wouldn't be spending much time there or sleeping all that much. "Thank you, this looks far more comfortable than I expected."

The gnome beamed. "You are most welcome, Adventurer Mason."

I turned to Dayena. "Feel free to get settled in. I'm going up front to be ready for departure."

She slipped past me into the compartment. "Let me know through party chat if anything is needed."

"Will do."

I gave Wrefen a nod and headed forward up the corridor. The doors at the end of the corridor slid open automatically as I approached, and I stepped out of the car and into the vestibule that bridged the passenger carriage with the upper level of the workshop car ahead. From the inside of the vestibule, I got a good look at the articulated armoring that shielded the connection between the train cars. The vestibule could be opened to access the exterior of the cars on either side, but I left those mechanisms alone for now.

Inside the next car, I found Nargen seated on an elevated stool before a long workbench. Tools covered the wall above the bench's work surface, fastened securely to ensure nothing fell loose in transit. On either end of the bench sat numerous pieces of high-tech appliances that I didn't recognize—probably equipment for maintenance of the train or the tracks. Shelves lined the upper sections of the walls on either side, filled with boxes of supplies, storage containers, and ingots of various metals.

The dwarf glanced up, then returned to work as the door closed behind me. A small framework on the table in front of Nargen supported the partially assembled form of his dog drone, though most of the drone remained little more than a metal skeleton, a few strands of exposed wiring, and some partially assembled servo musculature.

"Thanks for getting me set up here," Nargen said without looking up as I walked behind him. "This equipment is top of the line."

"No problem. Once I found out there would be a mobile workshop to support the mission, it was an easy call to get you settled in here. This way you have access along the trip too, though I didn't realize it would be an entire car."

The dwarf nodded absently, already absorbed in his repairs.

"Good luck," I said and continued through the workshop for several paces until I encountered a single Pharyleri as the lone other occupant.

Eldri Giltwrench (Repair Technician Level 39)
HP: 480/480
MP: 640/640

The impressiveness of the gnome's neon blue mutton chops almost distracted me from his greeting. The Repair Technician wore beige coveralls underneath a harness filled with wrenches, ratchets, and pliers of various sizes. Goggles with multiple lenses were pushed up on his forehead, the strap holding them in place also restraining his unruly mop of hair.

"Adventurer Mason, welcome to my workshop." Eldri hopped down from a workbench stool and welcomed me by shaking my hand. "I can show you around if you have some time."

I shook my head. "Maybe when we have some downtime once we're underway I can take the time to appreciate everything your shop here offers. Right now, I want to be in position within the locomotive when we depart."

"Oh, I won't keep you then," Eldri said. "You should go. I think we'll be heading out shortly."

"Thank you," I replied with a wave.

Just inside the door at the far end of the workshop carriage, my eye caught on a matte black cabinet affixed to the wall. The sealed case looked noticeably out of place, more armored than the rest of the storage containers throughout the workshop. Unable to resist my curiosity, I swiped a hand over the sensor plate on the side of the cabinet, opening the segmented doors with an audible *snick* to reveal a half dozen energy rifles mounted to the inside of the weapons locker. Two of the sleek weapons were for human-sized humanoids, while the remaining four rifles were smaller models scaled for the Pharyleri.

I looked back at Eldri, who still stood in the middle of the car but with an annoyed expression now. Likely perturbed that I'd turned down his offer to be shown around the car but still found time to check out the weapons. I made an effort to appease the gnome by pointing at the locker and giving the workshop's supervisor a thumbs-up in approval.

The Repair Technician's sour expression morphed into a more pleased expression, at least slightly. Taking that as a win, I swiped my hand over the locker's sensor plate, and the doors snapped shut before I exited the carriage.

The door from the workshop opened up onto the vestibule that connected the lead car to the locomotive. I entered the engine's control cabin without any issues or running into any more earnest crew members.

Ismyna grunted in acknowledgement of my arrival but remained focused on the controls in front of her. Over her normal gear, the Pharyleri wore a dark brown jacket of a heavy, leather-like material with a fuzzy beige liner. The bomber jacket showed signs of wear, especially around the cuffs and elbows, and hung completely unfastened in the front.

Beside Ismyna stood a gnome I recognized from my first trip to the enginehouse, though we'd never spoken or been introduced. The midnight-haired Pharyleri turned toward me. Once again, a scowl flickered across his face as he saw me, though he cleared his expression and sighed instead. Ismyna glanced up at the sound and frowned at the gnome with a pointed look. Dicenyk swallowed and stepped over to stand before me.

I waited, noticing that Ismyna had paused in her checklist to stare at the other gnome's back until he finally spoke up.

"I'm Dicenyk, chief of internal security." The gnome extended a hand to me in an offered handshake.

"Nice to meet you, I'm Hal." I engulfed the small hand with my own before shaking firmly.

The tiny gnome shifted his grip and clamped down on my hand in an impromptu contest of strength. I raised an eyebrow at the Advanced Class gnome, who apparently needed to prove something, and let him squeeze away since I felt amused more than pained by the pinching sensation of the Pharyleri's miniscule hand. After a moment of watching the gnome struggle to get a reaction from me, I bore down with my own grip and watched the gnome wince. I held the pressure and glanced at Ismyna, who rolled her eyes.

Ismyna sighed before finally intervening. "Dice."

I returned my attention to Dice, as he was apparently called, and let my gaze grow cold. "Are you done?"

The gnome swallowed painfully and nodded hurriedly.

Point made, I released the gnome and perched myself off to one side of the cabin to stay out of the way. Dice returned to Ismyna's side while she went back to her work. I watched the two gnomes working through a departure checklist on a terminal window to the side of the central control console.

I couldn't help but curse at the way this entire thing was being rushed. Having time to meet with and speak with Dice, to smooth out whatever his problem with me was, and check over the additional cabins would have helped. Sloppy, unprofessional, and liable to cause problems.

Just about right for a military operation run by a brand new butterbar. At least with the train on rails, we couldn't get lost by misreading a compass.

Or so I hoped.

When they finished the list, the couple exchanged a quick hug before Dice left the control cabin.

Then Ismyna turned to me with a serious expression belied by the nervous tapping of her foot. "Is your team loaded and ready to depart?"

"We are."

Instead of replying, Ismyna spoke into a small microphone attached to the collar of her jacket. She pressed a hand to her ear and the wireless earpiece as a faint voice replied to her question. The gnome grinned with barely constrained excitement and slammed her hand on a red button near the primary locomotive controls.

A blaring noise blasted out from above us, the sound a cross between a foghorn and a tornado siren. It rattled the control cabin and reverberated deep in the spaces of my chest.

The cabin's viewscreens showed gnomes scattering away from the train to gather by where we'd left Nesdyna. A handful of others, most of whom carried duffel bags or other bits of individual gear, pushed through those leaving and hurried to board by using a ladder at the rear of the train.

Amongst the stragglers, I noticed several non-Pharyleri boarding the train. I glanced at Ismyna, who watched the crew boarding with her hands on the control console. From her lack of reaction, it seemed the others were expected. I found that a little surprising and made a mental note to look into the other Galactics later.

Once the half dozen latecomers had climbed onboard and disappeared into the last passenger car, Ismyna pushed forward on the throttle controls. A shudder ran through the engine as it eased ahead, jolting slightly as it took up the coupling slack from the cars behind.

The train accelerated as Ismyna throttled up. A slight sway from side to side accompanied the acceleration. Beyond that, only a barely perceptible shudder traveled through my feet as the locomotive moved forward. I watched as the viewscreens showed the enginehouse behind us growing farther away.

Ismyna throttled up to full speed once we'd cleared the crowded area, and it didn't take long for us to depart the starport. Her head twitched from side to side as she shifted her gaze between the various readouts and the display of the track ahead.

"The first several miles should be pretty clear," Ismyna explained. "I've already got our track drone out at the transition point, and I'll kick it into automatic mode when we get a little closer. Once we transition from our new tracks to the main rails of the pre-System freight transit lines, we'll have to slow down to a crawl in order to engage the rail conversion systems. That's where I expect we'll start running into monster problems."

"Any particular reason for that?" I had my own suspicions, but I wanted to hear what the expert in the tech had to say.

"Anytime you have Mana churning like we'll have in reforming the rail lines, monsters tend to get attracted to the disruptions, especially before the process settles down," Ismyna said.

I frowned. "That makes sense, but since most big monster spawns tend to be territorial, won't the fact that we're just moving through that territory also rile them up?"

"That certainly won't help," she agreed. "We'll need your team to engage any large creatures or swarms as far away from the tracks as possible. We don't want to leave a line of carcasses along our route. That will just draw the carrion feeders in closer, and we'll end up having to deal with their trouble later."

"That should be doable since most monsters should try to flee back to their lair if we hurt them badly enough. We'll try to keep that from happening if we want to gain experience from the kills."

"Right," Ismyna said. "Gotta get that sweet, sweet experience."

Tilting my head, I looked at the gnome. "Do you need into my party to gain experience from our fights?"

Okay, so it was Dayena's party, even though I was nominally in charge.

"No," Ismyna replied. "Through one of my Class Skills, I have your party designated as the security section of the crew. I'll get a bit of a boost from your defense of the train without affecting your party experience at all. Since I'm more of an Artisan, most of my experience will come from converting all the miles of track along our route, plus Quest gains when the project is completed."

I brought up my own Quest log, revealing the details to the gnome as I toggled the window visibility. Ismyna displayed her window beside mine, and we compared the objectives we'd been given.

I pointed at the upper sections in both windows. "They're both the first in what appears to be a multipart Quest. Mine is to escort the train to Denver, while yours focuses on the track conversion during that leg of the journey."

"The experience payouts for both are significant."

"Dayena's Quest and Contract is identical to mine."

"Damn," Ismyna said. "Mom and Borgym really shelled out for this trip. These Quests aren't cheap. Neither is putting experienced Adventurers like your other team members on a combat retainer."

"Still cheaper than a full merc unit," I commented.

"Fair," Ismyna agreed. "Especially if you pick one of the top-tier units, like the Hakarta of the Sixty-Third Division."

I cocked my head and raised an eyebrow at the Engineer. "That seems like an oddly specific example."

"It pays to keep tabs on the major players when so much territory on this world is in flux. Platinum-ranked mercs don't usually show up on Dungeon Worlds unless they're brought in by someone making big moves,"

Ismyna explained. "That unit works for a Truinnar that's taking over Canada."

"Duchess Kangana," I said, making the connection.

Ismyna looked at me in surprise.

I gestured with a thumb toward the carriages behind the locomotive. "I have reason to pay attention to the Truinnar powers on Earth. Duchess Kangana. Duke Zuka. Viscount Nivoosi. The Marquise of Pourbet."

Ismyna frowned. "Those are seriously major players. You're not in trouble with them, are you?"

I shook my head. "Not directly, as long as we stay out of their territory. Truinnar politics are so complicated that it's better to stay clear of them all the same. I didn't know the specifics about the Hakarta unit though."

"There are a couple other outfits on the planet, but none of the others are anything near top-tier."

"Good to know," I said. "Still, most contract-following units won't be the ones giving us trouble unless we somehow cross their employers."

"For the most part," Ismyna agreed. "I don't think our plans for the railroad system have attracted any attention from potential competitors. Still, without a real intelligence network across the continent, learning for certain would require spending more Credits than it's worth. Better to just make the attempt and find out if there's trouble on the way."

I regarded the gnome with a serious expression. "If we get hit by a serious military force, there's probably not much my team will be able to offer in defense. I'm not going to send anyone to die in a hopeless situation."

Ismyna sighed. "I know. We don't expect you to fight anything on that level. We're hoping that it's not an issue. Just like the starport, once we've got the rail infrastructure in place, the industry will fund its own growth."

"That starport infrastructure had a cost in blood," I reminded the gnome. "Not everyone who walked into that monster-infested terminal walked back out."

Ismyna blanched, her normally pale skin growing even more translucent for a moment. "I know. The story is well-known with every Pharyleri clan on the planet."

I hadn't realized the extent that the story had spread around. It did explain the looks I'd received from the gnomes when the Countess and I first walked through the starport terminal.

The silence between Ismyna and me dragged out as we watched the terrain roll past on the control cabin's display screens. A central display showed the feed from a hovering sensor drone, which floated far ahead of us and scanned the tracks for broken rails or obstacles to allow the train to be stopped in time.

Eventually, the view showed the track curving to merge into another line that looked significantly more worn. The railroad ties showed signs of aging and the rails themselves showed clear need of repair.

Fortunately, the track repair drone was already on the job. Another display showed the unit quickly leveling a broken section of track and fixing it with a solid weld. A job that would have taken hours before the System now took moments with the additions of Mana and high-tech equipment.

"Main line's just ahead," Ismyna said, backing off on the throttle by a significant amount until we'd slowed enough that a jogger could match the engine's pace. "I'm going to engage the track conversion system, so be ready."

"Got it," I confirmed before notifying the rest of my team via party chat.

At my nod, Ismyna flipped a switch on the console, and a pair of arms extended out in front of the engine on the viewscreen. A bulky rectangular box sat at the end of each arm and rotated down over the rails in front of the locomotive once the arms reached full extension.

A channel appeared in the underside of each box as it dropped onto the rail and a blue glow emanated from within as a faint hum filled the cabin. The sound seemed to echo in my teeth, and I wasn't sure if the sensation affected me because of my enhanced perception or if it was a universal side effect of the conversion.

Ismyna didn't seem to notice the vibration as anything out of the norm, so maybe it was just me. I gritted my teeth and tried to ignore the annoyance as I kept watch on the displays for approaching monsters.

The shuddering beneath my feet increased when the locomotive rolled onto the older tracks. Even if the conversion worked, it seemed the rails were still worn from years of pre-System use.

Ismyna kept shifting her gaze between various readouts as the locomotive moved forward onto the adjoining main line tracks in a smooth transition. Once the engine had crossed onto the previously unconverted section without issue, Ismyna held her breath as she focused on her readouts, waiting to see the result of the track conversion system.

Several moments later, the gnome breathed out a sigh of relief. "It's working."

I nodded in acknowledgement but kept my attention on the displays for movement in the distance.

The conversion system wasn't my problem to worry about. Monsters were.

Greater Observation would alert me to anything close, but the specialized sensors on the locomotive exceeded the range of my Class Skill. Motion off to the left on the display screen drew my eye, alerting me to an approaching threat long before a trio of red dots appeared at the edges of my minimap.

"Contact west," I said, simultaneously sending the same message to my party. I turned to leave the locomotive's control cabin.

"Wait!"

I glanced back at Ismyna's shout and snagged the object she tossed toward me. The curved bit of System-tech was a communicator designed to fit securely over one ear.

"That'll tie you into the crew network. Keep me informed of any problems that break through."

The gnome trailed off and had the grace to look abashed at my glare, since establishing communications shouldn't have been a last-minute preparation that waited until monsters were approaching. I snugged the earpiece in place before slipping out and triggering the door closed behind me. Once on the engine's rear platform, I grabbed the edge of the roof and pulled myself onto the top of the locomotive.

A breeze flowed over me but nothing that troubled me, since we were only moving about as fast as a person could run. At higher speeds, I imagined standing on top of the train would be a challenge.

The elevated position provided me with a clearer view of the surrounding area than even the displays, and I realized that I felt the difference because of my Keen Senses taking advantage of the natural view. I'd have to remember that in the future, but that was as a problem for future Hal.

Through the forest off to the west, three large brown-shelled insect-like creatures headed in our direction. The monsters looked like a cross between a praying mantis and a centipede, with the torso and reversed-claw arms of the mantis extending up from a lengthy leg-filled body.

Long-range beam fire flickered across the approaching bugs, burning black lines into the carapaces. A quick glance confirmed that Dice and a half dozen other gnomes, likely the rest of the onboard security team, were firing out of the narrow windows of the passenger cars.

I frowned. Dice and I needed to have a serious discussion about coordinating our teams before our next engagement, but that little heart-to-heart conversation could wait.

It was monster-killing time.

"Kurak, with me," I sent over party chat. *"Dayena and Nargen, provide fire support from the train and make sure nothing hits from the other side while we're engaged."*

I jumped from the moving locomotive, rolling to spread the impact, and popped back up to my feet with energy pistols drawn. With the train crawling onward, I jogged toward the oncoming monsters at an angle to intercept. A massive thud at my back indicated Kurak's heavy landing, the plate-armored warrior dropping into a crouch to absorb the impact with pure strength.

The Yerrick charged ahead of me toward the monsters as I opened up with my beam pistols, joining my attacks to the furious fire flooding from the train carriages while I scanned the nearest of the beasts.

Khilopoda Soldier (Level 71)
HP: 2090/2180

Focused intently on the relatively slow-moving train, the lead creature ignored Kurak's charge. The first swing of the minotaur's halberd sheared away at least three of the smaller movement legs, and the monster's multi-segmented body rippled as it attempted to recoil from the source of its injuries.

With the majority of the beam attacks failing to pierce the insect's carapace and Kurak tied up with the first creature, I shifted my focus to the trailing pair of monsters and aimed at the compound eyes along either side of the monsters' heads. The large multi-faceted sensory organs were appealing targets, and my shots quickly found their way into the monsters' exposed vulnerable spots.

The second monster chittered in pain, one eye popping in a gory explosion of steam and ichor. The beast stumbled into the one in front of it, and the first creature jerked at the surprise contact, offering Kurak an opportunity to hack the axe of his polearm into his target's arm joint.

The insect swung with its other arm and batted the minotaur away with a savage strike. Kurak kept his grip on the haft of his polearm as he went flying. The force of the Khilopoda's blow ripped the halberd free of the wound, leaving the nearly severed joint hanging by a few threads of muscle.

The half-blinded insect circled around the now-wounded lead bug and rushed me. I backpedaled, continuing to fire. My shots forced the oncoming insect to slow since it kept jerking its head away to protect its remaining eye. Several smaller eyes lay in the center of the creature's triangular head, and I sent energy beams into them whenever the monster turned the larger eye away.

The fast-moving beast reached me as my fire left smoking craters in the center of its head. A claw snapped out, and I instinctively dodged the lightning-fast motion. Though the attack came almost too fast to see, I realized that the clawed limb would have missed by several inches.

When I realized why the attack failed to connect, I warned the rest of my team. *"Take out the big eyes. It throws off their depth perception."*

Several more attacks jabbed toward me, pulling my attention from my party's responses, and I kept up a steady barrage while avoiding the monster's rapid strikes. Soon, the cracked and smoking center of the monster's head lay completely exposed to my fire, and I poured shots into the opening until the monster collapsed.

I looted the beast then turned to survey the rest of the fight. Kurak had downed his foe and moved on to engage the last Khilopoda Soldier before it reached the train. I hurried to join the fray, and the last bug fell quickly with my assistance.

Another look around confirmed no new monsters had appeared, though the locomotive had continued down the tracks and now was well ahead of us. I shared a glance with Kurak and then the two of us jogged after the train.

More red dots appeared on the edges of my minimap by the time we caught up with the last car, and we moved into position to intercept.

A beep sounded from the communicator in my ear, preceding a crew announcement from Ismyna. "All hands, obstruction on the track ahead. Prepare for braking."

The train's brakes squealed, the shoes squeezing down on the rolling wheels in a high-pitched scream. Despite all the changes brought about by the System, the mass and acceleration of objects as large as the train still, mostly, followed the fundamentals of physics.

I tapped the communicator. "Can my team do anything about the track being blocked?"

"Negative," Ismyna replied, her voice coming through clearly. "The obstruction is an abandoned freight train. My ground crew will work the problem after your team clears the monster wave."

A quick scan of the approaching monsters let me know what we were dealing with.

"It looks like more of the Khilopoda creatures, the ones we just took out. Let's hope there's not a hive nearby. Or an Alpha."

The gnome sighed. "That would be our luck."

"Then we'll deal with it. I'll signal you when it's clear." I tapped the communicator again, ending my transmission.

The train wheels continued to squeal throughout our battle with the mutated insect hybrids, which were dealt with similarly to the first trio. Finally, the train halted after traveling over a half mile from when the brakes were first activated.

Definitely not stopping on a dime here.

Once the last monster fell to a devastating blow from Kurak's halberd, I signaled Ismyna and headed to the front of the train. When I got to the locomotive, I saw the abandoned freight train in the distance and Ismyna on the engine's rear platform.

"I assume, with the track survey, you planned for obstructions like this."

"We did." Ismyna sighed. "They'll just slow us down. A lot."

She picked up a handheld receiver built into the side of the engine and issued orders. Within a minute, a crew of gnomes in beige coveralls were hauling equipment out from storage brackets underneath the workshop car.

I watched for a moment before speaking up. "You know, those railroad cars have been there since the System initiation. It might be a good idea to have them checked for monster spawns before your people go rushing into a lair."

Ismyna looked at me wide-eyed. Clearly the thought hadn't occurred to her.

"Dungeon World," I gently reminded the gnome. "If you're not in a Safe Zone, there will be monsters. Forgetting that will get your people killed."

The Engineer spoke into her communicator, and the assembling gnomes abruptly halted their preparations.

"I'll signal when it's clear." I gave orders over party chat as I jumped down from the locomotive. "*Nargen, you're with me. We need to check for monsters on a stopped train in front of us. Dayena and Kurak, keep an eye on our train while we're at it.*"

I headed to the train ahead while listening for my team's acknowledgements. Greater Observation wasn't picking up anything, but that didn't rule out stealthed monsters.

Reaching the rear car of the freight train, I called my knife into my hand. Looking over the carriage, the faded paint and rust along the edges showed the age of the boxcar. At the middle, a stamped metal band sealed the latch that held closed the pair of sliding doors. With a flick of my knife, I removed the seal.

Flipping open the latch, I pushed against the door, expecting it to slide back along the rails. The sound of stressed metal tearing gave me just enough warning to leap away as the door ripped free. The heavy metal plate slammed into the gravel ballast beside my foot, then slowly toppled away from the carriage to thud flat on the ground alongside the track.

"That looked like fun." Nargen walked up next to me and stared into the now-open boxcar. Shrink-wrapped pallets filled the space inside without any room for the load to shift. "I think this one's good."

"Only fifty or so to go," I said.

Eldri stood with the gnomes behind us, and I waved to indicate the first carriage was clear before heading to the next freight car.

While Nargen and I walked to the next carriage, the Pharyleri clearance crew maneuvered a pair of hovering devices into position under the inspected car. The floating equipment reminded me of pallet jacks on steroids and clamped to the tracks below the boxcar. Then the equipment operators raised the lift portion up to rest against the underside of the freight car. While the jacks were positioned, a couple other gnomes worked to uncouple the carriage before the entire crew ran clear.

The running gnomes prompted Nargen and me to halt our inspection, turning back to ensure the problem wasn't a monster we'd missed.

Eldri saw us looking back and waved toward a device held in one hand, an ominous red button glowing in the middle of it. The gnome punched the button, activating the pneumatic jacks with a loud hiss. The angled lifts drove upward, launching the car from the tracks entirely and flipping it sideways away from the tracks. The car tumbled as it hit the ground, metal frame crumpling as it rolled into the forest and tore through the trees alongside the track.

"Well, that's one way to clear the rails," Nargen said.

"It's not like that freight is doing anyone any good." I turned back to the next car. "Not anymore."

The day stretched on as Nargen and I hunted monsters, and the ground crew cleared the tracks, one freight car at a time.

It didn't take long to figure out which cars had monsters, since they usually bore obvious signs of habitation like doors busted open or holes torn through the walls. The occupants were all mutated terrestrial wildlife, easily dealt with. Slaying the beasts typically took less time than removing the blocking cars from the track, and it was late morning before the gnomes finally cleared the line.

After the pair of diesel electric locomotives at the front were launched with the same efficiency as the rest of the abandoned freight train, Eldri's crew hauled the hydraulic lifts back to the train and loaded them with smooth efficiency.

Then the locomotive moved slowly forward, and I swung up onto the back of the engine.

Entering the control cabin, I found Ismyna levering the throttle forward as the train picked up speed. "We lost too much time clearing that stopped train."

"I'm not sure how we could have gone faster, not without more of those hover jacks and additional crew to operate them." I shrugged. "Even then, it would still take time to clear any monster infestations."

I glanced over the readouts on the controls in front of the gnome. One display in particular caught my eye—the gauge measuring the Mana capacitors that powered the rail conversion system. The charge bar showed a significant drop since leaving the starport only hours earlier.

I caught Ismyna's attention and pointed at the gauge.

She sighed. "We've been using more Mana for the rail conversion system than we planned. We might need to consider stopping for the night to give the engine time to recharge."

"That would be wise," I agreed. "It's looking like we'll be in constant combat while the rail conversion system is running anyways, so stopping at night will give my team some downtime."

Ismyna's brow furrowed. "Let me bring in Wrefen and Dice for this conversation."

She jabbed a couple buttons on the console in front of her.

Dice rushed into the compartment, his face twisting into a scowl when he saw me. "What's the problem?"

Ismyna glanced at me before speaking. "We're changing plans. We'll be stopping each night."

Dice's eyes widened in surprise then glared at me. "That's going to put us completely behind schedule. What has this human done now?"

Ismyna gestured toward the console readout for the engine's Mana supply, already dropping from where it had been when I'd first pointed out the issue. "We're going to run out of power for the rail system, which is the whole point of the trip."

Dice stared at the power bar as if it had personally betrayed him. "Fine, but don't expect me to take any blame for the fallout from being behind schedule."

I turned to Ismyna. "Stopping at night is a good first step, but I'd also like you to reduce throttle and hold a slower pace while my team is engaged."

Ismyna frowned, apparently unconvinced. "Dice just pointed out, accurately, that we're already going to be behind schedule."

I folded my arms across my chest. "What happens if my team gets tied up due to heavy attacks and you run into a new group of monsters? We already fell behind after running into just a trio during that first wave."

"We can handle it," Dice asserted.

I raised an eyebrow. "Will you handle an entire nest? Or an Alpha?"

The Troubleshooter looked as if he was about to respond when Ismyna cut him off. "Hal's right. We need to take the time and do this right. If we rush, we'll run out of power and get swarmed."

"He just wants us to slow down so some human competitor can get their own infrastructure together," Dice ranted.

I glanced at Ismyna and rolled my eyes. "The 'humans' left in this country are too busy fighting a three-way civil war over what remains of the government to even notice Galactics taking over the former United States, let alone building their own infrastructure."

Ismyna shrugged in agreement, but Dice continued to glare at me. "You've got an angle, human. I just don't know what it is yet."

"My angle is that I'm getting paid a significant sum of Credits to get this train to Denver and then returned to Pittsburgh. I don't know what your issue with me is, but it ends now. I'm not going to spend the rest of the trip looking over my shoulder while I wait for you to stab me in the back. We both want this venture to succeed, so start acting like it." I stepped forward and loomed over the diminutive gnome. "Otherwise, I'm going to treat you like a problem to be removed."

Dice blinked in surprise then glanced at Ismyna for help.

"Don't look at me," she said. "Hal has the trust of the Sprocketsworth Clan for a reason. Mother wouldn't have contracted him if he wasn't dependable."

"Fine, go slower, do whatever the human wants." Dice stepped away from me and spat on the floor. "Don't be surprised when your mercenary here fails to live up to the hype."

The gnome spun on his heel and stomped out of the control cabin, pushing past Wrefen, and the conductor barely dodged out of the way before entering.

"Is everything all right?" Wrefen asked. "And what got Dice's mustache all knotted up?"

I chuckled at the apt idiom, which only served to perplex the conductor.

"Everything is fine," Ismyna spoke up, staring in disgust at the gobbet of phlegm Dice had left on the floor. "Mostly. We're planning on stopping at night because the rail conversion system needs time to recharge, and Hal has concerns over pushing straight on through the night with all the constant fighting his team has been doing. Dice opposed my decision but eventually came around. He wasn't happy about it though."

Wrefen nodded and patted the front of his waistcoat, tugging on the length of chain to slide a watch free of the vest's pocket. He opened it and checked the time before looking at Ismyna. "If we manage ten hours for today at our current pace, we'll cover about, what, thirty miles?"

She nodded. "Pretty close to that."

Wrefen snapped the watch closed and slipped it back into the vest pocket. "So maybe fifty days, or just around that, to reach Denver. If we keep that rate going."

Ismyna's brow furrowed. "Our provisions should hold out for that long. We may need to restock for the return trip though."

Wrefen sniffed dismissively. "We have an entire boxcar full of supplies."

"There's always monster meat, if you're worried about food," I interjected. "It shouldn't be a problem to butcher some of the more tasteful beasts if we don't damage them too badly."

Both gnomes looked at me in surprise.

"What?" I waved toward the world outside of the engine. "Almost every monster out there is edible. It's the most cost-effective meal an Adventurer can get. Portable grill, some seasoning, you're all set."

Ismyna looked at Wrefen. "It's not a bad idea."

He shrugged. "We do have a Chef for the dining car. She might turn out something palatable."

Wrefen hesitated over his last word. Apparently, the conductor's refined standards for charred monster meat were significantly higher than mine.

"I'll have my team keep an eye out for some of the more appetizing monster selections throughout the day. We can butcher them when we stop in the evening."

Ismyna's eyes lit up. "We could do a crew cookout! I'll talk to Eldri about putting together something before we stop tonight."

I shared a wry look with Wrefen. "Sounds like a plan. I'll brief my team and make sure we have the night divided up into watches when we stop."

"Watches?" Ismyna looked at me in confusion before glancing at the pocket where the gnomish conductor kept his timepiece.

"It's a military term," I explained. "One of us will be on guard at all times through the night. We'll rotate through who is on shift so we each get the same amount of sleep."

The Engineer nodded in understanding. "That's a really good idea. I'll set up a crew watch, so you'll have a clan member on watch too. Even if they just end up having to come get me."

"Rank has its responsibility," I said.

Ismyna cocked her head. "I've never heard that saying before."

I grinned sardonically. "People always talk about rank having privilege, but everyone always forgets that the obligations have to be dealt with before enjoying any of the perks."

"That is deeply insightful, Adventurer Mason." Wrefen peered at me. "I wouldn't peg you as a simple mercenary when you're spouting wisdom like that."

I waved dismissively. "I blame the added Intelligence that I'm getting with my Levels. Don't read too much into it."

"Sure." Ismyna snorted. "You're just a simple Hunter who happens to keep getting into all kinds of trouble."

I shook my head, pointedly ignoring the comment. Fortunately, I saw movement at the edges of the sensors around us as red dots closed in on the train again. "There are more monsters moving in."

I waved to the pair of gnomes, off to do what I did best.

Chapter 13

"Finally."

I sighed and stretched as the train brakes squealed again, not for any emergency, but because it was late enough in the day to halt for the night.

Blood stained the fabric of my jumpsuit around several ragged tears across my body, though the exposed flesh beneath the holes looked fine, my injuries already healed. I debated swapping out the ruined suit for a fresh one, but maybe a subtle point about the dangers of constant combat would make a good object lesson for the evening.

Once the train slowed to a halt, the silence of dusk fell over the area. It felt surprisingly peaceful without the sounds of constant conflict and roaring monsters that had filled the day.

Our combat party showed up as friendly dots on my minimap, so I didn't need to use any actual tracking skills to meet up with them. They waited by the last carriage of the train to ensure no late monsters arrived, the Mana churning of the rail conversion system shut down for the evening.

We made a bedraggled crew, even Nargen's armor showing signs of the day's encounters. The portly dwarf pointedly avoided melee combat as much as possible, so the fact that his clothing bore ragged evidence meant that the creatures had managed to get far too close for comfort.

Kurak looked up from leaning tiredly on his halberd as I approached. "Calling it for the night?"

I nodded. "Swing by the workshop and take care of any armor repairs or rearming your weapon systems, then get some food before you sleep. I'll take the first shift on watch once things settle down."

The minotaur yawned. "Sounds good. I'll be fine after a couple hours if you want me to take the second shift."

Before we managed any further plans, one set of side doors on the workshop car opened. Eldri directed a crew of gnomes in the groundcrew's beige coveralls to haul out several pieces of equipment.

I shared a glance with the team then headed up the train toward the activity, the others following. By the time we arrived, several trough-like grills, tables, and benches were assembled alongside the stopped train.

Another beige-suited gnome guided an anti-grav sled out of the workshop car and down to where Eldri waited beside one of the grills. The sled carried a cylindrical Mana battery with blue-glowing coils, and once the gnome had grounded the sled, the Repair Technician plugged in a cable array for the grills. Once Eldri had secured the connection, the gnome hurried over to the grills and started them. The bottom of each trough glowed, radiating visible heat that shimmered above the grated surfaces.

Despite the obvious working nature of the equipment, Eldri still nervously bounced between each of the cooking surfaces while he made minor adjustments.

I stepped over to the fretting Technician. "It looks like they're working. You did a great job getting this all put together on such short notice. So what's the problem?"

The gnome stopped and blinked at me. "They have to be perfect."

"It's a grill, Eldri. You heat it up, slap some meat on it, and let it cook."

A disdainful sniff from behind me let me know that at least one approaching gnome disagreed with me. I turned and found another member of the crew that I'd yet to meet. An apron-clad gnome glowered at me from beneath a floppy white toque. Strands of pink hair escaped the chef's hat, curling out along her ears.

Ulyndra Sizzlebone (Governing Gourmand Level 31)
HP: 960/960

MP: 1180/1180

She shook her head at me. "The proper preparation of fine cuisine is not an endeavor to be taken lightly."

"It's grilled monster," I replied. "I'd hardly consider that fine cuisine."

Ulyndra clicked her tongue. "Then you have yet to see what a true Chef Class can produce with the bounties of a Dungeon World. You're the one who is providing the raw materials for this evening's feast, yes?"

I nodded. "Where do you want the best of the stuff we've butchered today?"

The chef pointed toward a flat table at the edge of the clearing.

"I'm looking forward to sampling your work." I nodded to the Gourmand and headed in the direction she'd indicated.

A gnome with a Sous Chef Class waited beside the table along with two non-Pharyleri, the first crewmembers I'd seen who weren't a part of the Clan. The green-skinned Hakarta held the Class of Boucher and spun a cleaver the size of my head around her finger while waiting for me to provide the day's monster harvest. The final member of the trio was of a race I hadn't encountered yet and looked like a humanoid rabbit, which Greater Observation identified as a Lagomorah. Class: Kitchen Porter.

I unloaded the day's haul from my Meat Locker storage space onto the table and the Boucher started hacking away with her cleaver, chopping the monster parts into grill-sized steaks. At the same time, the Porter removed the now-cut pieces from the table, loading them onto a large tray and clearing space for me as I continued disgorging my Inventory. Once heaping piles of meat filled her tray, the Kitchen Porter skipped over to where the Gourmand waited by the grills.

Ulyndra waved a hand in front of herself, as if spinning through a series of options, then pulled a set of grilling tongs from out of the air. Since Meat Locker placed my kills in stasis, there was no need for the steaks to rest at room temperature like there would have been when using refrigerated meat.

The gnomish Gourmand then flipped the slices of fresh meat into another pan already filled with a liquid marinade. Once each piece was coated in marinade, Ulyndra snagged the slab from the pan. Flicks of the tongs sent the now-coated steaks onto the grill, Mana-fueled flames sizzling as the meat cooked. Once each side of the steak had seared to seal in the flavor, she moved them to a section of the grill with a lower flame to finish cooking.

The display of Class Skills at work to simplify and hasten the cooking process put the abilities of any pre-System chef to shame, let alone my meager attempts at meal prep. I really did just eat charred monster meat when compared to the cuisine being readied here.

The rich aroma of searing meat and savory spices filled the area, saliva filling my mouth at the flavorful scents. I didn't really expect any monster attacks now that we were stationary and the rail conversion system shut down. Still, if there were any monsters nearby, they would certainly be drawn by the fragrant smells that wafted through the air.

After I'd finished emptying the stored monster parts from my Inventory, I stepped away as the orc carved up the last of my offerings. No longer ferrying between the Boucher and Gourmand, the Porter pulled finished steaks from the grill to let them rest on a series of large platters.

As the chef worked over the grill, the remaining crew assembled alongside the train. It was the first time I'd seen the entire staff for this expedition, let alone all together in one place.

Most of the crew were Pharyleri, but there were a number of exceptions. The first notable was a Gimsar female currently making doe eyes at Nargen, much to the latter's discomfort and my amusement. Another was a golden-furred leonid, like the ones I'd noticed in the starport, who looked on hungrily as she stared intently at the selection of sizzling meat on the grill.

My analysis of the crew halted when I noticed Ismyna jump up onto one of the tables and pound her foot several times to command the group's attention. Once the murmur of conversation died down, the gnomish Engineer cleared her throat.

"I hope you all enjoy this evening's cookout, courtesy of our external security force and chef brigade. Please take a moment to thank Hal, Ulyndra, and their teams for tonight's feast."

A round of applause echoed from the assembled crew before Ismyna spoke again. "You may have noticed that we've slowed down and are now stopping for the night. If you haven't heard yet, this trip will be taking longer than originally planned, but our mission remains the same.

"Our goal is still establishing a secure ground transitway between the starport and the Rocky Mountains. Your hard work is going to make it possible, and you all will continue to be paid your full contract rates for the entirety of the journey."

A few cheers broke out at comments about pay, mostly from the non-Pharyleri.

Ismyna grinned. "Now, enjoy dinner tonight and get a good night of sleep. We'll be back to work at first light."

Another round of polite applause followed the Engineer as she jumped down from the table, only to be handed a plate with the first of the rested steaks.

Meanwhile, the rest of the cook staff assembled a full meal beyond the monster filets, filling her plate with salad, potatoes, and a few dishes I didn't recognize offhand.

I signaled Dayena and Kurak to grab food while Nargen and I patrolled the perimeter. I chuckled at Nargen's sigh of relief when my instructions allowed him to avoid the other Gimsar, who had been attempting to get him to sit next to her at one of the tables.

The dinner went until the entire crew had eaten their fill, our team swapping out so that each of us got a chance for a hot meal. I did notice that Kurak avoided the offered meat and pulled his own rations from Inventory for his dinner.

I was forced to admit that my attempts at charring monster meat over a grill stood up dismally when compared to dishes properly prepared by someone with actual Class Skills in cooking.

When I returned my empty plate to the kitchen staff, I stepped over to the Gourmand. "I owe you an apology. That meal put almost everything I've eaten in the past year to shame."

Ulyndra actually smiled and nodded politely. "Thank you, Adventurer Mason."

By the time the kitchen brigade cleared their cookware from the tables and grills, the rest of the support crew were already well into disassembling the grilling equipment. It didn't take long for the technicians to clear everything, leaving behind little evidence of the gathering.

Looking around the area, I found only two of the internal security team remaining on guard, in addition to my party, as Ismyna herded the last of the crew back onto the train.

I walked over to the Engineer. "This worked out well. We had no surprise monster attacks and plenty of food."

"Yes, Ulyndra put out quite a spread. I doubt that every evening will be to that quality, but they probably won't be far below it either."

"No complaints here," I said, then sent her a data packet. "Here's my team's watch rotation. I'll make sure my team is geared up for tomorrow, then get things buttoned up for the night. Signal me if you have any issues since I'll be taking the first guard shift."

Ismyna acknowledged my comments and turned to her assistant, launching into a maintenance discussion that I quickly tuned out.

While the last of the crew filed back onboard the train, I rounded up my team. Kurak and Nargen confirmed they had restocked their supplies and fixed any broken equipment after they'd eaten dinner, so they plodded off to rest.

I held up a hand to stop Dayena before she could follow. "If you don't mind, I'd like to start spending more time sparring. It's been a while since we did any serious training. I want to be ready for the next time we face your family."

Dayena stared at me, then nodded. "That is a sound plan."

The dark elf stepped away from the train, drawing her short swords as she moved into an open space.

"I was hoping you'd use a long blade."

The Countess peered at me intently, her face nearly inscrutable. "You want practice for the next time you're up against my cousin."

It wasn't a question. I shrugged. "She didn't seem too happy about having to bring you in. Maybe if I'm good enough, we won't need to kill her. Though I have no qualms about taking out your other cousin. He seemed like an asshole."

Dayena snorted. "You will need much practice before you're up to Truinnar standards, but I will do what I can to teach you."

"Thanks, I think."

She stared at me seriously for a moment. "You have improved significantly since we began our partnership."

The dark elf sheathed her twin blades before holding out a hand and summoning a basket-hilted saber from her Inventory, one that appeared similar to the one I'd looted after our fight with her family.

The moment I drew my melee weapons, the dark elf launched herself at me in a furious assault. Despite my attempted defense, Dayena's blade flicked past my ax and knocked aside my knife to carve chunks from my arms and legs with every swing. Each cut felt painless at first, skin and muscle sliced to flap free with my movements, blood pulsing from my wounds and watering the ground.

Then the pain set in with fire burning in distracting lines across my body as the injuries made themselves known.

A viscous chop to the back of my knee severed tendons, and I collapsed as my leg gave out.

Dayena sauntered over, the tip of her blade tracing a line across my throat as she cut a shallow channel.

"You have improved." Quiet and defeated, her voice sounded like someone on the edge of despair. "Nowhere near enough."

Dayena dismissed the sword and summoned a healing potion, crouching at my side to hand me the small bottle of liquid while avoiding my questioning gaze. I drank the concoction, boosting my natural regeneration, which was already hard at work sealing all but the worst of my injuries. Storing my weapons, I pulled my knees up and rested my arms on them.

When the silence between us stretched out with no sign of the dark elf speaking, I asked, "What was that about?"

"What do you know of Truinnar children?"

My brow furrowed at the apparent non sequitur. "Nothing really. The information I've been reading from the Shop has been focused on the political structure and current major players."

The dark elf sank down beside me and held out a hand. "Let me see your knife."

I pulled the weapon from the sheath on my chest and passed it over. "Okay…"

She spun the blade in her palm, flipped it over her hand completely, then flicked it upright to balance on the end of her index finger.

"When I was three, my mother gifted me my first sword." Her eye remained fixed on the blade where it stood on the point. "Not much longer than this knife but just as sharp." Her eyes met mine. "On the morning of my fourth birthday, my father pushed me into a sand-covered arena to face my first monster. It was only a Level 1 creature, but it injured me gravely before I managed to kill it with that very same blade."

She ticked the knife slightly upward and caught the blade between two fingers before passing it back to me, hilt first. I took the offered weapon and returned it to its sheath as Dayena continued speaking.

"I slew a different monster first thing every day for the next year. As I improved, the Levels gradually increased. No matter how badly I was injured in the fight, the rest of my mornings were filled with schooling and training. Martial techniques, weapon styles, court etiquette, academic learning, and everything else expected of Truinnar nobles."

I shook my head. "That's insane. There's no way children should be raised like that. Families should protect their kids from the dangers of the world."

"That is not the way of things under the System. Most Council races train their children in some manner, though Triunnar methods are acknowledged as the harshest. Coddling will only raise adults unable to face the truth. The reality is that the System only respects strength and those who wield it effectively. At least as a noble, I had the finest of tutors and the mostly highly skilled weapons masters to instruct me." Dayena looked at me intently. "However, you have missed my point."

"Which is?"

"I have nearly three decades of training and instruction under the System. Class Skills and spells will only get you so far. At a certain point, your individual talent and skill count just as much. You need to fully integrate your Shop-implanted Skills so that they are part of you. You have relied on your Advanced Class attributes and Skills to get you this far, but they will not be enough should you continue to face foes of an equal tier from the wider galaxy."

Part of me didn't want to admit she was right. I'd used my higher attributes and versatile Class Skills as a crutch without dedicating myself to any particular combat style. I'd switch as needed between ranged and melee combat based on the situation.

That flexibility offered advantages when facing monsters and foes with lower Agility or Strength. However, when it came to squaring up against enemies of higher skill and attributes, this sparring session with Dayena had proved the weakness in my jack-of-all-trades strategy.

A true combat expert would prevent me from making full use of all the extra equipment stashed in my various Inventory spaces.

I pushed myself to my feet. "You're right. I need to get better, so we're going to do this again and again. And again, until I have the skill to stand on my own against you or your family. If I have to get turned into a bloody, ruined wreck repeatedly, then so be it."

Dayena stood, her brilliant white teeth shining in the evening gloom. It was an ominous smile that promised pain, but I could only believe my efforts would be worth it in the end. The saber reappeared in her hand, and she beckoned me forward.

I moved to draw my knife, and Dayena lifted her saber to pin my hand in place, the tip of her blade embedded in my skin as she shook her head. "Your blades are not the answer here."

"What do you mean?"

Dayena pulled her sword free of my hand and gestured to the projectile pistols sheathed at my hips. "You have those fine pieces of hardware. Use them. Master them. Learn to fight with them instead of relying on your Skills alone. Then we may stand a chance."

I flicked my wrist to clear the blood from the back of my hand before grasping the holstered pistols on my hips. My hands wrapped comfortably around the fitted grips, and I regretted not taking time out of the busy day to use them against the monsters we'd faced. Dayena nodded approvingly, then paused in a ready stance for a moment before launching herself at me once again.

My weapons cleared their holsters, and our dance began. The echoes of clashing weapons, gunshots, and the sounds of my body being cut to ribbons continued on for several hours into the night, the ruckus ensuring that any nearby monsters knew to stay well clear.

It was a good thing the train was well insulated or I'm sure we'd have had more than a few complaints.

Chapter 14

The next few days fell into a routine. Progress with the rail conversion through the day, feast at dusk, and develop my evolving close-quarters pistol combat style late into the night. That last part ended up being just as bloody and painful as the monster fighting during the day.

Ismyna started the locomotive with the first light of dawn each morning. My team spent the hours under the sun slaying monsters as the rails were converted, and the train powered farther along the tracks. We provided perimeter security when the train halted for the crew to clear blocked sections of the tracks.

Usually that blockage involved abandoned trains, but we also encountered washed-out bridges, rockslides, monster corpses, and fallen trees, all of which slowed our progress. Whatever the impediment, Eldri's team had a contraption to deal with the problem. Sometimes it seemed that every intersection we passed had a stopped truck, stalled out during the System-initiation like a bad public-safety video.

The locomotive probably could have plowed through most of the minor obstructions, but nobody wanted to take the risk. Not when the tools were at hand to resolve the problem without risking damage to the engine.

The pneumatic jacks worked just as well on personal motor vehicles and semi-trucks as they did on freight cars. More so actually, launching the lighter cars hundreds of yards through the air. An automated bridging system dealt with the washed-out bridges by framing supporting tracks and driving pylons into the ground beneath the newly assembled framework. A track-mounted drilling and digging system sorted out the landslides, clearing the rails of sediment and shoring up either side of the newly dug channel for the future.

Of course, the track clearing operations disturbed monster nests. My team managed to respond quickly enough each time that none of the ground crew were critically injured, but there were several near misses.

Like the stealthed rat monster that avoided detection by hiding on top of a boxcar's axle, only jumping out to attack the ground crew when they launched the freight car into the air. Two gnomes lost an arm and a leg each before Nargen's robot dog wedged itself down the monster's throat as we killed it.

Of course, that meant Nargen spent the entirety of the next night repairing his beloved creation.

Tensions with Dice and his security team remained high. The Troubleshooter kept having his team open fire early, luring monsters away from our group when we had them under control. I ended up instructing Kurak to let the monsters go.

Kill stealing was annoying and rude, but if the gnome wanted to play at being a professional, I'd give him enough rope to hang himself.

Our course led northwest from the starport, passing housing developments and along the outskirts of smaller towns, each empty and abandoned with the buildings crumbling or shattered by passing monsters. The desolate structures reminded me of humanity's fall, and everything lost post System. System notifications had coldly informed us that ninety percent of the human race had died in the first year, but how many more had been lost since?

It wasn't like the world suddenly went back to "normal" once the Mana flows stabilized. No, people were still dying. It's just that the System notifications weren't updating us of humanity's status anymore. Especially not now when so many Galactics were pouring onto the planet and setting up shop.

Sometimes literally.

The empty remains of the once-thriving communities only emphasized the broken and shattered world that was left.

Maudlin thoughts, especially for me. Even Dayena saw it, as it drove me to train ever harder.

Six days after leaving the starport, we rolled into Cleveland, Ohio.

Before entering the City Center and the Safe Zone around the Rock and Roll Hall of Fame, we stopped for several hours. While Dayena stayed out of sight in our cabin, I played the role of stoic bodyguard as Ismyna negotiated passage and transportation rights with a Truinnar delegation from Viscount Nivoosi.

Led by another dark elf who turned out to be the Viscount's majordomo, the greeting party met us at the edges of the territory carved out against the edges of Lake Erie. The staff carried by Seneschal Balver Fyrik radiated so much power, I didn't need Greater Observation to identify the old elf as a serious threat. Never mind the way the old elf hunched over and leaned on the staff to support himself. The Mana-infused gemstones in the intricately carved staff glowed with ethereal energy, alternately growing brighter and dimming throughout the discussion between the envoys.

The Viscount himself never bothered to put in an appearance during the negotiations, which worked out fine for everyone. In short order, Ismyna worked out a deal where the Truinnar would receive favorable rates for goods transported between the settlement and starport in exchange for access and ongoing security for the tracks.

Once the negotiations were wrapped up, the train pulled up to Cleveland's Union Station. Most of the crew took the opportunity to use the nearby Shop, only a skeleton group left behind to be rotated through later.

We joined the crew at the Shop, myself selling off a full load of monster carcasses from my Meat Locker, but I didn't spend many Credits beyond restocking my ammunition loadouts and a few extra jumpsuits. At the rate I was going through the armored clothing, part of me wondered if buying them in bulk might be cheaper in the long run. Maybe a crate of them would fit in my expanded storage through my Right Tool for the Job Class Skill.

Despite my more pessimistic beliefs, our group didn't encounter any problems while in the Viscount's territory.

Departing from Cleveland, the tracks stayed within sight of the Lake Erie shoreline for several miles before turning inland to the southwest and running through the ruins of Elyria.

Monsters thoroughly infested the ruins of civilization through this area. They rushed the train in massed waves that reminded me of the first several months of System initialization, when the creatures were being pushed around by the fluctuating Mana concentrations.

Good times. Good experience.

The increased monster density forced the locomotive to slow further until we cleared the area, lengthening our journey yet again.

One bright spot came as a result. Dice's team turned out to have purchased a crew-served weapon during the Shop visit in Cleveland and deployed the tripod-mounted energy cannon on top of the workshop car.

I grudgingly admitted that the new weapon was a wise investment when a Monster Wave poured through the ruins of Elyria to attack us. The barrels of the gatling cannon glowed for hours as monsters surged. The constant need for the firepower was so bad that the gunners had to be swapped out after their fingers cramped from holding down the triggers for so long.

It took an extra two days of fending off the monster attacks before we cleared the way through the city ruins.

From Elyria, we headed west most of the way across the former Buckeye state, then back up to the Lake Erie shoreline until we reached Sandusky Bay. There, we were forced into a full day's stop to rebuild the collapsed railroad bridge over the estuary. Fortunately, the nearby Edison Bridge remained mostly intact, so we got a second work crew to the far side of the bay to start on the other end of the bridge and work back toward the middle.

The water-based monsters that spawned in both the bay and the lake didn't appreciate the disturbances, so the ground crew worked under literal fire as flame-breathing opossum shrimp crawled up the bridge pilings to assault the workers and their equipment. Grenades launched into the water at short intervals seemed to deter the monsters, but we went through a literal ton of munitions during that twenty-four-hour period. An armament station in the workshop car cranked out a tray of simple handheld explosives every few minutes that we lobbed into the water or ferried across to the other side to do the same thing.

Besides the shrimp, the makeshift depth charges also left a fair number of fish floating on the surface of the water beneath the bridge. About the only thing going for us was that Ulyndra managed to make an amazing shrimp boil from the monster corpses and more mundane fish, refilling our larder. No one even had to climb down into the water to grab the corpses. The Kitchen Porter deployed a Class Skill for quick retrieval that teleported bodies over to the larder in safety. A dish of beer-battered walleye proved especially popular amongst the crew.

Once the final assembly of the new bridge fit together, Ismyna drove the train across, and we left the frothing Sandusky Bay behind.

Before departing, the ground crew deployed extra sensors along the bridge just in case the native wildlife became a future problem. Despite the challenge faced by rebuilding the bridge, the crew hoped that the Mana stabilization of the rail system would keep the creature difficulties minimized. If not, Ismyna was talking about setting up a nearby fish and boil spot, for the more adventurous visitors to the world.

Galactics.

And they called us humans insane.

With the sheer number of monsters slain during the last few days, it finally pushed my experience high enough to earn Level 39.

Dropping the newly earned Attribute Points into Perception and Willpower, I boosted the lowest of my stats. I stubbornly continued with my plan of hoarding the Class Skills points though. Level 46 still lay ahead of a long grind before I unlocked my final tier of Class Skills.

Back on track with the worst of the water troubles behind us, our overland journey continued with the return to the steady pace of day-long monster slaying and nightly stops. Monster attacks came constantly. No matter the Levels of the nearby creatures, the disturbances of the rail conversion system drove them into a frenzy, and they charged the train recklessly.

Higher Leveled creatures began breaking through our perimeter as we crossed from Indiana into Illinois, adding additional pressure to my team. Luckily, their ability to damage the reinforced armor of the locomotive remained slight thanks to the enchantments that bolstered the train's defenses. Even so, we were run ragged with the constant fighting, the mental wear worse than the physical thanks to the System's constant regeneration.

Tempers grew shorter, Dice's people and mine snapping at one another as tensions rocketed. Requests for a break were denied though as we grew further and further behind their timetable.

After rounding the southernmost tip of Lake Michigan, the tracks gradually angled to the north into the outskirts of Chicago's suburban sprawl. That's where our journey was brought to a screeching halt by a congested snarl of derailed and tangled freight trains.

Intermodal containers lay like a jumbled heap of damaged and piled blocks. Formerly dry goods like cement, grains, and gravel poured from burst hopper cars, leaving solidified or soggy messes strewn everywhere. Rolled and toppled gondolas added their scattered loads of scrap metals, logs, and sand to the detritus that mired the railyard.

Clouds muddled the midmorning sunlight that peeked through as Ismyna stood atop the engine and cursed loudly, staring over the cluttered chaos. Standing behind the Engineer, I scanned the wreckage a hundred or so yards ahead for any signs of monsters beyond the scattered red dots appearing on my minimap.

She turned to Eldri and gestured to the clogged tracks. "It looks worse in reality than on a Shop scanner. How long will it take to clear this mess?"

The Technician frowned and shook his head. "Not quickly. This job will take days."

Ismyna sighed. "Then we better get to work. I'll have everyone who isn't occupied assist whenever they can, even for just general labor."

"There are a few monsters to be removed before you get started," I interjected.

Ismyna ran both hands through her hair and growled. "Of course there are."

I chuckled darkly. Even after all this time, life in a Dungeon World still hadn't made its way through her.

Leaving the glaring gnomes, I dropped down to the ground alongside the stopped engine. A quick exchange of messages through party chat updated my team about the situation.

"Are you sure you can handle that many?" I felt the skepticism in Dayena's voice over party chat.

"I'll be fine. Stay here and guard the train. The Levels for the zones have been climbing again, so until we get a better feel for the local threats, most of our group should stick close."

Only once I was sure that Nargen and Kurak were also ready to keep an eye on the perimeter around the halted train did I start forward into the tangled jungle of metal and broken machinery blocking our route. Gravel crunched underfoot as I clambered up a spilled mound of granite chips and onto the broken hopper car from which the pile spilled.

The red dots on my minimap closed in on my position as I ascended the pile, probably drawn by the noise of disturbed stones cascading down over the mountain of debris. In response to the approaching threats, I pulled my named pistols once I reached the top of the car. The next car in line, a jackknifed centerbeam, lay derailed at a canted angle with only one set of trucks still on the rails. The centerbeam's load of plastic-covered lumber, shifted from the collision and derailing, provided convenient ramps up to the top of the car for the onrushing monsters.

A series of high-pitched barks and shrieks preceded a streak of orange breaking cover from beneath an autorack.

Red Feathered Fox (Level 63)
HP: 1280/1280

From a distance, the beast appeared similar to native red foxes. Further examination revealed the differences. The cute, cuddly animal of frolicking, pre-System nature documentaries bore only a slight resemblance in color and form to the monster. Tiny orange feathers covered the creature instead of fur, and oversized raptor talons curved up between the bounding creature's toes.

I opened fire at the rushing beast, the crack of the gunshots echoing through the railyard. The projectiles rippled across the feathery layers and blood spattered from the wounds. My barrage of fire shredded the creature, and it stumbled to a halt, slumping over against the bottom of a lumber pile as two more popped out from different places in the wreckage.

Splitting my fire between the pair, I ran along the top of the narrow truss in the middle of the centerbeam car. Before I could drop either of the creatures, my weapons ran empty.

Holstering my left-hand pistol, I summoned a fully loaded cylindrical magazine from my Inventory into my open palm. Swapping out the empty magazine in the right-hand pistol, I dismissed the depleted cartridge back to my Inventory to reload later as I jammed the loaded weapon into its holster. Drawing the other weapon, I repeated the reloading process.

I really needed to figure out a better way to reload in combat. Swapping out depleted weapons worked great for generic beam and projectile weapons, but that tactic didn't help when I needed to keep using my new, higher quality hand cannons.

For now, the best I could do would be to get more practice at reloading under pressure.

The twin foxes snarled as they lunged at me, having climbed up the scattered lumber piles and onto the centerbeam while I was reloading. With my weapons now full, I kicked the lead creature in its snapping maw and knocked it into its companion.

The two monsters tangled briefly at the surprise impact with each other, and I took the opportunity to leap onto the next car. The monsters quickly sorted themselves out and pursued me. While I fled, I spun around to fire along the top of the narrow I-beam truss at the lead fox.

Three more of the orange-and-red feathered foxes approached from the surrounding wreckage, so I needed to finish this pair off before the full skulk encircled me completely.

A barrage of pistol fire dropped the first fox, but the second never slowed, leaping over the carcass of its fellow and launching itself at my throat. I brought my weapons close together, shooting directly into the monster's mouth. The shots punched through the back of the monster's skull, but it was already airborne. Ducking, I turned and ensured that it was truly dead as it flopped bonelessly, the landing creating an echoing hollow thud while blood pooled around the corpse as its heart shuddered and juddered its last few times.

A fast check of my surroundings showed that I still had three of the monsters to go.

I emptied my weapons into the nearest, a nimble beast that outraced its companions. My attacks punctured through the feathers shrouding the upper forelegs of the creature, crippling one limb badly enough that the fox slowed to a limp, letting out a low keening noise that set my teeth on edge.

The other two drew closer as I reloaded. As the monsters clambered up the centerbeam car's uneven load of fallen drywall and construction materials, I greeted them with a hail of bullets, my ears ringing from the repeated explosions.

Thank the System for perfect healing, or else I'd probably have permanent hearing loss.

The next ten minutes were spent in a frenzied combination of parkour and gunplay as I maneuvered to keep the skulk of fox creatures from overwhelming me with their numbers. Several times, I failed to evade them all and took injuries before breaking free.

The end of the fight came down to me limping over to finish off the last fox with my knife, while only a few strands of tendon held my knee together after my leg had been jointly savaged by the previous two beasts.

Moving to a loose pallet of lumber, I flopped onto the conveniently improvised seat and reloaded my pistols with fresh magazines. Once I'd readied my pistols, I pulled a case of standard projectile ammunition from my Inventory and refilled my spent magazines while keeping an eye on the red traces moving around the edges of my minimap. The threats were distant enough that I wasn't worried, but still near enough to keep track of while preparing to take them on.

When I'd finished rearming, I jumped down from the pallet and stretched, feeling the tight pull of newly knitted tissue across my torso and abdomen as I twisted and bent through a few exploratory movements. My knee felt a little stiff, but the time spent readying my weapons had provided my body with the time it needed to heal.

The encounter had certainly showed me where I needed to improve. I could have done a far better job of isolating my opponents and forcing them to engage one at a time. Pushing myself was a worthy goal, but taking on the last monster with limited mobility probably hadn't been particularly smart. Instead of jumping down to take on the wounded fox right away, I could have fixed the worst of the damage by drinking a potion while holding the high ground.

Sometimes I really could use someone to smack me upside the back of my head and call me a fool.

Still, things had gone rather well for consciously not using my Class Skills during the encounter. Hinder alone would have easily swung the fight in my favor. Good weapons really made a difference, though that fact had been evident since day one of the Apocalypse.

Limbered up and with my health pool nearly topped off, I headed into the tangled wreckage to track down the next closest series of monsters. The wispy strands blowing in the slight breeze indicated the next round of creatures would likely not be of the friendly neighborhood variety.

Chapter 15

Traces of webbing wafted in the wind, broken in places where once they'd stretched between the leaning cars and other bits of debris. Dammit, now I had to deal with mutated spider monsters again.

Just a few strands of web appeared at first, then the density increased until the gossamer fibers blocked off various routes through the debris and I was forced to backtrack multiple times. Giving up moving along the ground, and not liking the way the webs closed off overhead in addition to blocking off passages, I looked for alternatives.

Fortunately, the narrow, built-in ladders at the ends of the intermodal containers provided a route for me to climb onto the top level of the pileup. However, even the tops of nearby cars were coated in a layer of webbing.

My concerns grew when I realized that most of the few red dots that remained on my minimap were huddled together and glowed only dimly, showing reduced threat.

A scrape from behind me provided a moment of warning, and I jumped forward, turning back toward the noise as I drew my pistols. The monster skittering toward me was exactly the kind of hideous mutation I'd come to expect from the System's takeover of Earth.

The brown-furred body and head of a rabbit, grown to the size of a rottweiler and with the addition of eight insectoid legs, clambered along the top of the container. Mandibles extended on either side of the bunny-spider amalgamation's mouth, and a viscous green fluid dripped down the pair of pointed fangs that replaced the typical blunt incisors. As the mint-green liquid struck the top of the container, it sizzled and burnt the paint, drawing my attention to the penny-sized markings all around that I'd missed earlier.

As I raised my guns and sighted down it, the six red eyes on its rabbit-like head fixed on the motion. The monster hissed and its torso seemed to inflate. With a huff, the beast spat a ball of the green substance. A quick juke turned the attack into a narrow miss, for all but a few spatters of the secretion.

Where the liquid landed, my jumpsuit bubbled and my skin burned. Despite the pain, my return fire stayed on target, and the rounds shredded the monster. It collapsed, oozing blood and viscera. From the matted fur around the wounds, it looked like these creatures lacked the hardened exoskeleton of most insect mutations.

More skittering sounded from several directions, though nothing showed on my minimap. Some kind of stealth ability was in play, but they weren't especially quiet. One of the problems with rampant mutations was that not every one was a winner. The advance warning allowed me to pull back in the direction from which I'd approached the nest.

Keeping to the highest points of the wrecked trains allowed me to deal with several of the monsters as they pursued. The monsters went down surprisingly easily, but there were far more of them than there had been foxes.

When I left the webbed areas behind, I noticed that the bunny-spiders appeared on my minimap. It seemed their stealth and ability to hide from detection was tied to their home turf and webbing.

I lurked around the perimeter of the webbing, luring them out and running when the creatures showed. Their reluctance to travel beyond the ends of their webs left me plenty of room to rearm and reload my weapons after each sortie.

The monsters responded more slowly each time as I whittled away at their numbers, forcing me to probe ever deeper. The number of creatures and the density of the webbing left me with an unsettled feeling, but attempts at burning down the webs saw little effect. Not your average cobweb, it seemed.

To prepare for the likelihood of an Alpha I knew was in the wreckage, I laid proximity mines to cover my exit.

Sneaking through the tangled paths and cutting away the worst of the webs when I could no longer progress, I found the lair not long after. A pair of boxcars lay in a V-shaped tangle, completely shrouded in webbing that stretched overhead between the wrecks and blocked almost all of the afternoon sunlight. White cocoons of varying shapes and sizes indicated that the spider-like monsters preyed on a variety of creatures from the surrounding area. The largest number of entombed victims lay cluttered across the ground and affixed to the sides of the boxcars.

Crouching in one of the few areas clear of the webbing, I peered into the dimly lit space. Occasional twitching of the webbed cocoons drew my eye, but I saw no immediate signs of spiders.

Then a half-dozen red glowing eyes flicked open in a white mound in the middle of the lair, peering directly at me. The mound heaved upward, revealing a monster significantly larger than the other spiders, a creature about the size of a pre-System minivan. The white fur of the mutant's rabbit-like body blended with the spider silk draped around the lair, giving the monster extra camouflage within the space.

Chelixia Spider Alpha (Level 73)
HP: 5940/5940

I dropped a mine at my feet, and the device beeped softly as I leapt backward. Clawed forelegs slashed down as it leapt toward me, digging into the ground with a muffled thud.

Activating Hinder on the dangerously close monster, I bolted back the way I'd come. The lightning-fast jump must be an ability unique to the Alpha, one that had a cooldown. It didn't jump after me again, instead scurrying after me. I'd have to watch out or one of those pounces might pin me in place.

The mine exploded beneath the monster a moment later, the monster shrieking loudly as the blast peppered the back of my armor with shards of shrapnel. The armor held up to the hits, leaving me with only bruises. So far anyways.

With a pistol in one hand, I summoned a grenade into the other and pivoted to aim at the spider as it skittered after me. I pitched the grenade at the monster and squeezed off a handful of shots before sprinting away.

Soft beeps alerted me that I'd passed another set of the mine emplacements, and I continued on for another dozen steps before I lobbed another grenade at the spider. Mines exploded beneath the enraged monster, halting its rush just in time for my grenade to bathe the giant spider in flames.

As the fires died away, all of the white fur looked burned away from the monster's head, leaving only charred and blackened flesh. The skin cracked as the spider mutant hissed in pain, its wounds leaking ichor that dripped down and sizzled on the ground beneath the creature.

With the creature stunned, I emptied the magazine of my pistol into the beast's face. My attacks added to the injuries and punctured at least two of the Alpha's eyes. But despite the amount of damage dealt, none of my attacks really restricted the creature's mobility. Singed carapace on the spider's legs creaked as it sprang forward, clawed forelimbs slashing.

I dove to the side as claws raked through my armor, drawing a pained gasp. Barbs from the first leg dug into the side of my chest and glanced off my ribs, while the other scratched a shallow furrow into my leg. Ignoring the pain and the uncomfortable sensation of blood flowing from the wounds, I rolled to my feet and reloaded my pistol. My hands swapped the magazines thoughtlessly as I dodged the Alpha's stabbing and slashing forelegs.

With my weapons once again full of ammunition, I drew my second pistol from the holster at my waist while dancing clear of the enraged spider's constant attacks. The thunder of my hand cannons roared in the narrow confines of the wrecked train cars. My fire traced a staccato line of destruction across the monster's head, tearing away chunks of flesh and destroying another pair of eyes as the monster recoiled in agony. The Alpha's health dropped, each shot stripping away a noticeable sliver of its vitality.

Taking advantage of its distraction, I backpedaled and continued to fire steadily as I increased the separation between us. Once I was far enough away, I jumped over the coupling between two boxcars and ran on. I passed the last set of my emplaced mines, which activated as I went by.

Skittering claws scraping over and tearing through the metal walls of the cars behind me let me know that the Alpha still pursued me. I couldn't help but allow myself a wolfish grin, as I'd counted on the monster following.

Of course, then the monster went up and over the last boxcar, moving to cut off my path instead of following me. The Alpha paused on top of the car, peering at me through its last pair of undamaged eyes, then the monster vaulted itself straight at me. The springing lunge pushed off from the boxcar with such force that the car rocked up off the rails.

I saw the attack coming and, with the now active mines behind me, launched myself under the arc of the diving spider. The creature slammed into the ground, shaking the earth around me as I tumbled clear. I pushed myself back to my feet and turned to find the nearly blinded monster spinning in my direction. Its legs stabbed into the ground beneath it as it searched for me by feel.

I slunk behind the Alpha as it continued to rotate, staying behind it while keeping my steps light and quiet. I reloaded my hand cannons, one after the other, then holstered both of the weapons.

It was time to finish this fight.

Summoning my hybrid rifle from my Inventory, I pulled the stock tight to my shoulder and watched the flailing spider from within its blind spot as I planned my next attacks.

The Alpha slowed, growing cautious as it failed to find me.

Crouching, I scooped up a piece of gravel from the loose ballast near the tracks. My arm whipped forward, skipping the rock off the boxcar on the far side of the spider, and the stone bounced back to hit the creature on its side. The monster, already turning toward the sound of the rock hitting the metal, blindly lashed out.

The Alpha's movements exposed the creature's flank, and the noise of its flailing covered the whine of my rifle's building charge as I squeezed the trigger. The weapon's radiant discharge propelled the railgun's projectile directly into the side of the monster's head, blasting out a crater of flesh and knocking the creature off balance. Staggering from the hit, the Alpha toppled over as the legs along its side gave out. I charged, dodging between the scrambling legs, and jumped onto the creature as I fired another shot into the monster's head.

My third shot, triggered at almost point-blank range to the back of the Alpha's head, punched through its skull. The creature went limp as the round pithed its brain. I rode the collapsing monster to the ground and paused with my rifle readied for another shot while I checked my experience notifications to confirm the monster's demise.

I hadn't even lost a limb in this Alpha fight.

I read through the updates then checked my minimap for any threats, finding it clear for now.

Swapping out the rifle's partially used magazine for a full spare, I stored the weapon in Inventory then looted the Alpha. Spider legs, fangs, a poison sac, and a pristine pelt large enough to blanket a king-size bed were my rewards for slaying the creature.

After that, a few handfuls of gravel tossed at the unused but still activated mines detonated them to clear my path back to the monster's lair.

When I reached the Alpha's den, I used Greater Observation on the webbed cocoons while finishing off any of the trapped monsters that still lived with a few stabs of my knife. No sense in wasting ammunition, though I only earned minimal experience from the almost-dead creatures.

Halfway through the lair, I stopped in surprise as I read the results of my analysis.

Lyrra Valjyn (Combat Medicae Level 41)
HP: 42/620
MP: 0/650

My knife, already plunging toward the bundle of webs, shifted trajectory enough that I slashed along the length of the cocoon instead of stabbing into it. The enveloping silk split open along my cut, revealing an emaciated woman with pallid skin and matted golden hair. Her chest raised only slightly with each shallow breath, so I cast a round of healing spells on the unconscious woman and pried her free from the silken shroud encasing her.

The tacky strands clung to everything, and I constantly wiped my hand on the ground as I attempted to clear away the worst of the sticky filaments that clung to the woman. While I managed to get the majority removed, when I tugged at where the substance stuck to her hair, it reminded me of bubblegum pressed into hair as a horrible prank. I ended up cutting away the worst of the sections.

My hacking revealed her pointed ears, and I sat back on my heels while I digested the discovery that I'd rescued a Movana. I managed to peel her away from the cocoon, and almost immediately, her health climbed as the draining effects of the web stopped working on her.

Huh. Maybe the webs could be used for something...

Looking around the rest of the lair, I analyzed the rest of the web-wrapped bundles as I used more healing spells on the elven woman. None of the remaining cocoons held living sentients, so I left the Movana to recover while I finished off the rest of the cocooned monsters.

Once I'd looted the last of the creatures, I returned to kneel beside the senseless elf. Lyrra's breathing had grown deeper and some color seemed to have returned to her cheeks, but she still looked deathly pale. Her status showed her above half health with her Mana pool regenerating now that I'd cleansed the poisons from her blood and removed her from the cocoon.

Lyrra woke suddenly, bolting upright with a startled shriek, her emerald eyes wide in panic. The elven woman's chest heaved as her cry cut off. On the edge of hyperventilating, she locked her gaze on me for a second before looking around the area in confusion.

I snapped my fingers to grab the elf's wandering attention. "Take it easy, you're safe now!"

Lyrra looked back at me, and her breathing slowed as she reined in her emotions, though her brow furrowed when she took in the admittedly ragged state of my armor. "Safe? Who are you? Where are Malyn and Sharya?"

"My name is Hal, and you're sitting right where I found you." I shrugged. "I couldn't tell you anything about your friends."

"There was an Alpha." The elf's voice trailed off as she inhaled sharply and looked around at the nearby cocoons.

"The Alpha's dead."

Lyrra seemed to not hear my words as she climbed shakily to her feet. I stood and offered her a hand, but the elf waved me away before staggering over to kneel beside a nearby bundle of webbing, one that I hadn't disturbed. Greater Observation had returned no result of anything still alive within. A glimmer of metal appeared in her hand as she pulled a small knife about the size of a scalpel from her Inventory. Immediately, she cut away strands from the tightly wound mass.

Tears streamed down Lyrra's face as a few minutes of work revealed the desiccated corpse of a white-haired Movana, so shriveled I couldn't even identify whether the elf had been male or female.

Once Lyrra had cleared the webs away from the remains of her friend, she checked several of the similarly sized cocoons. Soon she found the second of her missing compatriots. Other than having golden hair, the second dead elf lay in a similar condition to the first. Lyrra clearly knew the dead elves well and bowed over the second body, sobbing into the corpse's chest.

The display of grief left me feeling uncomfortable. The elven woman's obvious pain at her losses tugged at me, but I had nothing to offer her besides the healing I'd already given.

I turned away to walk out of the lair, intending to leave the Movana to her grief.

"Wait."

Stopping, I looked back at the kneeling elf and waited for her to continue.

"I have nowhere else to go now. Could a lone Adventurer such as yourself use the support of a healer?"

Sweeping my gaze over the gaunt figure of the listless elf, I considered her offer. "A healer could prove useful. If you're someone who can be trusted. But I'm not exactly alone."

Lyrra nodded, looking slightly confused. "All right. Let me gather what I can, and I'll go with you. It may take me a bit of time to get back to normal, but my Class Skills can remove all of my present afflictions."

She only took a few minutes to strip the equipment from the pair of dead elves and store it in her Inventory. During the process, I noticed that each of the Movana had the emblem of a slender silver tree prominently displayed somewhere on their armor.

As we left the lair, I asked, "What's with the tree symbol?"

Lyrra sneered. "The Silver Saplings Guild, which I just left. If they couldn't be bothered to send someone after us, even when Malyn was related to the Guild Master, then they're not worthy of my allegiance."

I nodded in understanding. Loyalty within an organization, at least any decent organization, needed to flow from the top down as well as from the bottom up.

Lyrra looked at me. "Are you part of a Guild?"

"No. My employment isn't anything so simple as membership in a Guild."

She snorted. "Cryptic."

"You'll see shortly. Just don't start using Class Skills on anyone."

The elf's stomach growled loudly, interrupting the conversation. I pulled a water bottle and a ration bar from my Inventory, passing them over without a word. Lyrra drained half the bottle in one gulp before tearing ravenously into the ration bar. I'd never seen anyone excited about ration bars, but the Movana stuffed it down and drained the rest of the bottle while we walked.

With the Movana's weakened condition, it took far longer to exit the maze of wrecked trains than I'd have liked. Before we got within sight of the train, I used party chat to inform the rest of my party of the situation and warned them that I was bringing back someone new.

Dayena didn't hesitate to launch a quip. *"Picking up strays now?"*

"Don't worry, I'm sure you'll get along great." It was all I could do to keep a straight face and all inflection from my voice. Triunnar and Movana hated each other.

"What did you do?" Suspicion tinged the dark elf's question.

"Killed a few monsters, rescued a damsel in distress. You know, the usual day's work."

"Right."

She didn't believe a word I'd said. This little prank would be *epic*.

The Movana beside me noticed my sudden amusement and gave me a side-eyed glare as she voiced her suspicions. "What is going on?"

"The short version is that I'm working with an organization trying to get the rail system back into working order, while I'm also contracted as a bodyguard and guide for another Adventurer."

"That doesn't really explain why you got all giddy."

"I'm just amused by anticipating my contracted employer's reaction to meeting you."

Lyrra's eyes narrowed. "And who is your employer?"

I grinned.

Despite the elf's continued questions, I remained silent the rest of our journey through the wreckage of derailed trains. We reached the end of the debris field and stepped out to find an assembly waiting, which included the rest of my team. Everyone paused in their discussions and looked over, though their looks swept past me to examine the skeletal Movana.

Breaking the silence, I stepped forward and pointed my thumb back at Lyrra. "Hey, Ismyna, would you be interested in hiring a healer for the Adventuring team?"

The gnome in question blinked at me in surprise before glancing at Dayena, who she'd been conversing with when Lyrra and I appeared. A furious expression twisted Dayena's face as she glowered at the newly arrived Movana. When Lyrra slid behind me, the dark elf shifted her ire to me.

It was a bad idea, but I chuckled anyway.

"You knew how I would react to this," Dayena said.

"Of course," I replied, completely unrepentant. "But we could use the support of a dedicated healer."

Dayena frowned as she considered my words. Finally, the Countess scowled and marched around to the elf behind me, schooling her expression into neutrality. I turned with her advance, just to ensure she didn't lash out at the still-traumatized Movana.

"Countess Dayena Baluisa." She bowed curtly as she introduced herself.

The pale elf hesitated before lowering herself farther than the Countess had. "Lyrra Valjyn."

Following the introductions, Dayena nodded once to Lyrra before marching back to the train.

Ismyna then took Dayena's place. "Well, that was exciting. You're a healer?"

Lyrra nodded, still off balance from the rapid shift in conversation.

"Great!" Ismyna exclaimed. "I'll offer you standard Adventurer contract rates, plus meals and quarters on the train for the duration of our journey."

"That sounds reasonable, but I'm not going to be in condition to assist much until I've healed myself, removing my status afflictions."

"Of course, we'll get you fed up and healthy before expecting you to keep up with this maniac." Ismyna gestured toward me.

Lyrra said, "Hal does seem reckless, even taking on the Alpha monster alone that disabled my entire party."

I scoffed in mock disgust. "I see how it is, Lyrra. I saved your life and got you a job, and this is the thanks I get in return."

Ismyna chuckled, while the hint of a smile crossed the Movana's face for the first time since I'd met her.

"All right, that's enough, Hal," Ismyna said. "I'll have Wrefen set her up with a cabin and put together a meal for her while she gets cleaned up."

When Ismyna beckoned, the conductor joined us, and she explained the situation. Wrefen led the elf back to the train, and Ismyna returned to organizing the work crews in preparation for the undertaking ahead of them. I noticed Nargen off to the side of the gathering, deep in discussion with

Eldri as the two bent over one of the Gimsar's drones, and I walked over to the pair.

"Think the targeting computer and the focusing lenses will be enough?" Eldri asked.

"Yup." Nargen nodded. "The scanning system will map out the wreckage and get you a survey your teams can use to plan out their work."

"What do we need a map for?" I asked as the drone lifted off the ground and hovered between them.

"There's too much debris," Eldri replied. "We can't just launch things out of the way like we've mostly been doing so far. Not and have enough space to clear everything with the city closing in around the tracks. If we want to make a path through, we'll have to be strategic, and that means planning out where we'll put everything we need to move."

Nargen pointed at the drone as it zoomed off in the direction Lyrra and I had come from. "That's what the drone is for. The mods we made will give us a better idea of what needs to be moved and where there's enough space for it."

"Sounds good. Let me know if I can help out."

"Well, about that . . ." Eldri trailed off, and I looked at the gnome, who pulled a shovel from his Inventory. Of course, the tool was sized for a gnome.

I raised an eyebrow at Eldri, nonplussed. After a moment, his serious expression broke as he cackled in amusement.

"Very funny. If you really need me to dig something, I have my own tools." An appropriately human-sized collapsible shovel appeared from my Inventory.

Eldri's amusement turned to puzzlement. "Why do you have a shovel?"

I grinned. "Semper Gumby. It pays to be prepared, and you never know when you might need a foxhole."

The gnome blinked and looked at Nargen.

The dwarf only shrugged back. "You're a maniac, Hal."

"You know, Ismyna said that too."

Eldri sighed. "She's usually right."

Chapter 16

For the next several hours, I shoveled spilled gravel so that it could be moved away from the rails. With my larger shovel, I moved more stone than any two gnomes combined, so my contributions to the track-clearing efforts amounted to the sweat of manual labor, with all of the local monsters now slain. Since the train engine was sitting in place with the rail conversion system shut down, monsters weren't drawn to us, but I kept a wary eye on my minimap for any threats anyway.

The Pharyleri broke out a number of collapsible hovering trays that worked almost like wheelbarrows. The floating trays lowered all the way to the ground to be loaded, and an adjustable energy field extended up from the sides as I loaded more material onto the tray. Once the hover-barrow reached capacity, the tray lifted itself from the ground, and a gnome would guide it off to whatever out-of-the-way place they were dumping the excess gravel.

With my high Constitution and Stamina, I never broke a sweat and soon lost myself in the relatively mindless labor. The repetitive grinding of my shovel digging into the massive gravel mound blended with the working sounds of the gnomes attacking the pile alongside me.

By the end of the day, the work crew I'd joined had managed to remove all of the spilled gravel, along with enough of the other surrounding obstructions, so that the gnomes could start clearing the derailed train cars along the main line, despite the wrecks still cluttering most of the rail yard.

Returning my shovel to Inventory after smelling the heady aroma of grilling meat, I cast Cleanse on myself to remove the chalky gravel dust lodged on every surface of my body and jumpsuit. Then I headed back to the train, where I found that the crew hadn't just been busy clearing the debris from the railyard over the course of the afternoon. Pieces of the wreckage now formed makeshift walls around one side of the train, providing a more defensible perimeter for the outdoor cooking and dining area alongside the parked train.

I jumped onto one wall and greeted Kurak as the minotaur chomped down on grilled corn. He held a handful of the husked cobs in one large palm as he faced away from the cooking area to scan the surrounding terrain for any threats. My mouth watered from the buttery scent of the steamed corn, a smell which overpowered the nearby grilling.

"Anything exciting I should know about?"

The Yerrick placed another corncob into his mouth and crushed it between flat molars, never looking at me. "Your Countess is pissed at you."

"Figured."

The minotaur snorted and devoured another piece of corn in two bites, so I hopped down from the wall and joined the line of crew waiting to eat.

Once I'd snagged a full plate, I barely finished scarfing down the meal before my earpiece pinged and informed me that Ismyna needed me in the dining car. I dropped off my plate in the bin of dirty dishware and headed into the train, then climbed to the upper level and passed through the carriages until I reached the dining car.

Other than passing through during the rare occasions I happened to be onboard the train, I hadn't spent any significant time in the dining car. The upper level consisted of booths on either side of the center aisle that ran along the front and rear thirds of the car, while the centermost portion consisted of a series of counters and elevators down to the kitchen on the lower level.

In the middle of the empty car, I found Ismyna seated in a booth across from Lyrra. Dice perched on the next table behind the gnomish leader, staring over Ismyna's shoulder at the Movana. A holographic map of the area floated between the two women, and I looked it over as I walked toward the pair, ignoring Dice, and leaned against the table across the aisle.

The map displayed the route I'd seen in Borgym's office when negotiating our contract, our updated position as a glowing orange dot along the southern end of Lake Michigan. The entirety of the path behind us was in green.

Summoning a tumbler from my Inventory, I held my free hand above the glass as I channeled Mana into a spell. The Mana shaped itself into a perfect sphere of ice that dropped into the tumbler with a clink. I reached into my Inventory again, this time pulling out a decanter full of amber liquid. I pulled the stopper from the large bottle with my teeth and poured several fingers of whiskey into the tumbler before storing the decanter away. Taking a sip and savoring the smokey flavor of the whiskey as the cool liquid slid across my tongue, I glanced at Lyrra.

The elf, along with the others, watched my actions with fascination. Some of the color was returning to the Movana's deathly pallid skin, though she remained pale and gaunt. "That's an impressive bit of Mana manipulation."

I shrugged and focused on the holographic map. "I like my whiskey with ice sometimes."

Ismyna ignored the byplay and let me observe the map for a few moments. "We have a problem."

I shifted my attention from the map to the gnome, raising an eyebrow and waiting for her to continue.

She sighed and waved at Lyrra. "We'd hoped to broker another trade stop in Chicago, like we did in Cleveland, but your new friend has been

Dungeon World Drifters

updating me on the current conditions in the city. Those conditions have changed even from when we left Pittsburgh."

Lyrra nodded emphatically. "There were four major Galactic organizations holding the City Centers up until a few days before I got stuck in that cocoon. Two of those groups worked together to wipe out the largest before breaking out in fighting amongst themselves. Now those three remaining powers are fighting over the City Centers, as well as a resistance force of local survivors making life miserable for any non-humans that venture out from the enclaves."

The map zoomed in as the elf spoke, highlighting the city in various colors to represent the areas controlled by the various factions. Within each of the territories, darker centers indicated Safe Zones that surrounded the individual City Centers, though I counted fewer than expected for an area with the size and population density of Chicago.

"There should be more Safe Zones by now, shouldn't there?"

Lyrra shook her head. "Several City Centers changed hands multiple times early on. Then the owners started selling them back to the System so they'd have fewer places to defend."

I stared at the elf. "That's insane. They'd be limiting the size of their own territory bonuses."

She shrugged. "It's not a bonus for them if they can't hold the territory."

"And all the poor suckers who bought houses in those Safe Zones just got left to fend for themselves, I bet."

Ismyna sighed and shifted the map's view toward the south, highlighting another section of the route. "It's a war zone, and I'm not going to make agreements with anyone who isn't going to hold the territory stable, so we're going to bypass the city on the freight lines. Maybe if things stabilize, we can look into setting up a branch line into the city proper."

I folded my arms across my chest. "Someone else can take that Quest."

Ismyna rolled her eyes and ignored me, looking back at Lyrra. "Do you need anything more to drink, or are you still hungry?"

The Movana shook her head. "I think I just need actual sleep for now."

"All right, Dice here will take you to the room we've got for you. Take your time recovering and let Hal know when you're feeling ready for more activity."

Lyrra bowed her head. "Thank you, all of you. Not everyone would be willing to offer aid to a stranger."

Ismyna gestured to the map, where the warring territories no longer showed. "We're in this business for ourselves, but there are lines that no one should cross. We're not like them."

The Movana stood and bowed to Ismyna and me, her eyes glistening with unshed tears as she turned away. Dice jumped down from behind Ismyna and brushed past me without a word before guiding the elf toward the sleeper cars.

I watched the two exit the dining car, then turned back to the gnome still sitting at the table. "I'm glad we're avoiding that mess. We don't have the forces for a conflict with anyone that's powerful enough to actually hold a territory."

"That's something we need to avoid at almost any cost."

After throwing back the rest of my drink, I stowed the tumbler in my Inventory before stepping over to the table. Reaching into the map's intangible terrain, I made a pinching motion along the highlighted route on the map to pull the view back then folded my arms. "Once we're clear of Chicago, there aren't really any major cities left along the route until we reach Denver."

Ismyna stabbed her finger down at a thick blue line that ran from the top of the image to the bottom, the view zooming back in on the place she'd touched. "Cities, no. That's our next major obstacle."

"Do we know anything about the bridge and whether it's still intact?"

Ismyna pulled her arm from the map and leaned back in the booth. "It was when we bought the route information from the Shop."

"I hope that intel is still good. We'll need to be prepared for surprises."

"Not much we can do until we get closer." The Engineer swiped her hand over the tabletop, and the map disappeared, then she looked at me and frowned. "You've been working all day. Go clean up and get some sleep."

I gave the gnome a mock salute. "Sure, boss."

Ismyna shook her head and watched me walk away.

On my way to the forward passenger car, I checked in with the team over party chat. I quickly found out that Ismyna had already rearranged the watch schedule for the night. Our gnomish employer expected me to follow through on her last instructions regarding sleep.

When I reached my assigned car, I stopped by the shower compartment, slipping inside the closet-sized space and locking the door. Divided into two sections, the outer part held a narrow counter and a shelf for personal items with just enough open space to strip down before entering the actual showering area.

Removing my gear and storing everything in Inventory, I got out a bar of soap and stepped into the shower. Somehow, the space felt even more constrained than the antechamber. Setting the temperature settings to a comfortably broiling temperature, I activated the overhead faucet. Hot water cascaded over me like a steamy, tropical rainstorm.

The Cleanse spell worked great for removing the funk, grime, and gore leftover after a day of monster slaying, but a hot shower felt infinitely more satisfying. I'm not saying the System spell wasn't great for day-to-day use—it certainly did wonders for cleaning yourself when you got an accidental mouthful of monster guts—but the magic lacked the tactile sensations that really triggered that relaxed feeling after a long day.

Soaping up and scrubbing down, I snorted at the ridiculousness of my situation while rinsing off in the luxurious downpour. Here I stood contemplating magic spells in the shower of a Mana-powered train. Before the System's arrival, I could never have imagined a life like this. Out of boredom on deployment, I'd once read Heinlein's *Starship Troopers*, but even the technology in that science fiction classic paled to the wonders of the System.

The shower beeped at me all too soon, reminding me that I'd used my daily allocation of the limited supply of hot water. The train's systems recycled and recirculated purified water while pulling in more from the atmosphere, but it had limits.

I changed the control settings on the shower, and warm, dry air circulated through the cylindrical chamber. The swirling air felt like being swaddled in sunshine, drying me like a massive version of those old electric hand-dryers.

Once the air dryer had finished removing the last of the water from my skin, I shut down the apparatus before stepping into the antechamber.

After slipping into a clean set of armored coveralls, I left the compartment and went to my assigned room.

When the interior lights kicked on as I entered and shut the door behind me, I found myself alone in the sleeping compartment. Probably still piqued by my actions, the Countess might avoid me for a while.

After killing the room's lights, I swung myself up into my rack and promptly allowed myself to fall asleep.

I roused briefly when the door slid open and Dayena slipped into the compartment. She sealed the door quietly and slipped into her bed across the room without turning on the light, so I returned to my slumber.

Chapter 17

Waking the next morning to pre-dawn light streaming through the window, I lay in bed for a minute and enjoyed the stillness as I roused to full wakefulness. I eased myself out of the bed, hearing the Countess still snoring quietly in her bunk across the narrow compartment.

I crept out of the room and headed to the dining car, where a portion of the crew ate breakfast. I slipped into an empty booth for a short wait until one of the staff stopped to take my order.

"Good morning, Huntsman," the cheery growl greeted me.

I looked up at the Demarcian who towered over the Pharyleri occupants of the dining car.

Sheera Valenstar (Handmaiden Level 46)
HP: 640/640
MP: 780/780

I raised a questioning eyebrow at the felinoid. "Huntsman?"

Sheera looked above my head and read my status before looking down, presumably embarrassed. "Apologies, Adventurer Mason. Hunter is the proper word. I went cheap on my translation pack for your world's languages, and sometimes it gets things wrong."

I shrugged, playing off my concern over the alien's slip of the tongue. "It happens."

This was the first occasion that I'd interacted with the Demarcian, so I really didn't have a baseline for her behavior. Still, with my actual Class masked by On the Hunt, she shouldn't have been able to see through my status without a significantly powerful observation Class Skill.

"What can I get you for breakfast?" she asked.

"Eggs, bacon, and coffee."

"Cream or sugar for the coffee?"

"No, thank you."

"That'll be right up."

The waitress turned away and headed toward the prep station at the center of the dining car, returning shortly with a steaming cup of black coffee. I thanked her as she set the drink on my table before continuing on to get the next table's order.

Sipping the scalding beverage, my resistances allowed me to ignore the heat as I looked out the window. Just barely visible in the overcast sky, the sun peeked over the distant skyline enough to cast dim shadows along the train. Dark clouds billowed on the horizon, and I enjoyed watching the gathering storm clouds roll closer until Sheera delivered a plate filled high with fluffy scrambled eggs and a pile of perfectly crisped, but not burned bacon.

Demolishing the food in minutes, I finished off the cup of coffee. As Sheena cleared away the empty plate and cup, I made sure to thank the waitress.

The dining car began to empty as I left, with most of the Pharyleri heading to the lower level of the train. Morning dew glistened over the surrounding terrain as I stepped down from the train. Humidity hung heavily in the air, matting my hair, and I felt the storm approaching.

Heading forward along the train to the workshop car, I found the gnomes slowly assembling and preparing their tools for the day. Nargen circled the perimeter, sitting astride his finally repaired robodog.

I made my way to the dwarf. "Quiet night?"

Nargen leaned forward to rest his arms on the head of his mechanical pet. "Quiet enough. No problems worth mentioning."

"Good. I'm going to sweep through the railyard before the work crews get going in case anything nasty moved in overnight."

Nargen gave a tired nod, and I left him behind to watch over the gnomes.

Rain fell as I made my way along the tracks. Lone drops splashed against my skin, and I knew that their arrival served as a precursor to the coming storm.

Sometimes I questioned my lack of investment in a decent helmet system, but I usually preferred the boosts provided by leaving my enhanced senses exposed to the open air. Whether sound, smell, or sight, those boosts kept me alive when foes found ways to mask themselves; only rarely could an opponent truly disguise all signs of their presence. For one thing, stealthy, carnivorous monsters typically reeked of terrible breath, and the scent of rotten meat often gave them away.

Maybe I should consider a brimmed hat?

The wind picked up as the sprinkles turned into a steady drizzle. My walk through the railyard wreckage discovered no surprises, and the crews started their work without any issues besides the weather. I joined in as general labor occasionally but continued to patrol the area while the tracks were cleared. Nobody enjoyed working in the downpour that turned the working areas around the railyard into a muddy mess.

A few wandering monsters showed up throughout the day, most easily dispatched. A long-legged jumping turtle shrugged off most of my attacks with its hard shell until I managed to disable two of the creature's legs. Once the monster was rolled over onto its back, it was easily finished off.

With the rail conversion system offline while the train stayed put, the lack of constant monster assaults almost made the mundane work feel like a vacation.

Still, I kept waiting for the other shoe to drop. Lyrra's report on the state of the factions within the city left me uncomfortable with how close we remained to that conflict, and I itched to get moving again.

The work crews finally removed the last of the wreckage late in the afternoon, although the rain continued. Ismyna made the decision to stay put, rather than push on for only a short time before stopping for the night anyways. The hospitality staff arranged feeding the entire crew through the dining car instead of the usual outdoor cookout, avoiding the misery of the deluge outside.

Well-rested from my full night of sleep, I took a double watch and let my team sleep extra as the rest of the crew cleaned all the mud-spattered equipment dirtied by the day's work.

The next morning, the rain finally cleared as the engine prepared to move out at the first light of dawn. The rail conversion system had just started up when a dozen figures moved out to block the tracks.

The group arranged themselves with heavily armored fighters in the front, lighter melee combatants and a handful of ranged support in the ranks behind them. The group consisted of a variety of Galactic species, ranging from a hulking cyclopian in cybernetically enhanced plate armor to a multi-tentacled purple-pink floating jellyfish wearing a gun belt cinched around its ovoid middle.

I jumped down from the back of the engine and walked ahead to meet them, looking them over.

The few humans, pushed to the front of the alien ranks, wore mismatched, hand-me-down gear. With Levels in the upper teens, the humans were clearly the cannon fodder. The Galactics ranged mostly through the twenties and thirties, seemingly relying on their numbers instead of individual strength.

The train's passage had been noted by one of the Chicago groups and they'd sent their B-team to shake us down.

Stopping a dozen paces from the group, I scanned the cyclops who stood at their forefront and folded my arms across my chest.

Prastyl Amnas, Warlord (Hulk Level 37)
HP: 470/470
MP: 280/280

Keeping my eyes fixed on the Warlord, I stared without a word. They clearly intended to force a confrontation, but after seeing how frail they were, I wasn't in any hurry to slaughter them until they did something stupid.

Eventually, several of the group behind the leader began fidgeting and nervously whispering to each other about my uncanny silence.

Prastyl raised the front of his helmet, hinging up to rest on top of his head like a welder's mask, and cleared his throat. "We'll let you pass for one thousand Credits per person and a tithe of consumables."

I didn't respond. Instead, I let the uncomfortable members of the group continue to become more agitated.

The Warlord glanced over his shoulder at the muttering members of the group before returning his attention to me. "Did you hear me?"

"I'll let you all live if you move out of the way now."

"What? No?" Prastyl looked confused. "You're going to pay a toll."

A ripple of thunder cracked as I drew my pistols and triggered a half dozen shots into the cyclops's large eye with Rend activated. The alien's head exploded like a ripe melon, flinging the welding mask helmet up into the air.

My sudden violence without warning startled the group into complete inaction. By the time Prastyl's body crumpled to the ground, my weapons were back in their holsters.

"I'll let the rest of you live if you move out of the way now."

The group scrambled to disappear, leaving their leader's body.

I looted the corpse—at least the armor would be worth selling at my next Shop visit—and the train got underway without any further delay.

Staying well clear of Chicago on the freight lines running south of the city, we headed west across Illinois. The terrain flattened significantly the farther across the state we went. Derelict wind turbines dotted the flatland fields that dominated the western reaches of the former state. Most of the towering structures sat unmoving or missing at least one of their giant blades. Surprisingly, a couple others still seemed to be in operation.

Scouting the pair of operational turbines with a silent and sulking Dayena, we found a small settlement of human survivors defending the towers. Earthen ramparts surrounded the village itself, dug from a ditch that ran the whole way around the colony in an oblong oval with the two turbines near the narrowing ends of the defensive barrier. A couple breaks in the wall allowed foot traffic passage to and from the outpost, with crude bridges spanning the impediment filled with sharpened wooden stakes and shallow muddy water.

Rough gates blocked the open entrances and looked like something constructed from broken turbine blades. Apparently, the hardened polymers used in turbine construction were better than nothing.

A farm sat roughly in the center of the settlement with a two-story house and a couple of barns. Other crudely assembled and more recently built structures surrounded the main house, maximizing the use of the area within the walls.

Ismyna insisted on visiting the settlement after we reported survivors and the existence of a Safe Zone extending around the tiny village of a few hundred people.

It turned out several Mechanics and Farm Engineers had managed to convert the operational turbines into Mana-generating structures. By hooking them into a series of large Mana batteries, they then used that power to run the settlement and establish a Safe Zone. So long as the sequence of jury-rigged devices remained energized around the settlement perimeter, they had a degree of safety.

The Pharyleri ended up generously exchanging desperately needed weapons and supplies for a trade agreement with the outpost's leaders, with orders for harvested monster goods to be fulfilled on the train's return journey.

During the negotiations, Nargen's robodog caroused with the contingent of surprisingly high Leveled farm dogs, much to the delight of the settlement's children. The kids were further enthused by Dayena handing out a collection of Truinnar sweets that put them all into an energetic sugar high.

We ended up spending the night parked outside the settlement and sharing our evening meal with the hungry survivors, who thanked Ismyna and the other gnomes profusely for their hospitality. Afterward, when the locals returned to their homes, I doubled our guard rotations in case anyone returned feeling less than grateful. The night passed uneventfully, despite my paranoia, and the train returned to its journey the following morning with only a few villagers waving farewell as we set off.

The next several days followed the typical routine of killing monsters by day and trading sleep shifts through the night, until we reached the Mississippi River.

The train halted in a forested stretch on the eastern bank of the river that divided the states of Illinois and Iowa. The town of Burlington lay across the river and seemed more functional than most of the abandoned remains of civilization we'd encountered. People moved around the city, the figures far too distant to make out any details, even with my enhanced eyesight.

Of significantly more concern, and the reason for the train halting, were the handful of aliens guarding both sides of the bridge and clearly waiting for us.

Ismyna sighed before hopping down from the train. "Let's go make a deal."

I motioned for Kurak to take point, then I followed with the Pharyleri Engineer. "You think they want to deal?"

"If they didn't, they'd have hit us at the edge of their territory."

"What if they just wanted us to bring everything to them?"

Ismyna shot me a pointed look. "Then we'll move on and find another way."

"Not all that many train bridges over this river."

"Stop creating problems that don't exist."

I chuckled. "It's my job to solve issues. Before they become problems."

Fortunately for the locals, the negotiation didn't become problematic, and we were soon on our way. The city had purchased all the adjoining bridges from the System, which ensured that the Safe Zone protections already in place negated the need for the rail conversion system. Without it, there were no monsters as we made our way over the lengthy span.

The tracks on the far side took a turn to the north before skirting around the edges of the town. Sitting in the engine's control cabin with Ismyna, I took advantage of the rare opportunity to just enjoy the view of the passing houses and signs of burgeoning civilization. I watched the plethora of people and aliens interacting on the streets, going about their daily lives and coexisting peacefully. It felt oddly surreal despite the number of Galactics I'd encountered over the past year.

Every adult on the streets looked strapped, with holsters and sheaths carrying a veritable armory, while dickering with vendors selling everything from meat on a stick to enchanted trinkets. Being similarly armed, none of the aliens seemed to care. There was an equality here, unlike some places I'd been. Better yet, no one was getting eaten. Probably.

For the first time in a while, thoughts of that early Quest came to mind.

The Krym'parke hiding out in Pittsburgh had deserved the destruction wrought upon them by the Gribbari. Very discreetly, I'd checked up on the aftermath of the fighting, but little seemed known about the fates of the losers, just that the casino-owning goblins' reach now extended across the river from the Downtown district all the way up to the University of Pittsburgh.

Part of me hoped that the Krym'parke's pet police officers had found their way free of the fighting, at least the few innocent of what had actually occurred to the prisoners in the Allegheny County Jail.

But I didn't really have much sympathy left these days. Too many dead and too much lost, the world left behind by the System now a place without law in the few places that some semblance of society remained.

Truthfully, that worked for me.

Looking out the windows at the peacefully crowded streets, I knew I didn't belong there. Civilization didn't fit me anymore. Not after fourteen months of surviving in between the pockets of safety that dotted the land.

Sure, hot showers and beds with sheets were nice. I liked those moments of quiet well enough.

But out in the wilds, when survival balanced on the edge of a knife blade or the accuracy of a pistol shot, that's when I felt most alive.

Maybe it was crazy. Okay, it probably was.

I'd fought almost every day since the System arrived. The days I hadn't killed a monster, or a person, could be counted on the fingers of one hand.

Grinding out experience always felt like a drag as I climbed the Levels, but each new Level delivered a rush as I earned those increased attributes and Class Skills.

My leveling had slowed significantly, but I hoped that my current activities would push me further toward that steep Level 46 threshold in the somewhat-distant future. Despite sharing experience with my party, the sheer number of monsters we slaughtered daily pushed me ever closer to that goal.

I'd already figured out a plan to spend all the Class Skill points I'd been saving up. I just had to climb across that barrier.

"Are you just going to sit there all day?"

I ignored Ismyna and folded my arms across my chest before closing my eyes and leaning back against the wall. "We're still in town. The monsters outside it aren't going anywhere."

The gnome blew a raspberry in response.

My break ended all too soon as we departed the settlement and I returned to the business of monster slaying.

It took several weeks to cross the prairies and fields of Iowa and then Kansas, with the daily routine persisting until we were just outside of Denver.

That was when things got weird.

Chapter 18

"I think we have a problem." A breath of steam accompanied the words as they left my mouth and then faded away in the crisp air.

Crouching near the crest of a snow-covered rise, I surveyed the tracks ahead of the train slowly moving through the rolling plain below. As close as we were to the mountains beyond Denver, I'd expected more rugged terrain, but the area near the famed "Mile High City" was more of a high desert prairie instead. Or would have been but for the current weather conditions.

The terrain wasn't the issue. The complication was the snow. Or more accurately, the snow covering the ground. Only wispy partial clouds intermittently floated through the azure sky and permitted the sunshine to gleam off the white covered ground.

Climbing up the rise to scout ahead of the terrain, I'd noticed that the farther I went, the snow seemed increasingly dense to the point that it almost became a solid sheet of ice. My boots dug not a fraction of an inch into the compacted snow.

I pressed a hand onto the white surface, the cold radiating from the icy precipitate. It felt something like the ice I formed from Mana for my drinks, bending the spell and formation of frigid matter to my will. Just a bit off, unnatural and forced. And yet the frozen crystalline formation called to me. Something drew me dangerously as the cold radiated up from my bare palm.

Ismyna's voice came over my earpiece, pulling me from my contemplation. "The snow and ice are getting worse, aren't they?"

It took a moment to find my words. "Yep. I would not have expected snow like this during the summer months."

Silence.

I tapped the earpiece. It had never had problems transmitting before. "Did you hear me?"

Finally, Ismyna released a lengthy sigh, clearly audible. "It's because of the dragon."

"The Frost Dragon in the Rocky Mountains? And what does that have to do with the snow all the way out here?"

"Yes. High Leveled creatures like that often have abilities affecting their environment. In this case, it's getting colder and snowier in the territory the dragon claims. It didn't help that the dragon got pissed off a few months ago after being disturbed by some Adventurers and proceeded to hit Denver in retaliation."

I dug my fingers into the unnatural snow beneath my palm. "That little tidbit got left out of the briefing."

Cold Effect Resisted

The notification jolted me from the conversation, and I pulled my hand out of the snow, turning it over to look at my palm. The skin of my fingertips looked white-ish blue, like hypothermia or frostbite setting in. Over a few seconds, my skin gradually returned to normal. Without my improved resistances to elemental effects, that detrimental reaction most certainly would have been worse.

I tuned back into the conversation as Ismyna was in the middle of an apology about not informing me about the dragon problem. I cut her off. "It's worse than even that. There's a cold damage effect that hits anyone touching the surface of the snow without some kind of insulation."

"What!?" Ismyna exclaimed, prompting me to detail the notification I'd received. When I finished giving the few details I'd gleaned from the

System update, the gnome stayed quiet for several seconds. "That's not good. We thought the curse just affected the parts of the city the dragon froze."

"There's a curse. After the local dragon hit the city. When exactly did you plan on mentioning those little facts?" Though I couldn't see her, I could practically hear the gnome squirming uncomfortably at the acerbic intensity of my tone. I let the silence drag out before I shook my head and dismissed my annoyance, knowing that we needed to move past this if I wanted to complete my Quest. "Your crew can't let this snow touch them."

"We have a way to deal with that problem. We just weren't expecting to need it until we reached the city."

I stood, looking at the slowing train that followed directly behind the track repair drone struggling to push through the buildup of snow and ice on the tracks. "I think you're going to need that solution now."

Ismyna grumbled softly and I chuckled at her Pharyleri curses, still audible over the communicator as the train halted. Sometimes translation packs proved worth every Credit spent.

A side access door slid open on the side of the workshop car, and a recognizable mecha hopped out and landed heavily enough to break through the surface layer of the icy snow. The armor looked like the ones worn by the Pharyleri at the starport, with a reflective canopy protecting the cockpit in the upper torso from which the pilot controlled the suit. Hoses ran from nozzles mounted on the sides of each arm, connecting to a pair of large tanks mounted on the back of the armor. The red tint of the armor and the artistically painted flames wrapping around the arms of the mecha indicated the suit's likely purpose.

The mecha plodded toward the front of the train, plowing through the several inches of snow without any sign of trouble. A crackle of static indicated the mecha pilot joining the communicator link when the suit reached the front of the stopped locomotive. "Need a light?"

Less than amused, Ismyna growled. "Har, hilarious, Eldri. Just fire it up."

Raising the mecha's arms to point along the tracks ahead, a spark briefly flashed at the tip of each nozzle before twin torrents of flame jetted from the arms of the mecha. The dual blazes swept over the rails, steam rising in a cloud from the evaporating snow along the path of the infernos.

Eldri stepped forward as the melting snow revealed the rails. After several steps, his progress slowed. "The ice over the rails is trying to reform. After it melts."

"I'm going to start moving the engine behind you, Eldri," Ismyna said over the communicator. "Hal, keep the monsters off him, since he's going to be standing in the middle of the rails without much between him and the active conversion system."

"On it," I replied, skating down the slick surface of the gentle rise. Mentally activating the party chat link, I updated my team on the situation and ordered Nargen up to the locomotive for added fire support.

A red smudge of multiple overlapping entities appeared on my minimap, alerting me to an approaching pack of monsters as a distant rumble filled the air.

"Incoming," I called over both communication channels. A quick shifting of my feet kicked up a spray of snow as I skidded to a halt, then changed direction and ran toward the new threat. "Nargen, cover Eldri while I thin out this wave."

Keeping my steps light, I bounded over the snow without sinking in and crested the next rise ahead of the converging monsters just in time to get a good visual of the stampeding herd of bison. Even with a quick glance,

I could tell that the mutated bovines significantly outmassed their pre-System relatives. Though the multi-ton creatures sank into the snow drifts with each step of their thundering hooves, it was obvious that the drifts failed to slow the monsters much at all.

More to the point, a herd of overweight bison could do actual damage to the train if they impacted. Derailment suddenly became an overarching concern.

Throwing plasma grenades as fast as I could pull them from my Inventory, I dashed toward the herd. Thunder and superheated air and flame erupted from the grenades just before I managed to reach the leading animals, disrupting the herd's unified wall. My own flesh burnt and crisp, my resistances only reducing the pain marginally, even as steam rose from all around us and choked the air.

Still, the fire allowed me to slip into the herd's midst with my pistols blazing. As I danced through the monsters, my gaze flicked over their Status information, taking in details of what I was fighting.

Mutated Stone Bison (Level 37)
HP: 702/1320

Individually fairly weak, compared to many of the monsters we'd faced on the journey, but the massed herd multiplied their threat.

I kicked off a dying bison in front of me when it tumbled to the ground, both eyes shot through with exploding projectile rounds. In the air, I twisted, my weapons barking at the next bison that came after me just before I landed on its back. A fraction of a second later, I jumped away before the wounded creature could buck me off. Repeating the process, I tore through the front of the stampede, slowing its progress as the beasts tripped and stumbled over their faltering front ranks and the suddenly altered terrain, slick with reforming ice and snow, boiling with rapidly cooling steam. The frustrated animals snorted and grunted, bellowing in pain and confusion.

Holding nothing back and draining my Mana like water, I cast spell after spell alongside the hail of projectiles. Monsters dropped from the accumulated damage, but the herd continued over the rise in a brown tidal wave despite the fury of my attacks.

A part of me wondered if this was what it had been like when the bison had roamed the land in ages past. Hundreds of the creatures, so many that a man might kill and kill and kill and their numbers still seemed never ending.

My strongest spells, mostly ice-based magic, managed to slow the beasts somewhat but failed to reliably penetrate their thick hides. My few weak fire spells caught on their shaggy hair and continued to burn, filling the air with a sulfurous stench as the monsters took damage from the persisting flames.

With my projectile pistols quickly emptied, I returned to my tried-and-true monster-slaying method of cycling through beam pistols from my Inventory as I depleted them one after another. The flashing energy beams only added to the smell of burning flesh and fur which filled the air.

Supporting fire from the rest of my party and the Pharyleri security team tore into the herd as the mass of monsters closed in on the train. Explosions from missiles and grenades blunted the momentum of the animals, while volleys of energy beams poured into the faltering herd.

I saw a few walls of metal and earth, mud and ice form only to be shattered under the press of the monsters. Some of those walls were doubled, tripled, such that they were channeled into the killing fields of my friends and the security team, slowing down the herd's charge. Despite being low on Mana and unable to cast more than a couple spells, I dove deeper into the herd to avoid the friendly fire.

Focusing my attacks on the back of the herd, in an attempt to break them apart, an impact knocked me from the air and drove me into the ground. The brutal landing and ensuing battering from the stampede tore both beam pistols from my grasp as the monsters poured over me. Damage notifications flashed as hooves trampled me, smashing my armor and crushing my left arm despite my best attempts to roll clear of the herd. Broken bones ground together with each movement, shooting spikes of pain along my arm.

My health dropped into the red before I found the clearance to regain my feet. Pushing off with my good hand and ignoring the pain from my trampled arm, I managed to kick myself off the ground.

Upright, I twisted and dodged bison horns as I grabbed a health potion from Inventory and slammed the injector into my side. Fire burned along my mangled arm as the potion's healing fused shattered bone and knitted mutilated flesh. The arm went numb a moment later, allowing me to focus on something besides the pain.

Like the deep swell of dread in my stomach, the heartbeat that had sped up, and the choking taste of vomit and blood in the back of my throat.

Fear Effect Resisted

A deafening bellow threatened to drive me back to the ground, but I bounced off the side of a running bison, barely avoiding the hoof that the beast reflexively kicked at me. I dismissed the notification as I continued evading the enraged bison around me. Turning toward the sound, I found the source of both the cry and the negative status effect.

Greater Plains Stone Bison Alpha (Level 76)

HP: 12,460/12,680

I read the status above the massive monster twice to ensure I'd actually read it correctly. The beast possessed an incredible amount of health, of which very little appeared missing. An angry crimson aura surrounded the Alpha, linking it to the nearby bison as the bull drew strength from the herd and strengthened them in return.

"The herd Alpha's here, could use some help if anyone is free." I sent over the party chat as I injected a health regeneration potion booster. A quick glance at my minimap showed a tide of red dots surrounding this side of the train, so I figured my chances of assistance were minimal.

Nargen replied first. *"Tied up keeping these beasties off Eldri, though they seem to be avoiding the fire."*

"The leading edges of the herd are battering themselves against the train. Kurak and I are trying to thin them out."

I supposed I should be thankful Dayena had decided I was worth speaking with again, but things were too serious to razz her about it.

"Understood. It's boosting the herd, so I'll do what I can to draw it away."

The Alpha's eyes flashed as it saw me in the midst of the herd, and the monstrous beast turned toward me. The huge creature, at least the size of a cement-mixer, pawed the ground and snorted. Clouds of steam rushed from nostrils the size of my fist and swirled around the Alpha when it charged forward.

I ran, pulling a new beam pistol from my Inventory as I led the Alpha away from the train.

The ground shook violently from the pounding hooves of the Alpha only strides behind me. With every step, I fought to keep moving as the ground heaved unsteadily. I felt the System tearing at me, Mana straining, as Efficient Trail struggled to ease my path. The Class Skill worked in direct opposition to the Alpha's ability to destabilize the snow-covered earth.

I fired my beam pistol blindly over my shoulder without bothering to aim. I couldn't afford to look back, not with the feel of the Alpha's scalding breath on my neck. If this thing caught me, I'd be smeared to paste in an instant.

Anyway, the damn thing was the size of a minibus. If I missed at this range, I should just hang up my pistols.

Every ounce of my concentration was on my next footstep as I pushed to sprint ever faster. It wasn't enough. I could tell that instinctively. I threw myself to the side a moment later, my feet caught by the monster smashing into them. I flipped through the air, smashing into the ground and plowing through snow.

Good news. The big bastard was slow at cornering.

Bad news... my feet ached.

I bounced back to my feet within seconds, throwing myself into a run as I stored my beam pistol. No more shooting at it, not right now as I ran at a new angle. As the monster started to near me, I shuffled through my Inventory, finding a few grenades that might be of use.

Phareesi Web Tanglers, to grip at legs and terrain and hold monsters still. Not as useful when the terrain was snow, but it caught at legs and fur anyway and forced the Alpha to stumble.

Absolute Zero Space Returners, to create zones of absolute cold for a moment. Freezing muscles, snow into planes of gripping absolute zero that tore at skin and hooves and sent bodies shuddering.

Lightning in a Bottle grenades, for electric stun effects.

All of them, thrown over the shoulder to impact and debuff the damn Alpha.

Eventually, the hot breath on the back of my neck faded slightly, Efficient Trail providing enough of an edge to gradually pull me away from my pursuer.

A tingle along my injured arm preceded the sensation of pins-and-needles as the potion-induced numbness wore away. I flexed my hand as my arms pumped to ensure the return of my fine motor control, then I grabbed more grenades from Inventory and chucked them behind me.

Enough buying time. Time to do some damage.

Plasma explosions far too close for comfort seared my back, and I hissed in pain as portions of my armor melted, though the Alpha's angry bellows drowned out my own exclamation.

I kept running and threw more grenades, adding in the occasional energy beam from my pistol. Even with my high Constitution, my legs burned from the exertion. Sensing the Alpha beginning to flag, I slowed when I reached the crest of the next rise and turned to fire at the beast.

Blood dropped from the Alpha's nostrils, and most of the shaggy hide around the monster's head and shoulders appeared charred from my attacks. Most importantly though, the strength of the red-tinged aura surrounding it looked significantly weaker now that I'd drawn the monster away from its herd.

Stopping to fire steadily turned out to have been a mistake.

One moment, the monster stood at the base of the rise. The next, the Alpha streaked through the spot where I'd been, and its ability sent me flying.

The shock of collision caved in my chest like a paper bag and crushed my ribcage. Somehow, I remained conscious by the slimmest margin, despite my inability to breathe or pump blood through my body with my organs pulverized. Ignoring the litany of notifications scrolling through my sight, I fought the overwhelming instinct to gasp for air and pushed against the darkness crowding the edges of my vision. Summoning another injector, I deployed the elixir directly into the cavity in my chest.

A moment later, gravity returned my soaring body to the earth, and I smashed through a copse of pine trees. The dense branches slowed my descent just enough that my impact with the ground failed to deplete the last remaining sliver of my health.

When I tumbled and skidded to a stop at last, pain racked my body. The extent of the damage prevented the elixir from dulling much of my agony. Staring at the cloudy blue sky, I found myself unable to move my limbs. I couldn't help but wonder if the Alpha had been baiting me, playing at being more injured and slower than it was just to set up that last attack.

Turning my head, I spat out a mouthful of viscera and bone shards. The coppery tang of blood remained thick on my tongue, even as bone and organs twitched in my chest. Faint vibrations beneath me indicated the ponderous approach of the Alpha, slowed after its instant charge ability. It was still some ways off, but no strength remained in my limbs as my body struggled to rebuild itself.

Coughing racked my torso as my lungs reformed, forcing me to spit out yet more blood and chunks of shredded flesh when my body rejected the organic matter after finding it in places it shouldn't be.

Despite the pain and heaving coughs, I focused on what I could still do. A couple spells came to mind, since the length of the fight had allowed even my abysmal Mana regeneration to partially refill my pool. Casting a round of healing spells on myself, the rest of my options looked limited as I waited for the spells to refresh. My chest pushed and pulled itself back together, my natural regeneration boosted by the healing potions, spells, and the properties of my Resilient Nature passive Class Skill.

My survival now became a race between my body repairing itself and the approaching Alpha. I closed my eyes and focused on reaching out with my senses to pinpoint the monster's position, but another sound interrupted my search.

"Well, we can't have you lying down on the job now, can we?"

Footsteps crunched on the snow after the feminine voice spoke up. I opened my eyes and Lyrra stepped into my field of vision. The Movana wore a combat jumpsuit shrouded in shadows despite the abundant daylight and carried a beam rifle slung across her chest. The Combat Medicae held her palm over my chest. A faint amber glow surrounded her hand, and a trickle of energy flowed down to wrap around my torso. Warmth radiated through my body, and I felt my energy rising as my wounds healed even faster.

The tremors beneath me grew, indicating that time grew short. I gingerly sat up and pushed myself up to my feet, the movement making me sway as pain spiked through me. I couldn't even imagine what it would feel like without my Resistances dulling everything. Everything in my torso ached, but I was functional despite the uncomfortable sensation.

I looked around for my beam pistol but couldn't find it. "Thanks. I was almost out of time."

Lyrra smiled wryly. "Just returning the favor."

Pulling two more energy pistols from Inventory, I stashed them in my empty underarm holsters before reloading my depleted projectile weapons. I glanced at Lyrra. "Stay on the move, especially if it turns toward you."

"Charge ability. I saw." She smirked, pulling her rifle tight to her shoulder.

"Right." I turned back to face the Alpha. "Let's finish this thing off."

244

Splitting away from the elf, I ran toward the clump of pine trees through which I'd been thrown. The oncoming Alpha shouldered aside a pair of the smaller trees and exploded through one of the mid-sized trunks. Squeezing off several beam shots, I gauged the monster's health as still well above two-thirds full.

Time for that to change.

With my health back up around the same percentage, and climbing thanks to Lyrra's healing abilities, I reentered the fight in better shape than I'd been when I initially pulled the monster away from the train.

The red glow encompassing the monster appeared weaker with the Alpha no longer surrounded by its herd. It probably helped that some of those herd members were also dead. At least everyone else should be having an easier time of things.

Or so I hoped.

Circling the few large trees within the grove, I took potshots at the Alpha while using the cover to break up the sightlines between us. The trees hampered the monster's movement and provided opportunity for flanking attacks.

Heavier rifle beams sniped at the beast whenever it turned away from Lyrra, though the elf wisely seemed to relocate in between shots and kept out of sight whenever the creature searched for her.

Twice more, the massive beast attempted the charge ability but never landed a clean hit. Without the boosts strengthening the bull and increasing its speed, I managed to mostly dodge the assaults. Even the grazing impacts of those near-misses knocked me into the air, doing plenty of damage. Fortunately, between dodging the worst of the attacks and the ranged healing provided by Lyrra, the fight with the Alpha swung in my favor.

I only lost one more beam pistol along the way, though I drained a half dozen others and significantly dented my stockpiles of fragmentation and plasma grenades, along with the more exotic ones, before the Alpha finally collapsed.

"Are you still alive out there, Hal?" Dayena asked through party chat.

I stood from looting the freshly killed monster, depositing the hide, horns, sinew, and a collection of bones into my Inventory. Definitely dumping the entire body into Meat Locker. I could see it being good eating. Bison wasn't something I'd ever eaten regularly, but I'd always enjoyed the subtle earthy flavor and tenderness of the lean meat.

"Alpha's down and we're about to head back. How are things there?"

"Mopping up the last of the herd. They've broken off and leaving at last. No losses here."

"Copy, see you shortly."

A casting of Cleanse on myself removed the disgusting bodily detritus and wastes that had leaked from my innards after all the damage I'd taken from the Alpha.

Jogging back to the train only took a few minutes for Lyrra and me, though we weren't in much of a hurry, with the threat of imminent danger eliminated and my minimap clear of any threatening red dots not running away.

For now, at least.

The nimble Movana matched my pace surprisingly well, despite my movement Skill, so it seemed likely that the Medicae possessed movement abilities of her own.

When we reached the battlefield, dead bison lay all around the tracks in the wake of the slowly moving train, which had never stopped during the frenetic battle. The scene reminded me of those haunting images from the history of the American West, the black-and-white pictures showing the aftermath of hunters slaughtering thousands of bison at a time from the safety of a train—only to leave the carcasses to rot, untouched and unused.

We would not do the same, not when the System provided loot. Lyrra headed on after the train, but I turned toward the fallen bison. Walking through the remains, I looted whatever I could and stored a few of the more intact buffalo into Meat Locker for the next crew dinner.

Hopefully, that feast would occur in Denver later this evening, as a celebration for finishing the first leg of the journey. I certainly looked forward to completing the first stage of my Quest. The experience gained should push me close to that coveted next Level.

Turning away from looting the last of the bison, I doubted whether we'd make it into Denver before dark. The speed of the train as it continued away from the battlefield failed to fill me with much confidence.

I caught up easily with the locomotive. Kurak stood guard on the roof of the rear boxcar and waved languidly as I passed his post. Continuing forward, I noted dents in numerous places along the side armor of the cars, the self-repairing defenses working to fill in gouges left by the bison horns.

When I reached the front of the train, I found Nargen keeping watch on top of the track repair drone, his own drones twisting through the air above him. The roar of Eldri's twin flamethrowers just ahead of him suppressed verbal communication, so I took advantage of party chat. *"Any problems?"*

Nargen waggled a hand in a so-so motion. *"Got a bit exciting when the herd tried to swing in front of the train, but they really didn't like Eldri's flamethrower pointed their way."*

"No, I'd imagine not."

"I'll say this though, those gnomes sure put out some firepower. They really stepped up in this final stretch." The dour Gimsar almost sounded appreciative.

"I'm glad they proved useful. I'll be sure to let them know." If I didn't end up punching Dice in his smug Pharyleri face. I'd continued avoiding the head of the internal security team whenever I could get away with it. *"I'm going to scout ahead and see if any more surprises are waiting for us. Keep an eye on Eldri."*

"Got it, boss." Nargen saluted casually.

An easy jog left the train behind without much effort.

The icy expanse of Barr Lake passed by without any surprises, though the sight of a lake frozen solid in the middle of summer could be considered a surprise in itself.

"Is it just me or have we been seeing fewer monsters since we hit this freak snow?" Dayena asked over party chat.

"It's not just you," I replied.

I'd expected the attacks to pick up again after we'd finished off the bison herd, though the slower pace of the train should also mean more time between encounters. Instead, nothing moved over the surprisingly flat terrain as I scanned the surroundings with my vision and System-aided senses of Greater Observation.

Glancing back toward the train far behind, I had no trouble picking out the engine, preceded by the fiery glare of Eldri's flamethrower. The glinting orange flames vividly marked the train's progress, which seemed absurdly slow compared to the weeks of travel so far.

With the rails sticking up through the snow to guide my path, I continued on while waiting for the rest of the team to alert me to the next threat.

Chapter 19

After jogging several miles, those threats had yet to appear, and the only noticeable change was the increased thickness of the snow covering the ground. The temperature felt just above freezing with the sun bearing down from overhead, but even the thinnest spots of snow cover refused to consider melting.

When the terrain opened up into gently rolling prairie without a tree in sight at the edges of the Rocky Mountain Arsenal, I moved over to run parallel to the train tracks on Highway 2. Devoid of any building or signs of civilization as far as I could see, the National Wildlife Refuge lay several miles to the northeast of downtown Denver.

Continuing along the highway, glinting structures soon rose above the snowy expanse in the distance. Futuristic architecture, the layout and form bearing some resemblance to the buildings of the Pittsburgh starport, they stretched out away from the railroad tracks with only a long, low-profile warehouse nestled up against the tracks themselves. Where the skies of the Pittsburgh starport bustled with activity, only the frigid wind and an eerie silence filled the air here.

From the first sight, something felt very off.

Growing closer, I found that the reflective sheen over the buildings was not due to their material construction. Instead, the shimmering tint covering every single structure resulted from their complete encasement within a smooth coating of translucent, blue-tinged ice.

Buildings, starships, and people still standing upright. All frozen solid.

The wrath of a dragon manifested in destructive permanence.

When Ismyna mentioned that the dragon had attacked the city, this was what she'd meant. The attempt to duplicate the success of the Pittsburgh starport here, swatted down by an all-too-powerful monster like I might step on an ant.

For a second, I felt small. Tiny, in the face of a creature whose might I could barely envision. It was the same feeling you'd get on a clear, moonless night staring up at the vastness of the Milky Way, knowing how inconsequential you really were.

Except this feeling had a few more fangs.

Gazing out over the uncanny vista, I saw several warehouse-sized bulk freighters and a half dozen smaller craft. Part of me wondered why no one was attempting to recover the ships until I realized that they would need to be flown out. No one without focused piloting Skills, and probably a bunch of stealth abilities, would evade the pissed off dragon who'd already devastated this place once. I doubted any remaining locals would look forward to a second visit from the creature.

Tapping the earpiece, I connected to Ismyna. "I found what's left of the starport."

The gnome sighed. "A damn shame. A bunch of Adventurers who should have known better got thousands killed."

"What exactly did they do?"

"Nobody really knows. Everyone affiliated with the group is a popsicle now, so it's not like we could ask anyone."

"You couldn't buy it from the Shop?"

Ismyna snorted. "Buying information about dragons? Come on. There are better ways to spend a fortune."

"I can't say I've ever tried." Though my System research budget tended to go for other formerly mythical creatures out of folklore instead of dragons.

"Well, I'll save you some Credits. Don't bother asking the Shop. Some knowledge isn't worth the cost."

"I understand and appreciate the warning. Are we doing anything about this starport or are we continuing on?"

Ismyna seemed to debate the question briefly. "We'll continue on. It's less than ten miles from there to the new transportation hub out of the old Union Station."

"I'll hold up here until you catch up. It seems the dragon's effects are scaring any nearby monsters from this area, but I'd rather be nearby if I'm wrong about that."

"Sounds good. See you shortly, Hal."

The transmission cut with a click, and I found myself alone facing the dragon's handiwork. A monster that powerful had to be over Level 100, if not higher.

I searched the once-living humanoid shapes frozen in the ice. Could a Master Class survive that fight? Or would it take a Heroic? A Legendary?

How many Levels did the dragon gain from the lives it ended here?

I'd gained almost forty Levels in about fifteen months since Earth's initiation into the System. Granted, Dungeon Worlds encouraged fast growth, but my progress seemed incredible by the standards of Galactic society, from what I'd picked up. Even then, my progress had slowed the higher my Level climbed. Earning experience grew increasingly harder.

Quests and bounties helped, when I could get them. Of the two, bounty work occurred more frequently and was much easier to find, though the rewards tended to be less than the larger Quest payouts.

I couldn't complain, not when the Countess paid me a significant salary to drag her along and fight alongside her. Despite the regularity with which she kicked my ass in training, I'd noticed the narrowing of the gap between us as my Levels climbed. If not for the full fifty Levels of her Basic Class that she'd earned well before arriving on Earth, my unique Advanced Class would have let me pull ahead of her in raw attributes alone.

A long road lay before me, but I was still fighting.

That was the key. Fighting on. Pushing myself. Gaining experience—both the System measured type, and the kind that couldn't be measured, only lived.

Something within the dead starport called to me and I felt the need to investigate the frozen expanse further once I completed my escort.

Rather than dwell on the mystery and waiting for the train to catch up, I summoned a case of projectile ammunition from my Inventory and held it awkwardly under one arm as I pulled out empty pistol magazines and reloaded them. Keeping alert to my surroundings while I worked, I managed to reload almost a dozen of the empty magazine cylinders before I emptied the ammo can. Then I switched to reloading the standard magazines for my more traditional projectile pistols, enjoying the fact that my thumb never got sore reloading as I pushed round after round into the double-stacked mags. Improved physical resistances meant things like blisters, splinters, and papercuts never happened as part of daily life.

Now, if those things were somehow a part of a Class Skill, all bets were off. The idea of a combat paper pusher amused me. There had to be some kind of Class out there dishing out death by papercut.

The roaring flamethrower announced the train's arrival and I stowed away a second ammo case, now half-empty, before Eldri passed. Another of the armored suits walked alongside Eldri, each focusing their flamethrowers on a single rail. Now, forward progress was at something barely faster than a normal walk. The repair drone fixed a broken weld right behind the suits while Nargen still stood on top of the rolling platform.

A third suit tromped up behind the leading pair and swapped out with Eldri. The gnome stepped to the side of the tracks, waited for the train to catch up, then swung the armor up into an open door along the flank of the workshop car. I jumped after him and watched as the suit parked in a framework that slid out of the workshop wall. Mechanisms on the rear of the framework swapped out the armored fuel tanks on the back of the suit.

"Fuel tanks were getting low," Eldri explained as the gnome climbed out of the mecha's cockpit. "We'll start rotating through the three suits to keep the rails clear and heated enough for the conversion system to stabilize them through the curse."

I rapped my knuckles against the armor on one arm of the mecha. "I didn't realize you'd brought any of these along. What other toys are you hiding?"

"I guess you'll just have to wait to see if we need them." The Pharyleri grinned up at me.

Shaking my head in mock disgust, I hopped down from the workshop's open door, easily managing the transition with the train's snail-like pace.

The strength of the snow clinging to the rails faded gradually after we left the silent starport behind, but the signs of damage continued as the train rolled into Commerce City. Though the weakening ice hastened our progress, the glaze still coated the mobile homes and single-story ranch houses along the outskirts of town. The lack of a Safe Zone notification only emphasized the devastation as we continued farther into the Denver metropolitan area.

Sitting on the roof of the locomotive, I finally got the expected notification after we passed under Interstate 70.

You Have Entered a Safe Zone (City of Denver)

Mana flows in this area are stabilized. No monster spawning will happen.

This Safe Space includes:

City Centers

City Dungeon

Marketplaces

The Shop

Training Facility

Transportation Hub

More...

Inside, I breathed a sigh of relief as the rail conversion system powered down. With the rails inside the Safe Zone already owned by the locals, the System maintained the tracks without need for further modifications. Though there still remained some risk of attack from human or Galactic forces, the Safe Zone meant that we'd passed beyond the reach of monsters for this leg of the journey and that my escort Quest neared completion.

"Hey, Hal," Ismyna shouted up to me from an open window set in the side of the locomotive, though her words still came through the communicator in my ear. "We're going to use a wye to change the orientation of the train and then reverse to backup into Union Station."

I hopped to my feet. "I'll head to the rear of the train and make sure you don't drive us into anything."

"Why would you say that when you know I can see everything on the tracks in both directions from here?" Ismyna asked. "I'm tempted to slam the emergency brakes to make you fall on your face."

Chuckling, I jumped from the roof of the engine to the top of the workshop car. "You really think that if you slammed the brakes, I would be the one falling?"

The Engineer declined to respond, leaving a smirk on my face as I worked my way along the rooftops of the other cars. I reached the end of the last supply car as the locomotive crossed over the South Platte River. An automatic switching unit just beyond shifted the train to a track that curved sharply to guide us onto a new track that led to the northeast. Once the train's entire length crossed fully onto the new track, Ismyna slowed to a halt before reversing directions and backing the train to head southwest once again.

After that, it only took a few more minutes until the train gradually reduced speed before coming to a stop at the platform outside Denver's Union Station. With a final jerk, the train reached the end of its journey, and a series of notifications demanded my attention.

Quest Completed!

You have successfully escorted the Pistongrinder Express to Denver's Union Station, completing the objective of connecting the rail transitway.

10,000 Credits and 10,000 XP Awarded.

Bonus objective completed: All crew members survived.

Additional 5,000 Credits and 5,000 XP Awarded.

Quest Received - The Pistongrinder Express II

Provide combat support against monsters and other hostile forces as you escort the crew and passengers of the fully loaded Pistongrinder Express cargo and passenger train to its destination at the Pittsburgh Starport.

Reward: Variable depending on the condition of the locomotive, freight transported, and surviving crew.

Level Up!

You have reached Level 40 as a Relentless Huntsman. Stat Points automatically distributed. You have 2 Free Attributes and 8 Class Skill Points to distribute.

Some of the updates in the follow-on Quest concerned me but couldn't stop the sense of satisfaction filling me.

Though I planned to continue hoarding the Class Skill Points, a voice interrupted me before I could assign any of the Free Attributes.

"Yo, Hal," Ismyna's voice echoed from my earpiece. "Can you meet me at the control cabin? We've got to meet with the local Clan leadership, and I'd appreciate some muscle."

"Sure, as long as there isn't a problem with that muscle being non-Pharyleri," I replied. "I'll bring Kurak along."

"That would be perfect." Ismyna chuckled darkly. "Mother wanted me to make the point that our allied clan can't keep expecting to do things without allies of their own. Bringing you and Kurak will help."

After the Engineer ended the communication, I sighed. First, I'd ended up involved in Truinnar politics and now drama between the Pharyleri Clans. Hopefully, this meeting wouldn't turn out to affect my life as drastically as my current employment situation.

I grabbed the Yerrick on my way back through the train, pausing in my cabin long enough to change into my last fresh and completely intact armored jumpsuit. The rest of the suits remaining in my Inventory looked rather ragged, despite my attempted repairs with Quality Over Quantity. The Class Skill worked to get them functional again after being torn to shreds, but they never seemed to hold up quite as well. Not like brand new, freshly created armor or gear repaired by a true crafter.

In short, I desperately needed another trip to the Shop to resupply, but that would wait until I managed some free time here in town.

Kurak and I climbed down the stairs to the lower level of my sleeper car and left out the open door. Stopping for a moment, I looked around and appreciated the station's modern construction. The cement platform outside the train was one of four extensions that divided three sets of tracks, all of which ended here at the station. A white multi-layered canopy covered most of the platform area, though an oval-shaped opening in the center of the cover gave a clear view of the sky above.

Kurak hadn't stopped to look around, so I hurried after him. When we reached the front of the train, Ismyna waited in a freshly pressed uniform with a pair of crew members whose names I'd never learned. Along with the trio in the olive-green Pistongrinder uniforms, two more Pharyleri-sized figures stood stoically a short distance away.

The two newcomers wore full-plate armor with thick panels of a bronze material that covered them from head to toe, with articulation points in the powered suits displaying pistons and gears that assisted the wearer's movements. Heatlines wavered from glowing energy panels and exhaust pipes emitted hissing steam from the backs of the suits, even with the pair standing entirely still.

A quick scan of the armored guards showed the locals weren't pushovers, despite the signs of destruction evidenced on the northern edges of the city.

Steamspanner Preserver (Level 39)
HP: 1890/1890
MP: 2140/2140

Steamspanner Sentinel (Level 41)

HP: 2260/2260

MP: 2210/2210

The stern expression on Ismyna's face conveyed the seriousness of the situation. I nodded respectfully to the Engineer before she turned to the bronze-armored guards. "We're ready to see the Clan Council now."

The blank faces of the full plate helmets blocked any vision of the wearers' expressions, but the delay in the response highlighted the noticeable hesitation.

Finally, the Sentinel spoke, a heavily modulated voice transmitted through the armor's faceplate. "Your presence does not require armed guards."

"My escorts are directed through Quest and contract to protect me," Ismyna responded and directed a pointed stare toward the pair of armored figures. "They will go wherever I do. Your Council has nothing to fear so long as they abide by the Clan Accords."

Several awkward seconds passed as we all stood there.

"Very well. Follow us." The pair of guards turned sharply and marched down the platform.

Ismyna followed with her assistants just behind her on either side. I glanced at Kurak, who shrugged, and we fell in at the rear of the odd procession.

The guards led us around the platform and over toward the historic Union Station building. Constructed of carved granite and terracotta, the rectangular structure highlighted the Renaissance Revival and Beaux Arts architectural styles of the early 1900s. Stone blocks composed the majority of the structure, with decorative carvings worked into the recesses set in the upper levels of the building on either end of the central portion of the building. Arches above large paned window panels were lit from the inside and stood out in the evening gloom. Double doors were set in decorative wooden panel entryways.

Atop the building, a lit neon sign proclaimed, "Union Station—Travel by Train" in red letters. The sign appeared as though it had aged in the intervening period after the System, as if surviving decades of weather.

Additional guards, in the same powered-plate armor as our escorts, were stationed at each of the entrances, but I noticed that most only held Basic Classes. Of those, all of them were significantly lower Leveled.

Our escort led the way through double doors held open by a pair of low-Level armored guards and into the building. The interior held benches near the doors, but the floorplan opened up into a more casual lounge beyond. Long tables with seating, couches and easy chairs were placed in a mirrored arrangement on either side of a slightly raised area with a pair of long shuffleboard tables. As per Galactic conventions, the furniture was a scattering of sizes, meant to fit everything from a four-foot-tall Pharyleri to a towering Yerrick. There were even backless chairs with divots meant for, I assumed, tailed creatures.

No nannite or metaform furniture though. That kind of luxury was only found in a select few places. We were on a Dungeon World, after all.

Flicking my gaze away from furniture and people, I took in the rest of the building. Chandeliers hung from the stark white ceiling that arched three stories above the square floor of the lounge. Balconies ran along two opposite sides of the upper levels, with a second-floor mezzanine above the Terminal Bar open to the ceiling on the third side.

Scents of cooking and cooked burgers wafted from that bar, competing with the varied aromas coming from the multiple eateries around the ground floor. I picked out curries and barbecue and some kind of fish.

I had to admit, my mouth watered.

A low murmur of conversations in numerous languages filled the lounge from the species comfortably relaxing in the area. Picking out the languages I recognized distracted me from my growling stomach. Listening carefully, I heard Truinnar, Pharyleri, Movana, Hakarta, and Gimsar, though there were several others, and I made a mental note to purchase a few more language packs at my next Shop visit. Everyone spoke Galactic, but it didn't mean they were comfortable doing so.

Scanning the crowd, I observed the lack of concern shown by the lounge occupants viewing our passage, so it seemed that guards escorting outsiders was an everyday occurrence here.

Our armored guides led us past a front desk that still bore the signage of the Crawford Hotel, now apparently repurposed as the local Pharyleri Clan headquarters. Passing through a lounge and down a hall, the guards posted themselves outside an ornate set of doors and directed us within.

A long boardroom table, with several gnomes seated at one end, filled most of the room. A young Pharyleri with a neon blue mohawk sat at the head of the table and leaned back as we walked into the room, folding his arms across his chest, his fingers fidgeting nervously over his uniformed sleeves.

Clan Leader Piklyn Steamspanner (Loadmaster Level 38)

_HP: 1230/1230_

_MP: 1540/1540_

"Piklyn?" Ismyna questioned. "What happened to—oh hells. Your father would have been at the starport."

The low Level and relative youth of the gnome made sense suddenly, along with the other similarly young Pharyleri in the apparent Clan Council meeting. With the dragon wiping out the entirety of the Clan leadership, the Pharyleri before us represented the new leadership. Suddenly, I had visions of fresh-out-of-officer-training lieutenants running the show and I had to do my best to hide a wince.

The young gnome looked at the table for a moment, clearly collecting himself before he met Ismyna's gaze. The blue-haired gnome cleared his throat before speaking with a voice cracking with restrained emotion. "Nobody made it out once the attack started."

Ismyna started toward the gnome. "I'm so sorry, Piklyn."

"Sentiment can wait. We need to talk about the details of our trade arrangement." Piklyn held up a hand, stopping Ismyna before she took more than a couple steps, and gestured to the open seats at the table. "My father neglected the details and the contract was never finalized, so I need to know what he agreed to, or we'll have to renegotiate the entire deal." The younger gnome sighed and smiled weakly. "I realize that this places me in a weak negotiating position, but I'm trusting in the friendship of our youth that you won't take advantage of us too badly."

Ismyna walked to the end of the table opposite Piklyn and took a seat in one of the well-cushioned executive chairs. Kurak and I exchanged a wordless glance, after which the hulking minotaur posted himself against the wall at Ismyna's back as an unsubtle reminder of the forces she brought in support.

One of the more junior-looking gnomes hurried over to Ismyna. "Would you like kipatchya?"

At Ismyna's assent, the assistant prepared a cup of the steaming beverage from a small cart at the side of the room. I decided looking around outside the meeting would be a better idea than sitting through the negotiations. Though I wanted nothing more than to find a quiet corner to assign my new Attribute points, finding more information about the locals could prove useful.

When I stepped backward out of the room, the guards peered at me through their expressionless helmets for a long moment before they shut the boardroom doors. Once they'd sealed the doors, the guards returned to the position of attention with their hands at their sides.

The smooth faceplates of the guards' helmets prevented me from having any idea of their expression, and they seemed determined to ignore my presence. Since they clearly weren't interested in a conversation, I wandered back toward the entryway and the front desk we'd passed on the way into the hotel.

A pair of human attendants, a man and woman wearing white button-down shirts with pressed collars and creased black slacks, stood behind the desk. The two masked their boredom with professional smiles, though a hint of confusion peeked through their polite facades at my approach from within the hotel.

"Can I help you, sir?" the shorter woman with blond hair pulled back in a ponytail asked.

"Just looking around and getting a feel for the place with my boss in a meeting," I replied, leaning against the counter and lowering my voice. "I'm surprised to see humans working here, since it looks like the gnomes have taken over."

The woman sighed. "Things have been hectic since the dragon attack. We do our jobs and keep our heads down. I can't complain about still getting paid."

She glanced at her coworker, but the stocky man pressed his lips together in disapproval. He gave his head a slight shake as if wanting to speak but didn't trust himself to do so. The man's black hair was parted on one side, neatly groomed like his close-trimmed beard.

"I'm Hal. I came in on the train." I extended my hand to the woman across the desk, and she gave it a tentative shake.

"Cara. Front Desk Clerk," the woman replied automatically, then her eyes grew wide as she processed my words. "You came in on the train? We'd heard that one was coming in, but I could hardly believe it even though the gnomes spent a bunch of Credit and work fixing up the place. There hasn't been a train through Union Station since the Apocalypse It's insanely dangerous outside the Safe Zones. I can't imagine how anyone survives out there."

I raised an eyebrow, slightly taken back by her thoughts about people living outside Safe Zones. "You'd be surprised. Lots of people are thriving out there. Combat-focused Classes and the proper gear make all the difference."

"I'm a clerk," Cara replied with a disdainful sniff. "That's about as far from combat as it gets, and I like it that way."

"You haven't been outside the city?"

"Not since the dragon showed up." Cara shuddered. "The fate of the starport and Commerce City cured me of any desire to venture out into the world."

I nodded. "The dragon lives all the way up in the mountains though. Does anyone know why it attacked the starport?"

The woman looked at her coworker. "You're the one plugged into the rumor mill, Jason. Heard any new theories lately from those old-timers you drink with?"

Jason sighed. "A party of high-Level Adventurers staying here disappeared around that time. Supposedly they had an elf recording almost all of their activities for some popular Adventurer reality show, but nobody has seen the group since the incident."

"People think they did something to rile it up?" I asked.

The stout man shrugged. "Lots of people are still frozen at the starport, so they could be somewhere in there too, but there ain't nobody signing up to go into that cursed place to check."

"Were they human?"

Jason shook his head. "Bunch of different Galactics. A walking tree, a wolfman, an orc, and a leonid."

"I would have thought I'd remember a group like that," Cara chirped. "That's quite the diverse bunch."

"Not really," I said. "Most groups worry more about finding complementary roles. It usually doesn't have much to do with the species as long as they're not generational enemies of some kind, like the Movana and Triunnar."

"There are just as many same-species parties around here," Jason said. "That group stood out for the dumb stuff they were doing, according to my drinking buddies."

"Like what?" I asked, my curiosity piqued.

"They got into a drunken brawl with the enforcers from the Binary Eclipse Sect that wrecked their favorite hangout."

"Binary Eclipse Sect?" I asked, only vaguely familiar with the Sect concept since I had yet to encounter any since the System arrived.

"Think of the mafia or the mob," Jason explained. "Only if they were a legitimate government on top of all the shady criminal activities."

I raised an eyebrow. "So, protection rackets and speakeasies?"

Jason nodded. "Add trafficking just about anything you can think of and debt peonage, yeah."

"They sound like a wonderful bunch."

Cara shivered in disgust. "Until a couple of them decide to follow you home 'for your own safety.'"

The woman stared at the counter and refused to look up, clearly unwilling to elaborate further on that particular subject. The part of me that really enjoyed taking down assholes and abusers took note anyway.

If I got the chance to settle the score, I'd take it.

I looked back at Jason. "So, these Adventurers got into it with the Sect?"

He nodded. "Supposedly trashed that bar for probably twenty thousand Credits in damages and forced them to bring in healers from across town to regenerate a bunch of torn-off limbs."

"From the sounds of things, the Binary Eclipse probably deserved it," I said. "Tearing off limbs is pretty hard core."

"For sure," Jason agreed. "The big lion guy did most of that, I heard."

"What happened after the fight?"

"That was right before the Adventurers disappeared, so maybe that disappearance was the Sect getting even?"

"Why would they wait?" I asked. "If the Sect could take them out, I'd think they'd want to publicize that they weren't to be messed with."

Jason rubbed his chin thoughtfully. "Good point. It sounds like nothing that happened in the brawl went to immediately fatal levels. Maybe neither side wanted to escalate things too far."

"Cautious and smart. Is that why the Sect has kept their hold on things around here?"

Jason chuckled darkly. "Not too many people around here with the Levels to fight back. At least, not before the Sect's primary administration and housing in Commerce City got wiped out in the dragon attack. Now they're just as hard up for leadership and resources as the gnomes."

"Sounds like the Adventurers had the Levels then," I said. "Though if they pissed off the dragon, no one would thank them for that, no matter how much they stood up to the Sect bullies."

"Not with everything else going on," Jason agreed.

"Speaking of things going on," I said, "what are some good things to do or places to visit around here?"

"There are shops along the 16th Street Mall and slightly farther south in Larimer Square," Cara replied. "Plenty of restaurants managing to stay in business too, since people still have to eat. The Museum of Contemporary Art is still open, though most exhibits are local creations now instead of nationally renowned works."

The clerk nodded toward me and a ping in my neural implant informed me that a location update packet awaited my approval for download. When I consented, new waypoints appeared on the edges of my minimap to guide me to the sites referenced.

"Thanks," I said. "I'm not really an artsy person, but I know someone who might be interested."

The short woman laughed. "No, you didn't strike me as one. Otherwise, I'd have recommended the Selfie Museum."

"Selfies are still a thing?" I asked, raising an eyebrow.

"No," Cara said, shaking her head. "The building is still there and maintained by the System. Some gnomes bought it from the Shop because they thought the whole thing was hilarious."

"Somehow that doesn't surprise me," I said.

Despite the fact that I had a neural implant connected to my brain that allowed control of advanced System technology—tech like my hovering motorcycle or powered armor—I didn't miss the lack of social media or other "conveniences" once provided by smartphones.

The two desk attendants stood up straight at the sound of stomping footsteps emanating from the power-armored guards echoing down the hallway beyond the desk. The two escorts from earlier reappeared moments later, followed by Kurak and Ismyna. The guards peeled off and waved Ismyna ahead of them, clearly only walking them out of the hotel rather than returning them to the train.

The gnome didn't seem bothered by the lack of escort and gestured for me to walk alongside her. I bid a quick farewell to the hotel desk clerks and joined Ismyna as she and Kurak continued around the edges of the semi-crowded lounge.

"Get everything straightened out?" I asked, pushing open one side of a set of double doors leaving the station and holding it for Ismyna and Kurak to follow me outside.

I had to admit, I was a little surprised we were already leaving. Everything I knew about business meetings spoke of hours-long negotiation processes. Then again, maybe the local clans didn't have time to spend doing things "right." Emergencies had a tendency to streamline bureaucracy.

Ismyna sighed and headed back across the platform toward the train. "We're going to take two or three days to make sure we've got a full load of goods to haul back. They were supposed to have the freight cars already loaded, but things are still being reorganized. Preparations are not where they should be."

Boy, did the gnome sound pissed with that last sentence. Then again, things not being exactly right drove most engineers mad, I'd found.

"I'd like to give my team those two or three days off then," I said. "There shouldn't be any need for monster protection while you're getting the freight cars loaded, if everything remains inside the city limits."

Ismyna nodded. "You'll have two days for sure. I'll let you know after that whether we'll need that third day to finish."

Turning to Kurak, I patted the minotaur's shoulder. "Hear that, big guy? You can take off now if you want. I'll let the others know."

"Understood," Kurak said. "I'm going to find a hotel for the night. One with a bar and a huge bed."

"Not a bad plan. Enjoy yourself."

The minotaur nodded before plodding away, leaving me to continue the rest of the way back to the train with Ismyna.

"Any plans for yourself?" Ismyna asked.

"I'll probably sightsee or check out some local shops tomorrow. After that, maybe find a nearby hunting ground and see what I can do about thinning out the local monster population."

"You're relentless." The gnome shook her head, the ends of her green bobbed hair bouncing off either side of her jaw. "You're completely unable to take a break."

I shrugged, well aware of that flaw but unwilling to back down. I gestured to the north, where the iced-over starport lay. "Just look at what happened here. Monsters don't take breaks. Like the dragon, they're always out there getting stronger."

"Dragons are a whole different stage of existence from us normal people. You can't go comparing your Levels against something like that," Ismyna said, stopping and looking up at me as we reached the last car of the parked train. The other cars extended farther down the platform, and groups had assembled to see to the tasks of servicing the train and reprovisioning from local suppliers.

I stopped beside the gnome and folded my arms. "Fair comparison or not, that doesn't stop creatures of that magnitude from stepping on the people of this world like bugs. If we don't get stronger, they'll just overwhelm the planet, and everyone will be dead."

"You're not wrong," Ismyna said, frowning. "Just don't get yourself killed. We need you for the trip home."

I kept my gaze on the Engineer as Eldri and Wrefen came over from the crowd of gnomes. "I got no plans on dying. Not now. Not anytime soon. Too many monsters out there need killing."

The two support crew leaders glanced between us for a moment before Eldri chirped, "No talk about monsters around here. Sleeping inside a Safe Zone is a luxury I intend to enjoy for a few days."

"Speaking of sleep, I'm going to go catch up on mine," I said, then pointed at my earpiece. "I'll keep this on while we're in town. Let me know if anything comes up."

"Enjoy your days off, Hal," Ismyna said, before the others echoed the sentiment.

I waved to the trio and headed up the train toward the sleeper car housing my room, bypassing the gnomes and other support staff hustling about the platform. A few local Pharyleri in Clan uniforms of navy blue helped out but stayed clear of boarding the train itself.

Before I boarded the open door to my car, Nargen exited the workshop ahead. The dwarf's robot dog followed him, the pair of hovering drones folded down into a compacted low-power mode and attached to clamps on the dog's back. I waved to the Gimsar and hurried over. Quickly catching him up on the plans, I let him know that the next two days were completely off with a good probability of also having a third day free. He thanked me and headed off.

The party locations on my minimap informed me that the last members of my party were actually in my shared sleeper compartment. I hoped the elven ladies weren't killing each other.

I boarded the car and climbed the narrow stairs up to the second level before taking the corridor down to my room. After rapping my knuckles against the panel twice in quick succession to inform the ladies I was coming in, I slid open the door and found the pair seated in the compartment's chairs. Both elven women turned their heads toward me, and Dayena raised a questioning eyebrow.

"Don't mind me," I said. "I'm just going to do some Status updates and then sleep for about twelve hours. Our team is off for the next two days and possibly a third."

Before either elf could respond, I jumped into my bunk by swinging myself up over Lyrra's head and rolling onto the mattress. Lying on my back and lacing my fingers behind my head, I brought up the pending notifications I'd been looking forward to since we arrived in Denver.

"Let me get this straight," Lyrra said. "He is your contracted servant and you let him talk to you like that?"

"He is rather informal, is he not?" Dayena replied.

"I'm right here, you know," I said, raising myself on one elbow and turning onto my side to look down at the pair.

The two elves ignored me.

"Surely your contract has penalty clauses?" Lyrra asked.

Dayena waved dismissively. "Not worth enforcing. Far better that he remains cooperative."

"Ah, the pelshua rather than the whip," Lyrra said. "That strategy often proves effective for high-performing and independent retainers, so long as they stay within the confines of their station."

I assumed the reference was the Movana equivalent of the carrot and the stick, but I wasn't worried about the penalty clauses, since I'd read the contract multiple times. The actual breach conditions could only result from willful negligence on my part, and I had no intention of welching. On the other side of that equation, the Credits that the Countess paid as my salary more than offset the restrictions that tied me to her.

Dayena acknowledged the Movana's statement with a noncommittal shrug that told me quite a bit. While the pair's discussion before I arrived clearly outlined the broader details of our arrangement, the Truinnar Countess still managed to keep the finer details under wraps.

No longer concerned about the direction of the conversation, I settled into the comfortable mattress and went back to my Status. Seeing my lack of interest, the pair moved on to a new topic besides needling me. With my Status updates floating in my vision, I tuned out the elves and reviewed the latest notifications before I got to the good stuff.

Closing out the blue boxes after I read them, I focused my attention on the unspent Attribute Points. Part of me wanted to continue adding to my lowest attributes of Perception and Willpower, as I'd been doing for the last couple Levels, but instead I went with my little tradition of using the free points on Luck every ten Levels.

When considering my survival so far, it seemed like that strategy continued to pay off.

After confirming the selections and finalizing the Level Up process, I confirmed once again that I did not wish to use my unspent Class Skill points before bringing up my status sheet.

Status Screen			
Name:	Hal Mason*	Class:	Hunter*
Race:	Human (Male)	Level:	40
Titles			
Dungeon World Delver*, Galactic Iron Bounty Hunter, Sharp Eyed* (*Title hidden)			
Health:	1260	Stamina:	1260
Mana:	910		
Status			
Normal*			
Attributes			
Strength	70	Agility	137
Constitution	126	Perception	85

Intelligence	91	Willpower	65
Charisma	90	Luck	24
Class Skills			
Efficient Trail	1	Expose	1
Greater Observation	2	Hinder	2
Implacable Endurance	1	Keen Senses	1
Meat Locker	3	On the Hunt	3
Quality Over Quantity	1	Rend	1
Resilient Nature	2	Right Tool for the Job	2
Non-Class Skills			
Blood Scent	1		
Perks			
Gut Instinct			

Combat Spells

Earth Spike (II), Firespray (II), Frostbolt (VI), Frostnova (IV), Greater Healing (I), Greater Regeneration (I), Lesser Disguise (V), Minor Healing (IV), Minor Renew (II)

When I closed the Status window, the elves seemed to be wrapping up their conversation and discussing their plans for the days off.

"One of the hotel clerks in the station here mentioned an art gallery and several marketplaces nearby," I interjected without sitting up.

"An art gallery?" Dayena asked, perking up.

Without a word, I sent her the location provided by the clerk.

Dayena's brow furrowed. "Museum of Contemporary Art Denver. That could be worth checking out. This planet is missing much in the way of culture."

I snorted. "It had plenty of culture before the System."

"Of course it did."

I practically heard Dayena rolling her eyes. Refusing to take her bait, I let the subject drop. "Have fun if you go out tonight. I'm planning to check the markets and hit the Shop tomorrow morning."

The two elves left the compartment and I shut off the overhead lights, then settled back into the mattress. My first night in a Safe Zone since leaving Pittsburgh. I looked forward to a full night of sleep without the worry that some monstrous thing would spawn nearby.

A content expression crossed my face as I released the conscious tension and alertness I maintained in the wilds. Only then did I let myself drift off, my dreams filled with screaming civilians, roaring monsters, and the soft call of horns.

Pretty much like every night.

Chapter 20

A hot shower just after dawn started my morning off right, washing away the last of last night's dreams. I followed my nose to the dining car, the rustle of my armored jumpsuit against my flesh continuing on. The smell of bacon permeated the air and I slid into an empty booth with my mouth watering.

Wrefen stopped by the table to collect my order and I looked at the gnome with a raised eyebrow after he noted my usual breakfast selections. "Where's Sheera? She's usually the one serving breakfast this early in the morning."

"She told me last night that she needed the next two days off from work and then promptly disappeared." The gnome paused before frowning. "I hope she comes back. She was one of my better staff members."

"She seemed nice enough," I said.

"Good help is hard to find." Wrefen sighed and shook his head before heading off to take orders from the next table.

The gnome returned several minutes later with a plate piled high with scrambled eggs and bacon. He slid the platter-sized dish in front of me and placed a steaming cup of black coffee off to the side.

"Can I get you anything else?" Wrefen asked.

"Nope," I said, picking up a piece of the bacon and biting into it.

Wrefen nodded in satisfaction and headed off to continue his other duties. I savored the bacon as I looked around the mostly empty dining car. Unlike most mornings, it seemed few of the crew opted to take advantage of the free meals provided for them on the train when the city offered so many other options.

Free being the operative word there.

With my metabolism increasing constantly since the System Advent, I'd take as much free food as I could and save the Credits for my ammunition habit. I certainly never seemed to gain any weight, no matter how much I ate. The gnomes somehow managed a supply of coffee, along with kipatchya and other popular beverages, so I wouldn't complain as long as my caffeine habit stayed sated. Coffee, bacon, and eggs certainly started my days off right.

When I finished clearing my plate, I thanked Wrefen and asked him to also pass my gratitude on to the cooking staff.

Breakfast completed and feeling full for now, I headed into the town and noticed an oddity on my minimap. The street grid in this section of the city angled the roads an eighth of a turn off the compass rows, so where most city streets ran north-to-south and east-to-west, here they ran northwest-to-southeast and southwest-to-northeast.

Wandering straight out of the station, I followed 17th Street for a block to the southeast without any real sense of purpose. Few shops were open this early, so I walked down the wide, pedestrian-friendly street as I took in the local sights. Quite a few people meandered about despite the hour, though my adventuring garb and armaments distinguished me from the civilian population. Many people shifted away uncomfortably, and most clearly gave me a wide berth on the sidewalks.

After yesterday's story from the hotel clerks, I wasn't really surprised that most people around here viewed Adventurers in a poor light—though I had to admit my currently equipped state probably didn't offer much assurance that I wasn't just another murderhobo out for glory.

Or a wayward Sect member out for his jollies.

Between the holsters on each hip and under each arm, I carried four visible pistols. Adding my armor on top of that gave me the appearance of a one-man SWAT team crossed with a gunslinger from the Old West. Pausing at the next intersection, I recalled the clerk's recommendation of shops along the 16th Street Mall, so I turned southwest down Wazee Street.

Halfway down the block, two men in jeans and fringed Western shirts with bold patterns maneuvered a rack of similar garments down a short flight of steps and placed it in front of one of the shop building's wide bay windows before reentering the store. Mannequins displayed through the glass showed off more of the uniquely designed clothing, along with cowboy hats, boots, belts, and a plethora of other ranchwear. The word "Rockmount" stretched across the front of the brick building just above the windows.

Since no other shops seemed open yet, I stepped over to the rack of apparel and browsed through it as the men returned carrying another clothing stand.

The first of the men finished placing the new stand, then stepped over beside my rack as I flipped through the menswear. "See anything you're interested in?"

"It looks high quality, but most of this stuff is a little bold for my tastes." I shrugged and glanced at the interior display through the window, a jacket on one of the mannequins catching my eye. "I'm not entirely sure what I'm looking for, but I wouldn't mind seeing some simple outerwear that offers protection from the elements."

The man frowned. "Like a jacket?"

"More like a cloak, something I can throw back easily," I replied.

His eyes lit up. "A poncho!"

I raised an eyebrow in question, recalling the standard issue woobie from my time in the service. "A what?"

"I might have just the thing," he said, hurrying toward the store entrance. "Wait here."

I looked at the second man in question, but he shrugged and returned to evenly spacing the clothing on the racks. The first man reappeared a few moments later with a rectangle of olive-green material thrown over one arm, clearly having heard my opinion about the bright and bold patterns on the displayed Western-style shirts. He jogged down the short steps from the door and presented me with the article.

Taking the fabric with both hands, I noticed that the material felt sturdy and smooth when I rubbed it between my fingers as I lifted it for inspection. A folded hood flipped down over the neck hole in the center of the rectangular garment. The dark mossy-green closely matched the Pistongrinder uniforms and, at a glance, would blend in with the other non-Pharyleri crewmembers from the train. It'd hopefully assist in maintaining a low profile for the return journey.

A subtle black pattern, woven in angular Navajo-inspired designs, traced across both the front and back of the poncho. With the similarities in the dark colors, the pattern remained subtle enough that it didn't set off my aversion like the brighter yellows and reds on the rack.

Focusing on the garment brought up its status.

No-Name Poncho

Durability: 125/125

This Spaghetti Western-inspired poncho provides protection from the elements and boosts the wearer's ability to blend into both crowds and wildlands. Wearing provides +15% Elemental Resistances and +25% Stealth.

On top of having something to keep the rain off, the bonuses to resistances and stealth transformed the item from a convenience into a piece of gear that really interested me.

I looked at the man. "Mind if I try it on?"

"Go right ahead," he said.

I slipped the poncho over my head and tugged it around so that the center seam lined up with my shoulders. The edges of the fabric hung down to the middle of my thighs. When I extended my arms, the poncho covered my torso entirely and extended out to just above my elbow. Reaching underneath the covering, I practiced drawing my pistols from each set of holsters.

It fit comfortably, covered my visible weapons, and appealed to my practical nature. Fine, perhaps a little of my impractical nature too.

"How much?" I removed the poncho and folded it over my arm as I asked the question.

He peered at me as if gauging my ability to pay, though he also seemed relieved I was asking. "Two thousand Credits."

"Fifteen hundred," I countered automatically.

The man shook his head. "Nineteen."

"Seventeen."

"I can't go lower than eighteen," he said with a frown.

"Eighteen then," I agreed.

The man nodded his head in a single jerk.

"Thank you." I transferred the Credits to him before throwing the poncho back over my head.

"We appreciate your patronage," he said. "Things have been tight since the destruction of the spaceport. We hear that trains are supposed to begin coming through again, so hopefully that will mean more trade flowing through town."

It seemed the rumors around the train's arrival and what it might mean for commerce in the city still flowed.

"I'm sure that would be good for business," I acknowledged, deciding that it wasn't my place to confirm the talk. "I hope things go well for you."

"Thanks," he said.

I gave a farewell nod and turned away as the man went back to arranging the clothing displays. Continuing southwest to the next intersection, I turned southeast onto the wide pedestrian-friendly 16th Street Mall.

Several shopkeepers flipped their signs from Closed to Open as I passed, though light poured out from the doorways and windows of other small businesses to highlight the availability of their goods. In contrast to the liveliness of the locally owned and operated stores, most larger chains sat dark and empty. The ones that showed signs of life appeared co-opted by Galactic owners, and a variety of alien species streamed in and out of the structures.

I paused outside of one such building, a bank on the corner of 16th and Blake which still displayed a Wells Fargo sign above the entrance despite the window displays proclaiming the new Pharyleri ownership. Another sign advertised the presence of a System Shop, though both signs were written in the gnomish language. That oversight probably accounted for the lack of diversity in the clientele, as only gnomes seemed to be entering the building.

Walking up to the red-brick-and-glass building, I pulled open the door and held it for a middle-aged Pharyleri couple walking arm in arm before I entered behind them. Several tellers stood behind a counter across the lobby, though the waiting area partitioned with stanchions was currently empty.

A bronze-plated guard stood just inside the lobby, keeping watch over the building entrance but remaining clear of the traffic entering and exiting the building. The guard's head shifted slightly as I came through the door. The smooth faceplate tracked me across the lobby when I followed the short couple over to the glowing Shop crystal on the far side of the room, but the guard made no other movements.

While it was possible to block access to Shop crystals and access, it was generally considered an active act of violence. The kind of thing that got people shot at or schemed over until someone shot at the blockers.

On rare occasions, Galactic politics were actually quite simple.

The pair in front of me disappeared with their activation of the Shop, and I took my turn before anyone decided to bother me. A moment's translocation later, I arrived in my default Shop instance and heard the booming greeting of my usual shopkeeper.

"Hal!" Ryk shouted. "Great to see you still alive, but you're looking a little rough."

"Thanks, Ryk. Nice of you to point that out when I'm sure you know that I'm down to my last suit."

The quadruped shopkeeper chuckled and rubbed his hands together in glee, knowing that my long absence likely meant plenty of purchases, with my Credits transferring into his furry hands. "Before I fleece you for your last Credit, do you have anything to sell on this trip?"

I sighed and nodded, allowing Ryk to lead the way to the sterile room that supported all the stasis systems that kept the harvested monsters as fresh as my Class Skills. By now, the shopkeeper was used to the large quantities of monsters and monster parts that I hauled in after a long absence. The exchange went quickly, and we soon returned to the main hall of Ryk's Shop, my account now flush with Credits from the sale.

"So, what can I get for you today, Hal?"

Rather than haggle over the details, I transmitted a prepared checklist of munitions, armor suits, rations, miscellaneous gear, and a couple weapons over to the shopkeeper. Ryk raised an eyebrow as he scanned the order in the System window that appeared in front of him.

"You sure about that last item?" Ryk asked. "It's not going to be cheap."

I grinned. "I'm sure. I'm good on everyday carry weapons and I want something with a little more oomph."

"All right then," the shopkeeper replied. "I'll put everything together. It won't take long."

"Sounds good," I said. "I'll just wander the hall."

"Let me know if anything else catches your eye. I'll be more than happy to add it to your bill." Without waiting for my response and chuckling at his own humor, Ryk headed toward the back of the building.

Ignoring the tinge of smugness that infused the shopkeeper's tone, I paced slowly down the hall. Instead of the purchasable goods in the cases that ran along the museum-like hall, I focused my attention on the exhibits of weapons and armor from across the Galaxy. A wry grin split my face when I saw one of the most recent additions.

On a raised platform extending from the wall, a humanoid mannequin clad in combat boots, cargo pants, and a Kevlar vest stood in a shooting stance, a familiar pistol extended toward an imaginary target somewhere over my head. The mannequin's equipment looked worn, the mundane equipment torn and tattered from surviving the first day of the System's Advent on Earth.

Memories from that day flooded back to me in an instant, memories of monsters and deaths burned into my brain.

Increased Intelligence and Willpower meant I rarely forgot things anymore, even when I would rather not remember bears the size of a truck or a tide of rats flowing over a street or the screams of the dying.

So many screams.

Among them, in stark relief, the face of a dying friend. Worried only about the safety of his kids as his life faded.

I still stood in front of the mannequin when Ryk returned sometime later and placed a hand on my shoulder.

"The past is a tricky thing sometimes," the shopkeeper said, his tone level and filled with understanding. "It's good to remember where we come from, but not so much that we lose ourselves in the pain of loss or the thoughts of what could have been."

"You're right. Dwelling on what we can't change fixes nothing." I breathed deeply, forcing myself fully back into the present. "Still, some things should always be remembered."

Ryk gave my shoulder a pat and stepped back as he sent me the bill from my shopping list. The hefty price lay within my expectations, so I transferred the Credits and the shopkeeper traded me the goods in turn. Fortunately for my Credit balance, the recently completed Quest reward helped offset my supply needs.

"Anything else for you today?" Ryk asked.

"What would it cost me for a map update that includes Denver and the surrounding areas?"

Ryk consulted his menu for barely a moment. "One hundred Credits."

I nodded and made the exchange, glad to have updated information about the settlement and nearby areas where I'd hopefully be able to hunt monsters for additional experience and loot. "I'm also looking to upgrade my defensive capabilities."

Ryk's head cocked. "Please elaborate."

For a moment, I considered my fight with Dayena's cousins. "I'm running into more melee combatants I can't evade, either due to speed or numbers. I need equipment to block or parry attacks, equipment that doesn't involve me sacrificing my weapons or taking my guns too far out of play."

The ram-like shopkeeper stroked his short beard with one hand and hummed as he looked over me, focusing on my numerous holsters. "Equipment specifically and not Skills or spells."

I nodded. "My combat regeneration is terrible."

"Then you're looking for bracers or vambraces," Ryk stated. "Unless you want to go with external help like drones?" He caught my shaking head long before he was done. I'd seen how costly those things were when they got wrecked. "Or an enchanted piece?"

"Enchanted shields sound good," I said.

"I'd advise against it for now," Ryk said.

I cocked my head. "Why?"

"Cost. You don't have enough Credits to buy something that will truly last. Maybe once you hit Master, but till then, you'll out-Level your equipment if it doesn't break beforehand," Ryk explained.

"Fine, armor it is. What's the difference between the two?"

"Bracers generally cover less area, while vambraces typically provide protection from wrist to elbow or even higher. Both options can be accessorized with utility gear and weapons."

More combat options sounded interesting. "All right, show me some options for both and I'll see how they feel."

Trying out several variations, I eventually settled on a pair of vambraces. Each of the slightly boxy sleeves of armor included a hinged elbow protector at one end and a mounting point forward just over the wrist. For the first mount, I opted for a grappling launcher that fired a hook capable of supporting many times my weight with a nano fiber line that could also be used to ensnare an opponent.

A micro flamethrower system attached to the second mounting point. The weapon operated from cartridges of a compressed napalm-like substance. It was capable of spraying out a focused stream of fire over a dozen yards for a short period before it had to be recharged.

Extra thick armor covered the housing for the fuel cartridge, making the vambrace on my left arm slightly bulkier, but I was happy with the trade-off that meant my arm wouldn't erupt in fire from an enemy attack. If I got really worried about the integrity of the armor, the fuel canister could always be ejected and discarded before it ruptured.

After saying farewell to the shopkeeper, I found myself transported back to the Shop crystal in the former bank. Just like on my way into the building, the bank guard's helmet turned with me as I walked out.

Maybe the poncho didn't disguise my "armed to the teeth" status as much as I'd thought, though it could be that the guard just didn't like Adventurers. Or non-Pharyleri.

The street looked far busier now under the bright mid-day sunshine. Beyond the open stores in the buildings along either side of the mall, vendors peddled their wares from a variety of simply constructed stalls. The shouts of street merchants clamored over one another as their owners competed for traffic while selling goods that included everything from handmade knives to armor crafted from some kind of insect chitin.

More often than not, there were non-combat items too, simple things like combs that kept hair silky and snarl-free, bolts of clothing or leather pants for everyday wear, or carving knives to aid in the making of better artisanal items.

Nothing caught my eye as I casually inspected the various displays, though I noticed that the goods simply weren't of high quality. I could obtain better items from the Shop. Only when I realized that the vendors were almost exclusively human did I understand what I saw. The crafters here were the inexperienced who'd gained their Artisan Classes solely from the System and only had just over a year of practice in their trade. Only those who sold their goods could afford to purchase additional materials to further Level in order to advance their techniques.

It was a vicious cycle, but not one that was my problem.

Pedestrian traffic still dominated the roadway and sidewalks, and vehicles seemed like luxury items for the more well-off, from the quality of the few transports I spotted. The owners of the vehicles, or their drivers, pushed through the crowds with only casual regard for the safety of those on foot, bumping the unwary or slow-moving from their path. I mentally shrugged at the lack of reaction from other passersby, though I supposed that the System could heal anything not immediately fatal.

Two blocks later, I reached Larimer Street and crossed the intersection to follow the road to the southwest. After another block, a line of stanchions blocked off the center of the roadway to prevent vehicles from traversing the square. Beyond the blockade, tables and chairs stretched out into the street. The lunchtime crowd flocked to the restaurants that served the square, though plenty of non-food stores also graced the area.

The scents of grilled meat wafted into my nose as a server stepped out of an eatery on the corner of the square, carrying a large tray with several plates of large steaks. My eyes locked onto the juicy steaks and my mouth watered from the aroma, pulling me into an almost involuntary step after the server. When the server deftly distributed the plates to the occupants of a crowded table, I found myself headed toward the hostess who stood at a podium outside the seating area.

After getting a seat and ordering one of the steaks done medium rare with a baked potato on the side, I only waited a short time until I dug into the meal. Though the steak certainly satisfied me, I grudgingly admitted that the monster steaks prepared by the train's crew exceeded the quality of the local fare.

I paid for my meal with a generous tip and took a quick pass through the rest of Larimer Square before I started feeling antsy. I hadn't gained any experience since completing the Quest yesterday, and the lack of progress needled my conscience.

Heading north, I left the more populated areas and pulled out my bike once the streets cleared. No one stopped me as I rode from the Safe Zone and crossed back out into the frigid desolation of Commerce City. Though the summer afternoon sun shone down through sparse clouds, the temperatures remained chilly enough that a layer of snow still covered the ice across every surface. My poncho flapped in the wind as I streaked through the abandoned streets to the frozen starport on the outskirts of town.

A few brave souls skirted the edges of the field of silent structures and sealed starships, but they scattered at my approach. I paid them no mind. I wasn't here for looters. The shimmering ice called to me in a way I couldn't put into words. I couldn't have explained it to anyone else if I'd tried.

The wind shrieked as it swirled through the abandoned structures, filling the air with the snow kicked up and reducing visibility to a dozen or so yards. Even through my armor, the cold sapped the warmth from my body.

In the middle of the empty starport, between what appeared to be a traffic control tower and a parked bulk freighter, I pulled to a stop and stored my bike. No sense letting it take damage from the elements. Here in the heart of the affected area, only my resistances seemed to keep me safe, though I felt the biting cold warring against the natural healing the System was providing me. A constant see-saw of reduced damage and healing.

My breath released a cloud of steam that dissipated in moments when the next gust surged past. Each inhalation through my nose seared the passages of my nostrils, freezing the tiny hairs within. Breathing through my mouth was no better, as moisture condensed on my lips and hurt my chest even as snowflakes clung to my eyelashes. I was forced to squint against the wind as I surveyed the surroundings.

I pressed my palm against the ice-coated tower, immediately feeling the frozen intensity burning my skin and finding the wavery surface surprisingly smooth to the touch. Closing my eyes, I pushed against the wall and stretched my senses into the spot beneath my hand. Manipulating Greater Observation, I narrowed my focus to a microscopic point on the surface of the ice at the center of my palm.

Though I knew this cursed ice wouldn't act normally, I still found myself surprised by what I sensed. Despite the heat from my body, the surface remained solid and radiated cold into my skin, rather than the warmth of my touch melting the ice. The structure of the ice itself looked like planes of interlocking hexagonal crystals, formed with no overlaps or gaps between formations.

I studied the crystals, the bonds between them, and the geometric formations. The mesmerizing patterns drew me into them, whispering of strength to be gained if only I could comprehend the power. Time flowed as I drove my senses further and further into the solid, almost maddening structure.

An explosion of pain stabbing into my brain rocked me from my intense exploration into the nature of the ice. Off balance and flailing backward, I found myself trapped by the arm frozen solid to the wall of the tower. My eyes refused to open, stuck closed from a sheen of ice that covered my face. I gasped from the intense pressure squeezing on my head.

After clenching my free hand several times to get the blood flowing, I wiped my eyes clear of the icy buildup that sealed them shut. Ice encased my arm all the way up to my elbow, the skin of my hand tinged blue beneath the glassy prison. Snow had built up around my boots, also trapping my feet. I tugged my boots free of the ground fairly easily, but my arm remained stuck.

Casting a round of healing spells through the painful fog in my brain took some effort, and the stabbing feeling of frostbite soon returned to my trapped hand. I flexed my trapped arm and stepped toward the wall in front of me as the ice broke with my movements. Blood coated the tower as I tore free, also dribbling onto the ground.

I looked around, only now noticing how dark the abandoned starport had become. Between the shadows and the buildup of the ice, I realized that I'd been standing unmoving for hours. A quick verification noted that it was well past midnight now.

Unread notifications blinked in the corner of my vision and demanded my attention, but I ignored them for now, choosing instead to stretch and focus on the physical sensations to distract myself from the pounding in my skull. My shoulders clicked as I spread my arms. My back cracked as my muscles pulled everything back into place.

Letting out a contented sigh, I summoned my bike from my Inventory and climbed into the seat before pausing with a frown. Somehow the cold seemed lesser now, almost as if it no longer affected me in quite the same way.

My breath filled the air with a cloud of condensation. At least that hadn't changed, though I figured I needed to check my notifications. Reading through the first dozen or so, I dismissed a long series of updates about resisting elemental damage effects. Then I found a completely different notification altogether.

Elemental Affinity Gained (Ice)
Affinity: Very Poor

Congratulations!
For gaining your first Elemental Affinity, you have been rewarded 2,000 Experience Points.

I kneaded my fingers into my temples, attempting to massage away the throbbing pain that refused to subside while I parsed through the update. With the System's usual opacity, I lacked any understanding of what abilities this new Elemental Affinity might grant, but my instincts told me that obtaining it was a good thing. A new ability without a Mana or Stamina cost seemed positive. The minor amount of experience didn't hurt either.

Resolved that I might just be dealing with this headache for a bit, I eased up on the massaging and throttled up my bike as I headed back toward town. All I wanted at this point was to sleep. Kicking my bike into hover mode, I streaked above the ice-covered streets with little regard for road conditions. I stowed the bike in my Inventory shortly after I reached the edges of the Safe Zone and walked the remainder of the way back to my berth on the train.

Fortunately, my room was empty when I arrived, so I avoided the need to answer awkward questions about my late night. Without bothering to change or clean up beyond a quick cast of the Cleanse spell, I swung up into my bunk and promptly fell asleep.

Chapter 21

Not long after dawn, my splitting headache subsided to a dull throb that, thankfully, seemed more like a hangover that would soon abate. Opting to deal with it in the same manner as the morning after a heavy night of pre-System drinking, I started with a hot shower before heading to the dining car in search of breakfast.

Neither Wrefen nor Sheera worked the dining area when I arrived and took a seat at one of the many open booths. Though the sun's presence indicated the early morning hour, most crew were opting to eat elsewhere while we remained in town. Only a single member of the serving staff occupied the car, sitting at a booth near the lifts that brought meals up from the kitchen below, completely engrossed in reading something on a tablet. The gnome blushed bright crimson when he finally looked up and noticed me waiting patiently. The tablet vanished as he hurried over and took my usual order before serving a cup of hot coffee.

I scarfed down the meal and a second coffee for good measure. With my Constitution, I doubted caffeine did much for me anymore. Still, I felt like coffee made my mornings complete even in this System world.

Thanking the server, who was already ignoring me in favor of his tablet, I left the train and took in the morning from the station platform as the last of the headache finally faded. A part of me wondered how much of it was real and how much somatic. The System healed you to full in ten minutes or so, minus lasting debuffs, and I hadn't noticed any lingering Status notifications. Then again, I was beginning to believe that the System might not be as all-encompassing as the Galactics liked to play believe.

The air felt crisp and clean. The hint of a chill lingered on the breeze that I absently acknowledged. Today needed to include monster killing since my only experience gained yesterday came from acquiring the Elemental

Affinity. With everyone giving each other space for the days off, I decided to continue doing my own thing. Finding a hunting ground outside town that didn't infringe on the locals would be the trick, but I figured I at least had an in with the Clan running things.

I tracked down Ismyna at a nearby trainyard and caught the gnome as she supervised a team loading a series of boxcars with pallets of Mana-infused ingots of precious metals. One of the local Pharyleri escorted her, wearing a bronze pauldron on one shoulder and carrying a tablet that the gnome consulted with each pallet loaded into the train car. Unlike most of the Pharyleri who wore their hair colorfully, this gnome's hair was cut into a gray flattop with straight sideburns and a neatly trimmed goatee of the same shade.

Ismyna regarded me with a raised eyebrow once I explained what I was looking for. "You were serious when you said you were going to hunt monsters. Even though you spent the whole way here killing things. And now, on your day off, you still want me to get you permission to hunt somewhere outside of town?"

I nodded. "I don't want to make trouble, just kill monsters."

The second gnome looked up from the tablet and gave me a once-over, locking onto the Status above my head. "The mines where we get the ores are always looking for Adventurers to clear out the local monster nests. There are bounties for killing Alphas open to anyone who turns them in."

"Thanks," I said. "That's exactly the thing I'm looking for."

The local gave me directions to the nearest mine, located kilometers outside of the Safe Zone, and I loaded the coordinates into my neural link. The gnome also told me to look for the foreman once I got there. "Tell Vokrum that Sparkie sent you."

"Thanks, Sparkie." I gave a salute in farewell, but the pair of gnomes were already moving toward the next boxcar in need of loading.

The directions led me west of the city, past the abandoned Colorado Railroad Museum and a destroyed small town, out into a zone rife with Level 60 plus monsters. The mountain foothills beyond that showed obvious signs of conflict with broken trees and smashed rocks that lay scattered across the highway.

A chill wind flowed down from the mountain foothills, blasting me in the face. With the poncho keeping me warm, on top of my innate resistances and whatever tolerance the Ice Affinity applied, the cold didn't really affect me beyond noting the cool breeze.

The trip allowed me to test out my new Affinity. A flicker of movement alerted me to an aggressive mountain lion just before it jumped from a ledge above the highway as it entered the hills west of Denver. Without even drawing a weapon, a flick of my hand fired a Frostbolt at the airborne cougar.

Mana flowed instantly at my command, easier and more efficiently than ever before. A swirl of ice packed densely into a jagged cone the length of my arm as it shot toward the leaping creature. The spike caught the mountain lion in the chest and knocked it from the air. Wheezing and whining, the severely wounded creature attempted to pick itself up from the ground, but I finished it off with a few shots from a beam pistol before stopping to loot the carcass.

After that aborted ambush, I ended up killing a number of other solitary natural and mutated creatures on the broken road. Ruts in the deteriorating asphalt evidenced heavy traffic before I reached the location provided by the Pharyleri.

A faint rumbling, felt in my chest despite my bike hovering above the surface of the road, shook the ground as I drove up a ruggedly winding road away from the highway. When I crested onto a somewhat level shoulder partially up one of the mountainous foothills, an explosion erupted from a reinforced tunnel dug into the far side of the incline. A flicker of flame subsided almost immediately, though the mine entrance was obscured by a cloud of dust and smoke that flowed out across the base.

Tower-mounted automated turrets around the perimeter of the cleared hillside rotated toward the opening as a number of figures stumbled out of the smoke and formed a loose defensive formation that highlighted the variety in the Galactic races throughout the group. The larger portion of the armed party consisted of short Pharyleri and squat Gimsar, but a few Hakarta and several humans filled out the group.

The tower's beam weaponry opened up at larger, indistinct shapes still hidden by the cloud obscuring the mineshaft. The energy rays lanced through the dusty haze and cleared the air enough that I could finally see their target.

A pile of rocks.

Then the rockpile stepped forward and I realized it was a creature.

Rare-Earth Elemental (Level 49)
HP: 3872/4280

Molten ore dripped in glowing rivulets from the elemental where the beam weapons seared its rocky surface but solidified before running all the way to the ground.

Behind the first elemental, several more blocky shapes rumbled toward the short figures arrayed around the mine entrance, all of whom were now launching attacks of their own at the leading creature.

Dropping my bike into ground mode, I coasted up behind the defenders as their ranged weaponry and spells tore into the elementals. Scanning for the most senior of the defenders, I rolled to a stop and rested my bike at a lean with one foot on the ground. "Sparkie sent me. Need a hand?"

A gray-bearded Gimsar in heavy mechanized armor looked at me dismissively before taking another shot with a large bore projectile rifle.

Foreman Vokrum Stonebelcher, Old Stone Hand (Expert Miner Level 27)

HP: 840/840

MP: 860/1220

A wad of what looked like chew seemed stuck inside the dwarf's lower lip before he spat out a stream of brownish liquid and spoke in a slow Southern drawl. "Aah, this'n just a little dustup."

I shook my head as the Gimsar went back to shooting at the plodding elementals. Sometimes System language packs got weird.

Lifting my foot from the ground, I prepared to pull back from the fight when the ground shook violently as an even larger elemental emerged from the mine. A new cloud of dust and debris shot out, flinging support beams from the entryway and collapsing most of the passage. The vaguely humanoid shape unfolded itself to stand about four stories tall. Two glowing orange eyes sunk within deep recesses shone out from a rounded mound on top of the monster.

Greater Rare-Earth Elemental (Level 91 - Boss)

HP: 9420/9460

The elder Gimsar glanced back at me. "Ah, since Sparkie sent ya all this way, we'll take the assist if'n yer still offerin."

I halted the bike and turned to the dwarf. "I keep my share of the loot."

"Agreed!"

Hopping off the bike with a grin, I stowed the vehicle in my Inventory to keep it clear of the coming fight before summoning my hybrid rifle and pulling the weapon tight to my shoulder as I stepped up beside the Gimsar. The rifle whined as I opened up on the giant monster, the shot digging into the core of the elemental. The attack chipped a small divot into the creature's granite torso, applying Rend's bleed effect and causing molten liquid to pour from the wound. Each attack also stacked the armor-reducing effect of Expose onto the boss elemental.

I kept my destructive attention on the boss, rather than combining my fire with the attacks and spells of the others as they demolished the first wave of enemies. The smaller elementals crumbled from the onslaught, leaving chunks of shattered rock across the ground.

As the others' attacks shifted to the boss elemental, the giant monster continued to plod forward as it roared a grinding reverberation that set my senses on edge. The noise of nails on a chalkboard and a wave of energy pulsed out from the boss, along with the sound. As the effect rippled across the battlefield, the broken and scattered rocks of the destroyed elementals rolled and tumbled toward each other as they reconstituted into smaller forms. Stumbling forward in a tightly packed throng, the reformed constructs belted out gratingly shrill cries of their own.

Beyond the boss, more of the creatures continued crawling from the mine entrance. Though none matched the sheer size of the greater boss, the new additions dwarfed the rebuilt forms of the elementals' frontline.

Despite the growing threats, the troop of miners seemed relatively calm. The group subtly shifted away from the semi-circle around the mine entrance, opening the range with the ease of long practice and repetition. Heavily armored individuals held their places longer, slowly giving ground as lighter-armored ranged attackers and magic users retreated.

The older dwarf glanced at me with a raised eyebrow, his expression silently asking if I really wanted to get tangled up in the midst of this fight.

Before I could offer any response, another wave of energy pulsed out from the boss. This time, the force picked up the newly reconstituted elementals and catapulted them into the surrounding miners. The disciplined lines collapsed into chaos as a furious melee broke out.

None of the launched elementals landed near the foreman and me, so I continued firing at the boss. The dwarf responded to the elevated threat by swapping out his rifle for a massive rotary cannon. End to end, the weapon probably stood at least as tall as the dwarf, but when held horizontally, it forced the Gimsar into a wide stance. The tri-barreled assembly whined as it spun up before spouting a stream of projectiles in an angry roar. Accompanying the projectiles was a gout of flame that extended several feet beyond the end of the whirling cannon.

The cannon's thundering storm of ordinance tore into the boss. Swirls of Mana and a light glow around the cannon spoke of a Skill in use, boosting the efficiency of the machinery.

Smart crafters learned to bend their Skills across a wide variety of items, including weaponry. "Increased Efficiency by 20%" seemed simple enough, but if you were talking about increasing the efficiency of damage and projectile output, damage numbers start scaling up.

Growling at the destruction of our attacks, the greater elemental slammed its arms into the ground. Twin lines of rocky spikes rippled through the ground toward us. The dwarven gunner dropped the minigun as he dove away from the attack, and I jumped in the opposite direction to avoid a particularly large set of spikes. As I rolled to my feet, I saw that the miners were slowly wearing down the reconstituted first wave. Though their formation remained scattered, only a handful of the elementals remained amongst them.

A small team, having cleared their nearest threats, broke away from the main group and circled the boss, rushing the mine entrance to cut off the stream of monstrous reinforcements.

"Rock and stone!" the cry echoed over the battlefield from an armored human at the head of the blockade team, charging forward and waving a pickaxe over his head.

Despite the commotion made by the party moving to bar the mine entrance, the greater elemental remained focused on the Gimsar gunner as he rolled to his feet. I split farther away from the dwarf, who scooped up the minigun and backed up as the boss rushed forward.

Still on all four limbs, the massive elemental shook the ground with each pounding step as it gained momentum. The creature's head drew back behind its shoulders as it crawled forward. The elemental's bulk shielded its vulnerable core from the attacks slamming into it from either side as the miners finished off the elementals in their midst and shifted to attacking the boss.

From straight on, my shots still impacted the elemental's head, alongside the stream of fire from the dwarven Expert Miner. Each attack sparked and chipped away at the monster.

Though the creature lacked a mouth, a gaping maw cracked open beneath the sunken orange eyes from my repeated attacks. The angry wound dripped molten liquid that sizzled when it splashed onto the ground beneath the charging monster.

The ammo counter on my rifle dropped to zero and I ejected the depleted magazine while moving farther away from the gunner's position. Dismissing the empty into my Inventory, I quickly swapped it for one full of explosive rounds in the hope that the concussive damage would prove more effective. While I reloaded, the boss focused its attention on the dwarven foreman. The minigun's roaring hailstorm of projectiles chipped away at the monster's health but failed to slow the boss by any appreciable measure.

The massive elemental reared up over the Gimsar and swung both arms down to smash the foreman. Before the blows landed, the foreman shot out a line from a pistol-like grapnel launcher and zipped away as he used the device to pull himself to a tree on the far side of the clearing.

Earth shot up like a geyser, sending a wave of dirt and snow flying. Lifting its arms to not find a smashed Gimsar beneath them, the boss roared in fury and hunched its back.

I fired again and explosions blossomed across the monster's stony face. In response, conjured stones spouted skyward from the boss. Several stories in the air, the rocks arced downward before slamming toward me and the miners attacking it. Dodging the deadly rain and moving farther away from the boss, I emptied another entire magazine of railgun rounds into the elemental, but it still appeared to stand strong.

Time to try out another new toy.

Stowing the rifle in my Inventory, I pulled out a cylindrical tube with a wide red band around each end. Arrows projected from one side of each band, all pointing in the same direction to indicate the forward end of the cylinder. I then summoned a handheld device that consisted of a viewfinder scope and trigger housing, which I proceeded to snap into place on the cylinder as I scanned the unit.

Hastati-VI Launcher Control System

This reusable launcher control system is the targeting and trigger unit for the two-part Hastati-VI Modular Missile System. When paired with the single-use MMS disposable firing tubes, the launcher control system allows the user to designate the appropriate target for the type of missile indicated by the color code on the MMS housing:

Red - Anti-monster Plasma Ignitor

Yellow - Anti-vehicle Armor Penetrator

Blue- Anti-shield Disruptor

Green - Anti-personnel Cluster Munitions

I placed the tube on my shoulder and rested my forehead against the upper lip of the viewfinder, using the integrated sight to focus onto the massive elemental. The control unit sounded a quiet ding to indicate a good lock on the target.

A squeeze of the trigger jerked the launcher against my shoulder as the missile popped free of the tubular housing and glided a half dozen feet before the rocket engines ignited in a roar. The missile streaked across the open space and slammed into the elemental. The shot exploded in a powerful detonation that ripped the arm from its shoulder and enveloped the monster in a glowing wave of plasma that interrupted the elemental's rockstorm. The off-balance creature plunged forward, the destroyed shoulder digging a furrow into the ground.

Several of the other attackers glanced at me in shock at the massive amount of damage dealt by the weapon. Though quite pleased with finally having a weapon that applied a massive amount of damage, I stored the launcher in exchange for my rifle and resumed firing as the fallen elemental attempted to clamber upright with one good arm.

For one thing, the Credits involved in buying one of those missiles was not something I wanted to dwell upon. Still, if the Marine Corps had taught me one thing, it was that you had to test your gear constantly, if you didn't want to get caught out when the shit hit the fan.

With the monster's mobility stalled, the attacks quickly ground away the rest of the creature's remaining health. A field of broken rubble remained spread around the elemental's fallen body by the time the experience notification appeared in my queue of System updates. Thankfully, the other team had wrapped up clearing out the reinforcing elementals at the mine entrance, so everyone moved to loot the field.

Taking my time to first reload the rifle, I stowed the weapon before I approached the grizzled Gimsar gunner.

Having climbed onto the elemental, the dwarf looked down at me warily. "Did Sparkie really send ya?"

"I mentioned I was looking for monsters to kill and he gave me a waypoint here."

"Can't say I'm sorry ta see ya. Usually takes a fair bit to put them bigguns dahn," Vokrum said.

Standing next to the defeated boss, I looted the corpse. Several stacks of metallic ores popped into my Inventory, though I only recognized about half of the minerals. The rest were more exotic System materials. "You get ones like that often?"

The Gimsar shrugged. "Reckon a small chance of a boss if'n we leave the mine shafts long enough. Come back and they all filled up with elementals."

"There are multiple mines here?"

The foreman gestured farther along the ridgeline. "This here is Mine #1, but we've got over a dozen o' them dug into the hills around here. Each got a killin' field cleared outside."

"You've got a fully defended outpost at each mine?"

"Nah," Vokrum replied. "Jus' this here base. Everything gets broke down inta teensy chunks at the mines, hauled here for smelting, then loaded into a convoy to be shipped back into town."

"Any opportunity for more elemental slaying today?"

The dwarf considered my question for a moment, turning to take in the work crews around the open field. The combat teams had shifted to breaking apart the elementals into easily transported lumps, moving with well-worn efficiency. Several vehicles with large all-terrain wheels and long trailers rumbled over, entirely driverless, and the workers loaded them full of looted ores and elemental parts.

"We did take down that boss a might quick, so we'll have this debris cleared up for processing inna jif. You give us a hand loadin' up them bits inta the haulers and you can tag along to the next mine."

"What can I do to help?"

Vokrum grinned and a pick appeared in his empty hand, which the foreman tossed to me. I caught the tool one-handed and found it surprisingly heavy. Vokrum's brow raised at my catch, clearly expecting me to fumble the grab.

I inspected the pick while keeping my amusement at the dwarf's surprise to myself.

Management-Issued Pickaxe

No respectable miner would leave home without it.

Requirement: 60 Strength

Base Damage: 45

Durability: 100/100

Special Abilities: +10 Damage to Earth-type Elemental Creatures. +1% chance to find rare gemstone loot in targets slain by this weapon.

The hefty Strength requirement explained Vokrum's surprise. Still only gripping the shaft with one hand, I raised the weapon overhead before swinging it down on the dead elemental in front of me. The tip of the pick stabbed into the granite-like surface, digging deep and opening a jagged crack that radiated around the circumference of the elemental's arm. The fissure gaped open beneath the Gimsar foreman above me, causing Vokrum to hop farther up the arm to steady himself. The broken rocks settled after the sudden shift, a noticeable gap between the now separated parts of the arm.

"Oops," I said with a complete lack of sincerity.

Vokrum frowned but kept his silence as I swung the pick into the wrist joint of the section. The wrist similarly split apart at my hit, and I hacked apart the lower portion of the elemental's limb into more manageable pieces as one of the haulers pulled up beside the carcass.

Other miners soon joined in, and the boss was quickly sectioned out before being loaded into the haulers.

I silently stowed the pickaxe in my Inventory when we finished and looked for Vokrum as the last trailer rolled off the field toward the mining outpost. The dwarf gathered up the crews with little delay and directed them to the next site. Only minimal grousing greeted the foreman's declaration that they'd be clearing another site today.

A collection of eclectic vehicles waited around the outpost's main structures, and the miners moved out into a straggling procession along a well-worn trail that zigzagged up over the ridgeline. The transports ranged from rugged all-terrain vehicles of the two-, four-, and six-wheeled variety to more exotic hovercraft that floated above the ground.

Nobody paid any mind as I summoned my bike and rode along at the rear of the cavalcade. It only took a few minutes to reach the next mine after crossing the top of the rise and making our way down the far side to the killing field there.

Everyone parked well back from the mine entrance, and I stored my bike rather than risk collateral damage. By the time I joined the others at the reinforced adit that entered the hillside at a shallow angle, Vokrum was already leading a small team down into the mine. The rest of the crew readied their weapons for the emergence of the elementals and formed an arch around the entry.

Several minutes of waiting passed uneventfully until faint explosions sounded from the depths. A muffled rumble grew slightly louder moment by moment until the echoes of pounding footsteps preceded the team scampering out of the mine and through the widely spaced perimeter. All along the curved line, power gathered in the hands of spellcasters as rifles and pistols pointed toward the dim depths of the mine.

Shadows moved within the darkened portal, and hell rained down on the barely seen elementals. Explosions of magical and mundane weaponry thundered into the enclosed shaft, magnifying the concussive forces that tore through the leading elementals. The destruction allowed the defensive line

304

to back away at a measured pace, keeping the range open as more elementals poured from the opening.

The initial wave of creatures rushed out into the killzone, just like the monsters at the previous mine. This time though, no boss or alpha emerged alongside the normal elementals, which seemed to be flowing out of the mine in an unending tide. Rocky mounds of broken elementals grew as the monsters continued exiting the mine, forcing the creatures to clamber over piles of their destroyed brethren in order to get to their tormentors.

Several elementals of a lighter gray material formed up at the entrance of the mine itself and launched a barrage of thrown rock. Several impacted, opening up holes in the defenses and giving the throng a respite to push out toward the perimeter.

I shifted my aim to the ranged attackers, though my focus drew their ire after I managed to drop one of the gray elementals. The incoming rocks forced me to move evasively, dodging the worst of the attacks and suffering glancing blows. Miners on either side of me moved away to avoid the onslaught, dodging about with glee.

The intensity of the barrage built as more of the elementals directed their rocky projectiles and I backpedaled away. Too many rocks rained down too fast for me to dodge entirely, the air clogging with exploding dirt and stone and obscuring my vision.

A large stone the size of my head slammed into my shoulder. The impact shattered my collarbone with a nauseating crunch, spinning me around and throwing me to the ground. Pain shot up my neck and my left arm went numb as I bounced off the solidly packed earth of the killing field. I groaned from the pain before dismissing my rifle in order to push myself up with my good arm.

Just in time for another rock to smash into my back and knock the wind from my lungs. The new attack forced me into the ground again. Several missed projectiles thudded into the earth around me, and I summoned a healing potion. With my good arm, I injected the remedy into the side of my chest. Wheezing breathlessly through aching ribs, I crawled to my feet and tried to ignore the worst of the pain as my broken collarbone fused back into place.

Another rock came thundering in close, and I got my good arm in place, the new vambraces taking the hit and helping me parry it sideways. It still hurt like the bitches, but it was better than getting plastered once more.

I looked around and found the majority of the miners now mixed into melee with most of the elementals. That limited the effectiveness of the ranged monsters since any projectiles were just as likely to hit another elemental as a miner.

I pulled out a plasma grenade and thumbed the activator before throwing the weapon in a lengthy Hail Mary at the cluster of ranged elementals. Without waiting for the explosion to follow, I drew my melee weapons and dove into the fray.

I elected to wield the pickaxe instead of my usual axe with my dominant right hand. The sharp edges of my knife were far from ideal against the rocky construction of the elementals, but stacking Expose allowed the pickaxe to find purchase with repeated strikes. Chipping away at limbs while avoiding their slow, flailing counterattacks let me build up enough stacks of Expose until I finally landed a devastating blow that proved effective. Those attacks often left a shattered core within the elemental's torso, causing them to collapse into a pile of dust and broken stone.

Gradually the slow-moving elementals fell, one by one. The ranged attackers were picked off by others who'd waded into the searing heat of my grenade. Finally, the field lay strewn with rubble and injured miners.

Several of the miners would certainly have died from shock or the severity of their wounds before the System, but now even crushed or mangled limbs were naturally repaired so long as they weren't severed completely. Even then, some Skills or the Shop offered remedies for such problems, a fix available for almost anything short of death itself.

Cleaning up after the fight took longer this time, though there was no boss to disassemble. The longer journey back to the mining outpost meant more time between round trips for the haulers before they returned for another load of ores.

I helped with my borrowed pickaxe as the crews easily smashed the broken elementals into manageable chunks by the time the trailers got back for their second payload. Once the final bits of the rubbled elementals had been shoveled into the haulers, the miners followed the last of the trailers back across the ridge to the outpost.

Vokrum beckoned for me to ride alongside him as we left the killing field. "It's been a productive day, we done tore up them elementals with your help."

"Yes, a productive day indeed," I replied with a nod as I quickly checked my Status, pleased at finding my experience grown by a slight but still noticeable amount.

Vokrum stayed quiet for a bit. "Expected ya to ask for payment beyond just loot."

I glanced at the dwarf and raised an eyebrow. "I never turn down Credits if they're offered."

The Gimsar rolled his eyes and focused on the trail ahead of us and remained quiet for the rest of the trip back to the outpost.

A cloud of gray smoke bloomed from several chimneys rising above a long building in the center of the fort. The haulers lined up at the end of the building, and the trailers lifted on powered pistons that tilted their filled beds, dumping their piles of ore onto a conveyor system that carried the raw materials away for smelting.

Large doors stood open at the opposite side of the building, and figures within maneuvered pallets filled with solid bars of refined metals onto long trailers for transport into town. The loaded pallets matched the ones I'd seen filling the boxcars and loading bay of the transport hub this morning.

"You fixin' to head back ta the city?" Vokrum asked from beside me.

"Yes, I need to see if my group is leaving town tomorrow."

"Since you're headin' thataways, will ya escort the convoy carryin' today's processed metal?"

"If you pay me Credits for the job, I will."

Vokrum sighed. "Figurin' as much."

He named a sum and I countered thirty percent higher. Vokrum raised his offering half again to my counteroffer, and I agreed rather than drag things out further. A short-term contract sealed the arrangement, with the Credits set to transfer upon arrival at the destination warehouse.

The smelters processed the ores faster than any pre-System facility could have, and a two-truck convoy soon pulled out from the outpost.

The trip back into Denver turned out to be easy Credits since nothing attacked the trucks. As dusk fell, I found myself at the same depot where I'd found Ismyna that morning. I left the trucks to unload, my escort completed and a few more Credits in my account.

All in all, a good day. Even if I expected things to pick up soon enough.

Chapter 22

My stomach growled a reminder that I hadn't eaten a full meal since breakfast, so I followed my nose into a local diner that served a massive, chili-covered omelet. A side of potatoes and biscuits with sausage gravy complemented my breakfast-for-dinner meal.

With my hunger sated, I returned to Union Station to find the train moved onto a different track. More passenger cars extended the length of the rearranged train, with two new coach carriages added just behind the workshop car and several additional sleepers at the end. The observation car now sat just behind the new coaches, followed by the diner then the sleepers. The rearrangement meant that standard coach passengers would get access to the observation lounge and dining room but wouldn't need to continue farther back to the exclusive sleeper cars.

All of the armored carriages gleamed as they reflected the station lights. The sight projected strength and durability, which seemed an intentional display to fill passengers with confidence. Confidence that the train would reach its destination successfully despite the dangers in the wilds of the Dungeon World.

Several Pharyleri crewmembers hurried about the train, performing minor tasks. I found Wrefen as the conductor supervised the loading of additional linens and towels to stock the new sleeper cars.

"Hey, Wrefen, have you heard if we're leaving tomorrow?"

The gnome greeted me warmly. "Evening, Hal. I think it's likely. Everything will be ready on our part as soon as we're done here. Ismyna would know for sure."

"Thanks, any idea where I can find her?"

The gnome shrugged. "Aren't you the bounty hunter who's supposed to be able to find people?"

"Generally I do that by asking questions. So, I'm asking you." I glared at the gnome, though my expression lacked any true heat.

Wrefen chuckled. "Fair enough. I haven't seen her lately. Check the engine?"

"All right, I'll start there."

Leaving the gnome to finish loading, I headed up the platform toward the locomotive at the head of the train. After clambering up to the control cabin entrance, I knocked before peeking inside and finding it empty. I closed the door and turned back to the workshop car that still followed behind the locomotive. The lights inside were on when the door opened, and the sound of quiet conversation flowed out.

The excitable murmurs continued as I entered and found Eldri alongside several of his technical crew gathered around a workbench where Nargen sat with his robotic dog on the raised table. The dwarf had side panels open on the quadrupedal drone and appeared to be discussing something about the inner workings with the group of gnomes.

Forward of the open panels, weapon mounts attached to the dog's shoulders and rose up to either side, where boxy micro-missile launchers sat on swivel mounts like deadly wings. The weapon assemblies pivoted to point in my direction when I walked in, and the gazes of the workshop's occupants followed.

I raised an eyebrow. "Is this a crafter-only discussion?"

"Oh no, just testing the motion tracking on the launchers," Nargen hurriedly explained. The dwarf bopped a fist on the back of the robot and the launchers reoriented themselves to point straight ahead.

I snorted and turned to Eldri. "Have you seen Ismyna?"

"Not since we had dinner together earlier," the gnomish mechanic replied with a shake of his head.

310

"Thanks. I'll let you get back to whatever tech stuff you were doing."

Eldri grinned, returning to the discussion with Nargen and the other gnomes as I left the workshop through one of the side doors and hopped down to the platform. The platform looked abandoned now. No signs remained even of Wrefen's team, now apparently finished with their last-minute preparations for tomorrow's probable departure.

Deciding that I was done tracking down Ismyna the hard way, I pulled my earpiece from Inventory and stuck it into my ear. Tapping the activator, I keyed the engineer's communicator.

The gnome's bubbly voice spoke up a moment later, a touch breathless. "Hal? Is something wrong?"

"No, I'm just checking in and seeing if we depart tomorrow."

I stepped away from the brightly lit train as the gnome stayed quiet for a moment. "I think we'll be ready in the afternoon, so have your team ready by noon."

"I'll let them know. I hope I didn't interrupt a date."

"Hmmph." Silence hung in the air for a moment as Ismyna seemed a touch irked at my comment. "Good night, Hal."

The communicator went dead, and I chuckled quietly as I stowed the device back into Inventory. It seemed pretty unlikely that I'd hear from Ismyna again tonight.

Movement in the corner of my eye caught my attention and I shifted my head to watch as Sheera Valenstar casually ambled across the platform toward the crew entrance on the lower level of the last sleeper car. She hadn't been a part of the crew loading up the new sleeper cars earlier, and I remembered Wrefen's mention of her disappearing for a couple days.

The leonine Demarcian caught sight of me watching and her gait hitched as she hesitated mid-step before continuing on and ignoring my presence. I glanced around the platform for anything that might have surprised her, finding nothing.

Sheera reached the train, and I shook my head at the Demarcian's behavior. It only reminded me of an adage in a science fiction book I'd once read on deployment.

Aliens were alien.

Assigning human motivations to species with distinctly different physiology and psychology rarely worked out, at least in pre-System fiction. Part of me wondered what those writers from the early eras of science fiction would think of how things had turned out with the System taking over on Earth. Or if they would have survived.

Maybe the guy who wrote *Starship Troopers*? Mobile Infantry in power armor would fit right into the System for sure.

The movie version, probably not so much.

Anyways, I needed to get the message out to the team instead of spending my night reminiscing about dated entertainment. Reaching out mentally, I activated my connection to Dayena's party chat and dropped an update to the team about the noon assembly before waiting for everyone's confirmation. Everyone seemed anxious and ready to depart, and I found myself in agreement.

It was time to move on.

With that chore completed, I had the rest of the evening free. Not feeling particularly tired despite the long day, I decided instead to find myself a drink.

I started off inside Union Station at the Terminal Bar, where the drink menu highlighted Apocalypse Ale. Though it turned out they only had a single case, most of which had already been consumed, I forked over the Credits for one of the few remaining bottles. Though I enjoyed the richness of the smooth malty beverage, I limited myself to nursing a single drink. I sipped from the ice-cold bottle and tried to ignore the itching between my shoulder blades warning me that Dayena and I had been in one place for too long.

How long would it take for her family to track her down again now that they'd already found us once?

Her cousins had first confronted us in a Safe Zone. They'd had to have paid off the local authorities and that hadn't turned out well for them, so I doubted they would repeat the same tactic. At least not in the same way.

No, my Credits were on the next meeting occurring just before entering or just after leaving a Safe Zone. Of the two options there, entering would be the more dangerous for Dayena and me. If they hit us leaving a settlement, there might be nothing stopping us from escaping back inside, so blocking us out would be the smart play. Either way, I had some new tricks in my bag to shift the odds in our favor after my latest gear pickup from the Shop.

The bottle of ale felt warm in my hand from idly holding it too long while considering the scenarios that might play out. Channeling the faintest flow of Mana into my palm, I forced a slight layer of ice around the bottle. Frost grew across the surface of the brown glass and spread out from my hand.

I focused on the creeping fractals and halted their spread up the neck of the bottle. Limiting the reach of the ice formation, I instead thickened it until the glass surface of the bottle appeared sheathed in a thin white beer cozy. The covering actively chilled the liquid inside the bottle instead of just keeping the beverage from warming to room temperature.

I'd manipulated ice from spells before but never with this ease or efficiency. It seemed like the Ice Affinity greatly improved my ability to control the spell formations as they formed, allowing me to improvise more readily. It still took effort, but I suspected that, like most things worthwhile, only dedicated training and concerted practice would increase my effectiveness.

I certainly needed another Shop visit before tomorrow's departure in order to broaden my repertoire of ice-based spells. More spells would give me a wider base to choose from if I needed to customize. I figured I wouldn't need more than the standard effects of spells like Frostbolt or Frostnova most of the time, but options were always nice.

Taking small sips of my now-chilled drink, I tried to think up a list of spells that would be the most useful. Something that provided armor topped the list. I needed more defensive options since my Class lacked Skills in that direction. An area effect for targeting multiple foes went on the list next. After that, I supposed utility spells, but I wasn't really sure what options I might need. I'd have to see what was available or if my shopkeeper had any recommendations.

I didn't have the Mana regeneration for prolonged spellcasting, and I still planned on keeping most of my focus on my weapons for dealing direct damage. Still, having more options meant being less predictable in combat and that was always good. Especially against competent foes.

My biggest fear was being pinned down and unable to soften enemies up at range before they closed into melee. Stronger or more numerous opponents could accomplish that task, and both of those feats lay within the capabilities of Dayena's family, if they were willing to spend the Credits.

They had sent two branch family members all the way to Earth, a not inexpensive feat. That those cousins then cheaped out with undertrained local mercenaries spoke to either frugality or incompetence. Relying on an enemy's continued incompetence was a good way to get dead, so I needed to plan for the worst-case scenario.

Which brought me back to my spellcasting tactics. My core doctrine of fire and maneuver, adapted from my Marine Corps training, laid the foundation for my strategy. Keep the range open, advance or retreat as necessary, and in the worst-case scenario, escape and evade to continue the fight later.

Satisfied with my rough plans, I finished my drink and allowed the spell formation around the empty beer bottle to dissipate. I left a few Credits as a tip for the bartender and headed back to my room on the train to get some sleep.

Chapter 23

I woke well before dawn and beat most of the crew to an early breakfast in the dining car. When I walked in and took a seat, only a few booths were full. Sheera was the server on duty, and the golden-furred alien took my order with her typical polite service.

The aroma of crisping bacon soon filled the car, and I could almost imagine the grease crackling in the pan while I nursed my cup of coffee. When my plate arrived, I ate quickly, then left the dining car before the sun peeked over the horizon.

The city streets were mostly empty as I made my way to the Shop housed in the former bank. Naturally, the bank building itself was still closed due to the early hour. With some time to kill before the bank opened, I wandered through the empty streets and took in a bit more of the city.

A paved footpath along Cherry Creek to the southwest made for a slightly more scenic walk. When I descended to the paved path, two shadows flowed out of an alleyway and followed along a short distance behind me, their heavy footsteps crunching on the walkway. It felt as if they weren't trying to hide their stalking at all.

The cold air settled within the slight depression, and my breath clouded in the air as I walked beside the partially frozen stream and kept a sense on the watchers at my back with a light touch of Greater Observation. The walking trail was wide enough for three or four people side by side, and tufts of frozen grass stuck up from beneath the snow and frost covering a small strip of uneven terrain along the bank of the creek.

I half hoped for a monster to jump out of the water, but the Safe Zone included the waterway and my desire for a bit of extra experience faded as the sun crawled above the horizon. Then the footsteps behind me picked up their pace and I wondered if my pursuers might make up for that lack of monster presence.

I stepped to the side of the trail under a bridge that spanned the creek and the trails along either side, intending to allow my two tails to pass me by if that was their intention.

Turning to look back as I stopped, I knew that my quiet morning was about to get interesting. Two aliens ambled toward me, slowing now that I'd stopped. Both had a few inches in height on me and nearly doubled my width, their tight jumpsuits bulging from their muscular bulk as they halted within spitting distance.

The first was an alien type I hadn't yet seen, with gray pebbly skin and a protruding snout with a curved ivory horn sticking up above the nose. The appearance reminded me of a rhinoceros more than anything. The second was a Scrofalori, one of the boar-like humanoids with brownish fur. The pair reminded me of a cartoon series I'd watched as a kid. All these two needed were a pair of purple punk rock shades and a combat helmet.

They eyed me menacingly as they stood side by side, nearly blocking the path. I returned the favor and scanned their status with Greater Observation far more deeply and unsubtly than polite behavior dictated.

Ro'khar'sar (Sect Bodyguard Level 39)
HP: 480/480
MP: 110/110

Bemparat (Sect Bruiser Level 38)
HP: 460/460
MP: 80/80

Other than the obvious Class names, the insignia of three overlapping circles adorning their chests proclaimed their allegiance to the Binary Eclipse Sect.

I folded my arms across my chest and waited for them to make a move, while the two glowered at me for a long minute.

Finally, I grinned. "I'm still waiting, if you're supposed to be intimidating me."

The aliens looked at each other in confusion before Ro'khar'sar, the gray-skinned rhino-headed alien, spoke. "You work with the train Pharyleri."

Tilting my head, I looked at the alien in puzzlement. "I can't think of how that would be any of your business."

Bemparat stepped forward. "Then maybe you need to learn a lesson about who is in charge here."

The Scrofalori swung a beefy arm in a roundhouse that seemed to float through the air toward my head. For all the power behind the blow, my Perception and Agility allowed me to avoid the attack almost trivially. Ducking beneath the haymaker and stepping behind the alien, I punched a fist into his kidney. If the boar-like alien had a kidney.

Even with the musclesuit's woven armor, Bemparat grunted in pain from the surprising strength of my strike and arched away from the blow. I hammered two more kidney shots before the alien twisted out of reach as the rhino-like alien charged forward with an attack of his own.

The gray-skinned alien's fist drove at me in a powerful cross as I backpedaled, raising my hands in defense, and I parried while pivoting away from the strike. Sliding sideways along the path, I maneuvered to keep the rhino between the boar and me before the second alien recovered its balance.

Oddly enough, neither one seemed to be using any active Skills, at least so far.

Then I remembered the hotel clerk's story of the missing Adventurers and their bar brawl with the Sect, notably the lack of deaths in the face of the abundance of property damage. Seemed like they were playing somewhat fair besides the two-on-one advantage, so I decided to humor them for a bit.

Once the Scrofalori reentered the fray, I worked to keep the aliens tripping over each other as much as possible. A few of their wild strikes glanced off my armor but still left bruises, even as I dished out more solid hits in reply.

Without any active Skills in play, wearing them down using fisticuffs would be a long fight. Doing enough damage to overcome passive healing was a pain and a half, which, feeling the smart along my arms from blocking one too many blows, was not an issue for the damn Enforcers. I had to wonder if Thugs and Enforcers got special Skills that let them stack health damage in a way that stopped them from killing their targets.

Yeah, the fight was boring.

The fray drifted along the trail, deeper under the bridge as I bobbed and weaved away from the aliens. Nothing really prevented me from turning and running. I knew the two couldn't catch me if I tried to get away, but two things stopped me.

On one hand, I doubted their lack of active Skill use would last if I turned my back. On the other hand, I hated bullies and really wanted to kick their asses in a lesson they'd be sure to remember.

Done boxing politely, I feinted toward Ro'khar'sar then jerked backward as Bemparat overcommitted at the perceived opening. Instead of pulling farther away as I had been, I kicked the side of the Scrofalori's knee and activated Hinder at the same time. The joint snapped with an ugly crack and the alien collapsed with a screaming bellow of pain.

Ro'khar'sar glanced at his wailing partner, taking his eyes off me.

Amateur mistake.

Before the rhino could look back at me, I'd closed the distance between us. I ran two steps up the retaining wall that blocked the side of the trail and hooked an arm under Ro'khar'sar's long snout. I launched myself off the wall, swinging around the alien's neck. Using the leverage of my momentum and weight, I twisted the alien from his feet and flung him to the ground not far from his partner. The pavement cracked beneath the impact of the large alien, who lay stunned from the heavy landing.

Drawing both pistols, I knelt on the prone rhino. I pressed the barrel of Ace on the alien's forehead as I jammed Last Word up the nostril of the Scrofalori, who had finally stopped screaming and pushed himself up onto his good knee. Both aliens froze at the touch of cold metal against their flesh.

"You boys know the deal," I said, my voice cooler than the icy breeze drifting through the underpass. "I ask questions and you answer them. Why were you following me?"

Ro'khar'sar tried to glance at his partner, but I pressed the gun harder into his skull to keep him from looking up.

Bemparat whimpered when I twitched the barrel sticking up his nose. "We were just going to rough you up a little to send a message."

A little. Right. "What message exactly?"

Neither alien spoke for several moments. So I pistol-whipped Ro'khar'sar. The *thunk* of the pistol butt striking a thick skull echoed through the underpass.

Then I prodded the rhino-like alien, who moaned before speaking. "Binary Eclipse owns the streets."

I snorted down my laughter. "All right. Here's what's going to happen. I don't want to hear about anyone from Binary Eclipse harassing anyone on the streets. Pharyleri. Human. No one. Or I'll hunt you two down first."

I let the threat hang in the air with a heavy silence.

"Are we done here?" Despite the question, my tone made clear that only one answer was acceptable.

The Scrofalori nodded slowly and carefully as Ro'khar'sar groaned before massaging the knot forming on his scalp.

"Ro'khar'sar, are you done?" I repeated the question intently, pressing the gun a little more firmly into the alien's head.

"Yes," Ro'khar'sar wheezed.

I pushed myself to my feet, keeping one pistol shoved into Bemparat's nose and applied a little more force than necessary to the other weapon as I rose. I stepped back a couple paces while keeping the guns trained on the two Sect members. "Good. Now get lost."

The two watched me warily for a second until I impatiently waved them away with one pistol. Ro'khar'sar scrambled to his feet and threw Bemparat's arm over his shoulder, helping the other alien limp away as they retreated back down the path.

I watched until they were out of sight before holstering my weapons and heading in the opposite direction. It was only a few minutes' walk back to the bank housing the Shop as it opened for the day, I used the crystal's teleport function to reach my personal instance.

Ryk stood waiting for me. "Early morning for you, isn't it?"

"Just as early for you," I replied before voicing a question that had long bothered me. "How are you always available when I use the Shop?"

The ram-like centauroid chuckled and gave a half-hearted shrug. "It's just part of the way the System works."

"Right." If I wanted the answer to that question, it would probably require more Credits than I cared to spend researching the answer.

"Are you here to buy or sell today?" Ryk asked.

"Both," I said, unloading the spoils of my fights with the elementals from my Inventory.

Most of the loot exchange went fairly quickly for most of the larger quantities of ores and only a minor bit of haggling over some of the precious stones.

"Now that you've got a solid balance of Credits in your favor, what can I offer to swing that sum back to me?"

"I'd like to see the ice-based spells you have available," I said.

Ryk looked at me in question. "You've mostly kept away from spellcrafting, other than healing and the typical Adventurer combat spells to round out any elemental weaknesses."

"At least I didn't buy fireball."

"So, you didn't get one ridiculously common spell." Ryk sighed. "Here's the list."

A console lit up on the counter beside the shopkeeper, displaying a lengthy list of spells and their descriptions. As I navigated through the list, a holographic display appeared above the counter that showed a translucent yellow humanoid figure casting the spell currently highlighted in the console.

The spell Blizzard showed the yellow caster selecting a wide area somewhat away from itself and raining down a hail of jagged ice and sleet that tore into a variety of enemies in a circular area around the spell's targeted spot.

Since the spell had area damage, I saved that one as a possible purchase despite the high Mana cost.

Moving to the next spell, the red enemies disappeared, and the yellow caster animation reset itself.

When I selected a spell called Chains of Ice, a second figure in red appeared and rushed toward the yellow humanoid. The yellow figure cast the spell, and pillars of ice erupted from the ground around the red target, flinging ice-covered chains around the enemy and holding it in place.

Since I already possessed Class Skills that slowed targets with Hinder, I passed on that particular spell but continued browsing through the catalog.

Ryk puttered around the lengthy hall as I perused the catalog, the shopkeeper quietly ignoring all of my playing and replaying of the spell animations.

Finally, I narrowed my selections down to three. I bookmarked a couple other spells for future purchases but decided to limit myself to three for now, ensuring that I wouldn't overload my already weak Mana regeneration in combat.

I brought up the final trio on the console and finalized my purchase.

Ice Armor

Effect: Creates a suit of armor made of ice on the caster. While cold to the touch, it does not harm the wearer, especially if applied over clothing or armor. Armor has 500 Hit Points.

Cost: 125 Mana

Ice Armor may be enhanced by using the Elemental Affinity of Ice. Armor durability increased by 10% per level of affinity.

Whiteout

Effect: Covers a 10-meter radius area with chilling frost and fills the affected zone with frozen fog, dealing 5 cold damage per second to hostile targets within the spell's area of effect and decreasing visibility for affected targets.

Duration: 1 minute.

Cost 50 Mana.

Whiteout may be enhanced by using the Elemental Affinity of Ice. Duration and coverage area increased by 20% per level of affinity.

Howling Blast

Effect: Blasts out a cone of frigid wind from the caster, dealing 100 cold damage to all enemies within the effect out to a range of 10 meters. Targets taking damage from this spell are knocked back 1 meter from the force of the gust. Cooldown: 60 seconds

Cost: 75 Mana

Howling Blast may be enhanced by using the Elemental Affinity of Ice. Damage and knockback distance increased by 20% per level of affinity.

The first spell, Ice Armor, served a purely defensive role to increase my ability to take damage. It might also save me some Credits, if it reduced the number of armored jumpsuits I went through.

The other two spells could affect multiple targets if positioned well, but I'd really chosen them for their utility effects. Whiteout created concealment and provided the option to break line of sight to enemies, even in wide open spaces without cover, while Howling Blast punished enemies approaching melee range and allowed me to open the range back up if an enemy got too close for comfort.

The line at the bottom of each spell description that noted the additional bonuses offered by the affinity reminded me that I had a pair of existing ice spells that might also be boosted similarly.

Digging into my status, I pulled up the spell information for my current spells.

Frostbolt (VI)

Effect: Creates a Frost bolt from the user's Mana, which can be directed to damage a target. The dart does 90 Ice damage and slows the target by 3%. Slow effect stacks up to three times (9%). Cooldown 10 seconds.

Cost: 25 Mana.

Frostbolt may be enhanced by using the Elemental Affinity of Ice. Damage and slow effect increased by 20% per level of affinity.

Frostnova (IV)

Effect: Creates a ring of Frost from the user's Mana which blasts outward in a 6-meter radius centered on the user. The ring does 42 Ice damage and may affect enemies with a Freeze effect, rooting them in place for up to 14 seconds.

Cooldown 30 seconds.

Cost: 50 Mana.

Frostnova may be enhanced by using the Elemental Affinity of Ice. Damage and Freeze effect duration increased by 10% per level of affinity.

The affinity consistently boosted the damage and secondary effects of my Ice spells at no added cost. The only downside was that I didn't have a clue how to actually increase the level of that affinity to really multiply the new bonus effects.

The shopkeeper returned to the counter when I finished my purchases and transferred the remaining Credit balance to my account, not that much remained.

"Anything else?" Ryk asked.

"What can you tell me about increasing an Elemental Affinity?"

The shopkeeper eyed me quietly for a moment. "Use it."

"That's it?" I quirked an eyebrow at Ryk.

"I'd be happy to sell you a guide if you want to waste your Credits." He shrugged. "There are plenty of manuals theorizing about Affinities."

"It sounds like you don't think much of them."

"It's a link to a force of nature that exists outside of the System. If your Affinity is able to increase, then using it repeatedly will allow it to grow."

I thanked Ryk, and after a quick goodbye, I was transported back to the bank building. The lobby bustled with a crowd of Pharyleri and a few humans. Most were lined up to speak with the tellers behind the counters, and I easily joined the flow of traffic out of the building.

A glance at the morning sun, now noticeably above the horizon, confirmed that several hours still remained before I needed to meet up with the rest of my team. Rather than heading directly back to Union Station, I detoured through the market areas. While browsing, I wasn't really focused on equipment or weapons so much as keeping my eyes peeled for consumables and interesting foods.

One vendor sold jerky made from various local monsters, and I bought a couple pounds each of the preserved bison and elk meat, along with a sampling of some more exotic meats from creatures not native to Earth. The rich smells wafting from the stall prompted my stomach to grumble, and the proprietor recommended a nearby eatery, promising the best hot dogs I'd ever had.

I followed the directions a couple streets over to a small shop at the end of a row of brick-fronted buildings with a red-and-white sign overhead advertising "Biker Jim's." Signage on the door announced the establishment as the premier place in the city for gourmet dogs.

After trying the elk jalapeno cheddar dog, I believed the sign's claim. The rattlesnake-and-rabbit dog also proved extremely savory.

I ordered at least one of everything on the menu after that, not worrying about the calories as my System-enhanced metabolism pretty much made it impossible to ever put on weight that wasn't strictly muscle mass regardless of how much I ate or drank.

Finished with my early lunch, I headed to the station and got back with time to spare.

A line of passengers waited on the platform along the train. Wrefen and several of his staff stood at the head of the line as they checked tickets. Each passenger was then directed to a seat in coach or, for the more affluent, guided to a room in one of the sleeper cars.

The staff waved me past the line when they saw me approaching, to the annoyance of several waiting passengers who promptly complained about special treatment. I rolled my eyes to the staff with my back to the whining passengers and received a few smirks in response, though the flickers of amusement were quickly replaced by the appearance of polite professionalism.

Before I reached the sleeper car, Dayena pinged me through her party chat interface. *"You're not wearing your earpiece are you, Hal?"*

"Nope," I replied. *"Just got back to the train after some last-minute errands."*

"Did said errand involve you purchasing any new weapons or ammunition?"

"Maybe!" My reply may have been a little too cheerful. Having more options in my arsenal always brightened my mood.

The dark elf sighed. *"Of course, you did. Anyway, Ismyna wants us both for something special. Meet us on the platform by the engine."*

"On my way."

Grabbing the communicator from my Inventory, I stuck the earpiece in place before I continued to the meeting point. The Pharyleri Engineer and

Truinnar Countess were bounding down from the locomotive's control cabin when I arrived.

"What's up?" I asked the gnome.

Ismyna glanced at my ear and saw the communicator in place before she replied. "VIP escort. We're taking a representative from the local Sect back with us for in-person negotiations at the starport."

"Oh, fun." My dry tone relayed my complete lack of enthusiasm.

Ismyna glared at me. "Is there something I should know?"

"I beat up a couple Sect goons earlier this morning, so I might not be the best individual to haul along if you're concerned about making a good impression with the sect."

"You left them alive?" Dayena gaped, clearly surprised, as Ismyna stared at me in a mixture of frustration and disappointment.

I answered in an attempt to placate them both. "I figured things were probably tense enough with the Sect and didn't want to bring more trouble to the local gnomes."

Ismyna rubbed her temples. "I don't need this crap. You're coming anyway. They won't start anything in the city, and if there's a problem, we'll deal with it right off."

We left the engine and walked back down the platform, passing the line of passengers still boarding. This time none of them commented as I escorted the Pharyleri leader around the end of the platform and over to the Union Station building.

The guards opened the doors for us, and we headed toward the hotel lobby. A small party exited the hotel as we approached, Clan Leader Piklyn at the forefront of the group with an alien that looked like a humanoid frog. Large, glassy black eyes stuck up from nubs on either side of the alien's wide head, blinking nervously as the frog-like alien looked around the busy terminal. The alien had no real neck to speak of, just a slight narrowing of the upper torso leading up to a broad mouth that stretched almost the full width of its head. Two spindly arms and a pair of backward-canted, equally skinny legs extended from the alien's rotund torso.

A quick scan with Greater Observation confirmed that the rotund amphibian served the Binary Eclipse Sect.

Jer'myeh Anura (Sect Assistant to the Regional Manager Level 41)

HP: 410/410
MP: 650/650

Each leader was escorted by a pair of their own guards, who followed behind as the leaders walked side by side. I recognized the two bulky fighters serving as the wardens for the portly Jer'myeh. Ro'khar'sar and Bemparat still wore their musclesuits, though additional armor plates now protected their shoulders, legs, and, amusingly enough to me, their kidneys.

Once the pair of bodyguards saw the approach of our party, they focused on stoically minding their subject and avoided looking anywhere near my direction.

"From the awkward shuffling of those Sect thugs, I assume those were your dance partners?" Dayena asked through party chat.

"Just a little bare-knuckle brawling with no Skills or weapons until I got tired of playing their game and drew down."

By the time I finished a quick summary of the fight, Piklyn was introducing the Sect representative to Ismyna.

"And this is Jer'myeh Anura. He'll be serving as the Sect's voice in the interplanetary trade negotiations with the other Pharyleri clans."

Ismyna bowed to the frog-like humanoid, who responded in kind, before the two launched into a round of small talk. Jer'myeh's voice sounded like a cross between a bubbly gasp and the expected croaking of a frog.

Eventually, the leaders wrapped up their discussion and Piklyn waved farewell, prompting Dayena and me to step aside as Ismyna led Jer'myeh back the way we'd come. The two guards finally looked at me as they passed, eyeing me suspiciously as they followed their charge.

I smirked at Dayena when the alien group preceded us, and the dark elf rolled her eyes.

The return to the platform went completely uneventfully. Only a handful of passengers were yet to board, and none of them voiced any comments as our party bypassed the queue. Likely, nobody wanted to piss off both the gnomes and the local Sect.

Ismyna led the group to the forwardmost sleeper and through the bottom level access door into the car. A narrow hall ran the length of the lower level, and the gnome led Jer'myeh to a door at the front end of the passage where Wrefen and another olive-uniformed gnome from the hospitality staff waited. Behind the two gnomes, Kurak stood stoically. The armored Yerrick's presence as a posted guard made a statement about the security protecting the train, on top of the escort already provided by Dayena and me.

Ismyna introduced Wrefen and the second gnome, Glumev, as the sleeper car attendant overseeing the passenger needs on the carriage. The pair of gnomes opened the compartment door, which slid open to reveal a luxury suite that took up the forward quarter of the sleeper's length. The chamber included a private bathroom for the suite's residents and partitioned sleeping areas for up to five individuals, so there would be plenty of room for the Sect envoy and bodyguards.

Ismyna entered with Jer'myeh, and the two Sect guards followed. The two heavies nodded respectfully to Kurak as they slipped by the minotaur, who returned the gesture. It was an odd interaction, given the way the two bodyguards had completely disregarded the presence of Dayena and me on the escort from the station.

"Since you're on the lower level, you'll feel less of the side-to-side sway that the train usually makes," Ismyna explained to Jer'myeh as she showed off the features inside the room.

"I appreciate that," Jer'myeh croaked. "I don't care for that much motion."

Behind the frog alien's back, the pair of Sect bodyguards exchanged a glance that betrayed their frustration with the envoy's sensitivity.

After settling the Sect representative into the cabin, Ismyna left the alien to the care of Wrefen and Glumev. Gesturing for us to precede her as she exited the suite, the gnome guided us out. I waved respectfully to Kurak as we left the VIP suite and headed back to the platform outside.

Ismyna stopped and rubbed her temples. "That Catesbeian is going to be a pain in my ass this whole trip."

"Probably." Dayena patted the gnome's shoulder comfortingly, which earned the dark elf a glare from the Pharyleri.

Ismyna gritted her teeth. "Twenty-four hours. I just have to make it one more day until he's Borgym and Mother's problem."

"After it took us so long to get out here, we'll be back that fast?" I asked.

The gnome lit up. "Yes! We'll be going so much faster now that the tracks are properly repaired and System recognized. I can't wait to open up the throttle!"

I raised an eyebrow. "So, you're not expecting monster problems?"

Ismyna shook her head. "Nothing outside of normal Dungeon World encounters. The train itself won't draw creatures anymore since we're not messing with Mana flows and the tracks are sorta 'Safe Zone'-ish."

"It should be an easy journey back then," Dayena said.

I turned to the Truinnar, incredulous. "Why would you say something like that?"

"What?" The dark elf's brow furrowed in puzzlement.

I sighed. "You never say things like that. Now we're probably going to get attacked by monsters the whole way back or something ridiculous."

"Nonsense superstition," Dayena retorted.

Shaking my head, I turned away from the two women and returned to my quarters in the staff sleeper to wait out the final boarding.

Yup, we were in the shit now.

Chapter 24

Lying in my bunk with hands folded behind my head, I felt a slight shudder travel through the car as the train lurched into motion.

After leaving Ismyna and Dayena outside, I'd confirmed that Kurak, Nargen, and Lyrra were all onboard the train and ready to depart. That left me no further responsibilities, so I'd been relaxing until we left the station.

Sitting up and swinging my legs over the side of my elevated rack, I looked out the window to watch as we departed Union Station at a crawl. After several minutes, the train slowed back down to a halt. Worried there might be a problem already, I toggled my earpiece to the general crew channel and listened. The calm inflection of the conversation allayed my concerns, and I eavesdropped as the gnomes worked with the local clan running a yard engine to hitch a lengthy string of loaded freight cars to the aft end of our train.

After a faint shiver ran through the train, the voices in the communicator confirmed the connection with the freight cars was completed.

I reclined back into my bunk as the train moved forward again, taking longer to accelerate but picking up more speed. After passing through the outskirts of Commerce City and the outskirts of Denver, the train sped up even further until we were moving far faster than we'd hit at any point on the west-bound journey.

A sway from side to side gently rocked the sleeper car, more noticeable at the higher speeds we were now traveling. The oscillation came from the interaction of adhesion and inertial forces between the rails and the wheel trucks of the train. I knew that at some point, the oscillation could become violent enough to derail the train, but I suspected that Ismyna had that aspect under control between Class Skills and System technology.

Outside my window, the abandoned starport flashed by as we raced northeast, and I watched the ice-covered structures recede into the distance as we left them behind.

Within an hour, the tracks shifted to head mostly straight east. With the late afternoon sun at our backs, the snow-covered plains alongside the tracks gave way to more greenery as we left the area affected by the dragon's influence.

I shot up from my rack at the sound of energy weapon fire and a cry of alarm over the crew channel in my earpiece. Jumping from my bunk, I bolted out into the hall as confusion erupted over the communicator.

"Sounds of attack on the crew communication channels," I warned the team over party chat, pausing in the passage as I debated which direction to go from here. *"Gear up and try to locate the source."*

"Lyrra and I are in the lounge car," Dayena replied. *"No sign of combat here."*

"The workshop car is clear," Nargen reported.

A cabin door slid open, and Kurak stepped out. The Yerrick nodded at me and waited for my direction.

"Nargen, you're closest to the control cabin. Head forward and coordinate our response with Ismyna, relaying any information so she can focus on the crew and train," I ordered. *"Kurak is with me. The rest of us will meet up in the observation deck of the lounge car."*

The minotaur hurried forward as I followed, though Kurak's hustle was more of a sideways shuffle with his large frame.

My gut told me the attack wasn't a monster attack. The sensors would have picked that up. This was something else.

We reached the observation lounge after passing through the other sleeper cars and the dining car. Though it had only been a minute or two since the initial warning, I hadn't heard any useful information over the crew channel or received any updates from Nargen.

I glanced over the two elves who waited for Kurak and me. The Truinnar and Movana were fully clad in armored jumpsuits. While Dayena's weapons remained sheathed for the time being, Lyrra held her beam rifle in a low ready position.

"Boarders at the rear of the train," Nargen announced, interrupting my inspection of the team. *"No confirmation yet on the composition of the hostile forces, but at least one of the security team is already down."*

"On our way," I replied.

Turning around, I led the group back the way that Kurak and I had come. When we reached the end of the sleeper cars, we found the door to the next car sealed. The armored boxcar beyond that door was the final car from the original train out from Pittsburgh. I'd never actually been inside it since the Pharyleri kept it locked down with one of Dice's security team members always standing guard.

One of the security team stood guard now, with an appropriately gnome-sized twin-barreled energy rifle held at port arms. "You can't go through here." Nervous sweat beaded her brow visibly beneath the brim of her black combat helmet. "Dice ordered me to let no one pass."

"We're headed to repel the boarders," I said. "You've already got one casualty on your team. If you want our help, then we're going through."

She bit her lip anxiously. "Fine. I'll let you through, but don't touch anything in the quartermaster's car."

The gnome turned and placed her hand on a pressure plate beside the door's locking mechanism. A red line appeared on the plate and scanned her palm. Once the scan swept completely up and down, the lock flashed green, and the door slid open.

"Don't make me regret this," the gnome said as she stepped aside, allowing us to slip past her.

I nodded but was already moving through the door with my team. Once I got into the car, I found numerous crates and pallets of metal ingots. An open central lane divided the car in half lengthwise and led to a rear door similar to the one we'd entered.

"You're not supposed to be in here."

The source of the raspy, shrill voice walked around from behind one of the many containers in the middle of the car as we walked down the lane between crates, revealing a gnome in a tiny, but heavily armored, suit. Though the Pharyleri stood with hands on hips, I still noted the integral launchers rising from each forearm and the multi-barrel energy cannon sticking up over one shoulder as I examined the gnome.

Jibryka Geargrinder, Combat Conditioned (Quartermaster Level 44)

HP: 440/440

MP: 590/590

The raised faceplate of the suit's helmet revealed an aged-lined face and strands of white hair that peeked out from underneath the armor.

"Do you want us to help your security team or just let them get overrun?" I bluntly asked the glaring gnome.

"Go." She sighed and her glare softened as she extended one arm, pointing a finger toward the rear door of the car. "I hope you have magboots though."

I hurried through the car, absently filing away the fact that a heavily armed member of the crew had been intentionally hidden from me for the entirety of the journey. Clearly, the Pistongrinders' trust only went so far with those outside the clan.

The door at the back of the car opened as I reached it, allowing a deafening rush of wind to flow through the aperture and revealing that the freight section of the train lacked the armored vestibules that connected the passenger cars. Beyond the door lay a narrow ledge before the coupling that connected the armored car to the following freight car. The force of the wind nearly tore off my poncho, even in the shelter of the car, and I stowed the flapping garment in my Inventory as I stepped onto the ledge.

The freight car after the coupling had no ledge on the opposite side of the gap, just a ladder running up the centerline and another ladder at either side. There was a small personnel door beside the central ladder but it looked sealed shut.

I glanced back at my party. *"Don't fall."*

Then I timed the oscillation of the swaying cars for a moment before jumping across the gap to catch the central ladder. Without another look back, I climbed up to the roof, where the wind caused by the train's speed nearly flung me onto the roof of the boxcar.

Now I knew why the old gnome had mentioned magboots. Even with superhuman attributes, standing unaided on top of the train would be nearly impossible with it traveling at nearly two hundred miles per hour.

I wasn't sure about the rest of the team, but I was covered, since that upgrade typically came with most armor rated for vacuum work. I always splurged on boots since I believed in taking good care of my feet. Boots also tended to last a little longer than my jumpsuits.

Except when we hit acidic grass. Gods, I hated mutated vegetation.

Activating the magnetic soles on my armored greaves, I crawled onto the roof on my hands and knees before rising to a crouch and confirming that my boots locked to the top of the boxcar. Then I pushed myself to stand against the force of the wind rushing against my back.

A random conversation with the Countess popped into my mind, how attributes didn't work linearly because a lot of the attributes functioned on other aspects of physics, developing areas that we might not necessarily think about. Like, for example, strengthening the bonds between molecules of the ground—or roof, as the case may be—so that excessive force applied by Status holders didn't rip them apart. Or in this case, I guessed, reducing the wind pressure effects on me, even if it didn't feel like it.

The train stretched out in front of me, dozens of boxcars with several gaps toward the end where ore-filled gondolas separated the more numerous rectangular forms of the freight cars. Flashes of light marked the location of the ongoing firefight between the security team and the boarders, but the rushing intensity of the wind stole any sounds of the combat.

It looked as though the boarders were advancing though, since the fighting appeared well forward of the end of the train.

Walking forward, I moved along the top of the boxcar with heavy clomping steps to ensure my greaves connected solidly with the surface. On my minimap, the friendly dots of my team appeared behind me once I'd cleared enough room for them to ascend.

Once I grew comfortable with the motions necessary for my boots to obtain a good magnetic seal, I picked up my pace until I hit an easy jog by the end of the boxcar. Leaping into the air and aided by the forward movement of the train passing under me, my jump easily carried me over the gap to the next car. Landing on my feet, I kept running toward the rear of the train.

I used the opportunity to familiarize myself with the peculiarities of magboot movements. Much of my usual agility would be limited since I had to keep my feet pretty much flat in order to engage the magnets on the metallic surface of the car roof.

After crossing a dozen or so boxcars, things got a little interesting when I reached the first gondola, filled almost to the brim with crushed ores. My options for passing the open-topped car were to crawl over the uneven rocks or stick to using my magboots on the narrow lip of the sidewalls. Opting for speed on the flat surface, I hopped down onto the narrow endwall of the gondola and shuffled over to the side before running forward along the slim, balance-beam-like width of the side wall.

I had to admit, I was cursing my inexperience at train security right about now. If we had taken more care about how we set up the trains and gondolas, all this would have been a lot easier.

I tottered along with the ground streaking by only eight feet below as the drag from the train's velocity battered me from side to side and threatened to throw me off. My heart rate shot upward, and my adrenaline spiked at the danger. Time seemed to slow as I concentrated on the placement of each step.

What a rush.

Focused on not falling, I never managed to work back up to a run, but I still made better time than I would have crawling through the unsteady ore mounded within the bay of the gondola.

After navigating a couple more of the open-topped cars, the actions became almost repetitive with my System-enhanced physiology and mind flowing through the motions to propel me smoothly along the top of the train like some kind of action star in a blockbuster movie. Except this was for real, not some kind of virtual reality or computer-generated imagery.

Leaping from the back of a gondola and clambering onto yet another boxcar, I almost ran over a retreating member of the Pharyleri security team.

The panicked gnome lifted his beam rifle as I hopped up onto the boxcar roof, but I grabbed the barrel and pointed it safely to the side before the startled guard could fire. Once the black-armored gnome recognized me and his posture relaxed, I released the weapon and looked for the rest of the team.

The gnomes appeared to be falling back in an organized fashion, leapfrogging in pairs toward us and the front of the train. One of each pair held up an energy shield that covered the width of their body as their counterpart fired around them with a short-barreled rifle like the one I'd just kept from shooting me.

Three pairs rotated in a tightly choreographed maneuver that had two teams laying down cover fire as the third fell back between them. The moving team then redeployed their energy shield and covered the next pair.

Another trio of rifle-armed Pharyleri slowly walked backward at the rear of the formation, laying down fire over the heads of the shield-bearing teams. While most of the gnomes were fully armed in their black gear, one of the rearmost three had his helmet stowed and I recognized Dice's blue-black hair as he directed the team's overall retreat.

At the far end of the boxcar, barely visible with the storm of energy beams flying in either direction, a shield phalanx of the hostile boarders marched forward in a three-wide formation. Tucked tightly behind their defenses, there were easily a dozen of the small figures advancing, but their tight huddle made an accurate count difficult.

The gray plate tower shields bore charred black streaks and melted rivulets of metal where repeated energy strikes had liquidated small gouges but failed to really penetrate beyond the surface. A cutout indent set into the upper corner of each shield allowed the carrier to stick a weapon barrel through and fire toward us without exposing any part of the shieldbearer.

Held just above the deck, the tall shields completely covered the attackers and prevented me from picking out any details of the assailants.

Checking the positions of the rest of my team on my minimap, I found the two elves not far behind me but well ahead of Kurak.

"Dayena and Lyrra, hold up," I ordered through party chat. *"Set up a firing position at the end of that last boxcar to cover us in case we have to fall back from here. Kurak, get up here when you catch up."*

Since energy weapons clearly weren't getting the job done, I pulled my hybrid rifle from Inventory and loaded a magazine of standard rounds. While I figured armor-piercing might have a chance of punching through the shields, my first thought was attempting to break up the tightly packed formation. Aiming for the bottom corner of the center shield, I squeezed the trigger of the Banshee II rifle.

Dice jerked around toward me at the whine of the energy capacitors cycling, audible even over the roaring wind, just in time for the brilliant discharge of the beam to shoot over his head.

Too fast to see, the gauss round impacted the bottom of the shield perfectly on target. The projectile dug into the armor and the lower portion of the shield shot backward from the force, pulling the shieldbearer forward and toppling the now-exposed alien onto its face. The opening revealed a second rank of tower shields behind the fallen foe. More interestingly, I noticed a tail sticking out from the backside of the prone alien.

Despite the surprise of my unexpected attack, the Pharyleri security team quickly capitalized on the hole in the enemy formation. The focused fire of their energy beams tore into the prone alien before it could climb back to its feet and vaporized the beige material of its armored suit. Beneath the armor, brown-green scales glinted momentarily until they, too, charred and burned away from the gnomish energy barrage.

I shifted my aim to one of the other shields in the front rank as the gnomes blasted at the fallen opponent. My second shot hit the outside edge of the shield and twisted it away from its owner. Though the target remained on its feet, the shield was pulled out of alignment and kept the alien from moving in front of its compatriot.

All that bought enough time for security as the tailed alien collapsed unmoving from the searing rays of gnomish energy beams.

Swinging my rifle toward the final member of the enemy front rank, I fired again. This time, the target managed to ground the shield before the impact of my shot, and it glowed from some reinforcing Skill. Firmly braced, the shield barely slid back a few inches. Rather than take another crack at the braced shield, I shifted my aim to my previous target, now under renewed fire from the gnomes as the alien swung its shield back into place in front of it.

My fourth shot hit the upper edge of the shield before it could be planted. The rim flew back and bashed into the alien's helmet with enough force to shatter the faceplate. Blood, tissue, and bone spouted from the impact, and the alien collapsed like a puppet with cut strings.

I frowned, despite having dropped an enemy. I hadn't expected a single shot to do that much damage to an armored opponent. Clearly the boarders weren't individually strong or resilient, but their heavy shield formation had been extremely effective against the security team's weaponry.

The phalanx slowed with the addition of my firepower, and the momentum of the fight shifted to us. Even with whatever Skill the enemies used to reinforce their plate shields, my railgun continued to break up the formation whenever it caught them unbraced. After two more of the boarders fell, the enemy fire slacked off and the enemies backed away.

"Square up," Dice shouted to the gnomes in front of him. "Push forward! We're going to kick these charvanfrey off our train."

I had no idea what the hell a charvanfrey was, but the beleaguered gnomes cheered at the security chief's declaration. The team, which had been retreating in pairs, formed up with two of their energy shields overlapping in the middle before advancing toward the enemy position. With my height advantage over the gnomes, I kept up my attacks over their heads as I targeted the tower shields whenever the enemies lifted them off the surface of the boxcar's roof.

The phalanx collapsed as the enemy tried to fall back onto one of the gondola cars, this one carrying logs that stretched the length of the car. The uneven footing of the round timbers prevented the aliens from locking their shields together, and several tumbled off the train from the impacts of my railgun fire alone.

The rear elements of the formation fled, leaving their counterparts to weather the deadly hail of energy beams and my rifle rounds. The shieldbearers facing us ran when they realized they'd been left to fend for themselves, though they still attempted to keep their shields forward facing.

Less than a dozen of the enemy remained by the time they fell back to the final car of the train, an armored caboose where they'd ascended. A black skiff flew just behind the caboose with a boarding ramp lowered onto the train car's roof. The ramp descended from the bow of the hovering craft, dropped in a manner reminiscent of the Higgins boats used in the Allied invasion of Normandy in World War II. Only the Allied GIs had charged off those landing craft on D-Day instead of scrambling back up the boat ramps in a complete rout like the alien forces here.

The final group of the aliens dashed onto the skiff's ramp as energy beam fire splashed harmlessly off the craft's armor. I popped off a shot at the last alien, my attack severing its leg at the knee, and it fell over sideways before tumbling backward down the ramp at an angle. The rolling alien leaked a trail of orange blood as it bounced down the side of the ramp, hit the roof of the caboose, and flailed uselessly before slipping completely off the side of the car.

"Nice shot," Dice commed over my earpiece, though I barely heard him over the rushing wind.

Surprised by the unexpected compliment, I glanced at the gnome, who continued to fire energy beams at the skiff.

With no more of the aliens left on the train, the boarding ramp lifted from the roof of the caboose and sealed the bow before slowly climbing away from the train. Then the skiff spun away and streaked off to the northeast, where it quickly vanished out of sight.

Chapter 25

Several of the gnomish fireteam collapsed, completely exhausted from the fight. Dice left the team and hurried toward the caboose. Curious to see what the security chief was up to, I stored my rifle in my Inventory and followed as the gnome clambered down a ladder at the very back of the train. I descended after Dice opened the rear door into the caboose but almost bumped into the gnome when he paused in the doorway without entering.

Looking over the much shorter gnome, I saw the reason for his hesitation. The inside of the cabin appeared completely burned out. Only a pair of charred husks remained of the security team members inside.

Dice finally stepped inside and knelt beside the dead gnome. I followed, which allowed the still functional door to close behind me. Firing slits lined all sides of the caboose, but they were all shut with armored coverings. A large, crew-served weapon sagged half-melted against one wall.

Despite the cabin being closed, the wind still whistled from a pair of holes in the roof of the caboose.

Looking up, I examined the two fissures.

"Shaped charges," I said after a moment, then looked at the familiar charring on the cabin walls. "And then plasma grenades through the hole."

Dice nodded sadly. "Probably laid by some kind of stealth users before the main boarding party hit."

Speaking with the gnome without any sign of his earlier abrasive behavior felt almost surreal, but I wasn't going to say a word about it. Not when he looked understandably upset about losing a subordinate.

The gnome's head jerked a moment later and he glanced up at me, touching his ear as if receiving a report. "They breached most of the boxcars up to the point where you joined us."

I frowned. "I didn't see them taking anything when they fell back."

Dice nodded. "We need to sweep through anywhere they got into and make sure nothing was left behind." He stood back up beside the body, clearly reluctant to leave the fallen gnome alone.

"I'll start checking on that and leave you to see to your team," I said. "I'm sorry for your loss."

Dice nodded without looking at me, clearly lost in thought.

I recognized the look; it was one I'd seen far too often on those losing companions and friends. It was a look I'd worn myself. I left the gnome to his self-recriminations and climbed back to the roof of the caboose.

Once I'd returned to the rest of the security detail, I organized the armed Pharyleri into three teams. The first policed the bodies of the slain while I led the second detail through the breached cars in the hopes of sussing out any hidden enemies or sabotage. Kurak joined my group while I kept Dayena and Lyrra on overwatch with the remaining gnomes. Just in case the unidentified aliens returned or if we needed a reaction force.

A blasted-out hole in the end of the boxcar directly ahead of the caboose marked the first breach, a gaping aperture of jagged edges large enough for me to fit through.

One of the energy-shield-equipped gnomes jumped through first and I landed directly on his heels, barely fitting into a narrow channel that stretched the length of the boxcar between stacks of wooden crates. I placed a hand on the gnome's shoulder, guiding him forward as I drew a pistol and aimed it down the empty aisle in front of us. A heavy thud at my back and a large shadow eclipsing the light streaming through the hole at my back announced Kurak's arrival once I'd cleared the space.

We crept forward, the rest of the security detail filtering in after us, carefully sweeping through the cramped quarters of the car in search of anything out of place, but we reached the end of the aisle without finding any of the aliens left inside. The lids from randomly selected crates throughout the dark interior of the boxcar appeared torn open, but nothing looked missing. The contents of several were scattered across the floor as if dumped in frustration by the aliens.

A couple of the security team used Skills normally employed against smugglers to search for any objects left behind by the enemy boarders. After a thorough search, the two gnomes looked at me with shrugs and headshakes indicating they'd found nothing.

Our group repeated the process through the next half dozen boxcars with similar results, finding no evidence of living aliens anywhere or signs of sabotage beyond the destructive searches.

After the completion of the search, we regrouped in one of the less filled boxcars with the rest of the security detail and my other team members. Kurak leaned against a side wall and pulled out a bag of trail mix, snacking on a blend of granola and raisins. The Yerrick's casual attitude contrasted with the macabre atmosphere of the car's interior, with the pile of the stripped corpses of the boarders lying beside a separate mound of their gear.

With the bodies laid bare, I finally got a good look at the aliens. The lizard-like humanoid would have stood at least a foot taller than the Pharyleri. A pair of short horns topped the elongated head, though the stubby, rounded nubs would have stood no more than chest high on me. A protruding snout jutted slightly forward above a maw filled with pointed teeth and a lolling purple tongue. The figure could only be described as wiry, and scales covered most of the thin body, including the lengthy tail that narrowed toward the tip.

While I examined the alien corpse, Dice was the last to enter. The shadow of a harrowed expression passed over the security chief's face as he glanced over his team, and I could almost see his thought process as he did a headcount to confirm no more of his staff were missing or dead. Then he schooled his features before anyone else noticed.

"All right, we're all here," Dice said. The gnome's voice echoed slightly over the communicator in my ear.

"What have you found?" Ismyna's voice came back over the earpiece.

Dice took one look at the piled alien dead and his face twisted in disgust. "Zabotkermanne."

The word wasn't a translation that my language packs picked up, so I assumed that the Pharyleri's statement identified an alien species. Ismyna certainly recognized the word from the cut-off curse that sounded over the comm channel.

"What's that mean?" I asked.

"Kobolds." This time my translation pack worked as Dayena stepped up beside me and loathingly kicked the body I'd been examining. "Pests and pirates. Usually the Zabotkermanne get employed as expendable troops for groups of dubious reputation."

Kind of a sad state of affairs that I could think of a half dozen such races that fit the bill too. The wider System galaxy was not a kind place.

I raised an eyebrow as I looked at the dark elf. "So, someone hired them to hit us?"

She half shrugged. "Likely."

"They were looking for something but didn't take anything when they retreated." Poking a toe into the haphazardly piled gear, I shuffled through it, looking at the cheap uniform fabric and low-quality beam rifles. The thick shields were the only half decent pieces of equipment. "They'll be back." Looking up, I found Dayena staring at me. "Tell me more about these kobolds."

"Zabotkermanne society consists of matriarchal dens, each led by a queen who lays large clutches of eggs. That queen imparts genetic memory and basic Skills to the male hatchlings at the cost of lowered initial attributes and a penalty in experience gain. Those infants grow to maturity quickly enough to be used as expendable troops, and the rare few that survive to true adulthood become far more dangerous after they hit the higher tier Classes and no longer suffer the initial penalty."

"So, they just throw their young into battle and hope that a few survive long enough to advance?" That sounded callous but fit with the behavior of the kobold infantry when their formation fell apart.

"They either overwhelm their enemy or die trying," Dice answered. "If you hadn't shown up with your heavy weapon, things would likely have been ugly for us. So, thank you."

I nodded solemnly. It seemed as though the security chief had gotten over whatever issue he'd had with me, but I wasn't going to rub his earlier attitude in his face. Not when he'd just lost two members of his team.

That sobering thought inspired my next question, and I turned to the gnomish security chief. "We know who attacked us, but why? What were they after?"

Dice rubbed his chin thoughtfully. "I don't know. Any thoughts, Ismyna?"

"We're mostly carrying bulk cargo that's valuable only in large quantities," she replied over the communicator.

"Oh," I said. "So, there's nothing precious in that locked down armored car that you've got supervised by your quartermaster?"

Ismyna went silent, and Dice sighed.

"You weren't supposed to ever go through there," he said.

I shrugged. "That's fine. I don't really care what you're hauling. I only care how it affects my job to see the train get back to Pittsburgh in one piece."

"Invaluable trade goods," Ismyna interjected. "Precious metals. Uncut, Mana-imbued gems. Charged crystals for energy weapons. All of them are raw materials for high-end crafting that can be traded at premium rates."

"That seems pretty normal," I said. "I really expected something spicier than that."

Dice looked up at me. "Like what?"

"Drugs? Dead bodies? Slaves?" I gave another shrug. "I really have no idea what contraband is with no actual government in charge these days."

"You really thought we'd be involved in that kind of trade?" Ismyna almost sounded hurt. "You're right about the lack of government, though I expect that to change as more members of the Galactic Council move in and expand their settlements. Eventually the System will enable territory owners to enforce their own laws and taxes."

I rolled my eyes. "I guess even in the apocalypse there's no escape from taxes."

A few gnomes chuckled.

"You certainly have not paid taxes on any funds I have provided you," Dayena commented.

"Nope." I grinned. "Uncle Sam doesn't really seem to be around anymore to pinch my paycheck."

Dayena's head tilted. "Who is 'Uncle Sam'?"

"Just one of the things we called the government for this nation before the System took over," I explained.

"I see," she said. "If enough of what remains of your government eventually reclaims enough territory, it might be possible for them to collect taxes within that area once again. That seems rather unlikely with the splintering of the various factions and influx of outside groups."

I waved dismissively. "Regardless of the future state of the American government, we're way off topic. Was anything in the secured car valuable enough to be what our kobold friends were after?"

The dark elf frowned. "Possibly. Many of those materials would be profitable to raiders, especially if they have low skill crafters to Level."

I glanced at the pile of discarded equipment next to the dead bodies. "Their gear was definitely crap, but I'm not sure that feels like the right answer here. I think there's something we're missing."

"What makes you say that?" Dice asked, apparently taking my concerns seriously.

"Just a hunch." I knew better than to voice aloud that a good portion of my intuitive feelings resulted from a Perk.

The gnome seemed to accept my response since he moved on from the topic. "So, what do you think we should do?"

I thought for a moment. "Patch up the damage as best we can and get ready for the kobolds to come up with a second strike force."

Sitting around, just waiting to get attacked, grated on me. I'd much rather take the fight to the enemy than concede the initiative to them. Unfortunately, without knowing where the kobolds were based, any attempt to intercept their forces would just be taking a shot in the dark.

"I hate being on the defensive. Is there any way we can hit these Zabotkermanne before they come back?" I asked.

Dayena shook her head, but Ismyna spoke up over the comm before the dark elf could speak. "We'd have to purchase the name of the clutch responsible. Only then could we acquire the location. Even if we were anywhere near a Shop, it's just too much information to buy and I don't have the discretionary funds for something that sizeable."

That ruled out going on the offensive. We'd need to beef up our defenses.

"You've still got that multi-barrel energy cannon your team used on the bison?" I asked Dice.

The gnome nodded. "Eldri mounted it to a gantry that can deploy from the top of the workshop."

"Good," I said. The fixed position atop the second car explained why it hadn't shown up for the fight at the back of the train. "The cannon should be ready to go at any time from here on out. Keep a dedicated squad to guard that gun and the front of the train. We can't afford to lose the engine, or we'll be sitting ducks."

"You think they'll hit the locomotive?" Ismyna asked, still listening in over the comm.

"It's what I'd do with forces like the kobolds," I replied. "Take out our propulsion and we're stuck where they can keep throwing those expendable troops at us."

Dice blinked in surprise as he thought through the implications of that scenario, then he shuddered. "Let's avoid that."

"Defending the engine is priority number one," Ismyna said. "The passenger cars come after. I won't trade lives for Credits, so the freight cars take the lowest precedence as we prepare for another attack."

Glad I wasn't responsible for the cargo, I nonetheless appreciated having fewer cars to cover in defense.

"They've already tried coming at us from behind," I said. "No guarantees, of course, but I suspect that they'll hit forward of where they've already searched for whatever they're trying to find."

"What do you suggest based on that assumption?" Dice asked.

"What do you think about stationing one third of our forces in defense of the workshop and engine, another third with the quartermaster, and the rest spread through the passenger cars?"

"Dice, does that make sense to you?" Ismyna asked.

"I like it," the gnome replied. "We can always shift our primary forces in response with enough warning, but I think we need to arm the full crew on top of that."

The comm went silent as Ismyna considered the proposal from her security chief. After several long moments, her voice returned, much quieter than before. "If we do that, we're going to take losses."

"If we don't do it, we may take those same losses. And more," Dice retorted without any heat. "This way at least everyone can fight back."

"All right, do it," Ismyna commanded, her tone resolute. "I'll have Wrefen inform the passengers. We won't stop out here in the middle of nowhere, but I'll halt at the next settlement. We'll let anyone off who isn't comfortable with the prospect of an imminent attack." There was a slight wince as she added, "And refund their passage."

After that, the meeting broke down as everyone split off to their preparations.

Eldri's technicians began making what repairs they could, patching up the breached boxcars and sealing the armor of the caboose. For a patch job, the welds were pretty well done and hard to spot without close examination. I couldn't help but wonder if it was a Skill or skill or just better tech.

Dice divided his security forces into thirds, keeping one group stationed with himself in the quartermaster's car while the other two teams went forward to position themselves in the passenger cars and the workshop.

I sent Kurak and Lyrra to the front of the train to join Nargen defending the engine and workshop. Dayena stayed with me as we moved to the lounge car as a reaction force to wherever we were hit first. My hope was to blunt the first of the follow-on attacks, with the thought that we might give pause to whoever was leading the kobold forces.

As we stepped into the lounge car, several passengers hurried past us. They all wore worried expressions as they returned to their assigned berths. Inside the lounge, Wrefen faced off in what appeared like a heated conversation with a human couple who wore far more finery than I would have expected for a journey across the open territory of a Dungeon World.

"I'm sorry." The olive-suited gnome gestured placatingly with both hands. "Your ticketing agreement expressly stated that there would be no guaranteed safety from piracy. That's why we'll let you off at the next stop and provide you with a refund."

The woman stamped her foot in frustration and the motion flailed her dangling earrings, the gem-studded chandelier-like jewelry swinging below the line of her blond hair cut in an inverted bob.

Her partner, wearing an impeccably tailored suit with silver cufflinks, ground his teeth. "It's simply unacceptable for you to leave us stranded in the middle of nowhere."

Wrefen sighed and looked at the man in exasperation, yet still made the attempt at a polite response. "If you do not wish to debark at the next stop, then you are welcome to stay onboard at your own risk."

"No," shrieked the woman. "We paid for passage to Pittsburgh, and you are going to get us there safely. I demand to speak to your supervisor."

Wrefen clearly had other priorities than listening to this couple complain, so I stepped up behind them. "Look, Karen, be thankful they're even going to stop and give you a refund."

"My name isn't Karen," she snapped at me.

I feigned surprise. "Oh, you could have fooled me with that act."

"Listen here, young m—"

"No, you listen," I interjected, folding my arms across my chest. "If you continue to be a problem here, then I'll throw you off the train now. Without stopping first."

Her mouth dropped open in surprise and she gaped like a fish out of water. Her partner stepped toward me, his face flushing in anger, and I fixed him with an icy glare that brought him to a complete halt.

"You can't treat us like this," he sputtered as he recovered from the intensity of my gaze.

"The conductor offered you two options. I gave you a third," I stated. "Pick one."

The man finally broke eye contact with me and looked away before putting his hand on the woman's shoulder. "Let's just go back to our seats. We'll get off at the next stop."

"Fine." She sniffed condescendingly, gave the dark elf beside me a disgusted look, then spun away on one heel. She marched forward to the coach cars as the man hurried along behind her.

I waited until the pair left earshot. "You know, I would have expected them to be in their own room, all dressed up like that."

Dayena chuckled.

Wrefen shook his head. "I could have handled that."

"I know," I said. "But you have better things to do than coddle idiots."

The gnome rolled his eyes. "That's at least fifty percent of my job now that we've got passengers onboard."

Grinning, I left the gnome to return to his duties as I looked through the lounge's large windows at the flat countryside rushing past the train. The golden light of the early evening was tinged with orange as the sun brushed low on the horizon.

"It'll be dark before long," I said. "Want to each take a side and keep watch as best we can while we wait?"

"Sounds good," Dayena replied.

I slipped onto one of the long, padded couches and placed a case of ammunition beside me, absently loading magazines for my hybrid rifle while scanning the flat Kansas terrain. This was going to be a long night, whether they attacked or not.

And I really wasn't going to bet on the not.

Chapter 26

As dusk fell across the countryside outside the train without any attack materializing, the crew raced to take advantage of the time given to us.

Eldri's technicians finished patching the holes across the train and began using the raw materials from the boxcars to weld ingots into defensive barriers on the roofs of several cars.

Wrefen's staff passed out energy rifles and the charge packs that served as ammunition to the entire crew. Even some of the passengers volunteered to assist in the defense effort and were provided spare rifles, though a couple members of the security team kept the volunteers under their watchful eyes.

Even the dining car staff stayed busy, with Ulyndra's cooks putting together sandwiches so that everyone was well fed before nightfall. In addition, they created a variety of durable finger foods to provide snacks that would last through the night. I had to admit, the minor boosts to Resistances and attributes were a nice perk, along with the tasty food. Too bad you couldn't stack the food boosts continuously by gorging on it.

Dayena and I shut down every light on the upper level of the lounge car and passed along the recommendation for an external blackout, in the hopes it would make it that much more challenging for our enemies to locate us in the dark. It also had the advantage of allowing us an unrestricted view of the moonlit night outside as we kept watch.

Hours passed, and I fought the monotone of watch through time-tested methods. Everything from pinching myself to moving seats. Thankfully, the increases in the Willpower attribute seemed to help my focus a little, making the mundanity of watching a little more passable.

A little.

"Movement," one of the security staff called over the communicator. "Coming out of the treeline to the north. Looks like they were waiting for us."

The extra guards stationed in the control cabin had been tasked with monitoring the external sensors until any fighting broke out.

With the direction from the guard, I located the black silhouette hugging the ground as it slipped across the open fields between the nearby forest and the moving train. The outline looked like the skiff we'd fought earlier, but in the dark, it was hard to be certain.

"Let them get closer before opening fire," Dice reminded everyone.

The shadowy shape slunk closer, heading toward the middle of the train and lifting from the ground.

"Get ready," Dice said. "Now!"

A storm of crimson energy beams flew from the Pharyleri firing positions on the roof of the train, and the cannon on top of the workshop car opened up a heavy stream of fire that stabbed deeply into the skiff. The craft veered away from the sudden attacks, breaking off its run at the train and accelerating to the north, chased by brilliant blue, red, and green beams of energy. The ground smoked and brightened as fires were lit, and a part of me hoped we hadn't just started a forest fire.

The gnomes cheered as the shadow disappeared into the night, but I felt no thrill at the apparent victory. It was too easy.

"Do you see anything on your side?" I asked over my shoulder, still peering out into the night to the north.

"Nothing," Dayena replied. "You suspect something?"

"They gave up too easily for a foe willing to throw lives away like the kobolds did in the last attack."

"That is a nasty but well-reasoned conjecture."

Though I couldn't see the dark elf behind my back, I could picture her frown.

Especially as my suspicions proved valid over the next several hours.

Twice more, the skiff attempted to intercept the train from different angles, only to veer off in the face of the gnomes' massed fire. I wondered, idly, how much more damage the skiff could take.

I also wondered how it was managing to keep up and not get eaten by monsters. Was someone clearing the way ahead of the skiff? Were their employers just that powerful that they could handle whatever random monsters they ran into? Or had they spent enough Credits to chart out problem areas beforehand, to ensure they could finish the job? Any of those options spoke to a rather worrying amount of planning.

On the enemy's third run, somewhere in the middle of Iowa, I left the lounge, moved down the length of the train, and climbed to the rooftop firing position closest to the skiff's approach. That brought me to the defensive works on the quartermaster's car, and Dice looked at me as I slid into cover.

"Hold off on firing a few more seconds, please?" I asked the gnome, just before he could give the order.

Dice looked at me in confusion, his brow furrowed. "Why?"

I focused on the approaching craft. "I think we need a better idea of what we're dealing with."

With a bit of extra concentration, I swept Greater Observation over the skiff. The vehicle's status flowed onto a Status update that I mentally shoved off to one side as I looked over the craft for vulnerabilities to exploit.

A grin crossed my face as a patchwork of red lines appeared across the surface of the vessel. Hidden beneath the smoothing effect of the uniform black paint, the actual armor plates were an uneven mess of plates that varied in thickness. The weakness explained the kobold's unwillingness to brave the gnomish firepower for any extended length of time.

"Got it. Fire away."

Dice gave the firing order and the gnomish gunners opened up on the skiff while I pushed the status screen toward Dice, sharing the information with him as I reviewed it myself.

Cargo Skiff (Modified Ariivis Cargo Transport Skiff)

Core: Class 6.72 Ariivis Cargo Transport

Speed: 600 km/h

Processing Unit & Software: Class H Xylik Core

Armor Rating (Ground): Tier V

Stealth Rating (Ground): Tier V

Crew Capacity: 2 (1 pilot, 1 loadmaster)

Cargo Capacity: 20 tons

Weaponry: None

Core Durability: 100%

For once, the System translated most of the units of measure into easily understandable kilometers per hour and tons, instead of something inscrutable like GMU. The speed of the craft explained how the kobolds could intercept us so easily, with nearly double the velocity of the train.

The fact that the skiff had "Ground" ratings for Armor and Stealth indicated that it was only a surface craft. Craft that operated outside planetary atmospheres received a "Space" rating instead, which operated on a whole different standard, and I doubted that our weaponry currently in play would have done much against a craft of that tier. The low tier of the armor rating indicated that heavier anti-personnel weapons might be at least slightly effective against the craft, and I could work with that.

The Core rating of the skiff's durability slowly dropped as the gnomish attack savaged the oncoming craft, but the fact that it had started off so high gave me pause. The 100% durability meant one of two things. Either the unit had been repaired after each run against the train or the vessel was a completely different craft altogether. The uniform paintjob on the skiff spoke against a hurried repair cycle, indicating that my theory of separate vessels was the more likely option.

"I'm pretty sure these attackers are using different skiffs," I said to Dice as the enemy craft disappeared into the night and the barrage of energy beams faded out. "Probing our defenses to see what else we'll show before they commit to a serious assault."

Dice sighed, the sound barely audible over the rushing wind. "That would fit with the way kobolds operate when they have a decently intelligent commander. I was really hoping they'd come in dumb and get slaughtered."

"I don't think we can count on that."

"No, I don't think so either," Dice said.

Cooperating with the security chief still felt weird after butting heads for the entire outbound journey, though it probably improved our chances for making it back to Pittsburgh alive.

Only one more attack probed at the train before we reached Burlington, on the edge of the Mississippi River. Stopping at the town's former Amtrak station just before dawn, a number of passengers chose to depart the train rather than risk the danger of the continued kobold assaults. Surprisingly, the Karen and her husband weren't amongst those who deboarded, despite the fuss they'd made.

During the brief stop, several crew members rushed to the Shop to pick up extra ammunition, supplies, and weaponry. I joined the group of shoppers, intending to pick up a few upgrades of my own, and Ryk greeted me warmly as I materialized in my default Shop instance.

"Adventurer Mason, welcome back on your abnormally quick return. Do you have your usual haul of goods to trade away?"

"Thanks, Ryk," I said. "Unfortunately, I think I'm just going to be handing Credits over to you on this visit."

"Splendid." The shopkeeper gleefully rubbed his furred hands. "Ahem, I mean, what can I get for you?"

I shook my head at Ryk's antics. "Remember that large weapon purchase I made previously?"

The shopkeeper's eyes lit up. "Of course!"

"I need more of the specialized ammunition for it."

Ryk smiled and gestured for me to follow as he led me to a glass counter at the back of the hall. Metallic tubes the length of my arm filled the shelves within the transparent display. A sealed cap covered the cylinders at either end, with a colored band wrapped around the circumference just before the end caps. A terminal on the counter listed the definitions of each color, and I read through the options quickly while considering the forces used by the kobolds so far.

"I'll take five yellow, four blue, and four green," I said, stepping back from the terminal.

Ryk raised an eyebrow at the size of my order, but the shopkeeper waved wordlessly, and the cost appeared on a blue System window in front of me. I accepted the transaction and winced as the Credits left my account, leaving my balance uncomfortably low. The munitions appearing in my Inventory slightly offset the blow to my spendthrift ways. I hoped that the completion of the Quest to get the train back to Pittsburgh successfully would recoup some of the loss.

We really should include expenses as part of my Quest bargaining next time.

"Anything else for you today?" Ryk asked, and I glared at the hope filling the shopkeeper's cheery voice, though I saw the worry which lay beneath the upbeat exterior.

"No," I responded firmly. "See you next time."

I left the Shop and hurried back to the station. Once I made it back, I checked in with Ismyna and found her with Eldri, the two gnomes in the middle of reconfiguring the control console.

"Long range communication module," Ismyna explained as Eldri finished closing the unit.

Lights appeared across the console's new addition, and the technician fiddled with the buttons for a few moments. Then he nodded to Ismyna, who stepped up beside him before speaking a greeting into a microphone.

A voice quickly responded in Pharyleri, and a hurried conversation went back and forth. The speaker lapsed into silence for several minutes, and I raised a questioning eyebrow at Ismyna, who gestured for me to be patient. Finally, a voice I recognized spoke in Galactic.

"What exactly did you do to get a contract issued to Zabotkermanne mercenaries?" Nesdyna asked.

"You know about that?" Ismyna responded.

"I pay attention to what trouble my daughter is getting into."

"What can you tell us?" I interjected. "Ismyna didn't think we could afford to buy the info from the Shop."

Nesdyna sighed. "I don't have much. It's a limited contract right now. The kobolds only had a small force available, with the rest of their clutches engaged in containing an outbreak of overflowing dungeons for a Movana Triumvirate in what used to be Michigan."

I frowned. "So that's why they're being cagey? They only have a small troop hitting us, but there are more out there?"

"Seems like it."

"Thank you, Mother," Ismyna said. "We'll monitor this channel so you can keep us informed if anything changes."

"Take care of yourselves." Nesdyna went silent for a moment. "I love you, Ismyna."

The gnome sniffed. "Love you too, Mother."

When the conversation wrapped up, we were still waiting on several crew members to return. The stragglers all showed up over the next ten minutes, and I saw the pride Ismyna took when none of her clan abandoned their crewmates.

I patted Ismyna on the shoulder in reassurance then climbed up to the roof above the train's control cabin. The sun peeked above the horizon as the engineer entered the locomotive and engaged the throttle, the train easing forward as it pulled out of the station and headed toward the bridge over the Mississippi.

We knew now the kobolds were coming. Good thing they'd left it so long though, because I was ready.

Then, of course, I looked around for some wood to rap. Just in case.

Chapter 27

The train crawled across the bridge spanning the wide expanse of the Mississippi River and, after a few winding curves through a small forest, accelerated into the straightaway. Unlike a real train, the chug-chug of the locomotive didn't sound. I wasn't sure I'd ever get used to that.

Another skiff announced the renewed Zabotkermanne attacks, swooping in to intercept before the train reached its full speed. A barrage from the turret quickly chased it off, and I crouched low between a pair of barriers on the roof of the engine. Easing down to sit with my back against the forward wall of the firing position, I pulled out a leftover wrap from the dining car. Savory strips of thin-cut meat with a mildly spicy sauce, tightly wrapped in a doughy shell that was something like a thick tortilla. With everything going on, focusing on the flavor wasn't a priority, but I knew I'd need the energy whenever the enemy made their big move.

Several more aborted attack runs harassed us throughout the morning, but the kobolds never followed through in the overwhelming assault I kept expecting.

"I don't get it," Ismyna complained over the communicator. "Why won't they commit to an assault? We're just getting closer to home the longer they wait. If this harassing continues after we get beyond Cleveland, we'll be in range to summon reinforcements from the starport."

"They're wearing us down," I replied when no one else spoke. "Harassing attacks keep us on edge since we're forced to respond in case it could be the prelude to a larger offensive. The uncertainty, constant tension, and spiking adrenaline all add stressors that we have to deal with individually."

"I don't like the sound of that," Ismyna said quietly.

"This tactic tells us something about them too," I responded. "It says they're concerned about their ability to engage us in a straight-up fight without sapping our strength first."

That seemed to reassure Ismyna and the others, enough so that the comm went silent again. I just hoped that my speculation about our enemy's ability was correct. It was entirely possible the kobolds were wearing us down to preserve their forces for whenever they got around to attacking us, but that went against the strategy of expendable forces they'd shown so far.

The mid-morning sunshine was raising the temperatures to the expected July heat, a relief after the altered climate of Denver, when that assault finally happened somewhere south of Chicago. It began with a pair of skiffs spotted sneaking around behind the train from either side and two more of the identical vessels closing in from the front.

"Here we go," Ismyna announced. "All hands, stand by to repel boarders."

From the top of the engine, I glanced back at the multi-barrel cannon rising from the roof of the workshop car to clear its lanes of fire over the welded barricades. Within the barricades, the Pharyleri defenders crouched, a few looking paler than before.

I assessed the approaching kobold craft and estimated that the one on the left would be the easier shot before keying my communicator. "Cannon gunner, take the forward skiff on the port side."

"Copy." The gnome in the seat behind the cannon gave me a thumbs-up as the cannon swung toward the indicated craft.

Accessing my Inventory, I pulled out one of the tubes I'd just acquired. Summoning the control assembly as well, I snapped the device onto the cylinder just behind the yellow bands that circled its end. Lifting the combined assembly onto my shoulder, I pointed the front of the tube toward the starboard skiff and looked through the optical assembly on the control unit as I sighted in on the approaching target.

Many veterans probably would have recognized the missile launcher on my shoulder as a weapon similar to the pre-System Javelins, but I hoped the kobolds wouldn't expect something like this. Not after the train's purely energy-based defenses so far.

After quickly checking behind me for friendlies in my backblast, I squeezed the trigger when the control unit locked onto the Zabotkermanne skiff. A torrent of fire shot from the rear of the tube as the missile popped from the launcher. The weapon shot forward, deploying stabilizer fins around its circumference at the front and rear of the weapon before the primary rocket motor ignited a dozen feet downrange.

The missile streaked forward and punched into the hull of the target skiff, instantly erupting into a ball of flame as the missile detonated inside. The momentum of the skiff carried the conflagration in an arc that descended almost gracefully toward the ground, impacting just shy of the train that blasted through the cloud of smoke and fire it left behind.

"What the fuck was that!?" Ismyna shrieked.

I chuckled, detaching the control unit containing the modular launcher's trigger and optics before chucking the spent missile tube off the side of the moving train. "That was me."

"Warn a girl next time," Ismyna said.

"I kinda figured you'd be a little more worried about the whole hostile boarder situation," I said, returning the control unit to my Inventory and looking around to take in the other parts of the fight.

The other forward skiff lay skewed perpendicularly across the top of the workshop car, smoking in multiple places from the hits delivered by the energy cannon. Even so, kobold troops poured out of ramps that lowered on either side of the damaged craft. With the grounded skiff in the way, I couldn't see the state of the cannon or the conflict at the rear of the train, where I assumed the other pair of skiffs had ended up.

The lizard troops coming out of the skiff on the side facing me were forming up to assault the locomotive's control cabin, which meant it was up to me to intercept them before they made that breach.

For the first time, I cast Ice Armor upon myself. As I finished the spell, a layer of frost crawled over my jumpsuit, forming a layer of frigid fractals that gradually thickened into plate-like armor while leaving my joints free to move. I wanted to focus on watching the fascinating process of the armor's formation, but I had a kobold problem to address.

I drew my projectile pistols and pointed them toward the mass of kobolds. The lizards lacked the protective shields of the initial boarding party, armed only with cheap beam rifles and a variety of crude melee weapons, and I opened up on them with abandon despite the sway of the moving train. My fire swept into the scrawny aliens, and several fell with critical injuries before the gaggle of lizards recognized the source of the attacks.

Beam fire lanced out at me, but most of the hasty attacks missed. The few that hit me swept across the plates of ice, hissing as the energy rays melted furrows in my protection but failed to punch through. In return, I focused my shots on the rifle-armed lizards and began dropping them one by one.

A few of the kobolds jumped down to the juncture between the workshop car and the locomotive, taking them out of my sightline. I moved forward with my magboots engaged, continuing to mow down as many of the aliens as I could before I reached the gap between cars.

More scrawny kobolds poured out from the skiff. The flow had ebbed since the initial rush, but the numbers still kept me from engaging the aliens below. I didn't have a clue how they'd packed so many of the aliens into the cargo bed of the skiff, but there were a ton of the little bastards. When the magazines on both of my pistols went dry, I slid the empty firearms into the holsters on either hip before drawing the beam pistols from my shoulder rig and lit up the kobolds with the fresh weapons.

By the time I cleared through the rest of the aliens on my side of the landed skiff, I'd swapped out the beam pistols for a second set from my Inventory. With the rooftop cleared of kobolds that I could see, I attacked the few aliens still trying to breach the control cabin. Once I'd eliminated that threat, I hopped over to the workshop car and climbed over the piled bodies then up the side ramp onto the skiff.

A few kobolds remained inside the craft, cowering from a hail of energy fire that shot through the open ramp on the far side. I wondered briefly why the beams were all from the gnomish rifles and not the heavier cannon before I took out the remaining aliens, before they turned to see me. With the interior clear of hostiles, I avoided the barrage of friendly fire to reach the vessel's pilot station, where a headless kobold sat slumped in the chair.

I pulled the dead alien from the seat and glanced at the alien controls. They were labeled in a script which consisted of lines and tiny triangles, not any language my translation packs recognized. Leaving the controls behind, I hoped that someone in the Pharyleri crew could fly the thing.

I really needed to upload a set of basic piloting instructions from the Shop. Maybe next time I had free Credits to blow.

The beam fire from the gnomes on the far side had died down without any sign of living kobolds inside the skiff, so I waved an empty hand out the opening before ducking back just in case anyone was a little trigger happy. When no one shot at me, I poked my head out and saw the effects of the kobold assault on the far side.

Bodies lay strewn across the roof, mostly kobolds at first, then a few dead gnomes close to the cannon. The cannon itself smoked and sparked beneath a pile of dead kobolds that had thrown themselves directly onto the weapon while it was still active.

A pair of gnomes with beam rifles peeked out at me from behind the barricades and I waved at them before keying up my communicator. "The cannon is down. We need a repair crew to get it operational if anyone is available."

"I'll be right up, Hal," Eldri replied.

"Could use your help at the sleeper cars, Hal." My connection to party chat lit up with Dayena's words. *"Kobolds are overrunning our defenses here."*

"On my way," I replied.

Picking up speed as I left the body-covered section of the workshop car, I ran along the roof of the train and let the wind help propel me across the gaps between the cars. Maneuvering across the moving train seemed to get easier the more I performed the potentially deadly stunts, but it could still go wrong far too easily if I grew careless.

Farther down the train, I spotted the other skiffs, grappled by their boarding ramps alongside one of the boxcars beyond the armored car. From the positioning of the firefight, it looked as though the kobolds had already taken the roof of the quartermaster's car. They'd isolated the remaining gnomes inside the heavily armored car and were pushing hard on the sleeper section.

My reckless pace slowed when I reached the lounge car as I kept my steps to the centerline of the curved windows, carefully avoiding the glass where my magboots wouldn't find purchase. When I looked up from making my way across the lounge car, the rooftop melee had reached the second sleeper.

Kurak stood at the rear of the car, using his halberd to sweep away the kobolds attempting to jump the gap. Dayena danced around the large minotaur, her quick footwork positioning the dark elf to cut through any kobolds jumping inside the Yerrick's guard. Lyrra stood a pace behind the two, tossing out the occasional healing spell as the Movana used her rifle to pick away at the outside edges of the throng of kobolds.

Only four of Pharyleri security guards remained standing. Two of those were hauling Dice's limp form between them. A quick check of the security chief's status showed a few points of health remaining. The other pair of gnomes tiredly fired their beam rifles around either side of my party members and into the mass of lizards beyond. A survey of my minimap showed no friendly dots left beyond the line Kurak held at the end of the sleeper.

I wondered how much this entire fight was frustrating my employer. If she brought her Artifact into play, if she went all out, I had a feeling she could have cleared the fight herself. But her self-imposed restrictions meant she was less effective than normal.

Well, I guessed I'd have to compensate with my toys.

Summoning the launcher control unit from my Inventory, I also grabbed one of the metal tubes with a green band. I snapped the assembly into place and pulled it up to my shoulder. The control unit's sight displayed a holographic reticle beneath an arching flightpath, which I adjusted until the target cross lay positioned on the middle of the lizard-packed sleeper car before squeezing the trigger. The launcher jolted against my shoulder as the missile shot forward and ignited with a whoosh. The missile flew upward at a steep angle before sharply reversing course into an abrupt dive.

"Brace yourselves for impact," I warned over party chat.

Just before the projectile came down into the middle of the swarming lizards, the cylindrical rocket exploded over their heads with a small puff. An instant later, the horde disappeared in a cloud of smoke and flame as the missile's rain of anti-personnel cluster munitions detonated amongst the kobolds. The force of the blasts sent bodies and parts of bodies flying out of the smoke to fall off the sides of the train. Best part of fighting on the locomotive—I didn't have to kill them, just knock them off.

The smoke cleared almost instantly with the train's speed blowing away the cloud to reveal the piles of stunned and injured lizards. Only a handful remained standing, and the heaps writhed as the least injured kobolds attempted crawling to their feet over the bodies of the stunned.

"Not that I'm ungrateful, but a little more warning would have been nice." Kurak didn't even look back before launching himself onto the lizard-covered sleeper car and stabbing the spearpoint tip of his halberd into a still-moving kobold.

"Everyone's a critic," I grumbled, detaching the launcher control unit from the spent missile tube and storing it before pitching the empty cylinder off the side of the train. *"Nobody asks, 'How many Credits did Hal just spend saving our asses?'"*

Chuckles over party chat greeted my complaint as Dayena and Lyrra trailed the Yerrick toward the rear of the train with three of the security gnomes in their wake. The group hastened to finish off the stunned and disoriented throng of kobolds.

I hurried to check on the downed Pharyleri security chief. The sole gnome remaining with the unconscious Dice looked like a medic, racing to treat the many wounds with a variety of powders, potions, and what looked like a staple gun to patch torn flesh back together.

I crouched behind the firing position where the two gnomes were sheltered. "How is he?"

"Bad, but he'll live," replied the medic. "He'll wake up soon, I think."

"Send him our way when he's up. I'm sure this isn't over yet."

The medic nodded and continued to work without looking up, so I left them and pursued the rest of my team. They were now engaged with the kobold rearguard on top of the quartermaster's armored car and pushing them back toward their docked skiffs.

Kurak's path through the carnage of the next car was easy to follow, the Yerrick having simply trampled through the fallen kobolds, booting them off and forcing their magboots to give way. His heavy footsteps further crushed and mangled the already ruined bodies of the few who were outright dead, leaving a navigable but gory route onward.

Even with the wind of the train's passage carrying away the worst of the stench, the stomach-churning aroma of death filled the air—a nauseating combination of charred lizard flesh, alien blood, offal, and voided bowels.

I caught up to the remaining security gnomes as they worked their way through the charnel slaughter. The trio searched through the piles of lizards and blasted any that still showed signs of life.

Before I passed the gnomes, the communicator crackled in my ear with a Pharyleri voice I didn't recognize. "Another skiff is coming in from the front. Looks like it's heading straight for the engine."

"You help Nargen deal with that, Hal," Dayena said, having also heard the warning. *"We should be able to handle these."*

I pivoted toward the front of the train, greenish kobold blood squelching under my boots. *"On it."*

Picking my way back through the dead kobolds consumed my attention until I reached the next car and my magboots once again managed a secure seal on the armor roof of the train. I plodded forward, pushing against the force of the oncoming wind as the train continued its journey at full speed. At least I couldn't smell the worst of the dead now behind me, though I still caught a whiff of the bodies from the forward assault.

"What are we looking at, Nargen?" I asked as I navigated the narrow path across the lounge car.

"Another skiff full of kobolds, coming in low," Nargen replied. *"They're practically hugging the tracks. If they don't pull up, Ismyna is going to run them down. That skiff's flimsy structure won't hold up to the armor on the train."*

Jumping from the lounge car to the roof of the rear passenger coach, I thought about the effect of any impact with those of us on the roof. *"Give an all-hands warning about the impact. It could get ugly for those of us on top of the train."*

"Ismyna says you'll be fine. She has a Skill for that."

Though I doubted the kobolds would just let themselves get hit, relying on a sole Skill wasn't a chance I wanted to take regardless. "Give the warning anyway."

Nargen just chuckled, and I ignored the dwarf as I hurried forward, though I took the opportunity to reload my empty pistols and swap out my used beam pistols for a fresh pair.

On top of the workshop car, Eldri's lower half stuck out from the guts of the energy cannon. Above him, the turret's control console sat with the cover off and two other Pharyleri technicians rewiring the tangled leads. Whatever repairs they were making looked like they were making progress since the turret no longer smoked or sparked as I passed.

Three security team gnomes were throwing kobold bodies off the side of the train. I shook my head at them and pointed at the skiff still sitting on top of the workshop car.

"Get rid of that thing so the turret has a clear firing arc," I yelled, hoping that my communicator picked up the words that were barely audible over the rushing air flowing over us.

Their eyes went wide, and they hurried to deal with the skiff that lay perpendicular to the train.

I ducked through the body of the workshop car and jumped to the roof of the locomotive. A straightaway in the track lay ahead. The oncoming skiff rushed toward us so low that it appeared to be scraping the rail. The skiff was closing in too quickly, and I worried that my launcher wouldn't be able to acquire the target, if I could even get it set up fast enough.

With only the length of a football field between the craft and the engine, the skiff spun a hard hundred-eighty-degree turn. The engines at the rear of the vessel flared as it slowed then reversed its velocity, gaining just enough altitude that the front of the locomotive slid beneath the skiff while the hovering craft continued accelerating to match the train's speed.

It was impressive piloting, far more so than what we'd seen from the other skiffs. A pit formed in my stomach that this one might be carrying a larger threat than the expendable troops the kobolds had shown so far.

The skiff dropped down and scraped along the armored roof of the locomotive as grapnels fired off along the sides of the vessel to attach it to the moving train. The engines cut out as the cabling affixed to the grapnels tightened down.

"*You seeing this, Nargen?*" I asked party chat.

"*Help is on the way,*" the dwarf responded.

"Help is on the way," I muttered under my breath, summoning my hybrid rifle and a plasma grenade from Inventory as I slipped forward. I pressed my back against the rear of the craft between the protruding engine nacelles.

Two shadows appeared on the lip of the craft above me, the aliens climbing onto the rear of the craft and looking down at the train. Both shadows stretched out on the roof of the train, too tall to be the expendable kobold shock troops.

"Find the sword," the more slender of the pair commanded, though I barely heard the voice over the sound of air flowing around the parked skiff.

My brow furrowed. The sword?

The stockier figure grunted in response, the sound deeper than the growling and hissing of the kobold hatchlings but of a similar tone.

I activated the plasma grenade in one hand and let it cook for a moment. Then I lobbed it up toward the figures as I spun around and brought my rifle to my shoulder, getting a clear look at the pair above me.

The first alien was a Movana with sapphire blue eyes and silver hair whipping in the wind. The second figure was a taller, more muscular kobold, clad in armor a clear tier above the shoddy garb worn by the more disposable lizard forces.

Both aliens stared in shock at the orb soaring up between them as my grenade reached the peak of its arc. The charge detonated in a brilliant flash of azure light that bathed the figures in blue flames as they were blasted apart, the explosion throwing the two screaming aliens in opposite directions. I grinned as it tossed them clear of the train, even as I blinked away afterimages of the flash.

I doubted the explosion and fall killed either, but they were out of the fight for now and would have to catch up later. If they could.

376

A moment later, a few singed kobold hatchlings peeked over the back of the skiff and my rifle took the head off the first to appear. Before I could shift aim, the others ducked out of sight.

I frowned at wasting ammo with the overkill. I'd expected another of the stronger juvenile kobolds, and the hybrid rifle clearly had more firepower than I needed to deal with the smaller lizards. Storing the rifle, I pulled my beam pistols as a wave of kobolds poured over the back of the skiff.

The first two carried boarding shields like the initial phalanx from the first attack. I ignored the pair, attempting to pick off the lizards behind them in midair as they jumped down into cover behind the shieldbearers. I swept the barrels of my energy pistols from side to side, catching each kobold two or three times before they dropped behind the protective barrier of the shields.

Eventually, one of the kobolds stayed still on top of the skiff long enough to shoot at me, forcing me to move evasively as I attempted to avoid the rifle shots from above while still returning fire. When I shifted my aim to the rifleman long enough to drop the lizard, enough of the kobolds made it into cover behind the shields that they began advancing.

Their progress pushed me back from the skiff and toward the end of the engine's roof, dangerously nearing the edge as the volume of energy fire from the growing mass of kobolds picked up intensity. My ice armor melted under the barrage and my health dropped.

"Get ready for some cover fire," Nargen advised.

"Anytime now would be great," I replied.

A roar of thunder sounded from behind me, and streaks of smoke wrapped me in a cloud as a wave of micro missiles arced around me to slam into the kobold troops. The detonating missiles sounded like extremely loud popcorn as they exploded against the boarding shields and amidst the lizards.

With the shieldbearers bowled over, the remainder were exposed to my return fire.

Unfortunately, the explosions halted the tide of kobolds jumping from the skiff. The lizards posted up on the rear of the vessel, and before I could take advantage of the disrupted formation, they fired down at me instead.

Charging forward into the disorganized mass of kobolds, I slipped the pistols away and drew my melee weapons. My knife and axe ripped through the weak creatures. The fire from above never slackened, though it hit the kobolds around me more frequently than my moving figure.

Another roar from behind announced a second wave of missiles, this time focused on the attackers above. The rippling explosions cleared the rear of the skiff, leaving me to finish the last of the living kobolds on the roof of the engine.

"Cover me while I take the high ground," I ordered Nargen, glancing over my shoulder to find the Gimsar's robot dog crouched in a wide-legged stance on the roof of the workshop car.

"I've only got one more round of missiles," the dwarf replied. *"I'll do what I can."*

Stowing my weapons, I jumped, then spider-climbed up between the engine nacelles. The metal remained warm to the touch from their race to intercept the train, but not hot enough to burn my skin as I ascended the rear of the vessel. Grabbing the back deck of the skiff, I hauled myself up and clambered to stand.

Below, in the bay of the skiff, a juvenile kobold with its back to me berated a half dozen hatchlings that cowered against the front ramp. It looked as if the smaller lizards were refusing to follow their brethren into the fight and the juvenile was pointing back toward me without looking.

I pulled out my rifle as the smaller kobolds caught sight of me and their beady eyes bulged in fear. The lizards shrieked and bolted away, mounting the front and sides of the skiff before throwing themselves off in terror.

The juvenile kobold glanced to either side in confusion before turning and spotting me aiming down the sights of my rifle. Like the smaller lizards, the juvenile's eyes bulged in surprise, but it dropped onto all four limbs and charged. Sparks flew from the lizard's claws as they scraped along the deck of the skiff, and I scanned the kobold with Greater Observation as I squeezed the trigger.

Zabotkermanne Juvenile (Coxswain Level 39)
HP: 490/490
MP: 620/620

The kobold pilot attempted to dodge my attack by bouncing off the sidewall of the craft, but my aim remained on target and the coruscating beam of energy carried the rifle's projectile into the center of the creature's chest. The impact caught the kobold mid-jump and knocked it tumbling.

Missing half of its health, the kobold slid to a stop in the middle of the empty skiff. The lizard pushed itself upright just in time for my second shot to tear through its neck, whereupon it collapsed back to the deck.

Snorting, I jumped down into the bay of the skiff and looted a few other hatchlings that appeared to have been caught by my plasma grenade. The dead Coxswain had a few Credits, but nowhere what I'd expect. Then I moved to the pilot's station, which looked like a phone booth stuck along one side of the skiff and set about three-fourths of the way back along the craft's length.

The stick-and-rudder controls were labeled in the same alien script as the last skiff.

"The skiff is clear, but we're gonna need someone up here who knows how to pilot one of these things," I informed the party.

"You should take it for a spin," Dayena said.

"Probably not a great idea when it's still grappled to the engine," I responded.

"Please don't," Nargen said. *"Not while I'm in the engine control room."*

I chuckled. *"I don't even know where to find the on switch."*

"A common problem amongst the males of most species," Dayena quipped.

I rolled my eyes as Lyrra voiced her agreement over party chat.

"Since you have time to make jokes, I assume that you're done clearing the kobolds from the back of the train."

"Yes, we are clear," Kurak said. *"Dice is working to detach the skiffs here."*

"Send him up this way if he figures it out," I instructed. *"Nargen, any sign of more kobolds?"*

"Scopes are clean for the moment, boss."

I nodded, though the others couldn't see it. *"Sounds like we've got time to repair and rearm. Once you're done with that, get a bite to eat while you can. No telling when the shit will hit the fan again."*

The team sounded off their agreement and went about their tasks. Following my own instructions, I checked my weapons and swapped out the few damaged bits of my gear.

Then a thought struck me about the positioning of the fight at the rear of the train. *"The kobolds took the armored car with the valuable materials, didn't they?"*

"They took down the quartermaster and Dice at the cost of a trio of their juveniles," Dayena replied. *"They had access for several minutes after pushing us back to the sleeper cars."*

"Did they take anything from it?"

The Truinnar took a moment to respond. *"I will have to speak with Dice."*

While I waited for that answer, I climbed on top of the rear of the skiff and sat with the wind blasting my face to clear away the stench of death. Pulling out one of the leftover sandwiches, I chewed through the densely filled amalgamation of meats and cheeses. I didn't know when Ulyndra's team could have baked fresh bread, but I had a weakness for a good sandwich and killing always made me hungry.

Mulling over the attacks so far, I sat with the intention to wait until someone either came to remove the skiff or until I got a better idea of what the hell the kobolds were doing.

I was really getting tired of being the mushroom in this relationship.

Chapter 28

My thoughts kept returning to the Movana and the elf's words nearly washed away by the wind before my grenade removed their presence from the train.

Find the sword.

They were after a weapon. A weapon worth throwing away scores of hatchlings and a half dozen juveniles so far.

The only things *that* valuable were relics.

Relics like Dayena's instrument, The Whispering Strings, which was the only relic on the train that I knew about. Its presence was so subtle that I kept forgetting about it, something I suspected was a Skill or ability of the relic itself. My Truinnar employer had yet to reveal the instrument to our party or anyone else on this journey.

Not that I blamed her, if attacks like this happened when word of one got out. Which begged the questions, what word was being spread and why hadn't we heard?

Time to speak with Dayena about my suspicions. She'd at least tell me if my reasoning was wildly off track.

The brakes squealed and the train slowed, the decrease in the flowing air highlighting the summer heat as the afternoon sun shone down from high in the sky. Frowning, I stood carefully to get a better idea of why we seemed to be stopping. I blinked as I recognized the silhouettes of the Great Lakes Science Center and the Rock and Roll Hall of Fame along the Lake Erie shoreline, off to the port side of the train.

We'd reached Cleveland around twenty-four hours after departing Denver. That still felt a bit odd, given the weeks it had taken us to make the journey as we'd repaired the track on the outbound leg.

The rushing wind that flowed over the train ceased as the engine halted at the station, and the lack of sensation set me off balance for a moment until I adjusted. I yawned and popped my ears before giving my head a shake.

Nobody had come to deal with the skiff yet, but I didn't want to wait around any longer. I pushed myself to my feet and climbed down from the rear of the skiff, finding some of the Pharyleri technicians tiredly pitching the kobold corpses over the side of the workshop car to the annoyance of the local Truinnar guards standing below.

With the rushing wind, I hadn't heard the work crew or I'd have tried to help out. Despite my still grumbling stomach demanding attention, I looted the bodies and cleared them from the roof of the engine.

It was only fair. I had killed most of the lizards here, after all.

Dayena showed up around halfway through the pile. The dark elf looked at the gristly jumble with disdain but joined in anyway.

"There was a Movana with this last group of kobolds," I informed Dayena, my voice pitched low so that it couldn't be heard by the work party of gnomes or the Truinnar guards eyeing us suspiciously from below. "The elf ordered a kobold juvenile to 'find the sword.'"

"A sword?" Dayena turned to me after pitching a lizard over the side.

"That's what was said," I replied. "It must be a pretty special sword."

I paused from my work and glanced at the dark elf, catching her gaze and flicking my eyes toward the empty space behind her shoulder where her relic remained hidden from sight. Then I looked back at her directly and saw her eyes widen before she nodded slightly in understanding with a frown.

She shook her head. "I have not seen any sign of a weapon exceptional enough to warrant the effort the Zabotkermanne have displayed."

"Neither have I," I said, throwing another body overboard.

"Do you think that we should try to find it first?"

I continued working while I considered her question. "A weapon like that wouldn't be hidden on its own, so either a person or a group is involved in concealing it. Until we know more, we're kinda stuck. If the Pharyleri have it, then exposing the weapon could affect our ability to finish our contract successfully. If someone other than the gnomes has it, then getting it the hell off the train would mean we stopped getting attacked and could finish the contract in peace."

Dayena nodded. "So, investigate quietly and if we figure it out, then we can evaluate further."

I grunted, tossing the last of the dead over the side. "Sounds good."

The Truinnar guards glared at Dayena and me as we jumped over to the workshop car, where the gnomes thanked us for helping.

Ismyna called out my name from the control cabin below, suspiciously not using the communicator. I walked back to the edge and hopped down to the rear of the engine as Dayena followed.

"What is it?" I asked, keeping my voice low.

Ismyna bit her lip nervously and looked around to ensure the three of us were alone. "There's no help coming from the starport."

I raised an eyebrow. "Why not?"

"The non-clan mercenaries are all contracted for defense of the starport only and won't take up a contract expansion that puts them in conflict with the Zabotkermanne."

"And Borgym won't commit the few loyal assets he has outside of the starport," I said.

Ismyna nodded. "Once we get to the starport, we'll be protected but until then…"

"We're on our own," I confirmed when the gnome's voice trailed off.

We left Ismyna at the control cabin, climbing back to the roof and heading off in search of something to eat while the work crew moved to deal with the skiff still attached to the top of the locomotive.

I led us past another crew of Pharyleri on top of the workshop, this group messing with the cannon, and made our way down the length of the train. My minimap showed the rest of the team at the dining car, but I didn't see them on the roof, so I slipped down the side of the train and through the emergency hatch integrated into the vestibule that linked the two cars.

Kurak sat at a table by himself while Dayena slid past me and into a booth across from Lyrra on the opposite side of the aisle. Half-eaten plates sat before them all with a stack of empties piled at the ends of the tables nearest the aisle.

I slid into another empty booth as the leonine server approached, clad in an armored harness over the standard olive uniform worn by the hospitality staff. Black straps affixed the armor plates over her torso, shoulders, groin, and thighs, with the bronze material matching the uniform buttons and the train's exterior plating.

"Limited menu today," Sheera warned Dayena and me as we settled into our seats.

"Whatever you've got that's fast and hot," I replied.

"Steak and potatoes, then?"

"A medium rare steak sounds great." I nodded and the server quickly took Dayena's order before she retreated toward the food prep area in the middle of the car. Despite the earlier sandwich, I was still hungry and had no intention of turning down a hot meal when I had the chance to eat.

The door behind me slid open and Nargen tromped into the car. He passed me and slid into the booth across from Kurak.

I looked at the others while waiting for my food. "Everyone ready for another fight?"

Nargen's head snapped around. "You don't think it's over?"

I looked at Dayena. "What did Dice say about anything missing from the quartermaster's car?"

The dark elf shook her head. "It was disturbed as if searched thoroughly. They were looking for something, but nothing appears to have been taken."

Sheera returned and slid a steaming plate in front of me before taking a similar order from Nargen. When the server turned away, I continued.

"They're clearly looking for something they haven't yet found."

Sheera hesitated mid step, drawing my attention, and a rounded ear twitched toward me before the departing server continued walking away.

"There was a Movana on the forward skiff," I explained further. "The elf was instructing a juvenile kobold about their search when I knocked them overboard with a grenade."

"What was the Movana's name?" Lyrra asked.

I shook my head. "I didn't catch it."

She frowned. "A family name might tell us who is paying the kobolds."

"Well, they're not dead. Just a bit crispy and blasted off a fast-moving train."

Lyrra raised an eyebrow. "You don't think that would kill someone?"

I shrugged. "That wouldn't kill me."

"Nor me," Kurak grumbled.

"You probably wouldn't even have been moved by the blast," I said, acknowledging the Yerrick's toughness. After Kurak nodded acceptance of the compliment, I took advantage of the lull in the conversation to cut a bite of the juicy steak and dug in.

"So, what are they looking for?" Nargen asked, bringing the discussion back on topic.

"They search for a sword," Kurak replied, his voice trailing off as everyone looked at him intently.

I forced myself not to show any further reaction. There was no way the minotaur could have known about the discussion between Dayena and me as we cleared bodies at the front of the train.

"How do you know?" I asked.

The Yerrick pulled out a communicator, and a holographic image popped into existence above the device. Within the display, a Movana with purplish-red hair ran across a snowy mountain. Though the figure spoke to the camera, no sound was audible. The view expanded to look over a group of adventurers locked in combat with a horde of drakes in a ravine below the broadcaster. The monsters were quickly slaughtered by the lead adventurer with a ridiculously massive sword, and the view zoomed in on the figure to highlight the lion-like features of the humanoid feline.

Sheera, who had been approaching while carrying a plate, slowed when she saw the display and continued watching after depositing the dish in front of Nargen.

A shadow fell over the display, revealing a white-and-silver dragon as it landed and smashed several of the party. The dragon promptly devoured the remaining adventurers. and Sheera gasped as the monster chomped down the leonine adventurer. The camera fell to the ground as that last adventurer's two-handed sword fell from the dragon's maw and landed directly in front of the view.

The recording sped up after that, showing day and night passing as ice built up over the sword, until the image cut out completely.

Sheera turned away, breathing deeply as if emotionally affected by what she'd seen, and slowly retreated down the aisle.

Everyone sat speechless for a moment until Kurak cleared his throat. "There are weapons so powerful they are passed from generation to generation within a family or ruling group, growing stronger with each wielder through the ages. Entire planets have been destroyed in the wars that are fought when the existence of such a weapon is revealed to those who believe they can take control of them. That sword is one such weapon."

The bit about planets being destroyed was news to me, though it didn't surprise me overly much, given how trashed Earth had been by the whole System initiation process. Never mind an actual war between Galactic powers. Still, it didn't seem that the conflict here had reached anything near that level. If Relics could grow in power as they aged, then it probably meant that planet destroying was only worthwhile for a few such items.

I hoped, anyways.

Nargen shook his head. "I can't wait to finish this contract. Between overflowing dungeons and heirloom relic weapons being hunted by pirates, I think I've had enough of this planet."

A predatory grin crossed my face. "Then where would you meet charming Gimsar like your friend Brostana?"

Nargen's eyes went wide, and his face flushed red at my mention of the only other Gimsar on the train. The dwarf sputtered through a mouthful of baked potato as the entire group broke down in laughter at the guilty reaction.

Finally, the Gimsar stopped choking. "How did you know?"

I chuckled. "I thought you were acting a little too hard at ignoring each other. I didn't know for sure until your reaction just now."

Nargen groused into another bite of his baked potato, and I also returned to scarfing down my meal. I'd hate for the steak to go to waste if the kobolds launched another attack while we were making jokes. By the time I cleared my plate, the discussion had returned to the mystery of the relic weapon.

The train's whistle sounded, audible even inside the dining car. A few moments later, the car jerked as the train moved. The final leg of our journey had started now, and with any luck, we'd pull into the Pittsburgh starport in a couple hours.

Dayena rubbed a hand over her face in frustration. "So, to sum up, we believe the kobolds think there is a relic sword on the train but have no idea where it might be or who might have it."

"Correct," Kurak said.

Nargen placed his cutlery on his plate and pushed the dish to the end of the table, as the others had done. Then he looked around nervously. "Are the Pharyleri holding out on us or playing us for expendable fools?"

"I don't think so. But I could be wrong. They did hide the quartermaster's presence from us." I slid my empty plate to the side and leaned forward on my elbows. "Kurak, where did you get that recording?"

The minotaur's nostrils flared. "I made some new friends in Denver."

I nodded in acceptance. The Yerrick's earlier interaction with the Sect bodyguards suddenly made sense if those were his new friends.

The conversation lapsed and the team took the opportunity to relax. Despite the filling meal, the exhaustion of fighting and the threat of constant attack showed itself in their weary posture. Even Kurak, with the highest Constitution on the team besides myself, slumped against the sidewall of the booth. It was a little comical since it barely fit his large frame.

I watched out the window as the suburbs of Cleveland gave way to the forests of northeastern Ohio and the train picked up speed once more, heading southeast toward Pittsburgh.

Part of me wondered if the kobolds had bad intel, but they'd committed and sacrificed enough forces that they had to be confident of their source. My instincts told me that the Pharyleri were as clueless to the relic's presence as we were. Still, I hoped that my positive impression of my previous experiences with Borgym's clan wasn't bleeding into my opinion of the Pistongrinder clan.

If the gnomish clan as a whole wasn't hiding the heirloom sword, then that left a passenger or an individual member of the crew. And if I had to bet on a passenger, it'd be that shifty envoy from the Sect. On the other hand, if I had to pick out a member of the crew, the behavior of our current server certainly seemed to indicate her as a likely candidate.

I glanced down the aisle toward Sheera. The feline humanoid stood a polite distance away with an ear cocked in our direction, still listening to the ongoing conversation.

Too many things didn't add up with the server. Too many coincidences and too much odd behavior.

After that awkward breakfast conversation, I'd strongly suspected Sheera knew my actual Class and not the counterfeit I displayed. Since On the Hunt disguised my Class from any observation Skill of a lower tier or level, that indicated her Class or Skills ranked higher than mine and she was likely obfuscating her own Status information.

On top of that, she'd disappeared in Denver and behaved suspiciously upon her late-night return. Looking back, I'd been the only person on that platform—which meant the entirety of the casual performance was for *my* benefit.

There were still pieces missing from the puzzle—namely how Sheera might have obtained the weapon in Denver, of all places—but the logic felt sound enough that she seemed the likeliest individual on the train.

Everything I knew was entirely circumstantial, but I tended to follow my gut feelings. I did have a Perk for it, after all.

Sheera's head turned toward our group and the server noticed me watching. Our gazes locked, and she blinked away tears from her large, amber eyes as I refused to look away in an unspoken accusation. Her eyes widened in surprise as I stared her down, her leonine expression lacking any sign of concession. The alien woman turned toward me and planted herself defiantly. Her chest expanded as her chin rose, and it almost looked as though she was about to roar.

"Alien vessels approaching from multiple vectors."

Ismyna's announcement over the communicator, broadcast to the entire crew, broke the stare-down between Sheera and me.

Everyone in the car climbed to their feet and worked their way out of the narrow booths. I gave the feline a glare that let her know this wasn't over before I launched myself out into the aisle and led my team out of the dining car.

Chapter 29

"Talk to me, Ismyna," I said over the comm, smacking the controls to open the door into the lounge.

"Another wave of skiffs, three of them this time, coming from behind to the west," she replied. "Two more vessels ahead to the east. They're new, something we haven't seen before, and they look like atmospheric or space craft. They're still at the edge of sensor range and haven't started closing in just yet."

A chill went down my spine at the mention of spacecraft. Even the most basic interplanetary craft possessed at least some form of self-defense or anti-meteor weapons, either of which put ground weaponry to shame. The train's armor could hold for a bit, but repeated attacks would punch through eventually and would certainly take out any of us on top of the train.

Seriously, who brought a starship to a train jacking?

Still, I had to try. That didn't mean I planned to lead my team to their deaths.

Stopping in the middle of the lounge car, I turned back to the four individuals in the aisle behind me and looked them over. Dayena halted and peered at me in confusion. Lyrra stood just behind her, with Nargen and Kurak bringing up the rear.

I pointed at Dayena. "Stay inside the train, no matter what."

The dark elf stared incredulously at my finger for a moment before her face twisted in anger. "No, I will not hide away while you take all the risk."

Her anger flowed over me, and I let it pass without changing my expression or stance. "If they take you out with a starship weapon, the penalty clause in my Contract activates."

The Truinnar's face froze as she thought through those implications and understanding blossomed in her eyes. The penalty clause was a short-term application of negative status effects that would make me useless until they expired. While it wouldn't directly lead to my death, that would be the likely outcome if that penalty was applied during combat.

I nodded, speaking softly. "If you're dead, I'm crippled. And then everyone on this train is pretty much hosed."

Dayena sighed and looked away, acknowledging my point without a word.

I kept my gaze fixed upon the dark elf. "Stay out of sight. Your shadow skills are best when you have cover and aren't exposed in broad daylight. I won't fail, we won't fail, this escort contract because you got taken out as collateral damage."

"All right." She addressed the whispered word to the floor instead of looking at me.

"Start off in the dining car."

Dayena's head shot back up and she looked at me questioningly. "What?"

Meeting her inquisitive gaze, I gave my head a slight shake before glancing over the other members of our party, who waited behind her. Her eyes widened in understanding and the dark elf nodded silently.

"All right," I said, looking over the group. "I'm going to take a potshot at one of the starships if I can. Lyrra, watch Kurak's back here in the lounge car. Nargen, you've got the workshop. Give ground if you have to. Don't let the expendable kobolds pin you down or surround you. If you get clear at any point, do what you can to take the pressure off the others."

The entire party looked solemn, knowing the worst fighting was ahead of us.

"One way or another, this will be over within the next two hours if the train stays moving. We make it under cover of the starport defenses and we're home free, contracts completed." I grinned. "The first round is on me tonight, and I expect to be buying all of you a drink. Don't disappoint me."

Giving a nod to each member of the party and receiving one back from all of them in response, I turned on my heel and headed forward.

"You have a suspicion about the Demarcian?" Dayena asked, and I noticed her question came through on a private link through party chat.

"Suspicions, yes," I responded. *"Nothing concrete."*

"Perhaps she will open up to me."

I sighed. Dayena could convince just about anyone of anything, given enough time. Damn Charisma. If that was what she wanted, then she would likely succeed.

I just hoped we had the time.

When I reached the locomotive, my minimap showed the others reaching their stations and meeting up with the few remaining members of the security team, as well as armed volunteers from the rest of the crew.

Slipping into the rear of the engine's control cabin, I closed the door and found Dice and Ismyna watching the sensors intently. Looking beyond the gnomes at the aircraft floating in the holographic display, I saw the shapes of the two vessels within the viewer.

Vessels I'd encountered before.

A rectangular hull made up the central body of the starships with four engines, one at each of the corners of the craft. The four engines pointed down at an angle, holding the vessels a few hundred feet in the air as they drifted at the edge of our sensor range.

I knew well the impression those craft would make if they were to set down, marking their outline into the ground. I'd seen the like before, outside a ruined school in the early days of the System's integration. If these were the same craft operated by the Krym'parke I'd faced before, then my day was taking a turn for the worse. Admittedly, I welcomed the opportunity to square off against the flesh-hungry aliens now that I'd gained a year of experience under the System. The ghosts of their victims might rest easier if I put down a few more of the people-eating bogeymen.

Stepping up behind the two gnomes, I closely examined the two ships. Unlike the vessels I remembered sitting parked on the roof of the Allegheny County Jail, these ships were in rough condition. Uneven gouges dug deeply into the armored surfaces across both craft, while large sections of hull plating appeared charred or slagged. Several holes showed where attacks had punched through the defenses completely, and patches of armor welded over breaches highlighted attempted repairs of similar damage.

Though the two vessels flew side by side, one tilted down toward one corner as if the engine there couldn't generate enough lift to keep the craft level.

If they were the same Krym'parke, they'd apparently missed more than a few repair and refit cycles. They also weren't using the cloaking field to make themselves invisible, as they had when fighting the Gribbari in downtown Pittsburgh. The listing ship seemed to be missing one of the two cannon barrels that protruded from a pivoting turret mounted beneath the cockpit.

"Do you have readings on any weapons besides those chin turrets?" I asked.

Ismyna tapped several buttons on her control console, and golden lines swept over the holographic display. I raised an eyebrow while watching the golden lines pass horizontally first, then vertically. The scanners dropped an outline over the chin mounted turrets on each vessel, then flashed that area twice to highlight the threat, confirming the cannons as the only weapons. "That's new, isn't it?"

Ismyna nodded, her eyes still on the display. "Yup. Picked up a pre-built sensor upgrade module before we left Cleveland. It's just a plug-and-play booster to our existing suite, but it nearly doubled our range and precision."

The positioning of the hovering starcraft made more sense to me now. "They don't know about the upgrade. That's why they're hanging out there. They don't think we can see them and they're waiting for the kobolds to hit us from the other side."

Dice frowned. "Are the starships part of the kobold forces?"

Debating whether to inform the gnomes about my past encounters with the Krym'parke, I hesitated.

Ismyna spoke up instead. "No way to tell unless we got a look inside their cockpits and see what's sitting in the pilot seat."

She was right, and I decided not to speak up. It very well might not be the flesh-eating aliens from my past, though I didn't really believe that.

"As great as the new sensors are, should I know about any other new surprises?" I asked.

Ismyna glanced at me, then looked at Dice before the security chief nodded and she spoke. "We added a few single-use launcher platforms, inspired by the way you took out that skiff earlier."

That sounded reasonable to me. "Anything capable of taking down a starship?"

Dice shook his head. "Nope. We just wanted something besides the workshop mounted cannon for fighting off the kobold vessels. We also got a few heavy infantry weapons if they manage to land boarders again."

I sighed. "Save your launchers for those skiffs then, and try for a coordinated launch to put down as many as possible. I doubt my anti-vehicle missiles will do much against starship armor, but I'll still try. Maybe we'll get lucky since they're so banged up."

Ismyna looked at me fully, weighing my words. "Thank you, Hal. I owe you an apology for my behavior when we first met. I see now why Borgym holds you in such esteem."

"You can thank me when we're out of this mess." Waving off her words, I headed for the door. "Tie my comm in with the cannon gunner. I'll try to coordinate a barrage with him on the starships when they begin their run."

"I'll send one of my guys forward to support you," Dice said.

I paused and nodded my thanks before slipping out. There weren't many of the security team left.

Exiting the cabin, I climbed onto the roof of the workshop car to brave the rushing wind once again. I nodded to the gnome seated in the gunner's seat of the turret before crawling into cover behind an empty firing position of welded metal ingots. Though I saw no signs of the skiff on the engine ahead, plenty of dried blood from the slain kobolds remained streaked over the roofs of both cars.

While I still had time for preparation, I cast Ice Armor over myself again and marveled at the crawling formation of crystalline water across my body as the frost grew into protective plates over my armored jumpsuit. Despite the gravity of the situation, a smile tugged at the corner of my mouth as I watched the fascinating formation of the icy fractals.

Once the armor had finished its growth, I turned back to my preparations and summoned the control unit for my launcher system and a yellow-marked anti-vehicle warhead. I fit the components together and set them across my lap while I waited for a signal from Ismyna, scanning the weapon in my lap one last time to confirm my readiness.

A chime sounded from the communicator, alerting me before Ismyna spoke to the crew. "The skiffs are sweeping in from the west and the starships are now moving in from the east."

Facing forward, I brought myself up on one knee to peer over the barricaded firing position and placed the launcher onto my shoulder. I scanned the horizon without looking through the launcher's targeting unit until the starships appeared on my minimap.

Then I pulled down the Status of the lead vessel.

Zetanis Heavy Shuttle

Core: Class 5.4 Zetanis Heavy Interplanetary Shuttle

Speed: 4.9 Doms

Armor Rating (Space): Tier V

Stealth Rating (Space): Tier III

Crew Capacity: 6

Cargo Capacity: 45 tons/100 Passengers

Weaponry: 1x Ares Beam Turret

Defense: 1x Polanca Interplanetary Force Shield (Damaged), 1x Marcinn Stealth Field (Damaged), 3x Point Defense Lasers (2 Damaged)

Core Durability: 47%

My eyebrow rose as I read through the information provided. That Core Durability was dangerously low for something still flying, and that was the vessel that had a functioning turret. The starship behind it was in even worse shape, showing up with a Core Durability of 42%.

Maybe we really did have a chance against these ships.

The first shuttle flew closer, and I pulled the targeting unit to my eye, holding the weapon as steady as possible with the swaying motion of the train. I swept the reticle over the vessel as it dropped down in front of the engine, looking for a weak spot to exploit but nothing triggered my instinct to fire. Stilling my breath, I steadied my aim but refrained from squeezing the trigger just yet.

"Should we open fire?" the cannon's gunner asked, a tremor in his words betraying his nerves.

"Wait for it," I cautioned.

Hurried footsteps beside me announced the promised arrival of one of the security team members, but I didn't have the time to even look to see who it was.

My patience paid off as the rear ramp of the vessel lowered, and I grinned. None of the armor in the world would do them a bit of good if I could manage to detonate the missile inside the bay. I zoomed in with the control unit, taking up the trigger slack and preparing to fire as the figures inside the bay appeared.

The image sharpened on the individuals within, and I blinked in surprise at the formation of Krym'parke infantry in brown armor. Then two spots of color drew my eye within the murky group of alien troops. I swore as I examined the pair of armored figures, one in white and one in red.

Armor that I'd stripped and sold off in the Shop. Along with my old friends, Dayena's cousins had finally caught back up with us.

"Fire!"

A stream of coherent light streamed over my head as the cannon on the workshop car opened up on the exposed bay of the starship. A much smaller beam stabbed out from beside me, the security gnome also firing.

Several of the Krym'parke in the doorway exploded into mist, vaporized by the sudden attacks. Then a shield of light sprang up to protect the opening as the Truinnar in white power armor stepped forward with upraised hands. The shield rippled under the intensity of the heavy energy cannon, and I knew that the barrier wouldn't hold for long.

"Keep up your fire," I ordered the cannon gunner.

The lithe, red-armored form of Dayena's other cousin slipped around the edge of the shield and down onto the roof of the engine, along with a quartet of Krym'parke. I ignored the boarders for now and focused on where Rhegnah stopped near the bottom of the lowered ramp.

The energy rifle shots from the security gnome beside me shifted to the boarders.

I needed to take out the ship to stop more Krym'parke from boarding, but I couldn't do that with the Truinnar's shield ability defending the bay.

The shield was fading, shrinking like a shallow puddle evaporating in the hot summer sunlight after an afternoon shower. Then the barrier dropped suddenly, the flurry of beams instantly blackening the Truinnar's white chestplate before melting through completely. Rhegnah's mouth distorted in a scream of pain, inaudible between the distance and roaring wind.

Any Basic Class individual would already have been atomized, but the injured Truinnar grabbed for a deployable shield generator on his armor belt.

"Nope, not happening, prick," I muttered. Despite knowing Dayena would be pissed over what I was about to do, I squeezed the trigger with the sight centered on the Truinnar's exposed chest.

The missile popped out of the tube and seemed to float forward for a moment, the rocket engine igniting an instant later. The projectile flashed across the roof of the locomotive, burning brightly. The Krym'parke pilot must have gotten some kind of launch warning because the shuttle instantly jumped forward to race ahead of the train as the rocket engaged, the motion nearly throwing the white-armored figure and remaining infantry from the back.

The evasive maneuver came far too late. The missile punched straight into the already blistered and burned center of Rhegnah's chest, exploding in a blinding flash that enveloped the aft end of the vessel in a storm of fire.

Smoke and flame spewed from the open bay, trailing behind the shuttle as the craft tipped forward. The ship lost altitude slowly, somehow maintaining its forward momentum until it plowed into the ground beside the tracks a hundred yards ahead. A bloom of fire erupted from the crash to form a column of gritty, black smoke that rose overhead.

Despite the inferno enveloping the crashed ship, an engine and the tail of the vessel still hung over the track. The train plowed through the obstruction and shuddered beneath my feet at the impact.

A notification pinged at the edge of my awareness, but I ignored the experience update to locate the enemies who'd landed on top of the engine before I'd fired at the starship. The smoke and fire washed over the roof of the locomotive before sweeping back across the workshop car, where I sheltered. The soot-filled cloud obscured the five figures that advanced across the engine, and only the fire being exchanged with the security gnome beside me showed their approximate locations.

Without taking time to detach the spent launch tube, I stashed the whole assembly into my Inventory and drew my projectile pistols as I stood from behind the barricade. The weight of Last Word and Ace felt comfortable as I raised the weapons to point at the oncoming Krym'parke.

Behind me, the cannon opened up on the remaining vessel. The alien craft veered away from the crimson streams that flashed across the sky toward it, the pilot already having started turning before it was even attacked.

The smoke cleared quickly as we left behind the wreckage of the starship, giving me a clear view of the group. I settled the sights of both hand cannons over the first alien and fired as I pulled down the basics of the Krym'parke's status.

Legh'k Am'tyve (Scavenger Level 41)

HP: 614/840
MP: 624/880

I'd almost forgotten how ugly the demonic-looking bastards were with the horns that jutted from their foreheads and chins. Despite their appearance, I nearly sneered in disgust at the attributes his status displayed.

They'd spent a year on the same Dungeon World, and it seemed the Krym'parke hadn't advanced much more than a few Levels. Maybe they were only good at killing imprisoned schoolchildren and defenseless teachers.

A half dozen more rapid-fire shots from my pistols staggered the alien, and I shifted my aim to the next charging Krym'parke, a Level 39 Corsair. The second alien also slowed beneath the weight of my fire, staggering to one side of the engine's roof before tumbling off completely, but my focus on the first pair of enemies cost me as attacks from the remaining trio raked across my arms and chest.

The ice armor protecting my upper body steamed and hissed beneath sweeping energy beams, while solid slugs from a projectile weapon cracked into my chest with enough force to stagger me under the repeated impacts. The defensive spell more than proved its worth, since my health only ticked down slightly despite the storm of fire around me, though I doubted the fracturing magical formation would hold up much longer if the barrage continued.

The aliens advanced toward me in a line with Dayena's cousin in the center, flanked between the two Krym'parke soldiers. The Scavenger I'd first targeted brought up their rear and appeared to be having trouble getting one of his boots to properly clamp onto the roof of the train. The alien's difficulties prompted a new strategy.

I glanced at the gnome hunched down behind the barrier beside me, seeing a Level 33 Sentry. "Aim for their feet. Take out the magboots and they won't get far."

The gnome, Kyvi Coglock, nodded and shifted his energy rifle to lower his fire against the oncoming aliens. I followed my own instructions to crack off several rounds at the Truinnar in the middle of the group.

Creynora fired a beam pistol at me one-handed while her other hand rested on the hilt of her saber. The Truinnar remained hauntingly beautiful despite the anger twisting her face into a mask of fury—probably due to the fact that I'd just blown her brother out of the sky.

My pistol rounds sparked off the armored train roof beneath the dark elf, her graceful, dance-like steps evading my fire. One lucky ricochet caught the good boot of the struggling alien in the back and the panicked expression on the Krym'parke's face was almost comical as he flailed to regain his footing. He failed, slipping and falling from the side of the train.

Two down, three to go.

The rightmost alien, a Vanguard with a beam carbine, sprayed a flurry of energy attacks toward me. On the left, a Blackjack fired a rifle that looked like a modified AR-15, complete with all the tacti-cool attachments like a laser sight, tac light, and red-dot sight.

The three attackers suddenly glowed red as Kyvi activated a Sentry Skill on them. The highlight magnified the damage of our combined shots on the trio.

Repeatedly activating Hinder, I managed to fire a few more rounds and spread my shots between them to slow their advance before my pistols emptied. Ducking down behind the barrier, I reloaded the pistols with fresh magazines and cast a refresh with the Ice Armor spell to restore the destroyed protection.

Frost seemed to flow from the fractures in the plates of ice, pushing out the rifle slugs which had been stuck to clank off the armored roof beneath me. Red lines flowed through the cracks in the icy plates from my wounds before the protection froze solid and smoothed the surface over the divots carved by the energy weapons.

Taking a crouched step to the side of where I'd ducked down, I popped back up and triggered my weapons as I swept them over the three aliens. The hand cannons bucked with each round fired and I focused on ensuring each shot hit one of the enemies, who were nearly at the edge of the engine's roof above the coupling to the workshop car.

For a moment, I worried they would ignore us long enough to assault the control cabin, but my fears proved unfounded as the two Krym'parke jumped the gap between cars and closed in on our position.

Creynora let the two aliens take the lead, and the brunt of fire, before she followed them, drawing her saber and activating her charge ability when she touched down on top of the workshop. The dark elf streaked across the distance between us and launched herself at me, sword-point first, as I began a spell-casting gesture.

Clearly, she'd expected a repeat use of Frostnova, bounding well above the surface of the train roof in an effort to avoid the binding effect of the spell. I grinned viciously as I completed the cast of Howling Blast, enjoying the expression of surprise that crossed Creynora's face as a swirling cone of hail-filled air projected from my gesturing hand. The frigid gust flowed over the trio of aliens and knocked the two Krym'parke back a pace, staggering them enough to halt their attacks. One dropped to a knee to catch his balance.

The airborne Creynora fared far worse from the effect of the spell. Without any ability to brace herself, the turbulent gale swept her away from me. She arced back to land hard on the roof and skidded toward the gap between the cars, her weapon bouncing from her grasp as she flailed in an attempt to halt her slide. Though the dark elf slowed significantly before sh reached the edge, her legs still slipped off. She finally caught herself with r lower half hanging over the end of the car.

With the threat of the Truinnar dealt with for the moment, I ted my attention to the remaining aliens before they could recover the effects of Howling Blast. A flurry of shots emptied my pistols, rating the still-standing Vanguard and the alien slumped to the roof train. I dropped my depleted weapons into their holsters on my hip the pair of beam pistols from my shoulder rig, and fired at the Blac

The torrent of my energy beams combined with rifle shots, searing the Krym'parke and melting through his a acket as the kneeling alien pushed himself to stand. The horned a the rifle back up to his shoulder and resumed firing at me.

Alien bullets crisscrossed with my pist n rays. I jerked slightly with each projectile that chipped aw e armor, but not enough to throw off my aim. The alien grit teeth in frustration and pain, coughing up blood as my contin urned deep into his chest before finally keeling over with his ptied.

Between the bodies of the two dead Krym'parke, Creynora scooped up her dropped weapon as she struggled to her feet. Her Luck must be as ridiculous as her Charisma, since somehow the blade hadn't fallen off the top of the train. I cast a Frostbolt at the dark elf, the jagged shard of ice catching her in the shoulder and punching through her red armor as she stood upright.

Despite wincing from the spike sticking out of her clavicle, Creynora raised her saber, and her parry Skill deftly deflected several energy beams as she stalked forward. Stupid, ridiculous System that let people parry literal light.

Not having any desire to cross blades with the skilled swordswoman, activated Hinder again to slow her approach and backed away while I lyzed the Truinnar to get a better idea of my chances of avoiding another ing.

Creynora Baluisa (Heart Guard Level 47)

: 520/880

720/960

the Truinnar had picked up a Level since we'd last faced off, she'd dr out a third of her health in the fight so far and held a decent pool of 1 eserve. I shoved my beam pistols back into their holsters in my sho hen drew Last Word. I reloaded the weapon quickly with a full maga olstered it, casting another Frostbolt at Creynora. Then I applied an der for good measure before repeating the reloading process with

Kyvi saw me backing off and hurried to get farther away from the Truinnar. Fortunately for the gnome, it looked like Creynora had tunnel vision locked onto me.

The dark elf grimaced in frustration as she struggled to reach me against the resistance of my Skill. Even with her face twisted in exertion, she remained damnably cute.

Despite the fact that she was trying to kill me. Fucking Truinnar and their ridiculous Charisma.

Rounds from my fully loaded pistols cracked out at the elven woman. Her blade swatted at the projectiles, but her parry Skill failed to deflect every shot. Several attacks bypassed her defenses and punched through her light armor, leaving wounds across her upper body. Stacks of Expose and Rend built as I applied the Skills with my repeated shots.

A whip appeared in the dark elf's free hand, and she flicked the weapon toward my face. Raising one arm to protect myself, the line coiled around my wrist instead of savaging my eyes.

"Hal, you were right about the need to defend the dining car," Dayena sent over party chat.

"I'm a little busy," I replied as the lash pulled tight between Creynora and me, the dark elf tugging on the handle of the whip. I tensed against her, and the Truinnar's eyes widened in surprise as she failed to pull me off balance. I continued firing at her with the pistol in my opposite hand. Still, with one hand wrapped up by the whip, she'd halved my firepower. *"Your cousins decided to crash the party."*

"Get unbusy," the Countess commanded brusquely. *"A swarm of kobolds and a half dozen elite juveniles are pushing forward from the sleeper cars."*

Then the lash flared with energy and my muscles seized from the current traveling through the electrified whip. Blood gushed in my mouth as

I bit halfway through my tongue. I choked from the fluid, unable to unclench my jaw.

Elemental Effect Resisted

The current still coursed through me, but the status message announced the return of control over my body, and I spewed a mouthful of bloody liquid before gasping in a breath of air.

The saber blade slashed toward me as Creynora reached melee range, and I leaned away from the strike, catching the edge of a slice that skidded off my chest in a spray of icy shards. Feeling the tug of Dayena's contracted order pulling me to follow her instructions, I knew I didn't have much time.

"I see the quality of your companions hasn't improved since our last meeting," I said with a pointed glance at the dead Krym'parke as I attempted to distract the Truinnar.

Creynora's growl indicated my jab hitting home. "What do you know of quality companionship?"

"Enough to avoid child-eating assholes like your Krym'parke friends there."

The dark elf scoffed, but her sour expression indicated another successful verbal riposte. "Convenient tools, contracted to bring in our cousin and nothing more."

That pretty much answered the lingering question on whether they were also coordinating with the kobolds. If the Truinnar even knew about the relic, they weren't seeking it out.

Dismissing my pistols to my Inventory and stepping forward, I grabbed Creynora's wrist with one hand to trap it across her chest before she could swing again. With my free hand, I punched the Truinnar in the face.

The blow staggered the elf, her nose crumpling and breaking with a spray of blood that cascaded down over her mouth and chin.

Creynora stumbled backward, and in the brief moment of separation between us, I activated the grapnel launcher in my vambrace. The line wrapped around her upper arms just below her shoulders to pin her arms at her side. The cord continued spinning until it snaked around her stomach, also trapping her forearms within the twisted cords, before disconnecting from my vambrace at a mental command.

I grabbed the dark elf and swung her to the side of the train as she blinked away the stunning effect of her broken nose. Before the Truinnar recovered, I pushed her toward the edge and delivered a Spartan kick to her stomach that doubled her over my foot as the blow launched the dark elf off the side of the train. As the slack from the whip still gripped by the dark elf and wrapped around my wrist played out, I summoned my knife into my other hand and cut the line free before the falling Truinnar could pull me off the train.

"Your cousins aren't a problem anymore," I reported to party chat. *"I'm on my way."*

Chapter 30

The turret cannon atop the workshop car fired another blast of energy at the second Krym'parke vessel as I ran past, forcing the craft to pull up from another attempt to drop more troops onto the train. After the destruction of their first ship, the aliens seemed reluctant to lose another. Leaving the turret to handle the circling starship, I hurried toward the aft end of the train where the kobold forces had managed to land at least two of their skiffs.

Dice and two battered members of his team held a firing position on top of the last coach car. From across the empty roofs of the lounge and dining cars, they sniped at a group of kobolds holding the roof of the forward-most sleeper. Around the Pharyleri lay a scattered handful of spent missile launchers, similar to the single-use tubes used by my Hastati-VI but sized for the smaller humanoids. Evidence of their effectiveness lay in the distance, two more ashy pillars rising skyward behind us in addition to the smoke from the Krym'parke starship.

Even with the heavy firepower, it wasn't enough. The Pharyleri may have upgraded their personal armaments slightly and picked up better armor at their latest visit to the Shop, but even their increased firepower only served as a temporary measure to hold back the tide of numerous kobolds.

One gnome used an ovular shaped device that emitted a beam that latched onto the shields used by the advancing kobolds, grabbing hold like some kind of tractor beam and yanking them out of position. One kobold failed to release the seized shield in time and was thrown completely off the train.

A second gnome used more traditional weaponry, a gatling beam cannon that let off a shrill whine as it sprayed a stream of orange light. The wave of energy pushed back the kobold force until their shieldbearers closed ranks.

The tired gnomes didn't even look up as I slid into cover beside them.

"My team inside?" I asked over the rushing wind, observing the dots on my minimap.

Dice leaned over to make himself heard. "Holding the dining car. The lizards haven't managed to push through there yet."

I nodded and pulled out my missile launcher, detaching the spent tube and pitching it over the side. Dice gave me a questioning glance as I summoned a green-banded launch cylinder and attached the control unit. Stepping out to the side from the cover of the firing position, I locked the targeting reticle onto the distant lizards and squeezed the trigger. The missile popped from the tube and whooshed into a tall arc across the space toward the kobold troops. The train roof erupted in fire as the cluster munitions rained down on the large group.

All three gnomes glanced at me in relief, and I grinned, unfastening the control unit and tossing the empty cylinder down to join the empty tubes of the gnomish launchers. I couldn't help the juvenile thought that crossed my mind. Size mattered and mine was bigger.

"Here," I said, handing Dice the launcher control unit and pulling two of the missile tubes from my Inventory. "Green is anti-personnel. Yellow is anti-vehicle. Have fun." I started toward the back of the train and stopped after taking a single step, fixing Dice with a stern look. "I want that controller back later."

The trio of gnomes looked at the launcher, glanced back at the still-burning kobolds, and then turned toward me before nodding in agreement in unison.

Leaving the Pharyleri, I slipped down into the vestibule between the coach car and the lounge. The decrease in ambient noise was a relief after the roaring wind outside. I hurried down the aisle through the empty lounge and entered the dining car, immediately struck by the stench of blood, charred flesh, and death.

At the far end of the car, Kurak staggered back from the open doorway in a spray of blood as a juvenile kobold leapt over a pile of dead bodies to tear open the minotaur's chest with its raking claws. More kobolds packed the passage to the sleeper car beyond the juvenile and pushed their way forward into the breach.

Summoning my pistols into my raised hands, I fired down the length of the car. My rounds joined attacks from Lyrra and Dayena, who perched behind tables flipped over as barricades on either side of the center aisle just beyond the food prep elevators.

Another armored figure rushed into the fray from beside Kurak, forcing me to check my fire. Sheera tore into the kobolds with claws of her own, and I raised an eyebrow while I continued to snipe at the aliens, impressed by the savagery the Demarcian displayed. As I watched, she ripped an arm from the juvenile kobold. Ignoring the spraying arterial blood, the leonid pummeled the lizard with its own limb until it ceased moving.

Brutal, like the Adventurers who'd fought the Sect in Denver, or so I'd been told. A party which had had a leonine Demarcian who had a tendency to tear off limbs.

A party that had disappeared into the mountains, followed by an angry dragon attacking the city.

Kurak's holographic display had showed the inciting event of that dragon's rage, I realized, and my suspicions of Sheera crystalized into certainty. Especially with the way she'd clearly been affected by the death of the sword-wielding Demarcian in Kurak's hologram.

Nargen pushed up beside me, finally arriving from the front of the train too. He fired an energy rifle as his robot dog dashed the length of the car and launched itself at the throat of a kobold juvenile. We carefully picked shots around our allies until the last of the kobolds fell.

Sheera stood from finishing off a wounded kobold in the pile blocking the entryway, and Kurak slumped into one of the booths that hadn't been torn out for materials to build the impromptu barricade. Lyrra hurried to the minotaur and began healing his wounds, using some on-touch Skills I assumed. I approached the gore-coated Demarcian and helped her move enough of the bodies away from the door that it could be closed.

"Can we lock this thing?" I asked as the door slid shut.

Sheera shook her head. "No, it was designed to open at touch for ease of passage, not prevent unauthorized access from pirates."

I fixed the Demarcian with a glare as I casually leaned against the side of the doorway. "Pirates chasing a relic."

Sheera's head snapped around and she bared her fangs. "You know nothing of that."

"I know we've lost crew because of it," I responded. "The Pharyleri are paying the price for what you're carrying. We all might pay for it, if the Zabotkermanne keep coming."

"My family has carried that sword for generations."

"You're not carrying it now." I glanced at the Demarcian's extended claws, still dripping with kobold blood. "If you have a relic, then use it."

Sheera shook, anger and frustration rippling across her lion-like features. "I can't."

"Why not?" Dayena asked, approaching from behind us and folding her arms across her chest. "These attacks threaten the completion of our contract with the Pharyleri. If you will not fight them off, then there are other options we may explore."

Sheera growled at the threat then hissed in disgust. "No one can wield it."

The Demarcian gestured and a block of ice tumbled from Sheera's Inventory, thudding solidly to the floor of the dining car. Lying down, the roughly rectangular block stretched out nearly seven feet long with a cross section over a foot in both height and width. It was the same thick ice that smoothly covered the abandoned starport.

The once-pristine surface of the ice was covered with scratches and chips, evidence of Sheera's attempts to free the object within. Though none of the gouges ran deep, they still marred the surface in a sign that the regenerating effect of the ice had faded with distance from the dragon's domain.

Tinged blue and trapped within the translucent chunk was the sword from Kurak's hologram. Even encased in ice, the weapon radiated strength. The straight blade of the two-handed greatsword extended over six feet long and measured at least four inches from edge to edge.

A silvery light flashed over the icy block and slammed into my torso, throwing me backward and pinning me against the wall. Blood sprayed from my mouth as I gasped in surprise and glanced down to find the glowing axeblade of Kurak's halberd stuck halfway through my chest.

Even through the protection of my ice armor, the attack had dropped my health by over a third. I looked up at the Yerrick as the fully healed minotaur backhanded Lyrra across the car. Nargen fired his beam rifle into Dayena's back while the Gimsar's robot dog latched onto the back of Sheera's leg. She collapsed backward onto the dog as the two fell into the aisle in a tangle of alien and metallic limbs.

"We'll have the relic shortly." Kurak spoke into the same communicator he'd used to display the hologram earlier.

"Binary Eclipse paid you off." Blood dripped from my lips as I gasped the words, struggling to breathe with the halberd embedded in my lungs.

The Yerrick shrugged. "Sect Credits spend like any others. We don't fail the contract with the Pharyleri as long as the train makes it back to the starport, even if the Sect are the ones driving it."

"Not gonna happen," I said.

"You don't have much choice from where I stand," Kurak replied, tugging the halberd's axe head from my chest with a sickening squelch. "The Sect gets the train and the relic. Nargen and I split a bunch of Credits. The only losers here are you and your elf friends."

With the blade no longer pressing me against the wall, I sagged to my knees as the minotaur swung the halberd around for another strike. Activating Hinder on the Yerrick to buy myself precious time, I cast Whiteout to blind our opponents. A maelstrom of snow and tiny flecks of ice swirled through the interior of the dining car as the spell took effect. The precipitate caused little damage but completely occluded vision throughout the enclosed space.

Diving forward, I cast a round of healing spells on myself, which placed all of the spells on cooldown. My Mana dropped from the chain casting as I slid across the uneven surface of the iced relic sword. Pain jolted through the broken ribs and ragged flesh of my torso as I dropped off the far side of the slab before rolling to my feet. A scream threatened to slip out as shattered bones ground within my chest, but I choked it back, knowing that the noise would give the minotaur a target. The sound of the sweeping halberd slicing through the murk behind me was carrot enough.

Other sounds pierced the blizzard-filled dining car, rising over the howling magical storm. The shrill whine of energy beam shots, the scrape of claws tearing through armor, and the thump of flailing feet as the blinded combatants searched for their opponents. Greater Observation filtered the sounds, combining with Keen Senses to the point that I knew where each individual in the car stood—though I was just as blind as everyone else.

Drawing my pistols, I opened up on the Yerrick. Kurak's heavy armor blunted my initial attacks, but soon I punctured through as stacks of Expose built with every round that landed. It probably helped that his armor had been shredded and lost quite a bit of durability from the fight earlier.

The blinded minotaur sought me through the dining car in a deadly game of "Marco Polo," but between my higher Agility and the advantages of my Class Skills, Kurak rarely even came close to landing a hit with the unwieldy polearm.

At least, he didn't land a hit on me. I was pretty sure he got Nargen at least once before the Gimsar gurgled and went silent.

Reloading the slightly awkward cylindrical magazines for the hand cannons without being able to see them was an interesting experience. I added blindfolded reloading to my list of things to train. Still, I managed to replenish the weapons only slightly slower than usual.

By the time I finished the reload, I'd traversed nearly the length of the car. Then the duration of Whiteout's casting expired and all traces of the blizzard within the dining car evaporated as the dining car's overworked air circulation unit dumped the snow outside. Immediately, it revealed Kurak standing in the middle of the car, wrenching his halberd free from the food processing elevator. Holes perforated the minotaur's armor and several pieces hung from partially severed straps.

Nargen lay not far from where the Yerrick stood, prone on his back and staring sightlessly at the ceiling of the car. A bloody gash on the Gimsar's neck and a spreading crimson pool beneath his body told the tale of the dwarf's demise, though no other visible sign of Dayena remained throughout the car.

Lyrra stuck her head out from beneath one of the few intact booths remaining in the dining car, looking questioningly between Kurak and me as the elf debated whether she felt safe in our presence.

The crunch of crumpling metal drew our attention to the doorway beyond the block of ice. Sheera punched down a final time on the sparking and mangled metal shell of Nargen's robot before standing.

She no longer wore the olive uniform and bronze armor of the Pistongrinder train staff. Instead, smoke-gray armor with purple highlights clung tightly to the leonid's feminine figure. Thin plates of molded armor covered the inner jumpsuit layer, providing additional protection without significantly adding bulk. I took a mental note of how I might be able to upgrade my armor similarly. I also recognized the attire as the same worn by the leonine aliens I'd noticed guarding the bay at the Pittsburgh starport.

The armor wasn't the only change I noticed as I scanned the Demarcian and her Status.

Sheera Arfuriosa, King's Paw (Sworn Handmaiden Level 46)
HP: 1310/1640
MP: 1330/1780

Clearly, I wasn't the only one playing tricks with Status manipulation. Actually changing names was new though.

Kurak glanced at Sheera, who looked back impassively, and the minotaur's nostrils flared as he debated his options. Finally deciding he had a better chance at taking me down, the Yerrick swung his halberd at me and charged with the spiked point of his weapon leading the way.

I opened fire, some rounds sparking as they glanced off the plates. Others punched even more holes into the shredded armor.

Dayena stepped from a shadow of the passage to the kitchen below and sliced one short sword through Kurak's hamstring, then she stabbed the other into the back of his knee joint. The crippled Yerrick screamed in pain, slamming into the floor with an impact that I felt even over the movement of the train.

Kurak still tried to push himself upright, refusing to submit. I triggered two more shots at the fallen minotaur before Dayena pulled her weapons free. She scampered up Kurak's back and shoved both blades into the back of the Yerrick's skull. Kurak dropped limp, the last of his massive health pool destroyed. Even if he had any left, there was nowhere for his regeneration to go.

The Countess knelt on the dead Yerrick, sliding her swords free with a squelch of gore and flicking the weapons to splatter blood all around the dining car. I was so glad I wasn't on cleaning duty.

I reloaded, a much easier task now that I could see, before I slipped my pistols into their holsters and walked up to Dayena, tapping her shoulder to cast a Minor Heal. She nodded in thanks, then we turned to face Sheera.

The Demarcian crossed her arms and stared at us defiantly. "I suppose you're going to take the sword now."

I glanced at Dayena, who shook her head slightly.

"No," I said. "We have enough enemies. We don't need any more of a target painted on our backs."

Sheera blinked, not expecting us to reject the opportunity that literally lay before us. Her mouth moved silently, unable to form words.

I sighed. "Could you wield it if freed from the ice?"

The question roused the Demarcian, though her words were halting when she spoke. "I think so."

I knelt beside the trapped weapon. This close to its surface, I could make out several new cracks from Kurak's flailing halberd and lines where Nargen's stray beam shots had left thin streaks across the massive chunk during the recent fight. The attacks appeared no more effective in damaging the resilient material than the marks already on the block.

Just like the frost and snow around the frozen starport outside Denver.

I glanced up at Sheera. "I see your problem."

I debated whether to bring my new Affinity into play. It was an advantage that I'd kept to myself so far. Still, I'd already delt with Dayena's cousins, so if Sheera could use the relic to take the kobolds out then we'd be home free.

Placing a hand on the frozen surface, I pressed downward and closed my eyes. Reaching out with my mind, I pushed my will into the ice as the chill radiated up into the flesh of my palm. I pulled on my Ice Affinity, much as I had when I first gained the ability. Slowly, my awareness spread through the crystalline mass as I stretched toward the sword encased at its center.

The sword itself resisted my mental touch, but that barely registered in my conscious mind since I wasn't trying to claim the weapon. Instead, I wrapped my will through the ice around the blade. Once my consciousness sheathed the weapon from pommel to tip, I compressed the fractals that formed the icy chunk. Then I twisted the prismatic formations in an attempt to overcome their solidity with shear stress as I pushed a single command into the ice with my Affinity.

Break.

I felt the bonds within the ice weaken, but it refused to completely bend to my will. My nascent Affinity was too weak to overcome the remnants of the dragon's aura that infused the entirety of the substance. My head pounded and liquid dripped from my nose. I opened my eyes as a drop of blood landed on the ice, splashing onto the block's surface.

Glancing around, my eyes landed on Kurak's massive halberd where it stuck out from under his body.

I looked at Sheera. "Get the halberd. Hit the block when I tell you."

The Demarcian pulled the weapon from beneath the minotaur. She hefted the weapon like a lumberjack squaring up at a log splitting contest.

Once again, I pushed my awareness into the block of ice and strained to weaken the structure. "Now."

I barely got the word out before I felt the impact of the halberd's blade slamming down onto the surface of the block. The bonds flexed and I felt cracks run through the slab.

Still, it remained whole.

"Again!"

Sheera roared as she brought the head of the halberd down onto the block a second time.

With a crash like a sheet of glass shattering, the upper half of the ice block crumbled in a cascade of silvery shards that poured across the floor of the dining car. I fell forward without the support of the block, my hand landing on the exposed blade, and I instinctively pulled the weapon's status.

Tier I Greatsword (Judgment of the Dawn), Bane of Kings, Foereaper

Base Damage: 1097

Durability: 10,460 / 10,460

Special Abilities: Soul Drinker (Level 73), Armor Piercing (58), Shield Penetration (52), Reflection Barrier (Level 51), Furious Charge (Level 47), Cleaving Strike (Level 43), (more...)

Fuck me.

Now I understood why everyone wanted their hands on the weapon. The sword even had its own Titles.

The list of unique qualities scrolled on, and a faint understanding of each talent flowed into me as the blade reached into my mind, brushing my consciousness with a tentative connection.

With a shake of my head, I broke away from the mental contact with the strange blade and stood up, facing Sheera. "All yours."

The Demarcian cocked her head and looked at me questioningly. I didn't understand her confusion until I looked down.

The hand I'd used to push myself to my feet was clenched tightly on the bone grip of the sword just below the crossguard, with the tip of the blade angled down and still resting on what remained of the ice block. I frowned and tried to pass the weapon to Sheera hilt first, but my arm wouldn't move. Even when I simply tried to let go, my hand refused to cooperate.

"I'm not sure what's happening here," I said. I felt my heartbeat speeding up a little and I forced myself to breathe. No panicking.

Yet.

Sheera sighed. "I think I know."

Dayena circled around my side and peered closely at the weapon before glancing at Sheera. "It is a beautiful blade."

"Yeah, it's great." I tried storing the weapon in my Inventory, but nothing happened. "I just can't let go of it or even stick it into Inventory apparently."

Dayena looked at me sharply. "Why not?"

"If I knew that, I would let it go."

Sheera shook her head sadly and shuffled over to me through the ice shards covering the floor of the train. "Is this how it has to be?"

The words weren't addressed to me. She'd looked down as she spoke, staring at the sword in my fist.

"Daughter of Demarcia, this Dungeon World has already consumed one Arfuriosa." The words flowed from my mouth, but I wasn't the one speaking. **"I will not permit another to be lost here after your brother's foolishness cost his life. This vessel will suffice to complete your mission in your stead."**

Sheera nodded solemnly. "I understand."

"I certainly don't," I retorted, no longer performing my impression of a sock puppet but pushing down on the panic threatened by the lack of control over my own body.

The weapon was continuing to reach into my mind despite my attempt to reject its connection. The feeling was a little like silk fingers slipping my brain. Kind of nice in the soul screaming sort of way.

Dayena raised an eyebrow as she looked between us.

The armored leonid gestured to the sword. "Judgment of the Dawn is an heirloom bonded to the Demarcian heir when they come of age. The weapon is carried until the next successor is declared, at which time the blade is passed on to guard and protect their development."

"Except when that successor pisses off a dragon?"

"Arturios was a vain, attention-seeking idiot, but he was still my brother," Sheera growled. I shut up at the leonine alien's angry glare and let her continue. "My mission was to retrieve Judgment and return it to our capital. However, the blade tends to have a will of its own."

"None of that explains why I can't get this damned sword out of my hand."

"Judgment wants you to carry it back home," Sheera said.

I shook my head. "Not happening. I have contracts to finish here."

Closing my eyes, I sought out the mental links the weapon was forming between us. I refused to let them get a grip on me. Gripping one imaginary, silk-covered strand after another, I applied my considerable Willpower to it. I felt the System aiding me, helping to break the connections. Somehow, I got the feeling that Relics weren't exactly meant to have the level of control this one had.

Even as I severed the links, shattering them like so much ice, pain rippled through me. Shards of silky ice stabbed into my brain, leaving me biting my lip and bleeding from the nose. Damage notifications scrolled past, but I ignored them all, even as we jostled for control.

I would not give in. I would not be a puppet. I would not lose.

And finally, finally, the connections shattered, leaving me a final notification.

Mental Influence Resisted

A pressure I hadn't even registered feeling eased from squeezing my brain and I opened my hand, allowing the blade to drop to the floor. Broken shards of ice scattered from the impact as the massive blade clattered to rest.

Everyone stared silently at the weapon for a moment.

"You would reject the honor of wielding Judgment?" Sheera gaped incredulously.

"Honor?" I scoffed. "More like a death sentence. There are at least two interplanetary groups after the weapon now and who knows how many more will join in as your brother's little highlight reel spreads. I have no desire to play target dummy for a bunch of pirates. I much prefer being alive to spend my Credits."

"There weren't supposed to be any pirates." Sheera rubbed furry hands over her muzzle in frustration. "This was supposed to be a quiet op. In and out."

I shrugged. "That ship has sailed."

The Demarcian dropped her hands and stared at me. "Two-fifty."

"Two-fifty what?"

"Two hundred and fifty thousand Credits," Sheera replied. "Get the Judgment to my backup team at the starport and the Credits are yours."

That was a ton of Credits.

I glanced at Dayena, but the dark elf grinned at me. *"Take her for everything she offers."*

Raising a skeptical eyebrow at the Truinnar, I turned back to Sheera. "Five hundred."

Sheera didn't even flinch, and a Quest window popped up in front of me. "Deal."

As fast as she took the offer, I should have led with a million. I accepted the Quest anyway.

The train door behind the Demarcian slid open and through it stormed the largest kobold yet, carrying a battleaxe in each hand. A wave of lizard forces crowded the door beyond. Painted black and yellow hazard stripes decorated the hard surfaces of the juvenile lizard's pauldrons and

424

breastplate, the only solid pieces of armor worn by the kobold over its beige leather garb.

Zabotkermanne Juvenile (Marauder Level 19)

HP: 1490/1490

MP: 1120/1120

Sensing the threat behind her, Sheera slid one foot through the pile of ice shards and scooped up Judgment with a flick of her foot. I reached out as the blade seemed to float horizontally at the top of its arc and grabbed the hilt of the massive greatsword. Once again, information flowed into my mind, and this time, I allowed it as the weapon pushed a recommended action to the forefront of my consciousness.

The kobold stepped up behind Sheera, swinging an axe toward her head, and I engaged the sword's Furious Charge. Before the lizard finished its swing, the ability launched me forward. I shoulder-checked the kobold Marauder hard enough that its chest caved in, and an exhalation of orange blood splashed over my face.

When my rush finally stopped, the lizard collapsed to the floor unmoving after leaving my bicep aching and bruised. I flexed my arm as I wiped away the kobold blood from my face and looked around.

I'd plowed the kobold through the still-open dining car door and carried it halfway down the length of the sleeper car beyond, leaving kobold troops broken and twisted in bloody wrecks the length of the passage. Wind rushed in through the first window inside the door from the diner car, since I'd apparently been moving fast enough to generate a sonic boom. The other windows along the exterior were cracked and vibrating with the train's movement, while the interior wall and doors to the sleeper rooms had crumpled inward.

The Marauder twitched on the floor, not quite dead, and I felt a sense of satisfaction emanate from the sword as I drove it through the kobold's neck.

"All right," I addressed the blade. "I don't know if you can hear me, but here's how this is gonna go. We're going to kill a shit-ton of kobolds and then lead them away from the train. They'll come after us instead."

I caught sight of the circling Krym'parke ship through the spiderweb of cracks on the window beside me. "But first, we're doing something about that little problem."

Chapter 31

"Uh, Hal? Are you there? The Sect bodyguards are attempting to break through into the control cabin." Ismyna's voice echoed in my ear as I headed back toward the dining car.

Of course they were. Kurak and Nargen wouldn't have been acting on their own, and the Yerrick had mentioned the Sect wanting the train. Still, I'd forgotten about Kurak using his communicator with everything going on. He must have been signaling the Sect envoy and his goons.

I sighed and keyed the communicator. "Just the two heavies or is the envoy with them?"

"The two big ones and a bunch of goons who were disguised as paying passengers from coach."

"Be there in a minute."

Carrying the surprisingly light sword in one hand, I walked into the dining car and found Lyrra patching up Sheera and Dayena.

"Sect goons are pushing on the engine," I reported as I passed them. "I'll deal with them and then work on the starship."

"What then?" Sheera called.

"Kill more kobolds," I replied over my shoulder.

The lounge car beyond the diner lay empty, though a few beam shots flashed back and forth overhead as the gnomes on top of the car skirmished with the kobolds at the rear of the train.

In the first coach car, the bodies of several passengers lay sprawled into the aisle. I recognized the Karen and her husband among the dead. Despite their earlier attitudes and stated plan to leave the train, they'd stuck out the ride in their attempt to reach Pittsburgh. Their needless deaths at the hand of the Sect irked me.

Only a few surviving passengers remained, cowering on their seats or huddling against the walls as I stalked down the aisle with sword in hand. None of them attacked me or seemed like Sect members, so I left them in peace.

An armed mob filled the far end of the second car, crowding against each other to push through the door into the workshop beyond. Sounds of weapons fire and screaming wounded echoed from the vestibule that separated the cars, evidence of Eldri's technicians fighting back.

I lifted the greatsword into a ready position and advanced up the aisle. Scanning the rear of the Sect goons, I found a mix of species including a couple lower Leveled humans.

"Hal, the kobolds are getting reinforcements!" Ismyna's panicked voice sounded over the communicator. "Mother just transmitted a warning. Their contract is no longer limited. They're leaving the dungeon outbreak and sending all available forces this way!"

One problem after another just kept escalating our conflict and I had no patience left to take it easy on the Sect members in front of me.

"Hal, did you copy?" Ismyna transmitted.

"I heard. Dealing with the Sect now," I growled in frustration.

The sound of my voice caused one of those humans at the back of the throng to look over his shoulder at me just as I swung the sword. The blade bisected the man from shoulder to hip and passed through the leg of the dog-like alien next to him. The alien's howl of pain alerted the others, but it was already far too late.

Every swing of the sword left Sect members in pieces. With each clean cut, I diced my way through the passage as easily as a Sith Lord in a crowded hallway of Rebel fleet troopers.

The weapons fire from the front of the group cut out as I mowed down everyone and stepped into the workshop car. To my surprise, I found my old friends from my morning walk in Denver as the last pair standing. Beyond them on the floor lay an unmoving Pharyleri in an olive uniform, and I felt my blood run cold as I caught sight of a shock of orange hair.

I paused, spitting away some of the spattered blood now dripping down my face as I choked down my fury. "I see that kicking your asses once wasn't enough for you."

The pair glanced at each other but said nothing. Sparks danced over electrified brass knuckles as Bemparat squared up in a boxer's stance facing me. Ro'khar'sar stepped around the Scrofalori and leveled a large bore weapon.

A glowing shield flashed around me from the sword to catch the hail of metallic flechettes that blasted from the weapon. The shield rippled as the slender needles impacted the golden surface and stuck, hanging in the air for a moment before clattering to the floor.

Unfazed by the attack's failure, Bemparat lunged forward. The fist weapons glanced off the curve of the shield protecting me, the electrical discharges from the impacts spidering off the point of impact. Yet the attacks utterly failed to affect the shield or push me back even slightly.

I stabbed, the blade passing through the Scrofalori's armor and chest without any resistance. Bemparat looked down at the weapon embedded in his chest and blinked in surprise before I ripped the blade free in a horizontal motion that sprayed gore across the workshop and took off the alien's arm.

Ro'khar'sar gaped in surprise, an expression that would remain for the rest of the alien's brief life as I continued the swing. The sword moved around in an overhead sweep that removed the rhino's head from its neck as easily as running a lint roller over an inspection ready uniform.

A snap of my wrist flicked the rivulets of alien blood and ichor from the blade before I rested it on my shoulder.

"That's new," Eldri said as he peeked out from behind a hastily constructed barricade of crates stacked across the width of the car. The gnome froze as he saw the unmoving form of the conductor in the middle of the car.

The technician knelt beside Wrefen's body, tears trickling down his cheeks. The drops left dark spots on the olive uniform as he hunched over his friend.

If kobolds continued to bring more forces into play, we couldn't fight off the whole swarm. I had to get the sword away from the train or others would be joining Wrefen in death. And I'd fail the contract.

My resolve hardened. I refused to let others fall when I could stand in their place. I refused to fail a contract.

"I'm sorry for Wrefen," I said. "This sword is the shiny toy the kobolds are after. If you're good here, I'm going to wave it in front of them and lead them off before any more arrive."

Hopefully.

Eldri looked at the bodies, and body parts, of the Sect members strewn around the workshop doorway. He swallowed, visibly pushing away his grief. "I think we're good."

I nodded toward the side of the workshop. "Open the door for me then."

The gnome looked at me curiously but activated the door controls, filling the car with swirling wind and the roar of the train's high-speed passage. Improperly secured tools and packing materials scattered in the fighting clattered and blew around the workshop interior.

Pulling my bike from Inventory, I activated hover mode as it materialized before I swung a leg over and mounted the comfortably padded seat. I grinned at Eldri as I paused astride the bike. With the sword held in one hand, I snapped the blade up at a thirty-degree angle and held the crossguard in front of my chin.

It wasn't a perfect salute, since the "Present Arms" movement from the NCO Sword Manual was intended for a saber and not a greatsword, but it still looked impressive, judging from Eldri's expression. The Pharyleri's eyes bulged as I sharply lowered my hand to my side to complete the sword drill movement before kicking the bike throttle to max and shooting out of the bay doors.

The anti-grav system strained as I dropped from the open doorway, almost scraping the ground before the hover drive managed to float me several feet upward. Before reaching a steady elevation, the vehicle swung around in response to my one-handed twisting of the handlebars. The manual controls were more habit than truly necessary. My upgraded Neural Link was more than capable of maneuvering the bike remotely, but I still liked the tangible response.

Riding parallel to the tracks, I scanned the route ahead. A narrow overpass blocked the way and I slipped away from the obstruction, hitting the artificial hill in the middle of its vertical rise. The impromptu ramp sent me flying over the road leading to the overpass, higher than the top of the train roof, before reaching the top arc of the jump and curving back to the ground with a force that flattened the unmowed grass along the roadside.

The airtime from the jump provided a potential opportunity for getting the attention of the kobolds still on the train, but first I needed to deal with the Krym'parke. They still seemed focused on their mercenary contract to capture the Countess, despite the loss of a ship and the apparent death of the Truinnar contracting them.

A concerned thought of the dark elf possibly surviving that whole missile-to-the-chest thing led me to check my experience notifications, but I closed the status update in relief at the chunk gained specifically from the Truinnar's death.

Locating the remaining Krym'parke vessel on my minimap, I angled away from the train toward the circling starship. The ship still flew at an off-kilter angle, the damaged engine slightly lower than the other three. It barely cleared the treetops after all the added abuse from the gnomish turret, the harsh whine of energy beams racing outward punctuating the day. The energy beams might not be doing much damage, but they'd still managed to drop the starship's Core Durability another percentage as metal melted and left little dribbles on the ground.

The heavy shuttle broke off from its circling and shot forward to the south. Eyes narrowing at the change in behavior, I brought up my map to compare the trajectory of the vessel with the upcoming terrain and the train's current sensor feed.

The Krym'parke were heading toward a major highway overpass, likely intending on using the cover of the bridge where Interstate 76 crossed over the tracks to get low enough to drop troops from above. Maybe even from the span itself.

I used the map to plot an intercept and hunched low over the handlebars as I accelerated, following the waypoints projected into my vision. If I maxed the bike's speed and didn't get delayed at all, I'd get to the location just as the train passed below the interstate.

If I didn't... well, I probably wouldn't be able to catch back up. My bike couldn't match the full speed of the train.

The virtual markers guided me more south than east, and I intersected the highway just outside of Rootstown, Ohio, before turning to follow the broken asphalt surface toward the intercept point.

It didn't take long for me to confirm my conjecture about the Krym'parke plan. The heavy shuttle appeared to be sitting on the southern side of the overpass with troops waiting on the end of the lowered ramp. None of those troops looked my way as I rode straight for the ship hovering just over the old highway as I caught sight of the engine leading the way under the overpass.

Pulling the bike up to its max altitude, I streaked over the highway nearly fifteen feet in the air and pointed myself toward the wing-like structure supporting the forward engine of the Krym'parke ship. Swinging the massive greatsword beneath me as I passed over the wing, the blade sliced through the structure. This time, there was more resistance, but no more than you'd get pulling a knife across a tender steak. The ear-piercing shriek of rending metal marked the blade dragging through the vessel's armor.

The engine shuddered as my bike slipped over the front side of the wing, and I caught a glimpse of the Krym'parke pilot jerking to look at me as I dropped past the cockpit.

Then the wing I'd cut through buckled as the engine overpowered the support structure and twisted itself back toward the body of the vessel. The other forward engine strained against the increased load and flared out in a sparking cloud of smoke.

My bike caught traction hovering over the road again and shot forward as I swung around the tilting starship, ducking under the nose of the craft as it tipped toward the failed engine. The forward end of the vessel dug into the roadway as the rear engines of the ship continued their lift, unable to compensate for the damaged and destroyed front engines. It flipped the entire starship onto its back as the Krym'parke troops fell out of the open rear bay doors.

Pulling a U-turn, I headed back toward the center of the overpass and turned sharply just before reaching the passing train below. Aligned with the tracks, I gunned the throttle and shot myself into the open air above the moving train. Momentum carried me forward, airborne for several long moments before dropping on the dining car. Even from two cars ahead of where I landed, the incredulous expressions on the faces of Dice and his security team were visible as I jauntily waved the sword in their direction before spinning the bike toward the rear of the train.

The kobolds still held the rear cars, and I needed their attention if I wanted to pull them away from the train now that I'd dealt with the Krym'parke air support. And before the additional reinforcements arrived.

Unrestrained glee at the chaos I'd unleashed flowed into my mind from the sword as if the blade approved of the death and destruction left in my wake. I certainly felt the adrenaline rush from the insanity of my actions, though I wasn't sure what it said about me that a sentient sword approved of the sheer number of bodies I'd been dropping over the last few hours.

I just knew I wasn't done yet. I gunned the bike's throttle and accelerated toward the rear of the train with a savage grin on my face.

Chapter 32

Flashes of energy beams streaked toward me as I drove over the length of the train, hunched low over the handlebars with my sword-wielding arm cocked back. I ignored the incoming attacks as I rode. Most missed, and the few that should have hit splashed off the reflective barrier the sword raised around me. A man could get used to that. A saner, quieter part of me whispered words of caution, that all this was borrowed power.

I ignored it.

Swinging the massive blade forward, I drove directly into the ranks of kobolds streaming from a pair of newly arrived skiffs onto the rear cars of the train. Lizard blood geysered from bisected torsos and severed heads as the greatsword slashed from one side to the other, spraying ichor across the mass of troops already clambering over their fallen companions to throw themselves at me. The screams and cries of the enraged, wounded, and dying lizards rose over the roar of the wind and the roar of my heartbeat in my ears.

A juvenile pushed through the throng, and I flicked the blade's tip out to rip through the lizard's neck, adding a new source of spraying gore to the fluids coating the roof of the train.

Then I was through the far side of the crowd, the wailing from the kobolds fading after I passed the last of the skiffs and drifted my ride off the side of the boxcar. The side of the freight car passed beneath me in a flash before the nose of the bike pulled up and I leveled out, leaning over far enough to brush my knee through the tall grass as I turned back around.

Pushing the bike's throttle to the max, I accelerated alongside the train. A deluge of energy beams rained down over the side of the train as the kobolds figured out where I'd gone.

It seemed my reckless charge through their midst had certainly succeeded in getting their attention. Now I just needed them to chase me and leave the train alone.

The kobold attacks petered out as I left them behind, passing cars. Hunched low over the handlebars to reduce drag, I eked out as much speed as possible to pull ahead of the train.

Out of the kobolds' range, I used my free hand to send the axe on my back into Inventory before swinging the sword over my shoulder and letting the axe's storage clamps grab hold of the weapon. With the blade now locked in place, I had both hands free for the manual driving I so enjoyed.

Passing the workshop, flashes of light from the energy turret on top of the car drew my attention to a large red indicator on my minimap. The crimson marker floated in a curving arc away from the rear of the train, and I hazarded a glance over my shoulder to find a kobold skiff moving up.

A few kobold hatchlings peeked over the side of the craft before pointing their energy rifles at me and taking potshots. More joined in on the fire while hanging over the side wall of the craft.

Another barrage from the turret on the workshop car forced the skiff lower as it dropped to avoid the attack. The lower elevation of the craft gave the rifle-armed lizards better shots as the vessel pulled up beside me, clearly intending to pinch me between the skiff and the moving train.

No thanks.

I hit the brakes, dropping my velocity sharply for a moment then accelerating again as the lizards shot ahead. Before the skiff pilot could recover, I swung my bike behind the vessel as I pulled the greatsword free from the clamps on my back.

Heat from the skiff's engines washed over me, dropping my health a notch despite my resistances. Still, my speed carried me through the wake quickly enough and I sliced through the thruster on the far side as I passed.

The blade cut through the engine housing in a squealing spray of sparks, and the unit flickered before it lost power completely. The skiff turned sharply, driven by the other thruster still operating, and forced me to brake sharply to avoid running into the side of the vessel.

The skiff plowed into the ground a moment later, throwing lizard hatchlings off the side and pitching a number out of the troop bay. I swerved around the downed craft, aware that the movement of more red dots on my minimap proved that several of the kobold skiffs still remained in play.

Unfortunately, at least one of them had witnessed their companion vessel's demise and remained at range. The skiff's complement of hatchling gunners poured out enough rifle fire that even the greatsword's powerful shield was beginning to crack and let a few shots through.

Needing to change the game, I drove evasively alongside the tracks as I commanded my neural link to find another route, dense with cover and concealment. A waypoint popped up a moment later and I steered toward the objective marker, driving away from the rails and leaving the train.

The red dots followed, and I mentally breathed a sigh of relief. No more passengers or crew would suffer if the kobolds continued after me in the hopes of gaining possession of the relic.

I streaked across an open field before plunging into a wooded area on the far side. The trees provided cover against the barrage of energy fire. The beams streaked around me, and the missed shots ignited small blazes throughout the forest, leaving smoking ruins in the greenery

Something roared within a particularly dense thicket, but I passed before the monster reacted further.

Emerging from the woods, the divided highway of Atlantic Boulevard flashed beneath me before I broke through another wood line and into the outskirts of Alliance. My path showed multiple options here and I followed the selections at random as I skidded through empty streets and abandoned two-story houses with overgrown yards.

A line of fire erupted in front of me, blocking my path. Only my quick reactions saved me from a crisping as I turned away from the sudden spell formation. New red dots appeared on my map as more hostiles made themselves known with a round of energy and projectile weapons fire.

I dropped my elevation, and the undercarriage of the bike created a trail of sparks as I skidded across the asphalt and swerved across a parking lot. A glimpse of a stone building holding the attackers jerked my head around for a second look. There was a damned stone fortress in the middle of the town.

My neural link belatedly informed me of the existence of the fort at Glamorgan Castle, likely camouflaged by a defender's Skill until they'd initiated their attacks. The fort wasn't even a System building. Someone pre-System had built a modern castle in the middle of the countryside.

A trio of kobold skiffs appeared in the air to the north, flying in a spread linear formation over the ruined houses. The fire from the castle's defenders immediately shifted away from me to the new threats.

Righting my bike, I took advantage of the two forces firing on each other to accelerate through the empty lot before racing down a poorly maintained side road around the west side of the looming stone fort and out into an overgrown field. The forces keeping my bike aloft left a flattened trail through the tall grasses as I circled the castle and leaned into a sharp turn to the east.

A flash of light over my shoulder preceded a rumbling explosion as one of the skiff markers disappeared from my minimap.

One down, at least two more to go.

I hugged the tree line once I reached the far side of the open field and only left it behind once I'd reached the wide stretch of broken asphalt my neural link had tagged as OH-183. The waypoints directed me south and I followed, racing my bike with the throttle pushed to the max.

The paranoid corner of my mind noted the lack of any Safe Zone notification as I drove farther into Alliance. I'd have expected more survivors in the small town, especially with the strong defensive position the fort provided.

Side streets and abandoned houses flashed by as I streaked through the desolate city. A few glimpses of motion were all I caught sight of as the few living inhabitants ducked into cover, but I was gone before most fully disappeared.

One of the skiffs remained doggedly at the edge of my minimap's detection range despite my attempts to divert down side streets and break contact with my pursuers.

Though one fewer vessel followed me, I reluctantly admitted that while my headlong flight from the train had succeeded in pulling the kobolds after me, I didn't have any good way to break contact. Their craft were faster than my bike. Only my maneuverability and smaller size gave me any advantages.

An amused feeling flowed into me from the sword still in my hand, dismissing my concerns. No words accompanied the sensation, but the weapon's disdain for my pursuers came across clearly.

Several city blocks passed while I briefly considered my options. Noting a park ahead on the south side of the city, I steered between the short stone and cement columns that marked the entrance. Ignoring the 15 MPH speed limit sign, I cruised into another wild field in the middle of the park.

A line of explosions tore through the ground ahead of me, and I skewed into a sliding turn as I wrenched the bike away from the blasts. Looking around for the source of the attacks, my blood ran cold as a large shape floated ominously toward me from above the trees on the far side of the park.

Larger and more heavily armed than the pursuing skiffs, this craft held a trio of wide-mouthed cannons in the bow, and I saw kobolds on the deck of the vessel loading new shells into each of the weapons.

I swung back the way I'd come and slowed to a halt as the pursuing skiffs caught up and cut off my retreat. I looked down at the blade, feeling indescribable emotion emanating from the weapon as if it sensed my intent. "All right. Let's see what you've got."

I relaxed my mental defenses, lowering the walls brick by brick, until a pressure swept through my body and a force gripped my mind. I consciously avoided fighting the uncomfortable sensation and let it fill me as the pressure built. My muscles tensed and a surge of adrenaline roared through me, my blood pounding in my ears as my heart rate climbed.

Triumph. Anticipation. Hunger.

The swirling emotions continued building as the two skiffs split apart and turned broadside to me as they settled into place, a hundred yards from me and still twenty or so feet in the air.

My heartrate topped one-fifty and continued climbing as the sword's will consumed me. I heard nothing but the thunder of my beating heart as my vision narrowed, the sure precursor to a blackout.

An unsettling realization flickered through my mind as the darkness clouded my vision and my consciousness faded.

I no longer wielded the sword.

The sword wielded me.

Chapter 33

Consciousness returned, and with it came a wave of pain that filled my entire body. A deep ache seeped down through my muscles and into my bones, like a workout pushed too hard for too long and then multiplied tenfold.

The headache that pounded against the inside of my skull warred against the agony suffusing my body for several long moments until I opened my eyes to find myself slumped on both knees with my head bowed and an uncomfortable crick in my neck. Blood dripped from my nose and onto my chest. It had gone on long enough that a stream of sticky, half-congealed crimson liquid ran down my torso and along the inside of my leg.

A glance at my nearly depleted health bar, still blinking dangerously, warned me how close I'd come to death while under the control of the relic.

Mana fatigue from too many spells or Abilities used and my drained Mana pool explained the headache. Even my Stamina bar appeared dangerously low, something I'd never experienced since gaining Implacable Endurance. Only my elbow hooked over the crossguard of the greatsword in front of me kept me more or less upright, with half of the massive blade driven into the ground beneath me.

A few fuzzy blinks cleared my vision. I realized from the thick orange liquid that seeped around the blade that the sword wasn't embedded in the ground. The hilt of the weapon protruded from the center of a kobold torso. A kobold large enough that I also rested on top of the body with room to spare.

A full-sized adult kobold, larger even than the juveniles I'd fought before.

Slowly lifting my chin off my chest, I ignored the popping in my spine as I looked around before squeezing my eyes shut and opening them again.

The formerly green park lay ruined and burned, a charred waste of ash, mangled machinery, and broken kobold bodies. The savage vista reminded me of pictures of the aftermath of conflicts from the Civil War and World War I. Images where the dead lay cut down in windrows across the battlefields, piled ingloriously where they'd fallen.

So many dead that I couldn't count them by sight, though I felt certain the System kept a tally in my notifications.

Nothing moved anywhere that I could see, besides the dancing tongues of orange-red fire flickering around the wreckage of at least three skiffs. It was hard to get an accurate count with the amount of crumpled and broken pieces of metal scattered across the field. The armored gunship looked as if it had been cut in half. Lengthwise.

I shuddered at the power of the relic that had nearly killed me. I had no doubt that if the fight had gone longer, I would have been used up and tossed aside like so much used kitty litter.

I had no desire to possess something so dangerous, not when I lacked any control over my own fate under its influence.

After I snorted clumps of clotted blood from each nostril, my newly cleared nose was nearly overwhelmed by the stench of the battlefield. Smoke, blood, voided bowls, and the charged ozone of energy weapons fire combined into a pungent bouquet that left me momentarily dizzy.

My tattered armor still mostly covered me, but streaks of dried orange blood liberally caked both the gray fabric and the raw, barely healed skin beneath the ripped and burned sections of the jumpsuit.

Standing stiffly, I pulled the sword from its resting place with a liquid swish. A sense of sated satisfaction flowed into me as the blade rested dormant in my hands. I clamped it to my back with a shake of my head.

I needed to move on before anyone local decided to check out the battle in their backyard. Or something worse came along, like an over-Leveled monster or alien.

The thought begged the question, where was my bike? A check of my Inventory came up empty, so I activated the tracker with my neural link and followed the new waypoint that appeared.

I found the vehicle sticking out of the side of a skiff.

With another head shake and sigh, I got the greatsword back out and carefully cut my bike free before easing it from the slightly wider hole in the skiff's armor plating. Activating the bike's hover mode, I was surprised when it worked. Though the bike listed slightly to the side and down a bit in front, it appeared rideable.

Throwing my leg over the seat, I mounted the vehicle and throttled up as I steered my way out of the park. The damaged bike kept drifting, so I found myself fighting against the constant pull to the leaning side. Still, I made better time than I would have walking, despite the damage, heading back to link up with the train.

A new notification prompt appeared as I followed the highway south.

Quest Completed!

The Pistongrinder Express has successfully reached the Pittsburgh Starport, completing your objective of providing combat support on the return journey.

10,000 Credits and 10,000 XP Awarded.

Bonus objectives partially completed: Locomotive condition (good), freight condition (fair), crew condition (poor).

Additional 6,000 Credits and 6,000 XP Awarded.

Level Up!

You have reached Level 41 as a Relentless Huntsman. Stat Points automatically distributed. You have 2 Free Attributes and 9 Class Skill Points to distribute.

Another notification sat pending behind the quest completion, and I pulled up the blue box as I followed the waypoints leading me south.

Title Gained!

For slaying over one thousand members of a specific species, you have been awarded the title "Slayer of Kobolds" to acknowledge your conflict with the Zabotkermanne. All damage dealt to Zabotkermanne +5% and all damage received from Zabotkermanne -5%. Reputation with all Zabotkermanne factions now defaults to unfriendly.

Now that was a title I didn't mind showing off. I left it visible on my Status after closing the last of the blue boxes.

***

I zoned out soon after, too exhausted to focus on more than just following the waypoints that appeared one after another for the rest of the ride. Other than uncomfortably leaning forward and over to one side, the drive went smoothly. I even managed to outrun most of the monsters that popped up, with a few sticky grenades taking care of those who did keep up.

An hour later, the sky was nearly dark by the time I received the Safe Zone notification and cruised through the defensive perimeter at the western end of the starport, where I found a small crowd waiting.

Sheera stood beside the Pharyleri clan leaders, fidgeting as Borgym and Nesdyna chatted quietly. Dayena and Lyrra stood on the other side of the two elderly gnomes. Other armed Pharyleri stood around as an escort, along with a troop of Demarcian soldiers in sleek black armor that matched Sheera's.

A massive Demarcian pushed through the gathering as I dismounted and stored my damaged bike. The heavily armored Demarcian's focus drilled into me as the lion-like humanoid folded his arms over his chest. Refusing to be cowed, I squared my shoulders and faced the lion before looking him over head to toe while blatantly activating Greater Observation.

Knight-Commander Asaad, First of the Golden Pride (Ebon Breaker Level 39)
HP: 5240/5240
MP: 5460/5460

The Ebon Breaker Class jogged my memory and I realized this was the Demarcian from the stare down with the Hakarta mercenaries. The same ones Dayena and I had passed in the starport before we'd taken the Pistongrinder contract.

In other words, a real hard-charging badass.

After a long moment of unblinking intensity, the Ebon Breaker nodded in approval as the crowd behind him looked on silently.

"Kneel." The deeply voiced command nearly dropped me to my knees, so great was the natural authority and Charisma behind the order.

But I held firm and glanced at Sheera, who nodded in reassurance. I dropped to one knee, still not entirely sure what was going on.

The Knight-Commander held out a hand. "Present the relic."

I sighed. This little display reeked of politics and flashy showmanship. Resigned to playing the game, I pulled the greatsword from my back and held it across my palms as I lifted it toward the Demarcian's waiting hand.

The massive lion gripped the hilt firmly and snapped the sword vertical in a salute. The blade gleamed in the light of the setting sun.

It really was a beautiful weapon. For a moment, I regretted handing it over, but the thought quickly passed.

With a whoosh of sliced air, the Demarcian dropped the sword horizontal and ran his hand along the blade. Blood dripped in a blue-tinged stream from the alien's palm as he held it over my head. The warm liquid seeped through my hair and trickled down my forehead, streaking down my face.

I glared up at the lion, well aware of the sharp edge only inches from my face, but the Demarcian's expression gave away nothing.

When the leonid's regeneration sealed the wound and the blood stopped flowing, the Knight-Commander lifted the sword high and roared something furiously in his native language. After a long pause, during which the Demarcian resumed his serious expression, the lion nodded gravely to me, and the sword disappeared into the Knight-Commander's Inventory.

A notification appeared and I glanced at the text within the blue box.

Title Gained!

For service to the crown of Demarcia, you have been awarded the title "Knight Errant of the Demarcian Kingdom" to acknowledge the bravery and sacrifice of your actions. Reputation with Demarcian forces defaults to Honored, and Reputation with Demarcian allies defaults to Friendly. All transactions with associated factions shift 10% in favor of the title holder.

The Ebon Breaker smirked briefly as I looked up from closing the window. Then the Demarcian turned away and marched back through the crowd that parted before him.

Sheera waved and silently mouthed "thank you" as another notification informed me of a six-figure increase to my Credit balance. Plus the ten percent granted by my new title.

The King's Paw followed the Knight-Commander as the remaining Demarcian troops formed up around them and stalked off into the starport.

Borgym clapped his hands together in a sharp crack that drew the attention of the remaining assembly, and the old gnome chuckled as he gleefully rubbed his hands together before pulling his cane from the crook of his elbow.

"You don't see the Demarcians handing out honors often." Borgym chuckled again, leaning heavily on the grounded cane as he peered at me intently. "Knight Errant and Slayer of Kobolds, you're not getting out of taking credit for your actions this time."

With a shake of my head, I stood back up. The clan elder knew exactly how uncomfortable I felt receiving praise, especially after the way he'd put my name on the memorial for those lost in the early days of the starport's construction.

I glanced at Ismyna. "No trouble the rest of the way here then? I got the Quest completion."

"It was a smooth ride for the last leg of the journey," Ismyna replied with forced positivity, though her shoulders slumped.

No one seemed ready to acknowledge Ismyna's listless tone and thousand-yard stare despite the success of the mission. The loss of so many of her crew clearly weighed on the gnome.

I made pointed eye contact with Nesdyna, who stood just behind the engineer. The Pistongrinder elder nodded in wordless acknowledgment of my concern and placed a supportive hand on Ismyna's shoulder before pulling her daughter into a comforting hug.

Borgym jerked his head to the side and indicated for me to follow as he led the group away from the mother-daughter pair. Once we'd walked a respectful distance toward the starport administration building, the gnome elder glanced up at me. "What's next for you?"

"Reload, repair, rearm," I replied, wondering where the missile launcher control unit that I'd loaned to Dice had ended up.

"Rest," Dayena interjected forcefully as she came up on my other side.

I raised an eyebrow and looked at the Truinnar. "I blew up your cousin with a missile launcher. I don't think rest is an option when we need to grind Levels."

Dayena blinked, only now realizing what I'd meant when I said they were no longer a problem. "Both of them?"

"No, I only kicked Creynora off the train. She'll probably be fine unless she's ended up as a monster snack."

The Countess sighed in a mixture of relief and resignation. "While I am glad that she lives, my father will escalate this conflict with the death of Rhegnah. We must avoid drawing further attention. That Title will not help."

I fully agreed with her desire to stay under the radar. "You're right, it makes me sound like some kind of paladin."

Dayena looked at me blankly before smiling over her shoulder at Lyrra, who followed us. The Movana just stared at me with a raised eyebrow.

Ignoring the elves, I brought up my status and used On the Hunt to disable the Knight Errant Title. Except the Title remained clearly visible in my status, even after I'd hidden it.

I frowned as a new notification appeared when I tried disguising the Title's presence once again.

The bearer of this Title represents the honor and glory of the Demarcian Kingdom. This Title may not be suppressed or hidden from view.

Well, shit.

"You cannot hide that title, can you?"

My glare answered the dark elf's question. Dayena's and Borgym's laughter at my sour expression did nothing for my mood. Not at all.

So much for keeping that low profile.

Epilogue

Skidding to a stop after tumbling down the steep embankment alongside the tracks, Creynora lay still until the world stopped spinning. When she finally recovered enough to sit up, the Truinnar spat out the dust and grass from face-planting into the hillside during her fall from the top of the train. It took somewhat more effort to deal with the strands from the Hunter's grapple launcher.

Thoughts of the human brought on a wave of emotion that threatened to overwhelm her. She could still feel the wave of heat sweeping over her back as the Krym'parke's heavy shuttle erupted in fire behind her.

The explosion that had consumed her brother.

For several long moments, Creynora thrashed in anger against the bindings that held her arms pinned to her side. It was useless rage, energy and emotion that burned within her but had nowhere to go.

Finally, she lay spent.

The human had been right. Rhegnah had been an insufferable, egotistical, misogynistic bastard, but for all that, he was still the older brother who had always been there in her life.

Blinking back tears, Creynora forced away the anguish and focused on untangling herself from the wire that trapped her. Reluctantly, she admitted that she respected the human's surprising adaptability and resourcefulness. Even if she brimmed with overflowing anger over Rhegnah's death.

When she at last removed the final strand of the entwining grapple wire, Creynora stood and retraced her path back up to the tracks. She followed the route easily, her fall clearly marked by the knocked down grasses and furrows dug into the earth.

She found her sword, dropped to avoid injuring herself as she fell, at the top of the embankment beside the tracks. Scooping up the weapon, she looked southeast after where the train had continued on. A few columns of smoke in the distance showed the progress of the three-way battle between the Pharyleri, Zabotkermanne, and any remaining Krym'parke.

Instead of following, Creynora turned to the northwest and walked toward the faint wisps of smoke drifting up from the wreck of the initial Krym'parke vessel. It took several minutes to reach the crash site and only a single monster dared ambush the walking dark elf, though Creynora quickly dispatched the growling, four-limbed creature.

While the forward half of the fuselage remained mostly intact, the rear of the vessel lay in charred fragments. The end of the wreckage lay a field-length from the actual crash, spread along the rails by the train's impact with the aft end of the starship.

Creynora slowed as she passed twisted armor plates, smoldering electronics, and the bodies of Krym'parke troops, dreading what she knew she would find.

A pile of wreckage moved suddenly, startling the dark elf. Creynora jumped away from the motion and instinctively raised her sword defensively. A heavily charred suit of white armor stood, casting aside a hunk of hull plating as it rose to reveal the entire front breastplate missing. Though the armor around the destroyed section showed cracks and heavy charring, unblemished dark flesh rippled over a muscular torso with every movement.

"You live?!" Creynora gaped at the standing figure as armored gauntlets pulled off the suit's helmet.

Rhegnah shook out his lustrous hair and breathed deeply as he stowed the armor's helmet in the crook of one arm. "Yes."

Creynora lunged forward and wrapped her brother in a hug. "How? You were gone from our party?"

Rhegnah's lip curled in disdain as he extracted himself from the embrace. "Enough. Here. This is how."

Creynora choked back the emotional pain felt by the dismissal of her concern and read the System message that appeared before her eyes.

False Report (Level 1)

The task of the Adjudicator is a heavy burden, facing the foes of a kingdom and often doing so alone. It is inevitable that the weight of this task will lead to the Adjudicator being overwhelmed by their enemies in the line of duty, but failure is unacceptable when the fate of the kingdom is at stake.

Effect: Permanently sacrifice 10% of user's Health and Mana, which are placed in reserve until such time as the user receives fatal damage. When the user's health drops to zero, the user is dropped into stasis and unable to be damaged further. This effect registers the user as slain to all damaging entities and gives full death experience. Once the stasis effect wears off, the sacrificed Health and Mana are restored to the user in order to prevent death. This effect may be triggered no more than once per 50 Levels.

The sounds of other figures emerging from the broken fuselage of the vessel drew Creynora from the System display. An unlikely pair of a Krym'parke and a human in an armored jumpsuit led several others of the demonic-appearing species over to where Rhegnah and Creynora stood.

Rhegnah looked at the group. "I'm glad to see you survived, Jahgg'd."

"Your words are welcomed," the horned alien replied with a nod, then looked at Creynora. "You made it onto the train. Were you unable to catch your quarry?"

"No, the Countess's pet human Hunter knocked me off the roof shortly after your crash." The dark elf frowned and shook her head before glancing at Rhegnah. "That Hal is a problem that needs to be dealt with. He is far too capable for a human."

"Did you say Hal?" the armored human spoke for the first time that Creynora could recall, a surprisingly feminine voice sounding from beneath a featureless helmet.

"I did," Creynora responded, watching the human and Jahgg'd exchange a wordless glance.

An unsettling hunger crept over the alien commander's expression, bringing Creynora's thoughts back to Hal's assertion that the Krym'parke ate children. She no longer held any doubt that the human had history with the barbaric species.

Jahgg'd smiled, revealing a maw of sharp fangs framed by the spiked horns protruding from the Krym'parke's chin. The expression felt far more menacing than encouraging and Creynora felt a chill travel down her spine as the alien spoke.

"We would very much be interested in 'dealing' with this human Hunter Hal."

The adventures of Hal will continue in

Apocalypse Grit

Glossary

Relentless Huntsman Skill Tree

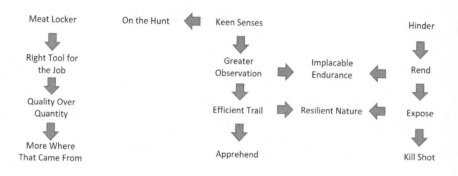

Hal's Relentless Huntsman Skills

Hinder (Level 2)

Effect: All physical movement by a designated target within 15 feet is significantly impaired for 1 minute.

Cost: 40 Stamina + 20 Mana.

Keen Senses (Level 1)

The user is more in tune with their body and more accurately interprets information gained from their surroundings. This manifests in the user as increases to vision, audition, gustation, olfaction, tactition, and proprioception. Mana regeneration reduced by 5 Mana per minute permanently.

On the Hunt (Level 3)

The Relentless Huntsman has a reduced System presence and increased ability to disguise their visible titles, class, level, and stats. Effectiveness is based on the user's Skill level and Charisma. Mana regeneration reduced by 15 Mana per minute permanently.

Meat Locker (Level 3)

Effect: The Relentless Huntsman now has access to an extra-dimensional storage location of 60 cubic feet. Only deceased bounty targets or slain creatures may be added to this location and must be touched to be willed inside. Mana regeneration reduced by 15 Mana per minute permanently.

Right Tool for the Job (Level 2)

Effect: The Relentless Huntsman now has access to an extra-dimensional storage location of 10 cubic feet. Items stored must be touched to be willed in and may only include weapons, armor, equipment, or supplies owned by the Relentless Huntsman. Any qualifying System-recognized item can be placed or removed from this inventory location if space allows. Cost: 5 Mana per item.

Greater Observation (Level 2)

Effect: User may now detect System creatures up to 50 meters away and is provided an analysis of the subject upon detection. Increased Skill levels may reveal additional System information not normally available. Depending on comparative overall level and Skills in effect, the target of focused Observation may know that the user has gained some level of information. Mana regeneration reduced by 10 Mana per minute permanently.

Rend (Level 1)

Effect: Physical weapon attacks that cause health damage apply a bleed effect, causing the target to bleed for 15 damage over 15 seconds. This effect can be stacked if the health damage occurs at a different location on the target.

Cost: 10 Stamina.

Implacable Endurance (Level 1)

Effect: Reduces Stamina cost for physical exertion and activated physical abilities by 25%. Does not stack with other Stamina reduction skills. Mana regeneration reduced by 5 Mana per minute permanently.

Expose (Level 1)

The Relentless Huntsman's consistent and methodical attacks continually weakens their target's defenses.

Effect: Damage applied to shields, armor, or defensive abilities applies an additional 2% damage to those defenses. This effect is cumulative and remains for one minute, with repetitive damage refreshing the cooldown. Should all defenses fail with this effect active, the damage bonus is reset but can be reapplied with continued attacks to the target and will then stack again until combat ends. Mana regeneration reduced by 5 Mana per minute permanently.

Efficient Trail (Level 1)

Effect: Environmental and terrain features present reduced difficulty to the user, allowing the user to cover distance more rapidly. Mana regeneration reduced by 5 Mana per minute permanently.

Resilient Nature (Level 2)

Effect: Increase natural health regeneration and reduce on-going health status effects by 10% respectively. Poison and disease resistance increased by 12%. Relentless Huntsman may now regenerate lost limbs. Mana regeneration reduced by 10 Mana per minute permanently.

Quality Over Quantity (Level 1)

Effect: Equipped gear is resistant to environmental and passive aura effects. Only direct damage to the item will cause durability loss so long as it remains equipped and may have durability loss repaired directly by the user actively channeling Mana. The user may also designate a soulbound Personal Weapon. Personal Weapons cause an additional 5% damage. Mana regeneration reduced by 5 Mana per minute permanently.

Other Class Skills

Blood Scent (Level 1)

Effect: Select a scent present in the current environment and follow any object or individual to which that scent clings.

Cost: 30 Mana per minute

Spells

Minor Healing (IV)

Effect: Heals 40 Health per casting.

Target must be in contact during healing. Cooldown 60 seconds.

Cost: 20 Mana.

Frostbolt (VI)

Effect: Creates a Frost bolt from the user's Mana, which can be directed to damage a target. The dart does 60 Ice damage and slows the target by 3%. Slow effect stacks up to three times (9%). Cooldown 10 seconds.

Cost: 25 Mana.

Frostnova (IV)

Effect: Creates a ring of Frost from the user's Mana which blasts outward in a 5-meter radius centered on the user. The ring does 20 Ice damage and may affect enemies with a Freeze effect, rooting them in place for up to 8 seconds. Cooldown 30 seconds.

Cost: 50 Mana.

Lesser Disguise (II)

Effect: Creates an illusory visage over the target of the spell that changes the target's appearance. The caster's familiarity with the desired form of the disguise increases effectiveness. The spell does not provide any abilities or mannerisms of the desire form, nor does it alter the perceived audible or tactile features of the target.

Cost: 75 Mana plus 10 Mana per minute to maintain the illusion.

Earth Spike (II)

Effect: A jagged spike of rock erupts from the ground beneath the target, causing 70 earth damage if it impacts the target. Cooldown 25 seconds.

Cost: 50 Mana.

Firespray (II)

Effect: Sprays a rushing stream of fire at the direction of the caster. Does 50 points of fire damage. Cooldown 60 seconds.

Cost: 60 Mana.

Continuous cast cost: 5 Mana / sec

Greater Healing (I)

Effect: Heals 75 Health per casting. Target does not require contact during healing. Cooldown 60 seconds per target

Cost: 50 Mana.

Greater Regeneration (I)

Effect: Increases natural health regeneration of target by 5%. Only a single use of this spell may affect a target at a time. Cooldown 120 seconds.

Duration: 10 minutes

Cost: 100 Mana.

Minor Renew (II)

Effect: Heals 1 Health per second for 30 seconds. Only single use of spell effective on a target at a time. Target must be in contact during healing. Cooldown 80 seconds.

Cost: 15 Mana.

460

Ice Armor (I)

Effect: Creates a suit of armor made of ice. While cold to the touch, it does not harm the wearer, especially if applied over clothing or armor. Armor has 500 Hit Points.

Cost: 125 Mana.

Ice Armor may be enhanced by using the Elemental Affinity of Ice. Armor durability increased by 10% per level of affinity.

Whiteout (I)

Effect: Covers a 10-meter radius area with chilling frost and fills the affected zone with frozen fog, dealing 5 cold damage per second to hostile targets within the spell's area of effect and decreasing visibility for affected targets.

Duration: 1 minute.

Cost: 50 Mana.

Whiteout may be enhanced by using the Elemental Affinity of Ice. Duration and coverage area increased by 20% per level of affinity.

Howling Blast (I)

Effect: Effect: Blasts out a cone of frigid wind from the caster, dealing 100 cold damage to all enemies within the cone out to a range of 10 meters. Targets taking damage from this spell are knocked back 1 meter from the force of the gust. Cooldown: 60 seconds.

Cost: 75 Mana.

Howling Blast may be enhanced by using the Elemental Affinity of Ice. Damage and knockback distance increased by 20% per level of affinity.

Equipment

Silversmith Mark II Beam Pistol (Upgradeable)

Base Damage: 18

Battery Capacity: 24/24

Recharge Rate: 2 per hour per GMU

Luxor Series III Projectile Pistol

Base Damage: N/A (Dependent Upon Ammunition)

Ammo Capacity: 12/12

Ammunition Types: Standard, Armor Piercing, High Explosive, Tracer, Hollow Point

Tier II Knife (Soulbound Personal Weapon of a Relentless Huntsman)

Base Damage: 40

Durability: NA (Personal Weapon)

Special Abilities: Recall

Tier III Hand-axe

Base Damage: 25

Durability: 200/200

Special Abilities: None

Banshee II Gauss Hybrid Rifle

Base Damage: N/A (Dependent Upon Ammunition)

Ammo Capacity: 18/18

Battery Capacity: 40/40

Recharge Rate: 4 per hour per GMU

Cost: 5,400 Credits

Rudianos Class IV Outrider

Core: Class IV Hephaestus Mana Engine

CPU: Class E Xylik Core CPU

Armor Rating: Tier V

Hard Points: 2 (2 Used: Nano Garage Module, Anti-Grav Module)

Soft Points: 2 (1 Used for Neural Link)

Optional: Neural Link for Remote Activation

Battery Capacity: 60/60

Tier V Neural Link

Neural link may support up to 4 connections.

Current connections: Rudianos Class IV Outrider

Software Installed: Rich'lki Fire-wall Class IV, Rudianos Class V Controller

Ace (Tier I Projectile Pistol)

The twin enchantments worked into the frame of this hand cannon by Maestro Gunsmith Syx Cayde provide a minor enhancement to the wielder's reload speed and additional shield penetration to any ammunition fired through this weapon.

Base Damage: N/A (Dependent Upon Ammunition)

Ammo Capacity: 12/12 (Standard cylinder-style magazine)

Effect: +12% Energy Shield Penetration, +10% Reload Speed

Last Word (Tier I Projectile Pistol)

Customized by Master Armscrafter Malphyr, the enchantments engraved into the body of this hand cannon are guaranteed to deliver the final statement in any firefight with increased armor penetration added to any ammunition fired through this weapon.

Base Damage: N/A (Dependent Upon Ammunition)

Ammo Capacity: 12/12 (Standard cylinder-style magazine)

Effect: +15% Armor Penetration

Elysian Drop Harness Mk. IV (Modified)

This shoulder rig began life as a standard grav-chute issued to a member of the Elysian Home Guard. The air-mobile troopers of the Guard are known for lightning-fast deployments and guerilla attacks behind enemy lines. This particular harness was customized by a Guard trooper to carry twin pistols into battle and was promptly disposed of as surplus after the non-regulation modifications were discovered by a superior officer.

Hastati-VI Launcher Control System

This reusable launcher control system is the targeting and trigger unit for the two-part Hastati-VI Modular Missile System. When paired with the single-use MMS disposable firing tubes, the launcher control system allows the user to designate the appropriate target for the type of missile indicated by the color code on the MMS housing:

Red - Anti-monster Plasma Ignitor

Yellow - Anti-vehicle Armor Penetrator

Blue- Anti-shield Disruptor

Green - Anti-personnel Cluster Munitions

Authors' Note

I want to thank you, dear reader, for continuing Hal's adventure with me through the System Apocalypse world that Tao created. Things are definitely heating up for the bounty hunter and I'm looking forward to seeing what happens next.

I also want to thank Tao again for letting me play in his sandbox and explore the world that John Lee left behind here on Earth.

If you enjoyed this book, please leave a review! Seeing what you think of our works helps encourage us indie writers to keep creating.

~Craig

***

Here we are on book 2 of the Relentless series from Craig. Working on it with Craig is always a fun experience, though this time it was a little strange since doing so was between the writing of the end of my own series. Coming back to such an early period of the System Apocalypse timeline is fascinating, especially when we see things that come up in later works in the main book taken backwards.

Well, fascinating for me. Might look different for you readers.

Craig and I are already talking about how the third book of this series will look like and his overall goals over the next few books. I'm looking forward to seeing where he takes it, with some (minor) guidance from myself. Each book adds to Hal's journey and sees Craig's own writing level up.

Anyway, hopefully you all enjoyed the book. Thanks again for reading. Your support is, as always, gratefully received.

~Tao

About the Authors

Craig Hamilton

Craig Hamilton spends most of his day as a technical sales engineer, translating specifications and talking about IT infrastructure. While writing has been taking up most of his free time lately, Craig also appreciates playing tabletop RPGs or board games with friends. When his inner introvert demands a break from polite company, Craig can be found sprawled on a couch with a book or e-reader.

Follow what Craig is doing on his Author Page:
https://www.facebook.com/AuthorCraigHamilton

Tao Wong

Tao Wong is an avid fantasy and sci-fi reader who spends his time working and writing in the North of Canada. He's spent way too many years doing martial arts of many forms, and having broken himself too often, he now spends his time writing about fantasy worlds.

For updates on the series and other books written by Tao Wong (and special one-shot stories), please visit the author's website: http://www.mylifemytao.com

Or visit his Facebook Page:
https://www.facebook.com/taowongauthor/

Also, subscribers to Tao's mailing list will receive **exclusive access to short stories in the Thousand Li and System Apocalypse universes**.

About the Publisher

Starlit Publishing is wholly owned and operated by Tao Wong. It is a science fiction and fantasy publisher focused on the LitRPG & cultivation genres. Their focus is on promoting new, upcoming authors in the genre whose writing challenges the existing stereotypes while giving a rip-roaring good read.

For more information about latest releases and new, exciting authors from Starlit Publishing, visit our website or sign up to our newsletter list: https://www.starlitpublishing.com/

For more great information about LitRPG series, check out these Facebook groups:

- GameLit Society

  www.facebook.com/groups/LitRPGsociety

- LitRPG Books

  www.facebook.com/groups/LitRPG.books

System Apocalypse: Australia

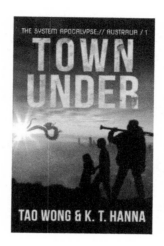

What's worse than Australian wildlife? *Mutated* **Australian wildlife.**

The System Apocalypse has come to Australia, altering native organisms and importing even more menacing creatures to the most dangerous continent on Earth. For Kira Kent, plant biologist, the System arrives while she's pulling an all nighter at work with her pair of kids in tow.

Now, instead of mundane parental concerns like childcare and paying the bills, she's got to figure out how to survive a world where already deadly flora and fauna have grown even more perilous - all while dealing with the minutiae of the System's pesky blue screens and Levels and somehow putting together a community of survivors to forge a safe zone to shelter her son and daughter.

It almost makes her miss the PTA fundraising sales. *Almost.*

Read more of the System Apocalypse: Australia series
https://readerlinks.com/l/2202672

The System Apocalypse

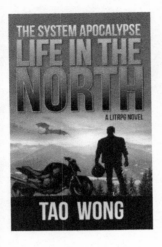

**What happens when the apocalypse arrives, not via nuclear weapons or a
comet but as Levels and monsters? What if you were camping in the
Yukon when the world ended?**

All John wanted to do was get away from his life in Kluane National Park
for a weekend. Hike, camp and chill. Instead, the world comes to an end in
a series of blue boxes. Animals start evolving, monsters start spawning and
he has a character sheet and physics defying skills. Now, he has to survive
the apocalypse, get back to civilisation and not lose his mind.

The System has arrived and with it, aliens, monsters and a reality that draws
upon past legends and game-like reality. John will need to find new friends,
deal with his ex and the slavering monsters that keep popping up.

Read more of The System Apocalypse series
https://readerlinks.com/l/2440485

Preview my other series:
The System Apocalypse: Australia

Town Under
(The System Apocalypse: Australia Book 1)

Chapter One: Timer

10:45 p.m.—15 Minutes Prior to System Onset

Usually, the stars gleamed through Toohey Forest at night, twinkling through the glass to remind me why I loved my work. Tonight though, the glare of the non-fluorescent lights reflected off the window and back to me, like it was trying to blind me. I hurried through my tasks as fast as I could trying to get the sample kits prepared before everyone got to the labs bright and early the next morning.

"Mum. Are you done yet?" Jackson's bored voice broke through my contemplation as I juggled several ecological sample kits. He was lucky I didn't drop them.

"You didn't have to come. I told you you could babysit." I kept my voice as soft as possible, knowing that Wisp was asleep over on my office chair. Jackson rolled his eyes at me but went back to whatever he was tinkering with on his laptop. It was true, though; he'd just turned thirteen. I figured he could babysit for a few hours, but he surprised me by insisting they come with.

Almost eleven at night. Just over another hour and it would literally be tomorrow. I would have been so much faster if I hadn't brought them with me, but sometimes I think they just liked to be near me. Not that they'd tell me that, of course. That wouldn't be on the cool scale at all. I stifled a chuckle knowing my newly minted teenager would assume I was laughing at him. I wasn't even close to in the mood for teenagerisms.

"Not too long. Just keep an eye on your sister while I check the progress on a few of these experiments and we'll head home. Just got to make sure the grafts are taking."

Jackson didn't answer but shifted in his seat with a wry grin. He always said I treated plants like they were kids too.

Glancing at the array of kits I still needed to check over, I couldn't blame him. After all, it wasn't difficult to get lost in my work. Ecosystems were an amazing thing, and helping them thrive when they'd almost been wiped out gave me tingles up and down my spine. With the amount of drought Australia went through on a regular basis, finding rare plants and trying to rejuvenate their habitats was everything I'd ever wanted to do. There I went again . . .

One more quick scan over the gear I'd gathered together so the field trip could leave in the morning and help gather the next round of samples we needed. Done, which meant I could check on the few running grafts I had percolating. I managed to suppress the sheer joy I felt at grabbing my clipboard so I could jot down my observations. There was this one fascinating plant graft that I'd had to use very specific soil mixture for, not to mention lugging back its native water source for testing—

The lights flickered, and I frowned.

That was odd. I was sure there hadn't been any storm warnings, not even an electrical storm. I'd have known, and I definitely wouldn't be in here for one of those. A few seconds passed. The entire university campus had back-up generators just in case. Turning around to comment to Jackson, the lights flickered again, and while I only had a brief moment to adjust as darkness engulfed us, I clearly saw a wave of bioluminescent air hit me in the chest.

My entire body tingled, and the power remained off.

"Mum. What the . . ." But Jackson didn't get any further, and my brain didn't have an answer for him anyway.

Blue flashed across my vision again, but this time eerily like the blue screen of death I'd grown up fearing as a child.

Greetings, citizen. As a peaceful and organized immersion into the Galactic Council has been declined (extensively and painfully, we might add), your world has been declared a Dungeon World. Thank you. We were getting bored with the twelve we had previously.

Please note that the process of developing a Dungeon World can be difficult for current inhabitants. We recommend leaving the planet till the process is completed in 373 days, 2 hours, 14 minutes, and 12 seconds.

For those of you unable or unwilling to leave, do note that new Dungeons and wandering monsters will spawn intermittently throughout the integration process. All new Dungeons and zones will receive recommended minimum Levels. However, during the transition period, expect there to be significant volatility in the Levels and types of monsters in each Dungeon and zone.

As a new Dungeon World, your planet has been designated a free-immigration location. Undeveloped worlds in the Galactic Council may take advantage of this new immigration policy. Please try not to greet all new visitors the same way as you did our Emissary; you humans could do with some friends.

As part of the transition, all sentient subjects will have access to new Classes and Skills as well as the traditional user interface adopted by the Galactic Council in 119 GC. Thank you for your cooperation, and good luck! We look forward to meeting you soon.

Time to System Initiation: 59 minutes, 23 seconds.

"Mum?"

This time, Jackson sounded scared, and if there's one thing I've learned about my two-week-strong teenager, admitting he was scared was no longer a thing. So much for vaguely hoping he'd played a practical joke. With his programming knowledge and penchant for fiddling with electronics, I was fairly certain a part of his brain was already trying to figure this shit out.

"It's okay. Probably just a gimmick of some sort." Even I didn't believe that lie, but he had the good grace not to harp on it. "Check on your sister for me."

I tried to keep my voice steady, not to give away that I might be freaking the hell out. That blue wave of whatever hit my chest had left a glowing residue behind in the project I'd been checking on. My fingers even felt like they'd been saturated, like they were swelling. The soft blue glow was our only light, because as I glanced at my phone, it was nothing but a glass and metal brick. Nothing I tried to do switched it on.

Breathe. I had to breathe. Maybe. What if the air was suddenly toxic?

This was the same old, though. What I'd done every day of my life for the last thirteen years and two weeks. My kids needed me. I couldn't and wouldn't panic right now. Later, when I'd figured out things, I could go somewhere and scream into a pillow, but right now I needed to gather my shit together and figure out what was happening and why the damned back-up generators hadn't kicked in yet. The samples, the supplies, the research . . . all of our work was going to die if their environments weren't maintained.

There was a part of me, though, that knew that screen wasn't a good thing, that knew I should probably swipe it back in front to read through again, and that knew none of our usual concerns mattered anymore.

Only the moonlight and stars shining through the massive, double-glazed windows illuminated the room now—like it mocked my earlier thoughts. I gazed around the room, past the desks to where Jackson stood watching over Wisp who was, somehow, still asleep.

"I . . . Mum, this is weird." Jackson kept his voice low, his words hurried, even if I could sense a hint of excitement underlying his tone. "It's like something beamed a video game into our heads."

My first response was to tell him not to be stupid and to take this seriously, that now wasn't the time for games, but since he couldn't legitimately beam anything into my brain and I had definitely read that weird shit only moments beforehand, I took another breath. A blue screen I'd basically swiped left on.

"What do you mean?" It was all I could do to fight that flight response, especially as I could have sworn that the soft blue glow in all of the testing tanks was rippling, moving, alive.

"Wave your hand, like you're using that VR rig dad got me for my birthday."

Yep. There was definitely excitement oozing out of his voice now.

I humored him, still wrestling that thing called panic. Surely, I could spare two minutes to indulge my slightly delusional son. Except maybe he wasn't imagining things. There, in the corner of my vision, was a golden glow, like it was trying to get my attention. Fine, then. My panic could just wait and sulk in the corner I'd relegated it to originally.

Congratulations! You have been spawned in Australia, Griffith University, Nathan Campus, Brisbane.

Australia is an exception under the Dungeon World Development Schedule 124.7.5.2. Just for being in the Down Under of Australia, not to mention being brave enough to eat Vegemite, you are assigned one Small Perk. Aren't you lucky? You'll need it.

As per Dungeon World Development Schedule 124.7.5.2, inhabitants assigned to a region with a recommended Level 25 or more (+25) will receive one Medium Perk.

As per Dungeon World Development Schedule 124.7.5.2, inhabitants assigned to a region with a recommended Level 50 or more (+25) will receive one Large Perk.

As per Dungeon World Development Schedule 128.9.6.2, inhabitants recognized as parental units must allow their spawns access to the System before they can have full use of all assigned Perks.

Your spawns awaiting approval are:

Jackson Kent—13 years. Enabling Jackson's interface allows him direct access to his Perks and abilities. Any choices will require your approval before being applied.

Whisper (Wisp) Kent—8 years. Warning: Wisp is only 8 Earth years old. It is highly recommended that she does not have full access to the System yet per Dungeon World Development Schedule 133.4.2—Protection of Youth Potential and the Abuse Avoidance Scheme.

However—Wisp will have one Small, one Medium, and one Large Perk at her disposal. You are responsible for choosing these. Please select them wisely.

Caution: As per Dungeon World Development Schedule 142.4.2.8, certain Skill sets are recognized as having abilities sympathetic to the System. Not applying these would be a grave violation. Swipe to let us know you're ready to choose a Class, upon which your life and the lives of your offspring will depend.

What. The. Actual. Fuck.

"Don't pick anything yet," Jackson urged, and he didn't have to tell me twice.

Maybe I was asleep; this was too surreal to be, well, real.

"Sure." My voice even sounded dull to me, and I reached down to stroke Wisp's hair behind her ear.

She was still wearing the leotard she'd been in when I picked her up from training. Silly thing, she'd get cold and only reluctantly put on her warmups. It was turning to winter out there . . .

"Mum. Pay attention. You need to allow me access to my abilities or I can't help you." His voice was soft, gentle even, like he was trying to take care of me.

What a shit-tastic thing for me to do to my son in what appeared to be an end-of-the-world scenario. "Sorry. Okay, give me a moment." Crap on a stick, Kira, what the fuck are you doing making your son be the adult?

This time I stood there, determined not to let him down. I thought at it, wanting it to show me how to give him permission.

Your spawns awaiting approval are:
Jackson Kent—13 years
Whisper (Wisp) Kent—8 years

With a thought, I activated his ability to choose himself. He knew more about stats and abilities in games than I did. Well, nowadays anyway. It had been years since I'd played seriously. Kids, post-graduate degrees, doctorates—they all ate right into that leisure time. Right now, I had a gut feeling that I was going to need Jackson's help at least as much as he'd need mine.

Parental Notifications. Do you wish to receive notifications when your spawn wishes to make adjustments to their Class, not restricted to abilities, Levels, and equipment?

Another hasty yes and I was done. I watched him as he clearly looked through whatever list of abilities he had in front of him, and I glanced at the notification and advisement about Wisp. I chose not to activate hers, especially since they were advising me not to. She was eight, and I was her mom. I didn't have time for any of that other crap right now. We just had to get to the damned carpark and get out of here so I could figure out what to do, before that glowing stuff in the terrariums blew up and took us all with it.

Jackson looked up at me, and I could see that excitement about a new game tempered by having no idea what was happening. Me too, kid. Me too.

So I did what any good mum would do: I told him what to do. "Grab two of those sample kits over there and we'll get one of the tents and ground sheets out of the lockers on the way out."

I quickly tallied what we had in the Jeep. Thank everything I grew up in America with a prepper for a dad. I turned to figure out how to carry Wisp, but just as I went to pick her up, she raised her head, bleary eyes blinking rapidly in the dim moonlight.

"Mummy . . . why are the tanks glowing like that?"

❖

Wisp was a good kid. But just after eleven at night, after a full gymnastics session and a nap, she was still in the middle of waking up groggily. Balancing her on my hip, I had one of the rationed backpacks on and carried a tent and supplies in my free hand. The halls were dimly lit, but if nothing else, humans adapted well, and my eyes could make out shapes and doorways, enough that we didn't walk into walls. I okayed the choices Jackson had made so far without paying much attention and just hoped I wouldn't regret that decision later.

No lights were visible anywhere on campus that I could see even though the science area was a little bit further away from the main portion of the campus, close to the trees, letting us study our ecosystem in fitting surroundings. But the lab creeped me out, the glow of the tanks and their movement seriously giving me *run now* vibes. I had this urge to just move away from there, to get away as fast as we could. My watch wasn't working, our phones weren't working, and for the first time ever, my son hadn't even blinked when he packed the laptop.

"Could it have been an EMP?" I asked Jackson. For all his young age, technology was his gift, in a way anyway. Gifted technological understanding, obsession with gadgets, disassembled everything whether or not he knew how to put it back together . . .

He hesitated. "It acts similar, but I don't think that's what it was."

Almost at the exit, I felt like a lifetime had passed since we left the ecology lab. I glanced out the corner of my vision, noticing yet again that there was something flashing there and realized it wanted me to make choices for myself. But I needed more information and time to go over them, so I didn't screw this up. For some reason, I didn't think I was going to be able to respec in this apocalypse.

I refused to make uninformed choices if the information was available to me. Whatever this screen in my vision shit was had the potential to be really scary and dangerous for my kids. And it would be just plain irresponsible of me to rush any decision that could impact my children's survivability.

Survivability. We needed to survive this. And while a quick choice on my behalf might help us in the short term, I didn't plan on dying any time soon. Important decisions were going to have to wait.

Shit.

I wished Mason wasn't traveling for work again. Maybe if he'd had the kids this weekend. . . Taking a breath, I shook my thoughts away from my ex-husband. Right now, I had to analyze what was happening.

Had the apocalypse really come? I tried to push open the entry doors and groaned. They were controlled by electricity. Shit.

"You two, around the corner. Wisp, stay with your brother." It probably added to the gravity of the situation that Wisp didn't even argue as I lowered her to the ground.

Glass fucking doors weren't going to stop me. I walked over to one of the displays. This month was for ecological awareness and highlighted the dangers of construction close to protected habitats. There were several bricks scattered around it. I remember thinking it was a bit gimmicky, but now I had never been so glad of a promotional tactic in my life. Hefting one of the bricks in my hand, I took aim, heralding back to that one season I played softball, and heaved the block right at the glass next to the doors.

The noise would have woken the dead if any had been around. Oh no, had I jinxed myself now? Were zombies going to appear too?

Breathe, Kira. Just breathe.

Shit.

I get it, brain—things are confusing. But I needed to get myself together and stop with the panicking. As the last of the glass clattered down, I turned and beckoned the kids. Wisp was properly awake now, her pale face scared but determined. She clung to my hand, gripping it like I was a lifeline.

"We have thirty-five minutes left, Mum. We have to get your Class chosen. We have to pick our Perks."

Jackson was just quietly urging, but it was all I could do to not snap at him. I knew I had to, even if the whole concept sounded absurd. Since when did the entire world turn into a bloody computer game?

Twenty-five minutes ago, my helpful brain offered.

We stepped onto the path outside the science building. The wrongness of the air and of the bush around us hit me immediately. I could feel something, the same way I could tell a bushfire was coming before the smell reached me. Only this was different; this was more dangerous, altering, devastating.

We needed to get to the car as soon as possible, which meant cutting through the campus and around to Park Road.

"Any guesses?" I asked the question quietly to buy time, and Jackson obliged with an answer.

"I don't know. I've never seen a game like this, and frankly, if it can insert itself into our minds, I have to think it's not just a game. I have to think we've been taken over by aliens." His expression didn't change or twitch.

He was dead serious, and I knew deep down he was also right. Maybe. The idea of aliens was insane. Then again, so was the idea of a game System world. Either way, this was outside of any game visuals I'd ever seen.

I nodded, not trusting myself to speak and still be strong enough for my kids right now. Half an hour left of this System initiation. Maybe I could get us back home and we could all just sit down in the safety of our own four walls and figure this out.

We wove among the buildings, along the paths, the breeze blowing the gum leaves in such a way I could smell the scent strongly. If I strained my ears, I swore I could hear the teeth of the koalas as they chewed their food, but that was just my overactive imagination.

All of the buildings held soft blue glows, even down to the fountain close to the quad where the students preferred to eat on sunny summer days. There were koi in there, but I wasn't particularly interested in taking a peek. No one else was here this late. I hadn't even glimpsed Steve or Jane. They'd usually be on rounds about now.

A shadow passed us on the path we were taking. Rodent-like yet larger than it had any right to be. My breath tried to stick in my throat, and the look Jackson shot me told me I hadn't been seeing things.

I'd always loved the campus for its place in the middle of the bush, yet as we neared the carpark and more creatures began to slither or creep close to us, I wished I'd taken that job at the uni in the city instead.

Continue reading Town Under:
https://readerlinks.com/l/2202672

To learn more about LitRPG, talk to authors including myself, and just have an awesome time, please join the LitRPG Group:

https://www.facebook.com/groups/LitRPGGroup/

Made in the USA
Las Vegas, NV
22 December 2022

63849631R00288